EMILY BAIN MURPHY was born in Indiana and raised in Hong Kong and Japan. She graduated from Tufts University and has also called Massachusetts, Connecticut, and California home. Murphy is the author of *The Disappearances*, which was shortlisted for the Waterstones Children's Book Prize. She currently lives in the St. Louis area with her husband and two children. Learn more at www.emilybainmurphy.com.

SPLINTERS of SCARLET

EMILY BAIN MURPHY

Pushkin Press
71–75 Shelton Street
London WC2H 9JQ

Published by special arrangement with Houghton Mifflin
Harcourt Publishing Company and Rights People, London.

Splinters of Scarlet was first published in Great
Britain by Pushkin Press in 2020.

1 3 5 7 9 8 6 4 2

ISBN 13: 978-1-78269-260-7

Offset by Tetragon, London
Printed and bound by CPI Group (UK) Ltd, Croydon, CR0 4YY

www.pushkinpress.com

To anyone who is still searching for home.
And for Pete—a plum.

Do you not know that there comes a midnight hour
when every one has to throw off his mask?

SØREN KIERKEGAARD

You can turn everything you look at into a story, and
everything, even, that you touch.

HANS CHRISTIAN ANDERSEN

Something is rotten in the state of Denmark.

WILLIAM SHAKESPEARE

CHAPTER ONE

THERE IS BLOOD ON EVE'S LACE.

I turn my palm as a fresh, incriminating bead blooms red on my fingertip. A new streak of crimson drips down the lace and onto the layers of tulle I just spent a week frothing to be as light as meringue.

With a yelp I drop my sewing needle and a hearty string of curses.

The most important performance of Eve's life is tomorrow, and I'm bleeding across her costume like a stuck pig. I suck on the tip of my finger, tasting rust, and throw a furtive glance around Thorsen's tailor shop. I am alone for once, tucked in the back behind reams of muted wools and intricate lace, silk scarves bursting with birds, a pincushion studded with needles and pearled buttons.

I could take more, I think. Thorsen keeps an unsorted stash of deliveries on the third floor. He might not notice the missing fabrics before I put aside my earnings from next week. I rise, remembering how I promised Eve I'd make her stand out tomorrow. I envisioned her in a costume dripping in glass beads so she'd reflect light like an icicle in the sun — not one that looks as though she practices arabesques for Nilas the butcher.

Tomorrow, a couple named Freja and Tomas Madsen are coming to the Mill orphanage, looking for a child to adopt. The thought of it makes my heart twist. I've poked around, wringing the barest answers out of tightlipped Ness, the orphanage director, and gleaning snatches from servants picking up their masters' tailoring at the shop. From what I can tell, the Madsens live two towns away — still within a morning's journey by carriage ride — and they might be Eve's best chance of getting picked.

If I hurry, I can grab what I need for Eve's costume before my roommate, Agnes, returns. Otherwise she'll snitch on me before I even make it back downstairs.

But just as I reach the first step, the bell over the door tinkles, and Agnes herself bursts in with a swirl of leaves. I freeze with my hand on the banister.

"What are you doing?" she asks, unlooping her scarf. We work side by side in Thorsen's shop and have boarded together in the cramped room upstairs since I aged out of the Mill myself three months ago. For someone who's barely older than I am, Agnes is as nosy and crotchety as a spinster. But worse, actually, because she has more zest for snooping.

"I just . . ." I say, but she isn't even listening.

"Did you hear?" She cocks her head and smoothes her hair from the wind. My heart falters. She looks positively gleeful. The only time she ever looks that way is when she's about to deliver bad news.

"What?" I whisper.

"The Mill's in a panic. That prospective couple, the Madsens—they aren't coming tomorrow anymore." Agnes squints at me, her lips curling up into a miserable smile. "They're coming today."

My mouth goes dry. The deliciously selfish part of me whispers, *Maybe now they won't pick Eve.* I kick at that thought like it's a dog that won't stop nipping at my ankles.

Agnes watches my reaction with growing pleasure, and when I turn, she follows. I stomp up to the second floor, trying to drive her away. "You know, I think I saw a mouse up here," I call over my shoulder. She squeals and hesitates for half a moment until she sees me bypass our bedroom and continue on.

"Where are you going, Marit?" she yells, charging up the wooden stairs behind me. No one ever wanted either of us, but I hope I hide it better than she does. She aged out of the Mill a year before I did, and the bitterness has settled into her like rot—the kind that repels people with one whiff, the kind that doesn't want anyone to have what she doesn't. *Don't be Agnes,* I tell myself. *You want Eve to have a family.* Even if it means they take her away—the last person I have left in the world.

Maybe this time my mind will finally stitch these lies well enough to hold.

"I don't know why you care so much," Agnes says behind me. "The Madsens have plenty of girls to choose from. Eve has almost no chance of getting picked."

"Stop talking, Agnes." I round the landing to the third floor. Agnes is wrong. Ness must believe that Eve has a very good chance, in fact. Because Ness is having the girls dance. And Eve is the best dancer of them all.

"Unless, of course," Agnes says, "Eve does something to . . . improve her odds."

I pause on the final step. It gives a shrill creak under my weight.

"What do you mean?" I ask coldly.

"Nothing, really. Just that there have been rumors." Agnes tuts her tongue. *"Of magic."*

My blood warms and beats faster. I take the final stair and stop in front of the fabric closet.

"She's always been good at dancing," Agnes continues. "Unusually good. Perhaps unnatural."

"Eve doesn't have magic," I say.

Magic. To excel in a single area since birth, like a savant, and do things others can do only in their dreams. Magic—the gift that comes with a hefty price. I shudder and think of my sister, Ingrid, of the blue frost that laced itself beneath the delicate skin of her wrists.

Agnes shrugs. "Using magic might get her picked," she says in a singsong voice, "until the Firn turns her blood to ice."

I kneel to sort through the boxes, gritting my teeth. Agnes is such a shrew.

"Eve doesn't have magic," I repeat. "If anyone would know, it's me."

I grab a handful of fabric and a spool of gold thread before Agnes suddenly seems to notice what I'm doing. "Hey! You didn't pay for that!" she cries.

I straighten. All I can think about is Eve, waiting for me at the Mill, her heart in her throat, her fingers tapping. How much I want the Madsens to pick her today; how much I don't.

"I'll tell Thorsen." Agnes crosses her arms and steps in front of me, challenge swimming in her cold blue eyes. "He'll kick you out, and I'll have our room all to myself again."

"In that case . . ." I shove past her and grab the small bottle of glass beads I've been dreaming about. "Might as well take these, too."

Her scandalized gasp is faintly satisfying and I whirl around to close the distance between us, so that for once I am the threatening one.

"Strike a deal with me, Agnes," I say. "What do you want?"

She narrows her eyes and thinks, smoothing the front of her apron. "Cover my lunch hours every day for a month," she says. "Starting . . ." Below us, the grandfather clock bongs out twelve noon. "Now."

I reach out my hand to shake and she purses her lips. But then she takes it and the agreement is made.

"Don't choke on your lunch!" I call, waving my contraband at her. She leaves me at the top of the stairs without acknowledgment.

Good, I think, trying to forget what she said. About magic and what it leaves behind, a Firn that frosts your veins until, eventually, it freezes you from the inside out.

My hands tighten around the beads.

Agnes has to be gone for what I'm about to do anyway.

CHAPTER TWO

I LOCK THE DOOR BEHIND AGNES and set the bor-rowed material on my work desk, pulling my chair closer to the glowing ink-black coal stove in the corner. The cobblestone street beyond the window is gray and wet with leaves, and the blunt edges of the windmill blades turn slowly beyond the roofs of the half-timbered houses. The people of Karlslunde hurry by the shop, heads ducked into the wind, pockets patched with stitches so ghastly they make my fingers itch.

I examine Eve's ruined costume, seeking out the lace not marred with red. My hands shake as I sort through the fabric. When I was young, there was a horrible rhyme that was whis-pered in the streets and sung by little girls spinning in circles at the market: *Magic flows like water; magic freezes like ice. Use too much and it costs a pretty price.*

I glance out the window now, waiting until the street is clear. Orphans who have magic are equal parts valuable and vulnerable. If we fall into the wrong hands, we'll be forced to use up our magic and burn out like a brief, bright flare.

I shudder even now, picturing Thorsen finding out what I can do.

The street clears, and still, I hesitate. I haven't used magic in almost two years. *Emergencies only,* I promised myself, and tucked away my magic like a weapon in a box, highly volatile and unstable. *Well, this* is *an emergency,* I tell myself. *For Eve.* I take a sharp breath as if I am preparing to dive into dark, cold water. Using magic is almost frighteningly easy—as simple as telling my lungs to fill themselves with a deep breath of air. It takes little more than a command, a slight concentration.

I close my eyes. *It's all right,* I urge myself, my hands clenching. *Such a tiny, inconsequential bit of magic won't matter.*

I uncurl my fists and immediately my fingers prickle and sing with long-dormant magic. I trace around each unstained piece of lace, faintly tapping each knot, and feel a thrill as something courses out of me and into the threads. I try not to think of the magic as something precious pouring out of me—or as a fuse being lit. The truth is, I forgot how quick and easy it is. How dizzyingly *good* magic feels. At my slightest touch, the knots untangle themselves and loosen.

The patch of lace falls into my hand, as delicate as spun glass, as intricate as a snowflake.

Without Agnes hovering over me, it takes all of seven minutes to reconstruct the tulle, a stiff, intricate honeycomb that would have cost me hours to do by hand. I work swiftly, heart thrumming, and transfer the old layers of lace onto the bodice like patches of stained glass.

I glance at the clock. *Maybe the Madsens will pick someone else*, I think. I uncork the gold and white beads I took and touch them to the fabric. The thread instantly winds itself tight to hold them in place, as easily as if I were pushing a plump berry into a frosted cake. *Maybe I can save enough money to adopt Eve myself someday.*

It's a thought I've never let myself look at too hard or too long, and my heart suddenly tightens along with the final knot. *Today,* I tell myself fiercely — *today* the best thing for Eve is to be picked by the Madsens. So I will give her the best chance I can — this tutu laced with magic.

And then I'll let the chips fall as they may.

I hastily throw the costume over my arm, lock the door behind me, and half run up the sloping street to the orphanage. I'm taking an enormous risk. If Thorsen finds the shop empty, Agnes and I will both be thrown out on the street. I run past the butcher shop that reeks of iron, the soot-soaked windows of the blacksmith, the tannery with its sagging roof. Waves of cholera and Denmark's two Schleswig Wars created plenty of drudges like me — orphans who run these places and spend our wages to board above them, half-starved and always in debt, our entire lives reduced to the span of one block. I quicken my pace as the warped roof of the Mill comes into sight. Ten years ago, my father was working in an underground network of limestone mines when the earth gave out over him and twelve others in the worst mining accident Denmark has ever seen. The Firn took my sister less than a month later, and suddenly, like a candle being snuffed out, I had no more family left in this world.

I don't want that for Eve. At eleven, she still has the slimmest chance of being picked. But today could be her last one.

I slip into the orphanage through the kitchen door, past the crooked back of Silas the cook, and dart up the side stairs. It smells like cloves and cardamom, which means he's making kanelstænger—cinnamon twists. In the drafty dormitory room on the second floor, Eve and another orphan, Gitte, are crowding in front of the mirror, slicking their hair up into high buns.

I exhale in relief. I'm not too late.

The tips of my fingers still tingle like frost.

Gitte finishes her hair first and nudges Eve. "You coming?"

Eve catches my eye in the mirror's reflection. "In a minute." She pulls at the dull pink costume that Ness scrounged up from somewhere. It hangs lumpily in some places and stretches too tightly in others.

Gitte nods to me on her way out. "Ness says the Madsens will be here any moment."

I remember the day Eve arrived at the Mill. Most of the young ones either mewed like pitiful kittens their first few days or cooed with lowered lashes. Eve was silent: dark haired, brown skinned, her deep brown eyes flashing. She barely said a word for half a year. Until her Wubbins caught on a spring one morning and ripped right down the middle. Wubbins, a horrible rag supposedly in the shape of a rabbit, missing an eye and with stuffing that never quite lies right. Eve came to me, holding him out, her eyes brimming. "Can you mend him?" she asked. I was the first — the only — person she ever asked anything of.

Now, petite at eleven, she is exactly eye-line with my heart.

"Marit!" she says, turning toward me. When our eyes meet, her face blooms into the loveliest grin. "How'd you even know to come?"

"Agnes was finally good for something," I say, holding out the tutu. "Unintentionally, of course. Here."

Eve leaps for her costume. "Look at this!" she crows, her fingertips admiring the fabric. "Are you *trying* to get me sent away?"

My stomach clenches and I turn my back. "Hurry."

She changes as I look at a small square of gray sky. The first week I aged out of the Mill, I snuck out of Thorsen's and walked here every night to gaze up at the dormitory room, surprised by my homesickness for Ness, for Eve, for my own bed. On the fourth night, I caught Eve through the window, practicing pirouettes in the mottled light from the street lamp when everyone else was asleep. I watched her for an hour, and by the time I returned to Thorsen's, hope had somehow brightened like coals within me.

I wonder, my heart closing up like a night flower, exactly how many minutes of separation it takes to turn someone you love into a stranger.

I squeeze my eyes shut. "Do you need help with the buttons?"

Eve gives a small squeal of delight in response. "Do I look like Helene Vestergaard?" she asks, twirling at her reflection. Helene Vestergaard, the Mill orphan who grew up to become one of Denmark's most celebrated ballerinas. When the other young orphans wanted to hear Hans Christian Andersen's fairy tales and the older ones wanted scary lore about the nightmare demon Mare the Vette, Eve always, always wanted stories about Helene Vestergaard.

"Even better than Helene Vestergaard," I tell her, and yet the embers of a deep grudge suddenly flare up within me at the name. Helene danced her way into a status none of us at the Mill had ever dreamed of—onto the Danish royal stage and into the glittering ranks of the wealthy Vestergaard family through marriage. I never told Eve about my own bitter connection to the Vestergaards. How their mines were the ones my father died in. How the Vestergaards barely sent enough restitution to cover my father's funeral, let alone the one that followed for my sister a month later. Instead I recited stories of Helene Vestergaard's legendary rise and then held my tongue, with her name still sitting on it long after Eve had drifted off, and wondered at how the ballerina's life was a strange mirror to my own: Helene left the Mill for a future with the Vestergaards and their mines—and the Vestergaard mines took my future and sent me to the Mill. A full circle of sorts, hers the light side of my own dark coin, this strange connection I could never shake.

"Marit," Eve says. She pulls on her shoulder strap and shivers with anticipation. "It could really happen today."

"It could," I say brightly. I blink, trying hard not to think about what she looked like at age four, when she climbed into bed with me at night because the sound of the wind scared her.

"Which means this might be the last time we're together . . ." she continues.

I turn away. I know what she wants from me, and I fumble with the ties on my apron, instantly uncomfortable.

"Please," she says softly. "I deserve to know, don't I? You promised you'd tell me someday." Her worn shoes whisper against the wood floor.

Years ago, she overheard the older girls gossiping about things that she was almost old enough to understand. That her mother had magic; that it had killed her. I've never outright *lied* to Eve about having magic of my own. But it's a secret I've never shared with anyone, holding it tightly to myself since the night my sister died. And talking about the Firn always sheared a little too close to other questions I didn't want to answer.

"All right," I finally say, focusing on a strand of hair that escaped her bun. "Yes, I suppose you're old enough now to hear it. I do think your mother might have had the Firn. I overheard Ness talking once."

Eve's shoulders turn stiff. "My mother was too careless with magic?" She swallows hard, as if I've confirmed something she's always feared. "When I was a baby? She . . . chose it over me?"

"It's never as simple as that," I say. I sweep back the wayward curl with a pin. "Try to think of magic as a strategy game with very high stakes." I sigh. "And sometimes . . . maybe it's worth the gamble. Maybe it's the best choice out of two hard choices."

"A game." Sadness shadows her eyes, as if it's pooling somewhere deep within her. The very thing I've always tried to keep away. "A game she lost," she whispers.

I give her a tight nod and think, *And my sister, Ingrid, too.*

"Eve?" Ness yells up the stairs.

"Coming!" Eve calls. She suddenly looks up at me, her dark eyes blazing in the gray half light of the dormitory room. "But are you certain, Marit? Because . . . *I* don't have magic."

I suspected this but now relief floods through me, strong enough that I could collapse. "That's good," I say softly. She wraps her arms around me, and I hug her back, feeling the delicate knit of her bones.

"Marit, wait. You don't either—right?" she asks, suddenly pulling away.

I remember her small, stunned face all those years ago when I handed her Wubbins back, miraculously healed. The feel of magic is finally receding from my fingers, the pleasant chill warming. I fight the sudden urge to look at my fingertips, at the thin skin on my wrists.

"Of course not." I push her toward the door.

When she reaches the hallway, she turns back, shimmering. The light catches in the beads I took.

"Good," she echoes me. She smiles. "Then we both have nothing to fear."

CHAPTER THREE

DOWNSTAIRS, IN THE MILL'S SITTING ROOM, the rug is pushed back from the worn floor near the fireplace to create a makeshift stage. The rickety chairs are arranged in a semicircle to flank the seats of honor, two grand wingback armchairs with splatters of tea and sunlight faded into their arms. The scene is the same as when I grew up here: all of us forced into some sort of show whenever Ness caught wind that a potential parent was coming to visit. She tried to make us look as desirable as possible: sitting in dirt, weeding the Mill's pathetic excuse for a vegetable garden for the woman who expressed interest in horticulture; positioning us with thick books around the hearth when an academic came to call. Most often, the girls with the golden voices were urged to sing while the rest of us sipped weak tea from the nice china and ate the flaky, cinnamon-flecked twists of kanelstænger. The children who could sing were always snatched up without fail.

But today is Eve's best chance to shine—because today, Ness has the girls dancing.

The girls who aren't performing take chairs in the audience. The fire pops, and there's a whistle of wind through the crack in the window. No one speaks to me, even though I've been gone for only three months. I know why. I am a reminder of a future they don't want to think about.

Ness glances at the clock.

The tea grows cold.

I left Thorsen's shop close to an hour ago and the seats of honor remain empty. Every minute I stay is reckless—another minute of idiocy. Eve has wrapped a long sweater around her to cover her costume and continues standing with perfect, expectant posture, even as the other dancers slump against the wall or slide into the audience seats. When she was seven, she spent hours flipping through a book of painted ballerinas, studying their poses until the spine shed its pages like leaves.

Helene Vestergaard was the one who sent that book to the Mill.

Now Eve bends to warm her muscles, and when she nervously taps a silent pattern into the wall with her fingers, I try not to think about all the wages I've just gone and wasted on the tutu.

"Perhaps they aren't coming today after all—" Ness says, but Eve's head jerks up at a cracking knock on the front door. A middle-aged man and woman step in, eyes bright. The man has a salt-and-pepper handlebar mustache and expresses his regret about the hour. Ness brushes away his apology and leads the couple to the sitting room, where a pretty girl named Tenna presents them with hot teas and a curtsy. I begrudgingly admit that

I like the woman's smile, and my throat constricts as they take their seats in the wingback chairs. I check the clock again as they settle in to listen to a trio of girls sing a simple harmony with clear, high voices. Tenna reads a passage of Scripture from the Mill's worn Bible, and then Ness gestures at the queue of dancers.

They trot out in a line organized by height, the smallest ones wrapped in mothy tulle with ribbon rosebuds sewn into their hair. I know Ness is doing the best job she can but it's awful, to feel like a piece of candy displayed behind a window, picked out by someone's particular taste, hoping that the person who wants you is offering a decent life and not a new kind of nightmare. I watch Eve as she strides out, her tutu still hidden beneath her sweater, and I flush with the sudden memory of the last time I used magic. It was two years ago, when I knew full well I was too old to ever be adopted. But in one last moment of desperation, I used magic to sew myself a new dress. I'll never forget the look on Eve's face when she saw me that morning and understood just how much I wanted to get picked—even if it meant leaving her behind. In the end it didn't matter, because that family chose Anja, who had a cherubic smile and a horrendous penchant for temper tantrums, and I cried hot tears into my pillow that night that I'd used precious magic and hurt Eve for nothing. I gave the dress away in the morning, casting it off along with my final dream of ever being adopted.

In fact, I see the dress right now, the embroidered high collar looking only a little worse for wear, on one of the older orphans setting out biscuits in the front.

And then Eve drops her sweater, and the entire room gasps.

I sit back in the shadows, a blush of pride and pleasure warming my face at the way she glows in her costume, but she doesn't seem to notice the audience's reaction; she juts her chin in the air, finds her pose, and waits, her muscles as taut as pulled string.

Elin sits at the toy piano to play something light and lively, and Eve waits behind the row of smaller girls. The tempo builds, and builds, until my foot is tapping along almost without permission; and when Eve's cue comes, it is as though she has spent years gathering the music within herself for this very moment.

Eve finally unhooks the latch and sets it free.

She bends and lengthens, fluid and lithe. The room has a draft from the gap where the window glass doesn't quite kiss the sill; there's a faint smell of mothballs that even the brewing tea can't conceal; but it is as though Eve steps out to dance in a space beyond it. Oh, I love her. She makes the other girls look as though their limbs have been hewn from wood and set on rusted hinges.

I want to grab Mrs. Madsen's arm and tell her that Eve's never had a true lesson in her life. That she simply feels the music and translates it into dance, as naturally as speaking another language.

Only imagine, I want to plead, *what she could be with a real home, actual instruction. What she could be with you.*

Eve dances as though her heart has melted and is now pouring in golden, aching fire through her veins. I almost can't tear my eyes away from her to observe the Madsens, who are watching with intent expressions. My heart knots in twin vines of hope and fear at the look that is dawning on their faces. A look as if they know they've seen their daughter for the first time.

As the music comes to a climax, Eve throws her legs into an effortless, improvised jeté. She finishes flushed and breathless and stares out at all of us with eyes that are fire.

The Madsens clap and the girls bow and drift into the dining room to set out dishes of meatballs, gherkins, dark slices of rye bread, chicken with brown sauce and rhubarb compote, gløgg flush with golden raisins. My heart is in my throat when the Madsens usher Ness over with a wave of their hands.

"We'd like to speak with one of the girls," Mrs. Madsen says, and I follow her long, thin finger to the side of the room where Eve stands. I draw in a shaking breath.

"Eve?" Ness asks. Eve curtsies.

"No," Mrs. Madsen says. "The blond one next to her."

My breath catches. She means Gitte. Gitte, who wasn't nearly as good as Eve, not by half. I see Eve blink rapidly. She has a smile plastered on her face that makes me hate them all, and myself, too, because if I'm honest, I am overjoyed.

"Gitte! Come here! Come speak with the Madsens, here, in the private foyer! And then . . . a feast!" Ness says, beaming.

I take a step toward Eve. I'm going to tell her my plan, right now. That I'm going to save up enough money so that maybe we could make our own future someday. That if no one picks us, then we can still pick each other. I'm halfway to her when I suddenly hear the sound of another woman's voice.

"Ness," the woman says softly, a whisper from the shadows behind us. The whole room turns toward her in shock. She must have slipped in when the girls were performing and I was distracted.

My head whips toward her, my heart pumping and pounding as I strain to see. The woman steps from the shadows into the light.

"I'd like to speak with one of the girls privately too, if I may."

What I notice first are her long ballerina legs and the glittering pins in her hair. Her glass necklace catches the light to show a hammer and pick. The Vestergaard mining crest.

I turn in slow motion to watch Eve. She's frozen, her breaths coming short and shallow. But I see the stunned look of disbelief on her face at the exact moment when she realizes who it is.

Helene Vestergaard.

The woman's eyes trace around the room until they come to rest on Eve.

She gives a small smile, extends a graceful hand, and says softly: "You."

CHAPTER FOUR

HELENE VESTERGAARD'S EYELIDS are outlined with ink, sweeping up into a delicate point. She has thick hair the color of hickory pulled up in a pin gleaming with glass flowers. Her coat is a lush coal-black velvet embroidered with intricate golden and pink blossoms that must be worth at least two years of my salary. Once upon a time, she was an orphan here, sleeping in the drafty room upstairs. Now she has turned into a stunning beauty, a commanding presence that sucks up all the air in the room. And she is the richest person I've ever seen in the flesh. When Aleksander Vestergaard died a year ago, he left his wife of seven years everything—including his vast mining empire.

The sight of her resurrects the resentment I've tried so hard to bury over the years. It slips out like smoke between the teeth of a steel trap.

I stumble forward as Helene leads Eve to the private room near the kitchen. They disappear inside, and the door shuts behind them.

My blood pumps hot and fiercely in my ears, and a copper taste fills my mouth. The idea of the Madsens was hard enough.

To lose Eve to a Vestergaard is unfathomable.

The other orphan girls turn and scatter.

But I follow Ness to the little office set under the curve of the stairway, charging in after her.

"You moved the Madsens' visit to today, didn't you?" I demand, putting my hands on my hips. "You asked them to come early?"

Ness shrugs and riffles through her papers. "I invited all of them here," she says dismissively. "I had a hunch Helene might take an interest in Eve. They are similar in many ways. And yes, I've found that a little competition never hurts to get one of you adopted." Ness is shrewd, and I do think she cares for us, in her own way. She is always looking to throw us a bone. Never one of her own, of course—but she wouldn't hesitate to pluck out someone else's, if it might help one of us.

"It is all working out exactly as hoped." Ness looks up at me, eyes sharp. "You should be happy for her."

"Where does Helene live, Ness?" I ask. I can hear the desperation creeping into my own voice.

"North of Copenhagen."

"That's a full day's journey from here," I say, nerves making my voice climb even higher. "I'll never see Eve again!"

Ness lets out an exasperated sigh. "Eat some bread, Marit." She jingles a key and kneels in front of her filing drawers. "Don't be naive. You know as well as I do that most parents in here took one look at Eve and didn't even consider her."

I noticed. But I tried to tell myself it wasn't because she stood out in the sea of white orphans and parents. That it had nothing to do with the fact that her mother was West Indian and her father could have been almost anyone.

"I've never known you to be selfish, girl," Ness continues. "At least *try* to think rationally."

"Perhaps I can't think rationally when it comes to the Vestergaards," I say through clenched teeth and with a tone I never would have used when I lived under Ness's roof. "My father died in their mines, remember?"

Her voice is frigid. "Yes, it was a terrible accident. Yet where do you think those linens on your bed came from last Christmas? Who do you think regularly sends money to pay for shoes —the king of Denmark?" She fixes me with the icy gaze that makes even the most grown orphans shrink back. "Marit," she says, drawing out her words slowly and unflinchingly, "can you offer Eve something better?"

I take a sharp breath.

Ness finds Eve's papers, stands, and ushers me out the door.

Eve and Helene are emerging from their meeting, and the look on Eve's face is somewhere between triumph and terror. When Mrs. Vestergaard gives Ness a slight nod, I see the glint of glass around Eve's neck.

No.

A hammer and pick.

The Vestergaard crest.

The wrong side of the coin, turning up in my life again.

Ness clasps her hands together and says, "A feast!"

Eve seeks me out as she and Helene walk toward me, and I can see in her eyes that she knows this is goodbye, this painful fissure of our old life and new splitting as clean as a rip. I swallow, trying hard not to cry. Instead I fix my eyes on Helene's coat as it trails behind her, the embroidered golden coils of vines and flowers spilling across the floor, and a deep, guttural scream builds within me.

Don't be selfish, something inside of me is pleading. *Don't be Agnes.* But I'm so desperate I suddenly don't care. Why do the Vestergaards get to keep taking the people I love?

At the exact moment the hem of Helene's exquisite coat sweeps across a jutting piece of a half-rusted pipe next to the bottom stair, I have a sudden, brilliant, terrible idea.

I step forward, putting my foot down on the coat with the full force of my weight.

The fabric catches and instantly rips with a horrible sound.

"Oh!" Helene exclaims, turning.

I retreat into the shadows.

"Heavens!" Ness says. She kneels to the rip and clasps her wrinkled hands together. "Oh, it must have snagged on this pipe, here. What an unhappy accident." She shoots me a look of daggers. "I'm so sorry, Helene. I've been meaning to have that pipe fixed."

I look at Eve's stricken face, her brief moment of happiness as ripped through as the coat, and I step forward to stand beside her. My emotions are fractals, turning wildly in a kaleidoscope. Sadness, fear, desperation.

"Excuse me," I say to Mrs. Vestergaard, and give a deferential curtsy, "but I'm a seamstress by trade. Might I mend it for you?"

"Yes—Marit can help!" Eve says urgently, as if Helene's misfortune might make her suddenly change her mind. "Marit is matchless. She's the one who made my costume." The curl I pinned earlier has slipped out again to graze the spattering of dark freckles across her right cheek.

"I'm not sure . . ." Helene looks at me. "This would be an extraordinarily intricate job. I think it's ruined."

"Then you won't mind if I try," I say, boldly holding out my hand.

Helene exchanges a look with Ness, who gives a slight nod.

"All right," Helene says, relenting. "Thank you. Do your best and let me know what the cost will be." She strips off the coat, revealing a cream patterned jaconet dress with a crisp necktie and tiers that pour out from her small waist like water spilling from a fountain. "We're staying at the Vindmølle Kro tonight," she says, offering the coat to me. Her eyes linger on mine for half a beat, almost as if issuing me a challenge. "And we leave in the morning."

"I'll bring it there," I say with confidence, and take the coat from her.

What I've done today might cost me my job, my board at Thorsen's, and any goodwill I ever had with Ness—but at least

I've bought myself a chance to see Eve one more time. I look her in the eyes and say, "I'll come to the Kro." Then I hug the coat, careful to keep my heart clenched tighter than a fist within my chest, and run.

ぉ

Thorsen beat me back to the shop.

As soon as I round the corner, I can see his meat-red face through the window, shouting at Agnes and pointing to my empty work desk. Cursing, I duck into an alley and clutch the coat to my chest. I could lie — say I was called out to pick up this job for Mrs. Vestergaard. But I suddenly feel too worn and raw to face either of them. I turn on my heel to steal up the back alley and sit on the cleanest stoop I can find, feeling the cold of the stone seep into my skin. At best, Thorsen will dock my pay for weeks — which is unfortunate, since I already spent it all on Eve's fabric. At worst, I'm fired, without so much as a single rigsdaler saved to my name. And after the stunt I pulled at Ness's, I'm probably not welcome there tonight.

But one thing at a time. I am alone in a narrow alley, and I consider the row of windows above me: the shutters all closed, the shades mostly drawn. The windmill blades turn lazily above my head. I've never allowed myself this much magic. Not so many times so close together. And never, ever in public.

I take a deep breath and smooth out Helene Vestergaard's coat, examining its mess of rips and spidering threads. I run my fingertips over each fissure, and imagine what the stitching used to look like with its golden tendrils and vines. Magic stirs within me and my veins feel a sparking rush; even beneath my dread of the Firn I shiver with the pleasant chill of magic. I let it flow through me, delicately running my fingertips along the coat's frayed edges. The threads find one another and knit themselves back together under my touch.

I think of what my father would say. He forbade me to use magic when he was alive. He feared it, and he was right to.

I'm glad he didn't live long enough to see what it did to Ingrid.

A few centuries ago, under a different king, we would have been burned at the stake for having even a whiff of magic. Now it's more or less understood that the greatest danger we pose is to ourselves. People avert their eyes and mostly pretend we don't exist, because the goods that underground magic can produce are useful—despite the unpleasant side effect that the magic might eventually kill us. But even at the age of six, I understood nothing good could come from someone who wanted an orphan with magic. The penny paper stories would make my toes curl up inside my boots: of people being kidnapped and forced to use their magic until the crystalline frost of the Firn filled their bloodstreams and killed them. Sometimes I joined in telling late-night ghost stories at the Mill so no one else would suspect; but it hurt to sit there, listening to the other children's voices in the dark. They whispered that we had deep blue bones and insatiable appetites, and that when we died we were jealous of the living. They called us *draugar*— "again-walkers"—because the Firn sometimes leaves people's bodies contorted in unnatural positions, sitting upright after their veins crystallize with ice, as though they're someday planning to return. The adults would shush the children, insisting that those were little more than silly legends and stories. Yet old fears and customs die hard. We may not be burned at the stake anymore—but they make sure we are always cremated.

I suddenly see Ingrid standing in front of me, the ghost of a memory from years past.

"I think," she whispers, blinking down at her wrists in a daze, "I think I went too far."

I grit my teeth, feeling the tense fear of the Firn build in a gathering storm along my jaw. I shouldn't think of that memory now.

Instead I examine Mrs. Vestergaard's coat and even let myself smile a little at my work. The rift has vanished, as though it was never there at all—as if the threads knew exactly where they were always supposed to belong. I don't have any money to spend warming myself with a coffee in a café, and I certainly can't return to my room at Thorsen's, so I wrap Helene Vestergaard's own coat around my shoulders and sink into its softness. There's the faintest hint of her perfume, lingering. It smells like spring and paper white blossoms.

Perhaps I can find my own way to Copenhagen.

I can still see little Eve blinking her large, dark eyes up at me, holding out Wubbins. How sternly she instructed me to mend only his tear, not the rest of him, because she liked him perfect and ugly just as he was. That was the day she started to thread her way into my closed heart, despite the fact I never wanted her to. Because I always feared this day would come. And I don't want to know what will happen tomorrow when all those reluctant stitches of hers are suddenly ripped out.

The sky inks with night as I make my way past Mathies's Bakery, with its torn gold-and-red-striped awning that sags a little bit more with each snowfall. At Christmastime, Mathies always gave each of us orphans a honey heart biscuit, hardened and brushed with melted chocolate, and I ate mine all at once, but Eve would wrap and hide hers under her bed and take one tiny bite each day to make it last until New Year's. I pause in front of his window, catching the scent of bread wafting from the inside, wondering what the world would be like if I could walk along and fix it all with the touch of my finger. Every tatter, every hole worn into the knee of a pant, every sad, old awning. How much good I could do, if it didn't threaten to cost me so much.

I wonder if there is someone out there like me, who can mend the rips and tears in people.

Hidden by dusk, emboldened by the magic that I can still feel humming in my veins, I hesitate. Then I dart my hand out and pass my fingers ever so briefly over Mathies's awning.

Maybe tomorrow, if my plan fails and Eve has left forever, I will come back and watch for the moment he discovers the awning is fixed.

It is still mending itself as I hug Helene's coat tighter to me and hurry away.

∼

The Vindmølle Kro sits on the outskirts of town, a white-and-olive-colored inn with a thatched roof. The chimney from the second cottage sends out puffs of smoke that are as thick and white as whipped cream. The air smells like cinnamon pears and burning leaves.

I rap sharply on the door.

"Who is it?" a voice calls from inside.

I clear my throat. "It's Marit Olsen. With your coat?"

I thrust it at Helene Vestergaard the minute she opens the door. Behind her, Eve is already wearing a new crimson dress with satin rose ribbons and black boots that are as shiny as oil. A new trunk is open at her feet, and inside I see the glint of the gold beads of her tutu.

I turn away from an embarrassing prick of jealousy—wondering what it must feel like, after all those years of yearning, to finally be picked.

Helene takes the coat from me and examines it. Her expression is unreadable.

"You work at a tailor shop?" she finally asks. I nod and she gestures me inside a room with exposed ceiling beams and thick quilts folded at the ends of the two straw beds.

"Marit did well, didn't she?" Eve asks. The fire crackles in the hearth, and the hammer and pick pendant gleams from her neck. She looks to Helene and me: her gaze bouncing between her past and her future. I desperately try to memorize her dark freckles, the mole just below her ear, the way her hair tufts up like soft down around her temples.

"Yes, Eve," Helene says. She runs her fingers over the whorls. "This stitching is magnificent." For the first time, I force myself to really look at her as she uncinches a small purse embroidered with flowers. Her eyes are a rich brown — honey dark and intelligent, surrounded by thick lashes and a high arch of cheekbone — and her wrists are small and delicate as a robin's egg. My fingernails seem so blunt and jagged, bitten to the quick.

"How much would you like for the work?" Helene asks.

"Actually," I say, "I'd like to request something different as payment."

Helene cocks a sharp eyebrow and watches me with interest.

Eve stills behind us, listening.

"I'd like you to recommend me to a tailor in Copenhagen," I say. "Based on the quality of the work I've done on your coat."

I look at her, biting my lower lip. Asking for a favor, from one Mill orphan to another.

Surely a word of recommendation from Helene will go a long way in Copenhagen. Surely she has a tailor who will be eager to please her. And I would still have a chance of seeing Eve sometimes, when they came to the shop. It's my last, best hope.

"You made Eve's tutu, as well?" Helene asks, studying me. "Have you done much costume work?"

"Some," I lie.

Helene shuffles through a healthy stack of rigsdalers. "It's an interesting proposition," she muses. "But I'd like to raise you a counteroffer. I've been looking for someone with truly exceptional skill to make my clothing, and now Eve's." The fire gives a loud crack from the hearth.

"Perhaps you would like to come work for me," she says.

The air in the room instantly stills.

"I recognize that the work you've done here is . . . *exceptionally* good," she says. "For its quickness, its high quality," she continues, looking down at the coat. "I'll pay you very well, and give you room and board. But I would insist on your work continuing to this very high standard."

Her eyes flick to me meaningfully, and a chill goes through me.

She knows.

She knows about the magic.

"Of course she will!" Eve cries, leaping to her feet. She takes a step toward me. "Marit, you can come with us!"

My heart quickens. I could go with them.

I could be with Eve.

It's everything I ever wanted.

But it's entering into an arrangement with the very family who took my father from me—and doing the one thing he begged me not to.

"You will have to decide quickly," Helene says. "We leave at dawn."

All I can do is nod, and Helene offers me the handful of rigs-daler bills—more than I make in a month at Thorsen's. "This is for your work today."

Eve rushes to embrace me. "Mrs. Vestergaard took me to a shop and let me choose anything I wanted," she whispers, and thrusts something into my hand. It's a silver thimble with tiny braided knots running along the rim. "I picked this for you, so you wouldn't forget me. But now, Marit—" She cuts herself off in excitement. "We can be together!"

My fingers close around the embossed knots, frozen and hardened in silver. The first gift from her new family, and she gave it to me. I brush my lips over Eve's forehead and feel the fluttering of fear, like wings dipped in iron.

Then I tuck the thimble in my pocket and sprint all the way back to Thorsen's.

I throw open the door and run past him, up the stairs, with him and Agnes hot on my heels.

"Where have you been?" Thorsen thunders behind me.

"I'm leaving," I tell them, hurriedly stashing my clothes and toiletry bottles into my beat-up carryall as Thorsen yells, his face purpling all the more, and Agnes watches with smug lips, lean-ing against the wall with her arms folded over her chest. I open the trap plank in the floor and grab the only sentimental things I have left from my old life: a book of Hans Christian Andersen fairy tales that my father used to read me, and the last letter he ever wrote. Then I fly down the stairs, fishing out half the bank notes Helene gave me and tossing them on my work desk. It's enough to cover the beads and fabric I took, and a little more for leaving Thorsen in such a lurch.

"Goodbye!" I shout, pulling Thorsen's door shut behind me for the last time, feeling reckless sparks of thrill and dread. I run toward the Kro. Toward warmth. Toward Eve. It's true that using magic for the Vestergaards could come at a heavy price. This job could actually cost me my life.

But if I stay . . . what life is left for me here?

I pound on the door.

"I'll take it," I say breathlessly when Helene opens the door a crack. I look past her and say directly to Eve, "I'm coming with you."

Helene moves aside to let me in, and Eve leaps forward to throw her small, familiar arms around me. "We set off at dawn," Helene says, locking the door with a final click behind me.

And just like that, the two sides of our coin come together.

Almost as if they were always meant to.

CHAPTER FIVE

Philip Vestergaard
1849
Faxe, Denmark

THERE IS BLOOD ON MY SLEEVE.

A stain, as though someone dipped the end of a paint-brush in rust and swept along where my shirt meets my wrist. I take in a lungful of sooty air and try to rub out the spot, but my fingers are dirty and the stain has set. I was nervous enough about begging for a job today—and that was before I knew I was wearing my own mother's blood.

I stand under a wooden sign that swings and creaks over my head. As a wagon with a rickety wheel rumbles by, I reach up and rap on the door, then carefully tuck my stained sleeve behind my back.

This is what I always told myself I would do, when my father and brother marched off to war last year singing "The Brave Foot Soldier." If the worst happened—if men bearing news of war came to our door wearing black—I would don my best shirt and go to the cloth factory set on the corner at the outskirts of town. The law may say that I have to go to school, but what good is learning if the rest of me is starving? I picture my mother, the shake of her thin shoulders as she dried the same dinner plate for close to an hour this morning, and shore myself up, warning my voice to not dare sound tinny.

When the door swings open, the man standing on the threshold wears spectacles and a sooty apron and looks down at me, with an expression both expectant and aggravated. "Yes?" he says.

I shift in my shoes, which are a half size too small. "I was hoping to speak about a job," I say, and my voice sounds only a little thin. I swallow. I can tell it is warm in there, the heat flowing out into the cutting chill. I've heard stories of people dying or maiming themselves terribly. But suddenly I want nothing more than to be inside—out of the bitter cold, and near machinery just loud enough to drown out my own thoughts.

"Come in," he says.

He leads me down a narrow hallway to a door marked MAN-AGEMENT and knocks. I remove my hat, and my nose suddenly starts to drip. The machines whir nearer and louder.

"This boy wants to speak with you," the soot-stained worker announces, and deposits me in front of a man smoking a cigar and examining paperwork on a desk cluttered with cloth samples. The office is dark and dim, with only a small window, and a Danish flag is spread across the wall behind his head.

"I was wondering," I say, clearing my throat, "if I could work for you on the cutting machines."

"No," the manager says, without even looking up. "I don't need any more your age. What are you, fourteen?"

I'm twelve.

"Please," I say, my voice faltering. I stare hard at the spot on the top of his head where his hair is thinning, like floss.

He finally looks up. "Aren't you a Vestergaard boy?" he asks, squinting. He wets his ink pen. "Your father can't give you work in his mines?"

I bite my lip. Our mines have been shuttered since the start of the war. Because no one needs limestone for building or chalk for paint right now. They need metal for rifles and cannons.

"Far died yesterday," I choke out. "In the war." I've said the words out loud, and now it's real.

"I'm sorry," the manager says gruffly. He nods at the Danish flag, then at me. "Take pride in knowing that he served Denmark well." He gestures toward the door. "Vestergaard, eh? I'll let you know if a spot opens."

I hesitate for a moment, kneading my hat in my hands. When the man delivered the sealed letter this morning, my mother became so inconsolable that she got a nosebleed. For one long, awful moment I didn't know who had been killed—my father or my older brother. I didn't know whose name I least wanted to read in that letter. I handed her a handkerchief, and when she took it from me, her blood got on my sleeve. I can see it now, out of the corner of my eye, when I stand and walk back out into the gray rain.

Don't cry, I tell myself fiercely. Men don't cry. I am a man now. But if the war drags on, if Aleks dies too, we might well starve. I lean against the cold stone of the factory wall and take a shuddering breath.

"Oy! Philip!" My friend Tønnes ducks out of the bakery across the road and jogs toward me, holding a hat down on his blond curls. When he reaches me, he puts a steadying hand on my shoulder. "I heard about your far." He thrusts a little piece of bun into my hand. "I'm sorry," he says. His father's fighting too.

They all made it sound so important, so noble. Far was so proud to fight, so that Denmark wouldn't continue to be "dismembered," as he called it. "Denmark has been shrinking for a thousand years," he announced in his booming voice. Remembering him now makes tears begin to fall onto the ground next to my feet. "The southern duchies of Schleswig and Holstein cannot be lost to Prussia." He pulled me into his lap, tracing down the veins in my wrist. "Those trading routes are like veins, connecting trade to Russia, and they are vital." So the mines, once filled with men unearthing limestone, suddenly emptied and went dark. There used to be life inside of them, and inside of me, but now it's gone, and all that's left is an abandoned, gaping hole.

I fight a sob. I don't care anymore about the duchies, or being noble. All I want is my far back, for Aleks to come home, to buy food for my mother, to save the mines. Instead I am twelve years old and little more than a handkerchief, soaking up blood and tears.

" 'Ey. You see that?" Tønnes's head jerks to the alley across the road. A little boy is crouching there, the shadows falling around him like a veil. He snaps his fingers and a little flick of flame appears between them, then vanishes.

Magic.

"You know that it kills them?" Tønnes asks in wonder, watching the boy flick the flame off and on, off and on, the shadows bouncing around him. Tønnes's eyes glitter with morbid fascination. I grew up learning to fear the use of magic: that it was the result of something bad, the natural world gone horribly wrong. But I understand why the little boy crouches there and ignites the burn between his fingers. Because magic is power. To have control. To bring something from nothing. I have the sudden unshakable sense that magic could save me, the mines, perhaps even all of Denmark. I watch that little flame with hunger that grows beyond the pangs in my stomach to something much deeper.

I snap my own fingers in the cold air all the way home, wondering if magic can ever be willed into being. Later, after I've seen Mother off to bed, I watch for even the slightest spark as my room begins to darken and grow cold with night. I change out of my bloodstained shirt, willing that flame to appear—snapping until my fingers are raw and I hear the quiet sound of my mother crying again—but that little blaze of magic never does.

CHAPTER SIX

Marit
November 8, 1866
Karlslunde, Denmark

I DREAM THAT NIGHT of being shut in a small wooden box. I smell the fresh pine. Feel the curve of a spoon clutched in my hand.

I hate this dream.

When I hear the dead bolt of a lock, I climb out of the box, just as I always do. My cramped legs burn like fire.

"Marit," my sister says, her eyes shadowing with fear. "I think . . ." she whispers desperately. Ice-blue Firn knits beneath her wrists, a horrific, mesmerizing beauty. *"I think I went too far."*

I wake with a start.

I am curled on the floor, wrapped in a quilt between the fireplace and Eve's bed. She's lightly snoring, that patterned breathing of her sleep I know so well. The fire casts flickering light and shadows across her face.

We leave Karlslunde together at dawn.

The Vestergaard carriage is black and sleek, pulled by two enormous Frederiksborg horses with thick, clean fur. We pass Thorsen's shop and the Mill on the way out of town. The windows glitter and all the candles are extinguished, and I'm secretly glad that our route doesn't take us past my old little thatched home on the outskirts of town, where Far's and Mor's and Ingrid's lives once filled the house like flames dancing within a lantern.

"I was worried I would wake up and it would all be a dream," Eve murmurs to me. She discreetly moves her feet so mine can feel some of the heat from the warming box on the floor, then raises her shoulder so I can smell her new coat. "Most people like flowers, you know," she whispers, elbowing me fondly as I take a deep breath. But to me, a fresh, stiff wool has always smelled even better than roses.

Helene's hair is pulled back in an elegant knot, and the train of her mended coat pools on the floor at our feet. "I thought we'd use the ride home to get to know each other better," she says to Eve. "Where shall we begin?" she asks. Her eyes are intense, her attention unyielding. She unscrews a silver canister and unleashes the rich smell of black coffee. The windowpanes fog with steam. "Your favorite food?"

"Plums," Eve says immediately. It's probably a tie between that and kransekage, the towering wreathed rings of marzipan cake and icing, but we ate plums only twice at the Mill. Last time Eve tasted one, she declared that people should give plums to show their love instead of flowers.

Helene looks pleased, rifling through a wicker basket until she somehow finds Eve a ripe purple-black plum. I stare at it with wonder. A ripe plum, in November? Eve takes a bite of it, revealing flesh the color of butterscotch. The juice dribbles down her chin.

I listen as Eve shares the beginning edges of herself: she likes staying up late and eating things that are tart; she has a scar on her knee from the day she tried to chase a butterfly and ended up falling onto a grate. *She's impatient, she used to have a lisp, she can't spell to save her life,* I want to add. But these things are really just the faintest shadow of Eve, how loyal and fierce and funny she is. She once pushed a girl who was twice her size bottoms-up over a log for saying that my hair was the color of dung hay.

"Did you have a favorite story growing up?" Helene asks.

Eve wipes the juice from her mouth and tries very hard to avoid my eyes while I bury my laugh in a cough. *Mythical tales about you,* I think. *Helene Vestergaard.*

Eve spies the worn bound copy of Hans Christian Andersen's *New Fairy Tales* peeking out of my bag. "'The Nightingale'?" Eve squeaks out. It isn't the same volume my father used to read to Ingrid and me when we were small—that one is long gone, sold along with the house to cover our debts after they both died—but I saved my first paycheck from Thorsen to buy another copy. Because it reminded me of my father. And because of what he wrote in his final letter, now hidden in my pocket.

Almost without thinking, I reach for the lines of practically invisible knots sewn into my petticoat: *Claus Olsen, b. 28 July 1825 in Karlslunde.* A few years ago I started sewing my family's names into my hems, where they were born, where they died. It's a comfort to know that I won't wake up one day and have forgotten it all—that those parts of them won't drift away like mist now that I'm the only one left to remember them.

d. 26 May 1856 is how my father's entry ends. *In Kalk Labyrint mines.*

Kalk Labyrint.

Vestergaard mines.

How could everything have changed so drastically since the last time I visited Copenhagen? Eleven years ago, I was here with him. I was still someone's child, someone's sister. A different king was on the throne. The southern duchies of Schleswig and Holstein were still Denmark's, before Prussia clawed them away. War and death have split through the years like an ax—wars shrinking Denmark's territories, and cholera weeding out its population. For a few years, the only things that seemed to be growing in Denmark were our graveyards and orphanages.

But perhaps the tide is finally turning, I think, as Eve uses a Vestergaard handkerchief to wipe her mouth and Helene tells her to keep it. There's a new royal on the throne now—King Christian IX. And at Thorsen's, we finally started selling more white lace than black.

Beyond the window glass, the countryside changes to long stripes of gray-blue canals. I first glimpse the spires of Copenhagen's stock exchange, its four dragon tails twisting upward. Wooden ships and jewel-toned houses reflect in the water; crowds of women and men in long, bustled skirts and black suits stream through the tree-lined walkways. There are so many colors here, each fabric like a different note, playing a sonata of crinoline and lace, of tiered ruffles showing below thick velvet capes. The city all but vibrates with the sound of boots and horse hooves and pealing bells, the air heavy with salt and urine and fresh bread and soot. Copenhagen looks the same but not exactly—sort of in the way I can still see the echoes of Eve as a young child, even though her features change each year. My heart clenches as we pass the corner where Ingrid once threw a coin in the bronze fountain of Charity.

I wonder what she would have looked like now.

"The Round Tower," Helene explains to Eve, pointing as the carriage rattles past. "Inside that garret is a wide, spiraled ramp instead of a staircase."

My father once stood right there at its base. "More than a century ago," he said, pulling at the ends of his mustache, "the Russian tsar Peter the Great rode to the very top of this tower on horseback, and his wife Catherine followed behind in her carriage."

"Fib or not fib?" I demanded, turning to Ingrid. She was twelve years old, and I was five.

She clapped her gloved hands with delight. "It's true!" she said.

Because that was Ingrid's magic. I may be able to stitch things back together, but she could always sense when people were lying.

"Stop wasting magic like that," Far said in a low, sharp voice. "Marit, next time, just ask me. Do I lie to you?"

"I didn't *ask* her to use magic. I could tell she was already doing it," I said stubbornly, pouting. Ingrid had this telling motion every time she was using her magic. Her hands closed into tight fists at her side, her fingers wrapping around her thumbs like the spirals of conch shells, as if she was concentrating very hard.

"Why do you do it?" he asked Ingrid that day. "Why do you tempt fate like that?"

"Do you worry every time you get into a carriage or mount your horse?" Ingrid shot back, red gathering at the base of her neck like a storm. "Or when you go to work in the mines? Every time you do, you risk death. But it's convenient, or it brings you some value, and so it's a risk you think is worth taking."

"That's different," Far protested, slamming his hand down on the iron railing.

Except, in the end, it wasn't. For either one of them.

꒰

We came to Copenhagen that day all those years ago to visit the Nationalbanken.

It hurts to see the building now, under a glittering eave of icicles that hang sharp as knives. My father and Ingrid stood right there, arguing about magic, and then we followed him in through the heavy doors of the bank so that he could open savings accounts for our futures. They were meager accounts, meant to help us in case anything ever happened to him in the mines.

I steal a glance at Helene, who is taking brown paper packages out of the basket and arranging them like pieces of art. Because something *did* happen to Far in the mines. But then we got the letter they recovered on his body. It pokes at me now, through my pocket. The envelope was delivered as part of his personal things, and it didn't occur to me until years later how strange it was that he should write us a letter if he was ever planning to come home to us again. I was too focused on the fact that it was the last thing he ever wrote—cryptic, spare. And that it was addressed only to my sister.

To Ingrid, he'd written in his scraggly handwriting. *I closed the accounts. I needed them. I'm sorry. Be a Gerda.*

Gerda, the goodhearted character from the pages of "The Snow Queen," which my father read to us every night. From then on I was determined to be a Gerda too—even if he had written the letter only to Ingrid. So I studied the book of fairy tales until I all but had it memorized. Gerda, who followed her dearest friend north to the snow queen's palace, to rescue him and make sure he was safe.

My eyes flick to Eve as she strains for a glimpse of Amalienborg, its four identical royal palaces set like heavy game pieces around a courtyard shaped like an octagon. What if my father's two instructions—*don't use magic; be a Gerda*—are directly opposed to each other? Which one am I supposed to follow more?

"I remember Ness being quite reserved with the butter," Helene says, unwrapping the brown paper packages to reveal open-faced pickled herring sandwiches. They are layered with shallots and bright purple beets and dotted with capers, crisp slices of cucumbers, and sprigs of dill. "Has that changed since my days at the Mill?"

"No," Eve says emphatically.

"Then we shall have it thick as a tooth," Helene says, slathering creamy butter on a slab of rye bread. My stomach rumbles —I haven't eaten since yesterday—and I feel a rush of surprise when Helene butters the final sandwich just as generously as the ones for her and Eve and promptly hands it to me.

"You've heard that our Princess Dagmar is marrying a tsar this week in St. Petersburg," Helene says, nodding toward the streets lined with rivers of deep red Danish flags. For the first time, I notice occasional glimpses of the Russian tricolor unfurling between them. "Half of Copenhagen came to see her ship off—including your Hans Christian Andersen," she says to Eve. She takes a dainty bite of her sandwich. "Perhaps you will meet him, someday."

Eve looks at me with dazed bewilderment, as if she's still worried she is caught somewhere in a dream. She savors her sandwich, taking nibbles that last almost the entire forty-five-minute ride from Copenhagen to Hørsholm, and falls asleep with the last of it still in her hand. I eat mine in five ravenous bites and then sit in uneasy silence with Helene as the carriage enters a dense, green-black forest and fills the space between us with shadows.

I'm starting to wonder if we will ever arrive when we suddenly burst out into the sunshine on the other side, turning down a long drive.

A blinding white manor house rises up in front of us, enormous and stately, with creamy gables that curve and build in delicate layers like a cake. I elbow Eve to wake her. Animal tracks deboss the snow around the house. Scarlet berries, cased in ice, melt and drip in the sun.

Eve straightens in her seat and gapes out the window. The house is sided with two expansive wings, each with slate roofs and spires that sharpen to a needle's point to prick the pearl-gray sky. The walls are covered with sets of glittering windows and an enormous second-floor balcony that overlooks a frozen pond.

"It feels like a fairy tale castle," Eve whispers. "Hidden in its own forest."

Someone in a vibrant red cloak is skating on the pond, lazily, as if she is floating above the ice. But by the time the carriage pulls to a stop and we climb out, she is gone.

The wind is harsh through my thin brown dress and coat, both made from the scratchy fabric Thorsen didn't think he could sell at full price. I tried to improve the garments with immaculate tailoring and embroidery around the hem and collar, but the cold still finds its way in with hardly any effort at all.

"Welcome home, Mrs. Vestergaard." A housemaid steps forward as soon as we enter the foyer. She appears old enough to be my mother, with round curves and cheeks that look like apples. "How was your journey?"

"It was fine, thank you, Nina."

Servants materialize in two mirrored lines, white aprons and smart black uniforms, neat and without a hair out of place. They bow symmetrically when we walk in. The foyer ceiling is vaulted, stretching for a mile overhead, culminating in a glittering pattern of stained glass and chandeliers. The floors and walls are covered in white marble tiles and layered with rugs and draperies, each the width of a palm, to absorb cold and echoes. A scent of lavender foxgloves overflows from a porcelain vase on the foyer table. I wonder, again, how something so out of season could possibly grow here.

Eve gasps at the staircase that spills into the foyer like a trumpet skirt made of marble, and the opulence sends an unexpected wave of anger over me. I brace myself against it. All I can see is Ingrid crying over the sink, wondering how to stretch the money after Far died, worrying that the collectors would come and separate us forever. Something within me stiffens further at the magnificent golden portrait of Aleks Vestergaard, Helene's late husband. Ingrid and I could barely afford to bury my father in a plain pine box, in a plot far from the prestigious places near the church door, marked with little more than a small, spindly cross.

"Nina," Mrs. Vestergaard says to the housemaid, "I'd like to introduce you to my daughter, Eve." An unmistakable ripple of surprise makes its way through the staff before they bow and curtsy again in their unified lines. "Eve, this is our household staff. You'll come to know their names and they will take excellent care of your every need."

"Welcome, Miss Vestergaard," Nina says, reaching out a hand to Eve. "May I take your coat?"

Eve flushes at the sound of her new name, and Helene turns

to me. "Nina, this is Marit Olsen, who will join our staff as my personal seamstress. Please find her appropriate quarters."

"Yes, ma'am." Nina nods to me. "Come along, Miss Olsen." She gestures to a staircase that leads down to a dark corridor.

I want to grab Eve in a hug or take her hand, but I cannot in the presence of these people. Cannot because I *should* not. So I avoid her eyes entirely to discourage her from doing something inappropriate in front of her new servants.

One of which, it suddenly occurs to me, *I* am now.

I nod at Nina and follow her as Eve mounts the steps behind Helene to the upper floors.

We part without speaking and I feel something shift between us the moment we take the stairs in two different directions.

CHAPTER SEVEN

I FOLLOW NINA THROUGH an underground corridor that veers right, to the servants' wing. She's cutting a pace, her low heels rapping against the floor and echoing.

"Seamstress, eh?" she grunts at me.

To my surprise, when I nod, she rolls her eyes.

The corridor is twenty paces long, lit with sconces that give off a dim light, and it's cold enough that for a moment, I can see my breath. Nina opens a heavy door at the end and we are hit with a wall of warm air and raucous laughter. The corridor is like a portal to a different world from the cold, white upstairs.

"Not that one!" someone fusses, and someone else adds, "Clod."

We enter a large kitchen and I hurry to keep step with Nina around a huge bronze wood-burning stove that hisses with pots and pans. Three servants crowd around a hulking slab of wood that serves as a table. A woman with frizzy hair is thrusting a husk of dried barley into a boy's face as he examines a cookbook.

A fourth person—a young man—is barely visible just beyond the corner, shining shoes made of leather black as pitch. He's dressed in a sharp black uniform like a butler, but his hair hangs long and greasy-looking.

"It clearly says *spelt*," the boy says.

"Well, we don't have any." The woman—presumably the cook—shakes the barley in the boy's face.

"Potatoes again?" The third servant, a girl who looks about fourteen, with hair plaited around her head like a crown, breaks into a burlap sack. "I heard Lara say that this much starch is making her harder to lift when she skates."

"I wouldn't have any trouble lifting Lara," the cook mutters, crushing the barley into the soup. "Right out that window."

Nina clears her throat and they look up in attention. "Mrs. Vestergaard's returned. And she's brought home a *daughter*."

The servants instantly whirl around, the barley forgotten. My heart squeezes to hear those words. Eve is not an orphan anymore. She's someone's daughter, again.

"What did you say?" The butler stands and in his haste sends the polish clattering to the floor.

"She's been looking for so long I thought she'd never find one—"

"A daughter, finally—"

"And without any notice?" the cook cries. She springs into action, whipping a towel from the table and tying an apron around her waist. "She'll be expecting a feast and I barely have scraps until the delivery tomorrow." She starts rummaging through the cupboards for cookbooks and flour and barking orders. "A pudding. Signe, check to see if we have any figs. Brock, run to the greenhouse and get me whatever smells the best. I'll make it work."

"I'll show you to your quarters," Nina says to me briskly, and seems anxious to rush me along before the other servants take notice.

We wind through a drafty hallway and up three flights of stairs to the east wing of the servants' quarters. They are toasty warm and well lit, crammed with nooks and storage closets and workrooms. It reminds me of the day I arrived at the Mill, with all the orphans watching me climb the stairs to the dorm room with my suitcase in hand. I was determined not to cry, even though it smelled so different from home and no one was going to braid my hair and read "The Snow Queen" when I was in bed with a fever. The next three years were the loneliest of my life, until the day Eve approached me with Wubbins and her fierce scowl. I picture her climbing a staircase right now, parallel to this one, with only a few walls to separate us. But how different a house must feel when you enter it as part of the family—not as a temporary arrangement, conditional on proving yourself useful.

Nina is rapidly going over the rules ahead of me, her breath shortening the higher we climb: "Dinner at seven prompt or you don't eat, no girls allowed in the boys' quarters and vice versa, we all head to town once a month, curfew's half past eight, and absolutely no leaving the house after dark. Make sure you never keep Mrs. Vestergaard waiting, and get all your work done neatly and on time. Early's even better."

There's an explosion of laughter through the door as we crest the third floor. Nina harrumphs. "I can only imagine what she's doing in there," she says, glowering and jangling the keys. "The infamous Liljan."

Nina slips the key into the lock and, with a jerk of her wrist, bursts through the door.

"Nina!" Liljan exclaims, scurrying to hide something under her pillow. "You might have knocked!"

I step into the room behind Nina. The infamous Liljan has hair the color of straw. Her blue eyes turn down at the corners and sparkle with light. She seems like the sort of girl who claps with glee over just about *everything*. Next to her, sitting on the bed that's probably meant to be mine, is a boy.

"You're not supposed to be in here!" Nina roars. The boy turns to us and he has mussed hair that sticks up, wire spectacles, and these dark eyes that make something in my chest feel funny. "And no eating!" She confiscates half-wrapped candies from them. "Do you want rats?"

They both look dutifully ashamed, but once Nina's back is turned, Liljan's mouth begins to quirk. The boy glares and throws a candy at her head when Nina faces me again. "No boys. No eating in the room," she repeats to me sternly. "Just don't do whatever Liljan is doing and you'll be fine."

"But, Nina, light of my life," Liljan says, "you haven't introduced us!"

"This is Marit Olsen. Marit, this is Liljan Dahl, housemaid and resident pain in my rear. And this," Nina says, grabbing the boy's arm, "is her brother, Jakob Dahl. Leaving." She leads him toward the door. "Mrs. Vestergaard will ring if she needs you," she tells me. "Wear your uniform in the main house, starched enough to stand up even without you in it, and *never be late!*" She shoves Jakob into the hall and slams the door.

"Hello, Marit Olsen," Liljan says, leaning forward on her elbows. "What'd you get hired for?" She unwraps another candy with a shiny red shell.

"I'm, um, the seamstress," I say, setting my bag down at my feet. To my surprise, Liljan's face falls. She heaves a sigh and rolls over. "That one's yours," she says, gesturing to the unmade straw mattress where Jakob was sitting. "Sofie only slept in it for about two weeks."

"Sofie?" I ask.

"The seamstress before you." Liljan presses her lips together. "They don't tend to be here for long."

"Why?" I ask too quickly, but Liljan merely shrugs and pops the candy into her mouth.

I steal a nervous look at my new bed. Suddenly, taking this job feels like stepping into clothes someone else died in.

I get to work making the bed, laying out the feather tick, admiring the underblanket and a quilt made of eiderdown. There's a small washstand and a matching tiled chamber pot, and the walls are covered with an intricate floral pattern of lavender wisteria knit like lace. When Liljan's back is turned, I run my fingertips over it. I've never heard of such quality in a servants' room before.

Liljan sucks on the candy. "Uniforms in the far trunk," she says.

I shake out and shape the straw sack mattress, then change into a crisp ink-black Vestergaard uniform. What would my father think, to see me here now? Working for his old employer —using magic?

His letter falls from my pocket and I tuck it carefully into the book of Hans Christian Andersen stories, wishing for the hundredth time that Far had written my name. This final thing from him, the last thing I have, and it wasn't even meant for me. It rankles me still, even after all these years, that he addressed it only to her. Why?

"Dinner!" Liljan suddenly trills. "Hope you're made of stiff stuff, Marit," she says, and though her tone is skeptical, it almost feels as though she's extending a piece of advice. "Coming?"

She opens the door and we're hit with the most intoxicating smell, as if the air itself has turned rich and golden. I tighten my apron across my front like a shield and follow her downstairs.

❧

The atmosphere at dinner is more raucous than Ness ever would have allowed, with people bustling in and out, gossip flying as the doors whip open and shut, servants heading to the main house with their tureens of red cabbage and platters of pork roast with crackling skin. The girl named Signe is whipping fresh cream, and the cook is pulling an apple cake out of the wood-fired stove, with browned cinnamon apple slices laced on top in a swirling pattern like the opening petals of a rose. My stomach rumbles. I think of Agnes, sitting alone in our room at Thorsen's, always sniveling and bent over her plate as if I were going to steal from it. For one half second, I almost feel sorry for her.

"So Mrs. Vestergaard's actually gone and brought home a daughter?" Signe asks. The staff is crowded around the thick wooden table, their faces lit by flickering wax candles as platters of food are set in front of them.

I stand in the doorway uncertainly—and then start with a sudden realization.

Magic practically shimmers around them all. I've never sensed it like this before—but then again, I've never seen so much of it collected in one place or so freshly used. Somehow I simply know it's there, an extra sense prickling along my skin, as if a low hum or buzz is radiating from them all. My breath catches in my chest as I remember the way Helene examined my work on the coat, and the realization that follows carves through me like ice. Of course she knew exactly what she was asking of me. Everyone working here must have magic. Because you have to be superior to earn a place in a house like this one.

And superior usually means magic.

I know now why she had a plum in November. I think of the gorgeous flowers overflowing from their vase in the foyer. What kind of woman fills her house with people who risk the Firn for her benefit? A woman from the same family who asked men to risk their lives in mines and ignored the orphans they left behind. And yet—I steal a furtive glance around the room. No one seems frightened or unhappy here. The atmosphere in this kitchen is actually warm and jovial. Even familial.

Until the moment when everyone suddenly seems to notice me at once.

Silence falls as they turn toward the doorway in unison.

They seem confused.

The cook says: "Well, who in spoon's haven is *that?*"

"That's Marit Olsen," Nina announces in a crisp voice. "Mrs. Vestergaard's newest seamstress." My arms keep trying to come up and cross my chest, but I hold them firmly at my sides.

The young man with long, dirty hair thunks his spoon down on the table with a deep growl in his throat. "I thought that job was finally going to be *Ivy's.*"

The cook half drops a glass platter on the table and a streaking crack appears down the middle of it. She swears under her breath and then looks up in anguish at a girl about my age, with a long blond braid and a mole perched like a cake crumb on her right cheek. "Ivy," the cook says, "we tried so hard. I thought this time you were finally going to get to stay."

"Oh, Aunt Dorit," the girl named Ivy says, her eyes bright. "It isn't your fault. I'm sorry I can't be what Mrs. Vestergaard needs. My sewing is good, but of course it isn't the same as being gifted with it." She places her palm over the glass, and when she takes her hand away, the platter is whole again. As if she *healed* it. My face heats. I've never seen anyone do magic so brazenly before—or speak of it so openly. It makes me feel exposed somehow. Like walking into a hall of mirrors and glimpsing an angle of myself I'd never seen before.

"Someone is going to want what you can do, darling," the cook says to Ivy. "And if Helene Vestergaard had half a mi—"

"Dorit!" Nina says sharply. "That's enough."

Dorit flings a heaping serving of salad down onto a plate. "I remember when Ivy lost her first tooth right there," she says, choking on a sob. "I promised my sister Rhody that I would always watch out for her."

Everyone turns once again to glare at me.

Oh, great.

Every seat is filled around the huge wooden table and no one makes any move to scoot over, so I sheepishly walk toward the wall and squeeze in at the small space left at the corner. I think of Eve and how knowing someone as a child can weave them into your heart like a web, no matter what happens next or who they grow up to become.

I understand that perfectly well. But that doesn't mean I'm leaving. I steel myself against the glares, pretending I don't notice them. I survived a decade in an orphanage and three months with Agnes the shrew—a welcome like this isn't exactly going to make me wilt like a piece of lettuce.

Especially when there's a platter of pork and crackling making its way around the table. Wax drips down the flickering candles as warmth rolls off the hearth fire. I eye the crackling, crisp and golden, and my mouth waters. I haven't had that dish since I was six years old.

The girl next to me takes a piece of roast. "Brock?" she says sweetly, offering it to the greasy-haired boy, who manages to grab the platter from her before I can get any. My hand curls into a fist in my lap. Brock sends the food farther away from me, then leans closer and says in a low voice: "Ivy grew up here, with us. She deserves that spot."

I look back at him without flinching. "Why don't you take it up with Mrs. Vestergaard, then?"

"Why don't you just quit?"

"No," I say defiantly, and as a result, the basket of rolls is passed right over my head. I clear my throat and ask for someone to pass the red cabbage to me, please.

My request is ignored.

I stand up to get it myself, but just as I reach for it, Dorit picks up the dish and whisks it to the kitchen counter. At least no one stops me from grabbing the soggy tomatoes left in the bottom of the salad bowl, even though I hate tomatoes. I feel Jakob Dahl studying me across the length of the table. When I look up, he meets my gaze, blinking dark lashes behind his spectacles. He isn't unfriendly—but he doesn't exactly smile, either.

I wonder if he notices me flinch when the gossip suddenly turns toward Eve.

"Who's seen her?" says a boy with dark, close-cropped hair,

shoveling food into his mouth. "The daughter? What's she look like?"

"She's a sweet-looking little thing, just a slip of a girl; I can't imagine she was being fed enough at that orphanage she came from—" says Dorit.

"She's *dark,* isn't she?" interrupts a girl with blond hair the color of dishwater. She chews loudly, showing her food. "Is she even Danish?"

I take a sharp breath.

"She's a dancer, like Mrs. Vestergaard," someone to my left says. "Lara saw a tutu when she unpacked her trunk—"

"I heard she comes from the same orphanage that Helene grew up in—"

"She's lucky as they come, ain't she? I wish Mrs. Vestergaard would adopt me!" says the first boy, and sets the table to laughing. He turns to the girl with the dishwater hair and obnoxious chewing. "Pauper to prince. I'd make you warm my towels by the fire, Rae, and feed me figs from the tip of your fork."

Rae shows him her tongue. "I'd lick them first, I would."

Anger grows in vines of fire through me to hear the person I love being passed around and picked apart like the meat on the platter. I start to rise, words that I'll probably regret burning in my throat, when—

"Yes, well," Brock says, his voice crisp and cold. He picks up his fork and examines the tines in the light. "I think *I'd* be forever looking over my shoulder if Helene adopted me."

I stop short, my words dying on my lips. I quietly,

inconspicuously sit back down. Listening carefully with ears pricked.

"Oh, stop," Rae says with a dismissive groan. "Not this again."

Brock shrugs, stabbing his meat with his fork. "Aleks Vestergaard was a healthy man in the prime of life—that's all I'm going to say."

From across the table, Jakob adjusts his spectacles, resting them on his cheekbones.

"He had a problem with his heart," Rae says with exasperation. "He wasn't *murdered,* you imbecile. Who would have murdered him? Helene?" She laughs.

My stomach suddenly turns.

"You *know* who," Brock says, his face darkening. He selects a bone and picks his teeth. "But good on Helene. It's a smart countermove. He takes out one heir; she adds another. It's like moving a pawn in front of your queen."

"Enough," Nina orders from the other end of the table. "You know I don't approve of this gossiping about the master's death. It's undignified, it's unprofessional, it's far outside the bounds of propriety."

I pull my collar from my neck, my heart loud in my ears. Who are they talking about? And surely Brock isn't saying what I think he's saying?

Surely Aleks Vestergaard wasn't murdered?

"Marit," Ivy says quietly, and I jump. The final tomato slips from my fork and splatters on my plate in a limp red puddle.

"Here," she whispers. She has piled her own plate with crackling and cabbage, and she pushes it in front of me.

My mind is still caught on what Brock said, and I look at her in surprise.

"Thank you," I whisper. My throat has gone dry.

"You're too nice, Ivy," Brock says, as if he's disgusted.

"You know I love you, and you know how much I want to stay," she says, smoothing her napkin. "But you don't need to drive Marit away. Someone else will just come. They always do."

Apparently the table is done discussing Eve and the potential murder of the late Mr. Vestergaard and has decided to return its collective focus to me. I'm fresher blood, anyway.

"I disagree," Brock says loudly, as if he's rallying them all to action. "Eventually, Mrs. Vestergaard will run out of magical seamstress replacements and realize she should just pick someone who already fits in with us all." He turns to me. "I'm Ivy's brother, and her aunt's the cook," he continues. "So will you prefer hair, sand, or glass in your breakfast?"

The whole table is watching him slowly smear butter onto a plump roll. And watching to see how I'll react.

My veins are buzzing. Somehow, I need to establish that I won't be trifled with by these people.

I pick up my knife and saw through an enormous piece of Ivy's roast.

"If I'm leaving the seamstress job, you'll be the first to know, Brock," I announce, brandishing the knife in a way that is at least vaguely threatening. "I'll submit my resignation by tying you to the banister with your own dirty hair."

For a moment there is gaping silence as Brock splutters, practically choking, and everyone else stares at me, mouths parted. It's no idle threat. With magic, I probably could.

Then Liljan erupts into a roar of delighted laughter and bangs the table. "Brock, do you need a formal introduction? Because this is Marit. I think she also goes by 'Your Match.'"

"There's your stiff stuff," I mutter. It seems I've won enough cachet from the staff to finish eating in peace, and they all move on, clattering their dishes into the sink and starting their evening chores. The only person who stays at the table is Jakob, his eyes glittering thoughtfully behind his spectacles.

"What?" I finally ask him with irritation, my mouth full of berry compote.

To my surprise he raises his glass to me in a wordless salute and then turns away, but not before his face lights with the most unexpected and magnificent smile.

CHAPTER EIGHT

M Y NIGHTMARES ARE LONG-DEAD GHOSTS that are roused anew by my coming here.

"It isn't like him," my sister says, "to keep us waiting."

She lets the curtains in the kitchen window fall.

Ingrid is thirteen, I'm six, and our father is late. He works three-quarters of an hour from here in the Vestergaards' southern mines, and he's always home in time to wash for dinner and change out of clothes coated in limestone dust. He whistles while he rinses the grime from his mustache, even when the water is cold enough to have little chunks of ice floating in it.

I wait, swinging my legs, knotting a dishtowel between my fingers.

Ingrid ties and reties her handkerchief and scrubs the wood table until her hands turn red and raw. She ruins the rye bread; it sinks into a soggy mess. She keeps looking out the window. Until finally, we hear it. The jingle of bells on his horse. We run to the window, breaths fogging the glass.

Ingrid makes a choking sound when she sees the black uniform, the golden tassels. The knock on the door sounds like a branch crack-ing under the weight of snow.

The man in black holds out an envelope stamped with the Vester-gaards' dark seal. The hammer and pick. Ingrid's slim fingers trem-ble so badly she can hardly open it.

The man waits as she reads the letter. He offers a formal "I'm sorry, ma'am," and tips his hat toward us. "I'm going to need to ask you a few questions. You and your sister."

"Please, not tonight," Ingrid says, her voice strangled. "You'll have to do that later." The door closing behind him is loud, but worse is the sound of the lock when Ingrid clicks it into its place. I know for sure then, as soon as Ingrid dead-bolts that door.

Because now Far can't get in from the outside. If he were still coming home.

I start to wail even before she turns to read the letter out loud to me. Sob and beat my fists against her when she says the words.

There was an accident at the mines.

Landslide.

Buried beneath.

We sit in the kitchen together long after darkness falls and the fire dies in the hearth. Still, she clutches that letter in her hands and doesn't let it go.

"What are we going to do?" I ask, and then, tired from crying, lay my head down on the clean wooden table. My breathing slows. Perhaps she thinks I've fallen asleep.

"An accident," she says, as if to herself.

I open my eyes to see her hands folding tighter around the letter, crushing it under her delicate fingers. The ink of the words is smudging into her skin. She blinks, once, twice, her blue eyes clouding.

Her fists curl like shells at her sides, the magic thrumming through her.

Someone else's fingers suddenly tighten around my arm.

"Marit. Are you okay?"

When I open my eyes, Liljan is kneeling by my bed, shaking me.

"You were . . . crying," she says softly.

"I'm fine," I say. I pull the sheets around me like a cocoon, around my hammering heart, and turn away from her. "Sorry," I say stiffly.

Now, in the brightness of morning, I can smell the coffee wafting up the staircase from the kitchen as well as something warm and doughy that instantly makes me feel hungry. I pull the sheets tighter around me as the nightmare fades, weary at the idea of fighting Dorit and Brock for some scraps of breakfast. Liljan squints at me for a moment as if to make sure I'm all right, and then she closes our bedroom door with a faint click behind her.

I rise, wash up, and am changing into my uniform when Liljan reappears in the doorway. She sets something down on my nightstand: a steaming coffee and a napkin that falls open to reveal a single freshly baked blackberry scone.

"Hair, glass, and sand free," she announces.

"Thank you," I say, and a warmth lit by surprise spreads through my chest.

"Just don't let Nina find out," she says. "If you have to, eat the napkin."

I smile at her shyly. When I take my first bite of scone, the blackberries are still warm.

Downstairs, Nina inspects my starched white pinafore and bonnet before giving me a key to my workroom and instructions on how to find Mrs. Vestergaard in her quarters. My steps echo through the cavernous main house. Rooms seem to spill out endlessly from one another, with corridors leading off in different directions, some blazing with light and others cloaked in darkness. The floors are a lattice of wood, shades of oak panels clicking together like intricate puzzle pieces, and gilded sconces seem to melt into the patterned walls.

My heart lifts at the thought of seeing Eve.

Helene Vestergaard is sitting at a dressing table as Liljan pins her hair into a sharp updo. Her bedcovers and curtains are heavy brocades embroidered with silvers and blues. A massive masonry stove is nestled in the far corner, and warmth pours out from behind its gleaming golden doors. The stove's pattern of white tiles and delicate blue flowers extends all the way up to the ceiling.

"Marit, are you settled in?"

I catch my reflection in the mirror. I wear the nightmare like hollows beneath my eyes, the memory of the wax Vestergaard seal on that horrid letter now fresh in my mind.

"Yes, Mrs. Vestergaard."

"Good. I have a job for you that will require quick work. I'll need several dresses for me and for Eve." Her earrings dangle in the reflection, hovering like water that dripped from her earlobes and then froze. "Liljan has left my measurements and designs in your workroom."

"I'll begin right away," I say.

"Eve's uncle—my late husband's brother, Philip—will be joining us for Mortensaften," Helene says. Liljan sweeps a dark wave of hair up to reveal the nape of Helene's neck. "I'll need the first two dresses by then."

Mortensaften—the dinner held the night before St. Martin's Day to celebrate the harvest—is tomorrow. There's a faint sound in my ears, like glass shattering. What she's asking for is two dresses' worth of magic in a single day.

Helene watches me in the reflection. "Will that be a problem?"

"Not at all," I say evenly, and take two silent steps backwards. As soon as the door closes behind me, I lean against the wall. Fear prickles just beneath my breastbone.

The door across the corridor is cracked just enough for me to glimpse the curve of a small brown foot peeking out from beneath the covers—Eve's right foot, the one that always ends up outside the blanket. "You sleep like a starfish," I once grumbled when we were forced to share a bed. She yawned and pulled her arms and legs in to make herself a tiny ball, rolling onto her back, her ballerina feet tucked beneath her. "Now I'm a snail," she said, giggling, and then made her snore noise, the one that's loud and obnoxious and sounds exactly nothing like an actual snore. *"Honch, honch, honch,"* she fake-snored, and it was so terrible that I started laughing and couldn't stop even when Sare threatened to hit me with the wide end of a broom.

I pause outside Eve's door, wanting to stop and climb into bed with her like I used to. But that's not appropriate now that she's a Vestergaard and I'm just a servant. Instead, I hurry on to my little workroom, which is tucked into a nook on the third floor of the staff quarters. When I find the corkboard pinned with the dress sketches, I half chuff in disbelief. The embroidery, lacing, buttons, and beadwork—each would take me at least a week without magic, even if I worked all day and all night.

I unearth a razor-sharp pair of silver shears and run my fingers longingly over the lush silks and thick brocades I find in the closet, wondering again at the staff last night. How the magic practically hummed off them, yet how settled they seemed together. How strange that they all *want* to stay here.

I bite down on a pin and consider as I drape the bodice across the dress form. I suppose it's the same thing as the men working in the mines. No one is forcing them to, just as no one forced me to take this job. *But is it right to ask people to work for your benefit if it poses such danger to them?* I think, jamming the pins into the soft flesh of the mannequin. *Or have I been wrong to begrudge the Vestergaards for all these years?*

Because they were easier to blame than my father for the choices he made?

I stand in front of the dress I've pinned across the form as though I'm confronting an adversary. I grit my teeth, feel the familiar tension mounting in my jaw. If I think too much about using my magic, I'll talk myself out of it. So I don't let the fear build any more. I picture walking to the edge of a dock, facing the dark waves below.

Then I brace myself and just plunge in.

Immediately, a tingling chill lights through my limbs, and it always shocks me — how *good* it feels — as if I'm doing exactly what I was made to do. But then fear chokes out any pleasure there is to be found. I wonder if small traces of the Firn have managed to build up within me by now, crystalline patches of frost, even though I've been so terribly careful with my magic through the years. Suddenly, all I can see is Ingrid. I remember the way her toes looked, stiff and blue, when the Firn spilled through her body and the cremator came to take her away.

Think of Ingrid happy, I tell myself. I picture her on the morning of Shrovetide, laughing as she pretended to hit Far with the ceremonial branch we'd made from birch twigs, feathers, and hollow eggshells. Far bellowed when I bounced it on his head to get him out of bed. Afterward he placed the rod in a vase on the kitchen table as if it were a lovely bouquet instead of a mishmash of ugly sticks. Later that evening, I became Queen of the Cats. I bashed a branch into a wooden barrel and sent candy gushing out like rain from a spout. But Ingrid was the one who had primed it for me. She had done the hard work on the turn before, so that all it took was the smallest swing, and I got the reward.

It suddenly hits me that I'm older now than she was when she died.

I work through the swell of the day until the sun is setting and beads glitter up the fabric of Eve's dress like delicate wisps of smoke. I can't imagine what damage the magic might have done to me on the inside. But when I catch my reflection in the mirror, I actually look flushed. Exhilarated. I feel alive. My skin and nerves practically crackle. Life is a blade that seems to grow dull with too much ease or assurance of what each day will bring. Tonight has none of that; it throbs with reality, and even the air has a slicing edge when I breathe it in.

I make sure to lock my workroom behind me, not putting it past Brock to sabotage the dresses before I can get them safely to Helene and Eve.

When I reach my room, there is a letter folded on top of my pillow.

"That's from Helene's daughter. For . . . you?" Liljan says. She looks at me with eyebrows raised, creasing the folds of her uniform before she puts it away. Her unasked questions hang in the air between us.

"Oh?" I ask, carefully turning my back to her when I unseal the paper. To Liljan's credit, the note doesn't appear as though anyone's tampered with it. I recognize Eve's familiar, uneven penmanship, the middle tine of all her *w*'s rising higher than the other two.

Mare,

> *Tried to find you. Where are you? Did you get lost in the corridors? Eaten by a draug? Did you wander off and smell too much wool? (Har, har) Were you taking a nap? (Honch, honch)*
>
> *Tried to save you a wienerbrød with that almond filling you like but that woman Nina wouldn't let me bring it out of the kitchen. So I ate it.*
>
> *come visit soon*
> *love from Eve*
> *and Wubbins*

I feel a warmth bloom in my chest and then realize Liljan is still looking at me. I think back to Brock's revealing comments last night—that Aleks Vestergaard might have been murdered, that Eve might even be a *pawn* of some sort—and wonder how quickly those inside observations would quiet if the other servants knew about my own friendship with Eve. Perhaps it behooves me to keep that hidden—and my ears pricked in the meantime. "Just some requests for the dresses I'm making," I lie. "Did you know Philip Vestergaard is coming for dinner tomorrow?"

It's a blatant attempt to change the subject, but Liljan takes the bait. "Dorit's Mortensaften goose will melt in your mouth," she says. "It tastes like butter. Like actually eating magic."

I pull out the Hans Christian Andersen book and slip Eve's letter inside with my father's. Then I roll up my sleeves to examine my wrists.

I breathe a sigh of relief. The skin there is blank, with no sign of the Firn.

But I'm walking a tightrope that will continue to fray, with Helene's impossible tasks and her house full of servants pouring out magic.

Sooner or later, Eve's going to find out that I've been lying to her for years. I roll my sleeves back down.

I can't risk her learning the truth about me from someone else, I think.

So tonight, I will tell it to her myself.

CHAPTER NINE

I WAIT UNTIL LILJAN'S BREATH turns even that night and the moonlight slices like a piece of white glass through the window before I sneak out of bed with Eve's new dress tucked under my arm. I don't dare light a candle, so I feel my way down the staircase, wincing when I find a creaky board. The corridor to the main house is cold and dark as a grave, and I feel along the wall with one hand and bite on the knuckles of the other out of a silly childhood fear that I'll run into a wight or draug. Or worse, Brock.

I listen for a moment when I reach the main house and climb slowly up to the third floor. I half can't believe myself, taking this risk of getting sacked, and I clutch Eve's dress tighter to my side when I tiptoe past Helene's bedroom. I give the five lightest knocks I can manage on Eve's door, in the telltale rhythm we'd use on the floor of the Mill when we wanted to talk, so she'll know it's me. When she cracks open the door, she's dressed in a nightgown, her hair oiled and tucked into a night scarf, and her face breaks into a dazzling grin. "What are you doing here?" she whispers, and ushers me inside.

My stomach turns a little.

"I brought your dress," I say. She brings it over to the window and lets it catch the moonlight. The beads are like liquid silver. She tilts the dress back and forth, admiring the clasps of the corset, the scalloped neck. "You did this all in one day?" she asks, and I hear the first note of suspicion in her voice. "Marit, how?"

Here is my chance. I wasn't expecting it so soon. I hesitate, looking at her deep brown eyes. How do you tell someone you love that you've been hiding something from her for her entire life? I flip the dress over to reveal the hem of the petticoat. At the Mill I used to sew secret pockets into our clothes so we could hide our little drawings and hard candies, feathers and pebbles, from Ness and the older girls. "H-here, Eve, listen," I stutter, trying to buy myself time. "If you ever need me — just claim one of your dresses needs mending and tuck me a note in this pocket." I slip my finger into it to show her. "Look, just like old times. Do you remember the Morse I taught you?"

My father was the one who taught me Morse. I peeked over his shoulder one day and asked him about the dots and dashes he was looking at, and he showed me patiently how to write my name. It became a game — we left little messages for each other in the dust that gathered on the windowsill, in the frost of the window. It was our way to communicate. And then, after he died, I passed what he'd taught me on to Eve.

"Why would I need to send you a secret note?" she teases. She tucks her fingers into the slip pocket. "I'll hide a bite of Dorit's cake in here to make sure you get some."

"Well," I say delicately, "things here are different now, Eve."

"What do you mean?" she asks, laying the dress out on her trunk.

"Our stations have changed. It probably isn't such a good idea for you to . . . fraternize so openly with the staff." I pause. "With me."

The light of realization dawns in her eyes. "I'm not ashamed of you, Marit."

"Oh, I know that." I take her hand. "But it's better this way. It can be our little game," I say lightly. I smile at her. "Send me a note, and I'll send one back."

I let go of her hand and examine the details of her room, with its walls somehow already patterned in pink roses and sketches of ballerinas. Incredibly, some of them even look just like Eve. I trace the images in the moonlight, and my stomach clenches.

To tell the truth now means admitting two critical things: first, that I've lied to her, and second, that I'm risking the Firn with each day I remain at the Vestergaards'. Both will infuriate and hurt her.

Knowing Eve, and how wily and clever she is, she'd probably accuse me of stealing something and get me kicked out—just to save my life.

I turn away from her. *No,* I decide, my nerve faltering. I won't tell her about the magic. Not yet.

"Do you have to go, Marit?" Eve asks.

"I should," I say. But instead I climb into bed with her, nestling under the warm eiderdown quilt, breathing in her smell of palm oil and toothpaste powder. "How is it?" I whisper, snuggling closer to her. "Being here?"

She exhales a long breath and tucks into herself like a shell. "It's like being hungry and then eating so much rich food you think you'll make yourself sick. Look at all these beautiful things." She runs her hands over her satin coverlet. Her voice is almost a whisper. "Sometimes I wonder why she picked me, Marit. What if it turns out I'm not what she wanted?" She rolls over, so that her back is to me and she is whispering to the wall. "Maybe she'll change her mind and send me back to the Mill. I'm almost afraid to let myself enjoy it. As if I'll wake up and it's all going to go away."

"That's not how it works, dear one," I promise her. "No returns allowed." I kiss the cloth covering her hair and feel a stab of guilt for the secrets I'm still hiding from her.

She turns and props her face on her elbow. "How is it downstairs?"

"Wonderful," I say quickly.

"Is everyone being kind to you?"

"Yes," I lie.

"They better." She giggles mischievously and wiggles farther into the covers. "Or I'll have them sacked. Now, will you do your face thing?"

"My face thing?"

"You know. The thing I love, with the stripes."

On the nights prospective parents came but didn't pick her, I'd tuck her in and graze my thumbs over the length of her eyebrows, from nose to temple, and then once along each cheekbone, as lightly as I could. "There," I say, doing it now just like I always used to. "I've brushed away anything ugly or bad left over from today. Now go to sleep, and we'll both wake up fresh tomorrow."

"I'm glad now, Marit," she says, already half-asleep, "for all those times I didn't get picked. Because then I wouldn't be here with you."

I look at her with a lump in my throat and kiss her forehead. Then I slip out of her room and am almost to the main floor when Nina emerges from the servants' corridor with a candle.

Oh, blast.

I dart down the rest of the stairs and manage to slip behind an urn just before she turns the corner. Three seconds more and we would have practically collided. My heart thunders. The shadow of another servant is behind her, blocking my exit to the underground corridor. They are doing one final sweep of the main house, and Nina will likely see me when she comes back down the stairs. I crouch in the shadows until she reaches the second floor, and then I open the front door a crack and slip outside. The night air stings, like a slap, and when the door closes behind me, I hear its lock faintly click. *Oh, curse it all,* I think, and draw a sharp breath. I turn around slowly.

Moonlight shears off the ice in the pond, which glows white, as though it spent the day gathering light within itself. Smoke from the chimney smells of deep wood and billows out into the night like steam from a teacup. I pick my way around the frozen ice toward the servants' wing, praying that the side door by the kitchen pantry might still be unlocked. But when I yank, the lock holds fast. I feel the first dull ringing of panic. If I get locked outside all night, I might very well freeze to death.

I always feared that's how I'd end up, eventually. I just thought it would be from the inside out.

I plunge my hand into the snow, looking for a piece of ice as small and hard as a pebble. Hoping that after this morning with the scone, Liljan and I have reached enough understanding that she might let me in rather than allowing me to freeze to death outside—or ratting me out to Nina. My teeth are starting to chatter as I wind up and prepare to fling the ice rock at our darkened window.

"Marit?"

Startled, I jolt back as Jakob skates out from the pond's shadows, the moonlight glinting on the blades under his feet.

"Horse's *bells*," I gasp. A gust of wind finds the bare skin on my neck. "You scared me!"

"Sorry." Jakob curves around sharply and my heart thuds as I plunge my naked hands into my apron. He clears his throat and takes in my coatless appearance. "What brings you out on this fine evening?" he asks. He skates to the edge of the pond, so that we are barely an arm's distance apart.

I sniff and silently curse to myself. This is not going at all according to plan. "I'm getting some fresh air. And I seem to have locked myself out. Is there, um, a way in"—I blink at him —"or do you sleep out here in some sort of fort?"

He smiles wryly. "There's a way in. As soon as you can come up with a better story than that."

I see the flicker of Nina's candle inside. "Quick, there's Nina," I whisper. "Hide."

He steps off the ice and we duck down just beneath the windowsill. I feel the pleasant warmth of him next to me. Nina's face appears above us, looking out. Then, after a tense beat, she and her candlelight disappear.

"I hope you really do know of another way in," I whisper, letting out a breath. When he turns toward me, I suddenly realize how close his face is to mine.

"Oh, we do!" Liljan's voice says cheerfully from my left. She laughs at my startled jump and finishes lacing up her skate beneath eaves glittering with icicles as sharp and crowded as wolfs' teeth.

"If Nina finds us all out here," she says, pulling herself up and shooting me a wicked grin, "she'll shave our heads and lash us all silly."

"Really?" I ask tentatively.

"Probably not," Jakob says, standing.

"But where's your sense of imagination?" Liljan asks, placing her hand palm-down on the window above her head. It instantly darkens, as if it's been stained with shadow. I stare at it, wondering if my eyes are playing tricks.

"No more Nina," she says. "She can stare out this window all she wants, but she won't see us anymore." She turns to us with a dazzling smile and then makes her way along the row of windows, turning them each into an opaque black shell. Realization feels like flowers blooming within me. I suddenly understand the intricate beauty of our bedroom walls. How quickly Eve's room was decorated just for her.

Liljan must have done all of it. With magic.

"My fellow Nina-defiers," Liljan says to us, stepping out onto the ice. "Shall we skate across Denmark tonight?"

Jakob offers me his hand and pulls me up.

As soon as Liljan places her bare palm on the ice, color seeps and spills out from her touch, over the thousands of air bubbles that have crystallized beneath her feet like fizzing glass ornaments. The ice becomes a living map of Jutland, Funen, and Zealand, with lush green mountains and grass that ripples in the wind. Bluebells and daffodils and violets are set blooming under the frozen stars. I feel lightheaded, seeing Denmark as a bird might, flying high above it all. I've spent my life wondering if everyone else with magic is as afraid of it as I am. But Liljan uses hers extravagantly, with pleasure, as if she's pouring from an endless well. Is she just a fool? Young and silly, with little thought for consequences, even more reckless than Ingrid?

Or does she know something I don't?

I watch her with the stirring of something deep within me that I soon realize is envy. I love the way magic makes me feel. I just wish that fear didn't seep in alongside my enjoyment like decay across a flower.

Jakob takes a step onto the ice and gestures to the map. "Marit, which part do you call home?" he asks.

"I came from Karlslunde," I say softly. "South of here."

"There?" He points at a spot just beneath Copenhagen. Miniature people walk through the streets, and ballet dancers raise their long legs in front of the Royal Theatre.

I shake my head. "Farther."

He smiles. "Here?" He points.

"More to the right."

He raises his eyebrows and points, and this time I laugh a little when I shake my head. I step out gingerly onto the ice. "I'll show you."

He comes to meet me halfway. The stars are a crystalline trail overhead. They do not look like the ones outside the Mill, muted and hidden behind coal smoke and clouds. Here the sky is a shattered mirror reflecting a thousand points of light.

"Do you skate?" he asks.

"No."

"Ever want to learn?" He adjusts his wool hat.

I wobble and stretch my arms out just in time to right myself. "No," I say.

It is eight painstaking paces from Hørsholm to Karlslunde.

"Here," I say, pointing to home. Picturing my little thatched-roof house, and then the Mill. I think of Ness; I taste cinnamon twists.

"Karlslunde," Jakob muses, pulling out a pocketknife. He has a thin, light scar along his chin, as if a cat once scratched him enough to draw blood. "Where Helene is from, as well?"

"And Eve." I look up at the sky, its glittering mess of stars, and wonder how the three of us could all come from the Mill and end up here, in the same house, yet the cards have fallen so differently for each of us. Jakob bends to the ice and carves an *X*. "Now you'll see a little bit of home with every glance out your window." He flicks the knife closed, and when he returns it to his pocket, I notice that his sleeves are slightly too short for his long arms. "You knew Eve? From before?"

Ingrid's voice suddenly whispers in my ear from long ago. *Secrets are like knots,* she told me once, *that bind people together.* "Yes," I admit, taking a chance. "We grew up together."

Forming friendships, I suppose, is a little like walking on ice that thickens underneath your feet with every step toward each other. I take another tentative step forward, testing the weight of it. "Do you think she will be all right here?" I ask.

Jakob tilts his head. "All right?"

"I mean . . . safe?"

At his quizzical look, I add, "What Brock said last night," trying to laugh. "It was all just nonsense? No one would have hurt Mr. Vestergaard on purpose, right?"

Jakob and Liljan exchange a glance.

"Right," he says.

"Probably," Liljan adds.

I was hoping for assurance, but instead alarm awakens within me like a fever.

"Wait. Why does Brock think someone would have hurt Mr. Vestergaard?"

"Brock's not the only one. Those mines are worth a fortune," Liljan says.

The mines. Something flickers inside me. The mines that killed my father might have cost Mr. Vestergaard his life too?

Jakob sort of turns away. "You heard Nina," he says. "I don't think you should concern yourself much with that. If you want to stay employed here." It feels like a door briskly shutting in my face, and I try to stifle the disappointment at the ice of friendship showing signs of cracking like eggshells beneath us.

But then I start to lose my footing and Jakob's hands strike out in a flash to steady me. He's stronger than he looks and he catches me without losing his own balance. For a split second, I'm surprised by how firm his hands feel on my waist. Then he draws back so quickly that you'd think my skin burned him. I tighten my arms around myself in protection from the wind and the disappointment gathering at the base of my throat. I say softly:

"All I want to know is if Eve is going to be safe."

He's very deliberate to leave a foot of cold night air between us, but he shuffles next to me, close enough to reach out again if I fall. He's thinking hard, and he looks at me differently. As if something happened, something that I don't understand, but it seems to be changing his mind.

"I don't think Helene hurt Aleks, if that's what you mean," he finally says. He's being careful choosing his words. "I was his valet before he died, and I believe she loved him. Eve wouldn't be in danger from her."

"But she might be in danger from someone?"

Jakob's jaw twitches and my heart beats a tick faster.

"Aleksander and Philip Vestergaard ran the mines after their father died," Jakob says. "When they found gemstones growing inside the limestone, the mines increased in value a hundredfold."

"Philip Vestergaard?" I echo, realization dawning.

The Philip Vestergaard who is coming here tomorrow for Mortensaften?

"When Aleks died, Helene inherited all of Aleks's ownership. The majority of the mines belong to her now. But perhaps that's not what Philip was expecting."

A prickle runs beneath my skin. Those bloody mines, coming up again and again.

"He's visiting tomorrow, to meet Eve," I say. "How often does he come to this house?"

"In the summers, he stays busier with the mines. But in the winter he comes for most holidays." Jakob ticks off his fingers. "Mortensaften, Christmas, New Year's. Helene's the only family he has left."

My throat catches. "Do you think there's any truth to it? That Philip could be dangerous?"

I don't miss the silent exchange between Liljan and Jakob as she skates past us, with the way siblings can communicate with only a look. When she nods, I suddenly feel as though I've passed some sort of test.

Jakob turns to me. "You know what happened with those mines. The landslide that killed all those miners." It's a statement, not a question, and he says it with such confidence. Almost as if he somehow already knows more about me than I've said. I narrow my eyes but give a slight nod.

"I don't think that was ever the whole story. I think there was more to it than that," Jakob says.

"What do you mean?" My stomach cramps with dread. "You . . . don't think it was an accident?"

The moonlight that catches in the silver of his spectacles suddenly seems shrill. "I think there's something in those mines they were trying to hide."

My voice is barely a whisper. "What?"

"Philip still manages the mines, but when Helene inherited their ownership, she wanted me to look into the logs, the blueprints—everything. To make sure the miners were reasonably safe, that an accident of that magnitude wouldn't happen again. But when I saw the blueprints . . . I found things that made me question whether it had been an accident in the first place."

"Can you show them to me?" I ask. My throat is tight and cold as steel. Something volatile is building within me, something that threatens to explode.

Jakob hesitates. "When I told Helene what I found, she . . .

she asked me to drop it. I think she's afraid that if something bad did happen, and Aleks had anything to do with it . . ." He swallows. "I understand, in a way, why she doesn't want to know. I cared for Aleks too. It would change him, in her eyes. In her memory. It would feel like he died all over again. So she's putting it behind her and moving on now. She adopted Eve. She's focusing on the future now. But to be honest" — he shrugs — "it hasn't been sitting right with me."

Liljan skates a half step closer to me. "It was a long time ago," she says gently. "Is there any point? To look into it after all these years?"

"Yes," I say immediately. "There is to me." It means learning the truth about what happened to my father. It was the event that changed everything, what sent me to the Mill. And I can't leave this place if there's any possibility that the Vestergaards are dangerous or have something to hide. Not with Eve sleeping right upstairs now.

Jakob blows out a breath and considers. "The blueprints are in the third-floor library. I can show you. Tomorrow. When Philip's here and everyone's distracted and busy with Mortensaften." He clears his throat. "Just . . . if any of this is true, no one can know you're looking into it. Not Brock, not Philip, not Helene. Not even Eve. Be careful."

Be careful.

I've spent my entire life up until this week being very, very careful. Careful with my heart. Careful with my magic. That familiar, simmering rage I've nursed toward the Vestergaards for years is back, as if somewhere deep down I always knew. I look from the slick ice below my feet to the sky that's inky above us and wonder at the idiocy of learning to skate. Why would anyone choose to, when the risk of falling is so great, caught between sharpened blades and ice hard enough to break you? *When skating is done right,* I suppose, begrudgingly, *it is beautiful.* As beautiful as ballet. But all it takes is one false move — one wrong split-second decision — for the beauty to become devastating, for bones and ice to shatter each other.

I clear my throat and hear myself say: "Perhaps I'm changing my mind after all."

"Perhaps?" Jakob asks. "About coming to Hørsholm?"

"About learning to skate," I say. I give him a tentative smile. *"Perhaps."*

The moonlight catches his spectacles again, the shadows cutting along the angle of his cheekbones.

"Then *perhaps,*" he says, "I might know someone who can teach you."

CHAPTER TEN

Philip
1854
Faxe, Denmark

I'M SEVENTEEN YEARS OLD, and tonight I will see two things for the very first time: a dead body, and the way my brother, Aleks, looks when he's in love.

He's been home from war for three years, but it still makes me glad to see him, straightening his cravat in the hallway's oval mirror. He flicks open a mustache comb made of silver and tortoiseshell as the grandfather clock strikes five from the foyer. His hands linger on the horn buttons on his coat. The scent of the oil on his tall leather boots is so familiar that if I squint, in the deepening twilight, he could almost pass for our father.

"Ready?" he asks now, and I nod. I'm growing out my own mustache, which I've waxed with pomade. I straighten my overcoat.

Aleksander looks every bit the hero, a man who came marching proudly home after Denmark won the Three Years' War, beating back Prussia with a stick to keep the duchies our own. I threw myself on him when he walked through the door three years ago and sobbed the deep, silent sobs of someone who has held in fear for so long that now it may never come out.

Aleks helps my mother into the carriage. We're taking her to the theater in Copenhagen tonight, like my father used to do. My father gave his life to that war, but at least it wasn't in vain. *That's the only thing that staunches the wound of losing him,* I think as the carriage rolls past the shuttered factory that turned me away those years ago. The alley where I saw the little boy with magic is dark and empty. My fingers itch to snap themselves together, something I practiced so much over the years it's turned into a tic.

"How were the mines today?" my mother asks with her voice that sounds like paper rustling. She uses the pet name she has for me — *min skat*, "my treasure" — and puts her hand on my own, the blue veins running through her skin like streaks of ore. Fine lines, as delicate as webs, fan out from the corners of her eyes. Losing my father, the worry over losing Aleks and the mines, too — how it aged her. It is good to see her with her hair clean, donning a gown. Like she once was, when my father lived, instead of the shadow self she became.

"Treasured mines, treasure mines," I say to play on her words, and when she smiles, I squeeze her hand reassuringly with my own.

After helping to save the duchies, my brother went on to save the mines. He threw open the chambers and stepped into my father's shadow, pumping lifeblood back into the Vestergaard mines, because the economy was buoyed by the nation's victory and limestone was needed to rebuild. Instead of debasing myself by begging for factory work, now I walk through a cathedral of mazes, forty kilometers of widening channels in a mine that bears my own name. There are secret caverns I've found that open up to entire glowing lakes hidden deep underground.

"Philip is finding new ways to make our tunnels hum like the combs of a beehive," Aleks says warmly. "He barely has need of me anymore." Aleks inherited almost all the ownership, but Father left me a small portion too. I am my brother's right-hand man, overseeing the miners and rising in stature, even while some days I spend more time below ground than above it.

I hold my mother's hand the whole carriage ride, through glittering Copenhagen, as the lamp man makes his way down the lane, lighting the gas lamps with his long stick. We disembark in front of the looming theater and Aleks seems to know everyone we meet, smiling his easy smile, shaking hands with vigor, and brimming with good cheer. I stay behind him, close enough to fall into his shadow, but also feeling a flush of pride when I see my growing mustache in the mirrored halls.

"Are you comfortable?" Aleks asks our mother, and she sighs happily, looks through the program, and remarks that there is a new ballerina taking Copenhagen by storm. Our seats aren't in the very best boxes, but they are respectable. My mother had to sell all her jewelry during the war and never replaced it. I want to see her with jewels in her hair again, someday.

When the lights go down and the curtains rise, the rumored ballerina steps onto the stage. She is young, with tanned skin, a long flowing dress, and hair dripping with rosettes. Her eyes are large, dark, and sparkling, but even from this distance there is something akin to a challenge issuing from them. Depth and fight, as if this girl has known sorrow. Her dancing is magnetic. She draws in the room as though she's pulling us on a string. The audience bursts into applause after her solo the same way a rag soaked in oil bursts into flame.

"How beautiful," my mother breathes, and Aleks sits at attention. As if he never truly used his eyes before.

"Who is she?" Aleks asks.

He sits forward, his eyes caught. His lips twitch; his fingers knead themselves together.

I saw it for a moment, but then I blink and look at her again. I don't see what he sees. The spell is broken. A woman up, down, up, down, on her toes.

After the final curtain, Aleks breaks through the flowing crowd, moving against its stream toward the stage. He leaves me alone with our mother. She leans against me slightly on the walk to the carriage.

When he returns, the look on his face is smitten. He keeps staring out the window, trying to mask a smile. He came home from war, victorious, invincible. But tonight is the night that we lost Aleks for good.

Helene Lind, that ballerina. She defeated him, with satin and lace and without a weapon or even a single word.

When the carriage pulls to a stop that night, someone is waiting for me. There's a rap on my window and my friend Tønnes appears, breathless and white as a ghoul.

"Can you come?" he says urgently. "There is something I want you to see."

I bid good night to my mother and brother and follow Tønnes out into the darkness, picking through crunching leaves and flickering shadows to the morgue at the edge of town.

My throat goes dry when we approach the door. I've never seen a dead body before. I'm sure Aleks has seen many, from his time in the war. Perhaps that's part of why Aleks was so smitten with Helene Lind tonight. Because she looked so fiercely alive.

But my father's coffin was closed and I was too frightened to look inside it, even to tell him goodbye.

I recoil when we step into the room and I am first hit with the stench. I try not to be sick. I don't know how Tønnes stomachs the smell, working here, but he barely seems to even notice it. Tønnes lights candles and then fishes out a handkerchief. "Hold it in front of your nose," he instructs. I look at it, crumpled in his hand. I've never forgotten, from all those years ago, what it felt like to be a handkerchief.

"Look," Tønnes breathes. "Have you ever seen anything like this before?"

I steel myself enough to look at the table. At the mangled body. My stomach turns.

"How did he die?" I ask.

"A tree fell on him. He was cutting it down, and it returned the favor." Tønnes is so unaffected by death. By the way a person can be breathing one minute, with all his dreams and memories, and then the next minute gone, as quick as a frosted breath dissipating. It's always struck me as unfair, how long it takes to make a life and how quickly it can end. Perhaps I'm looking green because Tønnes directs my attention toward the clothing he put aside to help a family member identify the body and the eight-pound blocks of ice he uses to help with preservation. "But, Philip—this time, when I performed the autopsy, it didn't go the way it usually does," he says, brandishing his knife so that it catches the light. His eyes are shining with excitement, his breath quick and shallow. "Do you see, here? This body doesn't look like it should." When I glimpse the neat and careful lines carved into the man on the table, my stomach nearly gives up its contents. Tønnes brings me over to the wood stove, where water is boiling away red blood, and it makes me think about how my eyes have seen things that are so beautiful and so monstrous all in the span of a single evening.

"Tønnes," I ask through the handkerchief. "Why did you bring me here?"

The color has come back into his face, and now his voice grows with excitement. "If I show this to my superior, he'll take any credit for himself and leave me with nothing. He'll have to —I'm not even supposed to be in here. So I thought . . . maybe we could ask Aleks if we could use the mines. Someplace private and hidden. Just until we can think about what to do next."

It doesn't escape me that he said *we*. I hesitate. "Tønnes . . . is it wrong?"

His jaw twitches. "I mean — what's the harm, really?" he says. "He's already dead. I think a lot of good could come from it, actually. A lot of good."

I stare down at that body, but it's as though instead I'm looking into a very deep crevasse, so deep I can't even imagine where it ends.

"Right. We're not really hurting anyone," I say slowly. I take the handkerchief away from my nose. "Since he's already dead."

"His family will never know" — Tønnes gestures toward the body — "and it's not as though *he* cares."

I think of the labyrinth of mines, of how I know the passageways like the back of my hand. Forty kilometers of tunnels, of dark corners and dripping echoes, of places the miners won't go because the walls themselves move with bats. How the miners have started answering to me, and how Aleks rarely descends beneath the earth anymore. He told me once, shaking, that it feels too much like a coffin, like the trenches of the war.

I think of his face, smitten with Helene, and know that he won't be venturing down into the darkness anytime soon.

"We don't have to ask Aleks," I say, with growing confidence. "We can use the mines."

I set the handkerchief on the table, because I can no longer smell the rot, and I don't need it anymore.

CHAPTER ELEVEN

Marit
Mortensaften: November 10, 1866
Vestergaard Manor

I N THE MORNING, WHEN THE LAWYER arrives to update Helene's will and accounts, a carriage waits outside to take Ivy to her new employment at a glass shop in Copenhagen. I steal a glimpse out the window as I'm tying a crisp, starched apron around my waist. A red-faced Dorit pushes a braided wicker basket overflowing with food into Ivy's arms; Brock is pulling her close to him and saying something into her hair. He looks anguished, and for a moment, I feel a twinge of guilt.

Then Ivy's carriage pulls away, a mixture of dust and snow pluming behind it, and I think: *But I'm not staying to hurt Brock, or any of the rest of them.* I run my fingers over the knots in my hem. I'm here to figure out what really happened to my father —and to make sure that Eve isn't one more name I have to add to my petticoats.

Nina puts me to work as soon as my foot touches the first floor. "Extra tasks today," she says, looking through her chatelaine of keys, "to prepare for Mortensaften." But I know that really I'm paying for Ivy's empty chair at the breakfast table. Nina sets me to finishing up Helene's dress for dinner, then darning holes in stockings and embroidering napkins and tea towels.

"Life isn't fair, all the way round, is it?" Dorit says, stooping down to the goose meant for our dinner. She picks it up. "So sorry that St. Martin tried to hide in a flock of your kinsmen. And now, you'll be served at dinner for their penance."

"Better than any other birds," Liljan says, grinning, "or perhaps we'd be eating crow."

"Or pigeon," Jakob adds.

"Owl?" Liljan counters.

"Swan."

"Dodo."

"Blue-footed booby."

Dorit rolls her eyes and cleans her knife. "Idiots."

I wind through the main house, the satin dress heavy as lead in my arms, the thread that holds it together somehow light as gossamer. The wind outside whistles with cold, but inside a servant named Oliver lights blazing fires in all the grates and Signe sets candles with flickering tongues of flame on the windowsills and tabletops.

Dorit is standing over the fire stove, brewing gløgg, when I return. "Marit, make yourself useful and go find Brock in the greenhouse." She begins to stuff a cheesecloth with cinnamon and cardamom and I pull a face at Liljan. "I need three lemons and an armful of elderflower blossoms."

"Back door," Liljan instructs me. She's bleaching tablecloths snow white. "Follow the pergola and you'll see the greenhouse at the end of the corridor."

I pull my coat on and make my way through the back gardens. The air is frigid and the sky is already darkening with night, but I stop short. Small flakes of snow are falling, yet a long arched walkway stretches out in front of me, where white, frothy wisteria hangs like lanterns sewn from lace. It curls up evergreen columns and stretches across the top of the pergola, a faint scent of jasmine mingling with fir, the best parts of spring and winter somehow intertwining. I part a curtain of strands and step into the veiled corridor, where the wind doesn't reach, and everything immediately becomes cool and still. There's a crunch of gravel beneath my feet as I take another step forward and gingerly reach out to graze one of the blossoms with my fingers. The very edges of the flowers are tinged the lightest lavender, and some are starting to etch with frost.

Someone here is keeping them alive with magic.

I shiver with pleasure that this exists in the world, and for this one moment, it's mine. I want to stay in this quiet passage for as long as I can, where the Firn and my fear suddenly feel very far away—where life can bloom even though ice encroaches all around it.

At the end of the corridor, the wisteria turns to darker shades of purple and then gives way to a door into a greenhouse. It is lit from within and its windows are tinted the color of green bottles.

"Hello?" I call, opening the door. I have to step down into the greenhouse like a cellar, and the first thing that hits me is a wave of warmth and the smell of something green and earthy. Glass orbs of varying sizes hang from the ceiling, some holding candles, the others herbs. I walk through the little pockets of scents, one step mint and the next thyme and lavender and basil, all wildness caught within glass. Narrow silver trays with leafy plants hang suspended from the roof like wind chimes and create the slightest semblance of aisles. I follow one to the back wall, which is alive and spilling over with pink and white flowers.

I'm so transfixed by them that I don't notice Brock crouched in the corner until I almost fall on him. Bunches of brightly colored flowers lie gathered in bundles at his feet, and he's arranging them in massive crystal vases for the dinner. I wasn't trying to sneak up on him, but still I notice him a half second before he notices me—and his eyes are wet and rimmed with red. Two things dawn on me simultaneously. He's sitting here crying alone.

And *he's* the one making all of this grow.

I clear my throat and he jumps to his feet.

"Ivy made all the glass bulbs," he says, hurriedly wiping his eyes. He adds curtly, "Did you come to take those, too?"

"Dorit wants lemons and elderflowers. Though I think I just found the lemon," I say, ribbing just enough so that he won't suspect I saw him crying. I wonder if he and Ivy played chase in the halls while growing up, if she ever popped into the greenhouse to sneak him a treat. I wonder if everywhere he turns, he sees memories of her. I pluck three bright lemons from a nearby tree and tuck them into my apron pocket.

"Elderflowers are here," Brock says gruffly. He shoves an armful of their stems toward me.

"Thanks," I say.

In response, he takes a long look at his muddy hands and then wipes them across my apron.

I glare at him, my sympathy dissipating, and stalk back through the wisteria pergola, which loses a bit of its spell now that I know the magic is Brock's. I hand Dorit the lemons and armful of elderflowers, and she promptly arranges the sprigs like a delicate crown around an almond bundt cake drizzled with elderflower glaze. The goose is in the wood-fired oven, browning.

Nina eyes my apron. "Marit, have you been playing patty-cake in the mud?"

"Come along," Liljan says, taking my arm. She grabs a cardamom doughnut dripping with orange blossom icing and pops it into her mouth, narrowly missing a slap on the wrist from Dorit. Signe is polishing the tiniest spoons I've ever seen, with Nina overseeing everything and making clucking noises. "She sounds like a hen," Liljan says under her breath as we head to the hallway.

"Turtledove? Mallard."

"Pelican, penguin, flamingo." She hands me a fresh apron from the cupboard. "Stand on the lookout for me. Oh!" A look of delight crosses Liljan's face. "And if there's trouble," she says, starting to giggle, "cry *fowl*."

She's still laughing at her own joke when she ducks into Nina's office and snags the chatelaine with its keys for the main house. She locates a key with a set of numbers on it and whispers, "With Philip here tonight, Nina will be distracted. But we'll have to find a way to get it back before she notices it's gone."

She doesn't have to say the rest: that if either of us gets caught, there will be a new spot opening for Ivy tomorrow.

"Marit!" Nina thunders from the kitchen.

"Quack, quack," I say to Liljan, and we part.

❧

Two hours later, Philip Vestergaard steps through the front door.

I've timed it exactly, slipping into the main house and out of sight when Nina goes to answer the doorbell. I don't know quite what I'm expecting to see, but I do know I want to be there when he meets Eve for the first time. A dark curiosity is swirling within me, and I clench and unclench my sewing fingers at my sides. It was all so much easier when these people were mere wisps in my imagination, simply destroying the people I loved most in the world rather than showering them with generosity and attention.

Even so, I steel myself anew. I'm not quite ready to let any of the Vestergaards off the hook yet. And a hard heart has always felt easier to bear than a broken one.

Philip stands in the foyer like a lord amid the cold white marble. His back is turned to me when he sheds his wool overcoat and hands it to Jakob, revealing a black dinner jacket so tailored it could slice someone with its edges.

I drop back and melt into the shadows, crawling beneath an alcove table in the hall where I can't easily be seen. My heart begins pounding loud and hard.

And then Philip turns, and I see his face for the first time.

He doesn't look frightening—not like the amorphous villain from my nightmares and daydreams about the Vestergaard family. He's dashing, with his structured jaw and his eyes the color of sea glass. He glances up the staircase, and all I can see of Eve from here are her fingers on the banister. They tremble as faintly as moth wings as she descends, and I want to whisper into her ear, *You don't have to win him, Eve—not anyone, not ever again.*

A twitch of Philip's eye, the straightening of his mouth, betray the faintest surprise at his first sight of Eve. But then, quicker than a blink, he dips into a silent bow, and by the time Eve reaches the bottom stair with Helene at her side, he's smiling again.

"Hello," Philip says to Eve in a voice that is surprisingly rich and low-timbered. "I'm Philip, your uncle. I must confess that I've never had a niece before." His face breaks into an easy grin. "I hope I'm up to the job."

"I'm Eve," Eve says, and the gown shimmers in folds of satin and beads that move like liquid around her legs. She curtsies, smiling uncertainly, her posture stiff and regal.

"Helene," Philip says, turning toward Mrs. Vestergaard in a simple greeting, and she allows him a chilly kiss on the cheek. Liljan says there has always been a current of tension between them; first a rivalry over Aleks's affections, and now an uneasy truce over managing the mines. Perhaps no one was more surprised than Philip to learn, when Aleks's will and testament were read here at the house, that the majority owner of the mines was now Helene.

"Shall we?" Helene says, gesturing them toward the dining room. Once they depart the foyer, Jakob enters the hallway with Philip's overcoat tucked across his arm. I dart from beneath the table to stand beside him at the wardrobe. Our eyes meet briefly as we wait there for Liljan's signal.

It doesn't come.

And then we both hear the servant door open at the same time. Rae is approaching with a silver carafe.

"Get in," Jakob whispers, opening the wardrobe door wider, and I step inside. He stands in front of me, straightening the coats to stall, and shields me with his body.

I can just see the dining room over the top of his shoulder.

Philip and Helene face off across the length of the table, surrounded by crystal: chandeliers above their heads, flickering candles sending shadows spilling through the goblets and onto the walls. Eve sits between them, her face betraying a look of panic at the amount of silverware. She tries to read the expansive table like a map.

"Eve," Philip says, unfolding his napkin, "Helene tells me that you are a dancer. Have you ever been to the ballet?"

Eve looks up uncertainly. "No," she answers.

"I plan to take you," Helene says to Eve, raising her goblet to her lips. "We'll go together, soon."

"The three of us should go. How about the day after tomorrow?" Philip proposes, and Helene noticeably bristles.

Brock passes the wardrobe, holding a tureen on a tray, and gives Jakob a funny look.

"I can't stall here much longer or he's going to come investigate," Jakob whispers to me. His eyes shine, liquid and dark. "I should probably be gone by the time he comes back."

I nod, hardly daring to exhale.

Brock places the tureen in front of Helene and lifts the lid.

"We are still getting settled in here," Helene says calmly. "We'll go at some point."

"But the royal family will be there the night after tomorrow," Philip says as Brock ladles soup into his bowl. "Wouldn't you like to meet the royal family, Eve?" he asks.

Eve drops her spoon into her soup and sends it spattering.

Helene seems careful to ignore the faux pas.

"I didn't realize you and the royals had become so acquainted," she says to Philip.

"I have a gift for them," Philip says. "A jeweled necklace for Princess Dagmar. A wedding gift, from us."

"My, how generous of *us*," Helene says crisply. "Next time, perhaps before you give away thousands of rigsdalers and invite my daughter somewhere, you might consider consulting me first?"

Brock puts a black rye roll on each plate.

"Come on, Lil," Jakob whispers.

One of Helene's furs brushes against my cheek. I'm starting to sweat.

Philip seems amused by Helene's annoyance. "It's building a relationship," he says. He smiles at Eve. "It can only benefit our family to be as close to their good graces as possible."

Our family. Eve's eyes light up, and Philip leans toward her, as if he senses an ally.

"Do you know they are beginning to call King Christian IX 'the father-in-law of Europe'?" he asks Eve conspiratorially.

Helene rubs her fingertips along the edge of her wine goblet.

"Why do they call him that?" Eve asks, clearly eager to encourage his plan. Meeting royalty—at the ballet, with her family. She could hardly ask for more of her dreams to come true.

"Because the king's children are marrying into dynasties across Europe," Philip says. He begins to draw an invisible map on the tablecloth with the tip of his knife. "This very week, his daughter Princess Dagmar wed the future tsar in St. Petersburg. His son George is the reigning king of Greece."

Jakob is listening. He's so close to me, yet he seems to be very careful not to touch me. "And another daughter," Jakob whispers. He meets my eyes. I can smell the scent of spearmint on him. His breath is hot on my neck. "Alexandra. The future queen consort of the United Kingdom and empress consort of India."

The tip of Philip's knife gleams. "And there are more heirs still to come. Queen Louise seems to be moving them like pieces on a chessboard." He laughs. "Like a game of daldøs. Do you play daldøs, Eve?"

His voice is as pleasant as ever, but Helene is looking intently into Philip's face, eyes narrowing. The way you would examine an opponent in a game of cards, trying to gauge their tells.

Or perhaps I'm just imagining it.

I'm drawn by a reflected light shining into the right eye of a painting of Gorm the Old. Liljan's signal. Finally. I touch Jakob's hand.

His skin is warm, and softer than I would have imagined.

He opens the wardrobe wide and I throw one last, hesitant glance over my shoulder before Jakob leads us to a door I thought was a closet. Behind it is a hidden back staircase that will take us up two floors. We close the door behind us just as Brock picks up his tray.

Liljan waits for us in front of the locked library.

"We almost got caught," Jakob says.

"Sorry," Liljan whispers. "Lara is turning down the beds, and everyone else is busy in the dining room or the kitchen." My mind is still half downstairs, but I force it to the task at hand when Liljan fits Nina's stolen key into the lock. "If Nina catches us, she'll make us stand outside until we turn into living ice sculptures," Liljan says.

"She'll use us as rat bait," Jakob says.

"She'll stick us full of needles and use us as pincushions," I whisper, and win an approving smile from Liljan.

We slip into the darkness. The library is a cavernous room with the musty smell of old paper and leather, built like a dark-paneled globe, with books curving around the walls and the rim of a banister marking a second level. The coffered ceiling is carved with a repeating pattern of the Vestergaard hammer and pick. Jakob draws the heavy curtains closed and lights a candle. Liljan locks the door behind us. My fingers itch to open one of the thick old books and hear its spine crack like ice.

Jakob glances at the clock. "We have roughly twenty-five minutes before dinner ends and they retire to the study for Philip's brandy and cigars." He slides a ladder along the shelves, which hold spines in shades of moss and sage and emerald. They stretch up the walls like climbing vines.

"I asked Liljan to make a copy of the blueprints, just in case, after Helene asked me to look at them," he says. Sleet patters on the windows outside as he begins to climb.

"I didn't realize you were an expert in mine architecture," I say. "Is that . . . part of your position here?"

Liljan giggles. "Jakob's position is being an expert in everything."

"I hid the blueprints in a book on ancient botany, but the shelves have all been rearranged since then," Jakob says. "So this will take a minute."

"A minute?" I ask. There are, by my best guess, ten thousand books in here.

But he begins running his hands along the spines, his eyes narrowing. They flick back and forth in concentration, his eyebrows twitching.

I watch him with amazement as he moves across one row in

a single minute, then two, simply pausing over each spine for a moment with the tips of his fingers. "Are you reading those just by . . . touching them?" I ask tentatively.

Liljan crosses her arms. "Jakob's the only person whose magic I've ever envied."

"It's like skimming," he says absently. "I'm not retaining much, just looking for something."

"He retains plenty," Liljan says.

But I am watching with a mixture of fascination and horror. "Don't either of you ever worry about the Firn?" I ask. How can these people pour out their magic without the fear of death always being there, haunting the back of their minds like it does to me?

Jakob's hand falters for the briefest moment. "I could spend hours and hours and hours looking through every book here, or I can use my magic," he says, moving on to the next row. "Yes, there's the threat of the Firn, but perhaps the hours it's taking are just the ones that I would have spent reading those books without magic. Do you see?"

"I never thought of it like that, I guess," I say, turning to Liljan. "And you?"

"I don't care to think of it much. Perhaps it will never happen to me." She shrugs, and my heart folds into itself, when I think of Ingrid lying cold on the floor. "And—well, even if it does, Jakob's going to find me a cure."

"Liljan, don't be a dolt," Jakob says from above us, heat spreading across his face. "A cure is probably a lifetime away, and that's if one even exists."

A cure, I think, dazed. I lean against the shelf. A way to use magic without worrying about the Firn? The thought of it never occurred to me. A cure like that would change everything. My world — my life. I could add beauty all around me, setting things right with a single touch, like I did with Mathies's awning. I could do what I love. Perhaps even *with* someone I love.

Even someone who has magic of his own.

I flush and try to forget I ever had that thought.

"You really think there could be a cure someday?" I ask, suddenly shy.

Jakob shrugs. "I'd like to study under Dr. Holm in Copenhagen to try to find one. I'm going to ask if he would take me on as an apprentice," he says, jaw tightening. "He's the one who researched the Firn so we could better understand it. The treatise he published explains that it's an icy sediment that collects in our veins as a natural castoff of magic — not a curse from the draugar." He smiles wryly. "The Vestergaards have all sorts of connections in society. I'm hoping my own link to them will help me get an apprenticeship with Dr. Holm."

"Connections to the Vestergaards can open all sorts of doors," Liljan agrees. She whispers: "They're using us for magic. We can use them right back, as far as I'm concerned."

But something else still bothers me, like an itch left from last night on the ice. "How did you know, Jakob?" I ask slowly. "That I already knew about the landslide, and the miners?"

"It's common knowledge in Denmark, isn't it?" he asks, but he won't look at me.

"No," I say. "It was more than that. You were certain." I whisper: "You can read books with a single touch. Can you read minds, too?"

He laughs and then clears his throat. "No, but I can read your . . . um," he says. He clears his throat again. "Your . . . um."

"Your undergarments," Liljan provides helpfully. "Did you write something on them?"

My memories of my father and Ingrid flood in front of my face. I can feel them in the knots on my petticoats.

"I'm sorry," Jakob says quietly. "I promise it was an accident."

I flush scarlet and cross my arms defensively. I feel more naked right now than if I weren't wearing clothes at all. Now I understand the strange look that crossed his face when he caught me last night on the ice, when he grabbed my waist so that I wouldn't fall. Why he changed his mind so suddenly after that moment. Helene didn't want to know what happened in those mines. But after that single touch, he must have known that I would.

"I think we have five minutes, at most," Liljan reminds us. "Tell her about the obituaries," she says. The words curl like steam out of her mouth.

"The landslide killed about half the miners working that day, right?" Jakob says. He uses his weight to slide the ladder to the next section. "Yet they were never replaced. I saw the logs. There's been very little turnover in the past decade since then. It's still the same handful of men."

"And there was another miner that wasn't working that day," Liljan says.

"As it turns out, he also died that very same week." Jakob swallows, his hands running over the spines of the books like piano keys. "Could just be a coincidence, I guess."

But a distinct chill runs down my back. I feel that bone-deep sense of true fear, a hint of something teeming just beneath a layer of tree bark. All you have to do is pull it back to see what's really there.

"Three minutes," Liljan says, peeking out the window through a sliver in the curtain.

"Got it," Jakob says, clutching a book. *"Pliny the Elder and Theophrastus on Botany of the Ancients."* He slides down and throws the book open across the table.

There's a paper hidden inside, with a map drawn on it. "Here are the blueprints Helene had me study. I examined all the books in this library on mine architecture, on reinforcements and support shafts and ventilation. And this is what I found: they said it collapsed here." He points on the map. "But that's impossible. The physics of it. The rocks would have fallen the other way, because of these reinforcements. It would need to have been done deliberately. Through an explosion of some sort."

I feel sick.

I take a deep breath and hug my arms tighter around myself, facing the wall.

Jakob says quietly behind me: "I thought you deserved to know the truth. If it were my father, I would want to."

Liljan comes up to me and touches me gently on the arm. "Are you all right?" she asks.

My father was likely murdered. And based on what he did with the bank accounts, and the letter he wrote to Ingrid, I think he might have known it was coming.

There's a distant burst of laughter downstairs, unmistakably Philip's.

My hand curls into a fist.

"I want to know what happened that day in the mines," I say. I hear the steel creeping into my own voice. "Can you keep those blueprints safe for a little longer?"

Jakob nods and folds them back into the book.

By the time we relock the door and return Nina's stolen key, I've decided something else.

Philip Vestergaard is taking Eve with him to Copenhagen over my dead body.

CHAPTER TWELVE

WHEN HELENE CALLS ME to her room the next morning and requests two more formal dresses for her and Eve, it doesn't take much to guess what she wants them for. The ballet, with Philip, and she wants them delivered immediately.

Something tingles in my senses, something with an edge of warning. Whatever happened that day in the mines is a secret that might well have died along with Aleks. After all, he was the Vestergaard running the mines back then. But until I find out what really happened to my father—and more importantly, *why* —I will keep the remaining Vestergaard brother in my sights.

Which means wrangling a ballet invitation for myself. And if that fails, then . . . perhaps sabotage.

I step into Helene's room on the day of the ballet, just after noon. I let her gown fall in a downpour of fabric, the beads hitting the wooden floor like frozen sleet. I see the pleased look on her face, and when she steps forward to accept the dress, I subtly hold it back.

"You mentioned that someday, you might want me to make dance costumes for Eve?" I ask.

She nods.

"I've never been to the ballet before. It would be helpful to observe how the fabric moves, in real life." I clear my throat and keep my voice steady and measured. "Perhaps I could use my salary for a ticket to the pit." A floor ticket, to the area where the servants, workmen, and officers stand.

Helene blinks, and for the first time, I'm surprised to see a hint of warmth in her eyes when she looks at me. It gives me the sense that she remembers what it was like to be an orphan, once, a long time ago.

"Yes, good idea," Helene muses. She takes the dress and examines the lines. "Bring Liljan, too," she instructs. "I'll pay for the tickets. Consider it research. I have a job for both of you."

I bite back a triumphant smile, and moments later, I manage to ladle a helping of rich-smelling, wine-soaked beef stew into a bowl just before Dorit takes the dish away.

"Liljan," I say, shoveling stew into my mouth. "Ever been to the ballet before?"

She snorts. "Sure, in the floating carriage made of butterscotch when the king of France was visiting."

"Well, I got us two tickets," I say. I rip off a piece of bread and dip it in my stew. "We're going tonight."

Her jaw drops open.

"Wait. That seamstress's been in employ for all of an hour and *she* gets to go to the ballet?" Lara says loudly as she scrubs the dishes, throwing a glare in my direction. "What am I, a chopped radish?"

"It's Mrs. Vestergaard's business. If you want to stew about it," Nina retorts, "Dorit can throw you in the pot."

Which is how, barely three hours later, Liljan and I find ourselves in our room, dressing for an unprecedented evening out with the Vestergaards. Liljan hums as she changes into a dress the color of honey warmed by the sun and then ties a vibrant red cloak around her neck. I pull my own dress on — it's a faded color that used to be green but now looks more like the fuzzy algae that forms in stagnant ponds — and Liljan fastens the buttons along the back. I'm halfway down the stairs behind her when I realize that the dress is beginning to change right before my eyes. A rich, jeweled tone somewhere between blue and green is sweeping across it, as though Liljan poured dye down my front.

"Mm, yes, so much better," she says appraisingly, turning when we reach the bottom of the stairs to admire her work. Then she twirls in front of the staff, who are sitting around the table in various states of excitement and jealousy. "If I don't return," Liljan calls over her shoulder, "I've run off with a dashing dancer and Jakob can have all my things!"

Nina splutters, *"Miss Dahl!"* and I catch Jakob's eye just as the blue-green color rolls down past my knees. He stands up and follows us to the door.

"Don't let her really run off with a dancer," he says, leaning against the doorjamb.

"I won't," I say. "Promise." I glance at him out of the corner of my eye as I tie my hat under my chin.

"You look nice," he says softly. A hot, quick thrill rushes through my whole body, and he turns and saunters away.

Outside, Eve is wearing her new coat with the gold embroidery along the sleeves, the silvery beaded edge of her gown peeking out from beneath, and she looks so elegant and suddenly older, as if she put on the Vestergaard name like a garment and instantly became someone else in it.

"I love this dress, Marit," she says, lifting up her coat to show more of the silver embroidery, "and you for making it," and then steps across the snow-dusted walk to wrap her arms around me.

Do you remember your mother at all? we used to whisper to each other in the dark, when the other orphans were snoring.

Do you remember what your house smelled like?

I steal a glance over her shoulder at Helene, at her mended coat that drapes like ink over the gown I made with magic. Helene's cheeks are rouged and her lips are a deep red, and the faint scent of narcissus and musk blooms from her like a flower. I can tell by the rigid way she stands that she heard Eve say those words to me, one of her own servants, when they likely haven't yet said it to each other. "And I you," I whisper, giving Eve a quick, earnest hug back. Then I extract myself abruptly— perhaps too abruptly. A brief frown crosses Eve's face just before she steps into the carriage.

On the road, there is a hushed quiet of anticipation as the country skies color with dusk. Eve can't stop smiling, or shivering.

"Are you cold?" Helene asks. She dips down to move the coal box closer to Eve's feet.

"No. I'm excited," Eve says. She takes a breath as if the air tastes sweet.

"I've hired you a tutor for schooling," Helene says. "But I plan to teach you to dance myself." She straightens. "As soon as I saw you dance that day at the Mill, I saw a raw talent in you—the sort you can't actually teach. It's rare, and you have it, Eve, just like I do. You've never danced on pointe?"

"No," Eve says.

"I will teach you that once you've learned proper technique. And," Helene says, leaning forward, "if you are willing, so much beyond that."

"What do you mean?" Eve asks. The city's edges begin glittering into view. Gaslights dangle in the night like glowing fruit from tree branches. A distant church bell clangs over the clopping of horse hooves, and the cobblestones shine with melted snow.

"Pointework right now is merely up, down, up, down," Helene says. She turns her wrists to demonstrate. "But I see it broadening to the newest things they are beginning to explore in Italy, in Russia. Leaps and turns, pirouettes, fouettés. Danish ballet is more interested in showcasing the male dancing, but there is so much more we can do. I'd like to push the boundaries."

"I would like that," Eve says slowly. "But . . . I'll never dance on stage, of course." A look flickers across her face, quick and then gone. "I don't look enough like those ballerinas."

My gut clenches as we ride through the widened lanes of Copenhagen toward King's New Square. I remember how the butcher in Karlslunde would pass right over Eve when she spoke to him, pretending as though she weren't there. Most of the prospective parents didn't give her a second look, but a few would look at her a little too long. And there was one cold morning on the street two years ago when a man staggered toward Eve with his sour breath and asked to see her "freedom papers." With how matter-of-factly that assertion just now slipped off her tongue, I wonder how many other moments there were that she never told me about. That I never saw, and that she bore alone.

"You're West Indian, yes?" Helene asks.

Eve traces the embroidery on her coat. "My mother was. I don't even know which of the islands she came from. She was a house servant for a family called the Ankers." Her voice drops to a whisper, as though her next words are almost a confession: "I never knew who my father was."

"As best I can tell, my father was some nameless, faceless Dane," Helene says. She straightens her gloves. "But my mother was from St. Croix."

Eve glances up at her in shock, her eyes large pools. I can tell by the way Liljan tries so hard to seem as though she isn't listening that she didn't know this either. I look at Helene more closely. Her tan skin, her dark eyes. I hadn't ever heard that part of the story.

"I didn't know," Eve says, and there's a look on her face that I've never seen before. But it dawns on me now that Ness must have known. I understand even more now why she invited Helene to come and watch Eve dance that day.

"Yes. Well. Not many people did know. I powdered my skin a little, and I played the game." Helene's face is carefully expressionless when she draws out a ballet shoe from her bag. Its satin is a supple pink, and the toe is shaped like a stiff box, reinforced with cloth darning. "I played the game long enough and rose high enough in its ranks that maybe now I might even be able to change it. Have you heard of a girl named Marie Taglioni?"

Eve nods. "Of course. She was the first to dance an entire ballet on pointe."

"Yes, and that wasn't even fifty years ago. You see, ballet seems so fixed, but really, it's in constant evolution. In the 1600s, female dancers were barely allowed. A century ago, ballet shoes had heels. Ballerinas danced in heavy gowns with layers that made it nearly impossible to leap. But then Marie Taglioni's father created a costume style that had never been seen before — light and airy, romantic." She shoots a look at me, and finally, I realize why she offered me the job that day in Karlslunde. The whole picture she was seeing, when she looked at me and Eve together. "The costume didn't reach Marie's ankles; it didn't even have sleeves. But her father trained her, designing choreography and costumes that emphasized her strengths. And they took risks."

Helene hands Eve the shoe, and Eve takes it without looking up. Deep in thought, she traces the curves of it with her finger.

"He had foresight, and she had talent, and together, they revolutionized ballet," Helene continues. "I want to do that too.

Evolve what ballet looks like. And what ballerinas look like." She gives Eve a small smile. "By the time Marie Taglioni was offered a contract in Russia, she was so popular that her pointe shoes were sold for two hundred rubles to be cooked in sauce and eaten by the ballerinas in training."

Eve is silent. After a moment she asks quietly, "But what if I don't want people to eat my shoes?"

I fight the strongest urge to take her hand.

Helene reaches out for it instead.

"That is more than all right," Helene says softly. "Eve, listen to me. You don't ever have to dance, if you don't wish to. I just want you to have the choice."

When she finally looks up, Eve says: "Well. I'd wager that if anyone could make my shoes taste delicious, it's Dorit."

Helene actually laughs, and it feels as though the thread of something substantial is knitting between them, something unseen and yet happening right in front of my eyes. I feel a pull of sadness, of jealousy, as if I just stepped off a train that they will continue on, together, to somewhere I have always dreamed to go and have never been before.

And then our carriage pulls to a stop in front of the columns of the Royal Danish Theatre. When the door swings open, the air outside smells of sea salt and sweet cedar smoke, the lights of the theater blaze, and Helene is mobbed by the crowd as soon as she steps onto the street.

⌒

Helene whisks Eve to the entrance of the theater, and Eve steals a look every few paces to make sure I haven't gotten lost. We are surrounded by a crush of people dressed in finery, the overwhelming smells of perfumed velvet and cigar smoke and pomade, and so many voices, and I notice, this time, the lingering looks at Eve and subtle whispers as Helene leads her through the crowd. We're enveloped in a sudden whoosh of warmth as we pass through the foyer. "The theater is too small for Copenhagen," someone sniffs, "and they're making plans for another," yet I've never been inside a building this vast, like a cathedral to marble, gold, and velvet. Liljan and I make our way toward the pit level with the other servants and laypeople, finding a stroke of luck and a place to sit on one of the few benches.

Eve and Helene move through the gilded rows above me. The fabrics become finer, the jewels larger, the higher my eyes rise up the tiers, and then the crowd stands in unison as the royal family is announced.

"His Royal Highness King Christian IX and Queen Louise."

My heart jumps into my throat as the king and queen of Denmark enter, flanked by guards. Beside me, Liljan cranes her neck for a better look. The light catches the crest around Eve's throat. She stands directly beside Philip Vestergaard and ten paces away from the reigning king and queen of Denmark.

The gap between us widens further.

I'm afraid of bats nesting in my hair, she once whispered to me in the dark after she woke shrieking and thrashing from a nightmare at the Mill. *I'm afraid of drowning,* I told her, lacing my fingers through hers. We never spoke of the fear we shared but wouldn't name:

I'm afraid no one will pick me.

I'm afraid I will end up alone.

Helene's face remains a tight mask as Philip leans over Eve to whisper something in Helene's ear, and it does nothing to ease my nerves as the doors shut heavily and the lights flicker and die.

The theater is cast in darkness as thick as velvet. I can't see Eve anymore, and it makes my pulse jump a notch. The music suddenly swells from the orchestra, with a deafening cymbal crash. The curtain rises, and on a simple, ominous violin melody, a ballerina appears on the stage. The spotlight catches every stone studded into her canary-yellow corset, structured with whalebone and rigid against a full, lush skirt. The servants are in rapt attention around me. They watch the dancing, but I gaze at costumes. To me the dancer's body is like a breath, bringing life into a costume as soon as she puts it on.

Liljan and I watch the performance in silence until the air itself begins to move. Little bits of paper fall from the rafters, creating a white blizzard of tiny snowflakes. The snow gathers in piles on the stage, and a row of dancers move in perfect symphony amid the flurries in their silvery satin shoes. The crowd gasps with delight and applauds. It is just little pieces of paper and cloth and ordinary humans, but as I'm watching, a chain mail of goose bumps rises along my arms and neck. I shiver with pleasure at the pure, transcendent beauty in front of me.

"Do you feel it?" Liljan whispers, and I recognize that the

tingling frost of pleasure feels like those first moments I call to my magic. Liljan glances around her at the audience, their captivated faces turned toward the stage like flowers to the sun. "Even people who don't have magic can feel it. When something is so terribly beautiful," she whispers in my ear, "when someone hits their perfect pitch or dances so exquisitely or plays that combination of notes that sends that tingle shooting up your spine—"

"Yes," I murmur, "you can feel the magic. On your skin."

I turn and watch Eve's face, her dark eyes reflecting the lights, but the next time I glance up, Philip is staring at me. I've drawn his attention by looking at them too many times. I turn around as quickly as I can and slink down, trying to disappear. I don't dare look up again for the rest of the night. But I caught Helene's face, and Eve's a mirror to it, in that final stolen glance. Both of them were watching the stage with yearning. Helene, because she was looking at her past—and Eve, because she was looking at the future.

⋖⋗

After the curtain falls, the sound of clapping flutters like birds rising around us to the rafters, and the open doors let in a slice of chill. "Come," Liljan says, and I dare to sneak another glance toward the upper boxes. Philip isn't looking at me anymore. He's in conversation with a man seated next to them, who is clutching a top hat in his long, thin fingers. He has hollowed cheeks, a high forehead, a prominent nose, and hair that curls around his ears.

Jakob's warning echoes in my thoughts. *Be careful.* I swallow and follow Liljan, suddenly so glad she's here with me.

"Who is that man speaking with Philip Vestergaard?" I ask as we make our way against the people who stream down the stairs around us, caught within the flow of their laughter and excited voices.

"It's Hans Christian Andersen," Liljan replies. "The author of fairy tales?"

I can still hear my father's voice reading to us from *New Fairy Tales. Papa,* I think, heart squeezing. The man whose words you read, from your mouth to my ears, and now you are gone and he is here.

The foot guards in bearskin hats and blue uniforms show interest in Liljan and me the closer we move to the royal family. My heartbeat slows in my ears as I take them all in: Philip and Helene Vestergaard. Hans Christian Andersen. The royal family of Denmark. Helene rose from the ashes of the Mill to pluck Eve from the orphanage and place her here, speaking with the queen. Helene is the impossible needle that is bringing Eve straight through a fabric she could never get through on her own —and me, too. Helene is sewing us right into the middle of it.

"We wait here," Liljan whispers, and pulls me into the shadows.

"In Paris they have more distinguished dancers than we, more decorations and extraordinary arrangements intermingled with the dancing, but such richness in truly poetic ballet composition as Bournonville has given, only Copenhagen possesses," Mr. Andersen is saying. He gestures to the man next to him, whom I take to be August Bournonville, the ballet master and choreographer. He has a long nose and dark hair parted to the side.

"It is the mission of art to intensify thought, to elevate the mind, and to refresh the senses," Mr. Bournonville says.

They both turn instinctively toward Queen Louise when she says, "You must return again to read the children your *Wonder Stories,* Mr. Andersen." She wears a glittering crown, lustrous satin in layers the color of iridescent shells, and glowing pearls that fall in strands over her décolletage. Despite the luxury of their appearance, the royals didn't go to St. Petersburg for the princess's wedding. This morning, I overheard Nina tell Dorit of rumors that they couldn't afford it.

"Please allow us this opportunity to present a small gift, as a token of appreciation and service to your family," Philip says, nodding at a guard who is clutching a rectangular velvet case. This guard doesn't wear the blue of the royal foot guard, but the black uniform with the Vestergaard hammer and pick embroidered on it in gold thread. "For Princess Dagmar," Philip says to Queen Louise. "With best wishes for a long and happy marriage."

I catch a glimpse of red stones as Queen Louise peeks inside the velvet case. Her eyebrows rise, her crown glittering like dew in her hair as she says, "How generous. We give our thanks to the Vestergaards."

The roar of the theater has simmered to a low hum, of pealing giggles hidden behind gloved hands, of glances up to the balcony box as if it has become the new stage.

"We are in your service," Philip says, bowing. "Pledging to

help Denmark in any way we can." Philip wears a heavy red stone on his first finger. Next to him, Helene dips into the most graceful curtsy. A golden circlet is threaded into her hair, understated and delicate.

It hits me even more than before how impossible it would be for me, an orphaned servant with no social standing at all, to uncover a conspiracy involving one of the most powerful families in Denmark.

"How extraordinarily lovely," Hans Christian Andersen comments, "that such beauty can grow deep within the darkness and the ground."

And such ugliness, I think, *that someone I loved died there, too.*

I found things, Jakob's voice echoes to me from the other night. Things that made him question whether it was really an accident at all.

I think there's something in those mines they were trying to hide, he said.

I picture the letter my father wrote, the one they found on his body, and I shiver. The letter that somehow he must have realized he was never going to send.

Be a Gerda, he had written in it.

And seeing Hans Christian Andersen standing there in the flesh, right next to Philip Vestergaard, I am hit by something I never considered before. It burned at me all these years, that my father didn't include me in that final letter. But maybe the fact that the letter was addressed only to Ingrid wasn't a slight.

It was a *clue.*

Because she could have read it in a different way than I ever could have.

I closed the accounts, he wrote.

But what if he didn't? Ingrid would have been able to decipher if any parts of his letter were a lie. What if he was trying to tell us something?

Be a Gerda.

What if Jakob is right and the mining deaths weren't an accident? What if those miners — and my father — stumbled on something that someone wanted to make sure stayed buried?

What if those accounts my father opened still exist after all?

Mr. Andersen catches me staring at him from the shadows and gives me the slightest nod, and I want to run to him and throw my arms around him. For the stories he gave me that I shared with my father — and for the fact that simply by coming to the ballet tonight, he might have given me a clue to a ten-year-old mystery I didn't even know existed.

CHAPTER THIRTEEN

I HAVE TO VISIT THAT BANK IN COPENHAGEN.

It's hard to persuade Nina to give me a day off, when I've only just started and have already taken a night off to go to the ballet. So I mete out my magic in mere drips and do as much as I can by hand, carefully watching for my chance. It takes six days for an opportunity to materialize.

And poetically, the person who hands it to me is Brock.

I'm still waking up on a cold morning, drinking coffee and scheming while fixing tablecloths burned with splattered wax, when Nina suddenly begins shrieking my name.

"Marit! Marit? Where are you?" she yells, her voice taking on a faint note of hysteria. I hurry toward her and my stomach drops —if I'm in trouble, I'll have to wait at least another week or even more to learn if there's something waiting for me in that bank.

I find her in the kitchen, clutching her apron.

"The drapes in the sitting room are shredded," she moans. "They're in absolute tatters, as if a small animal got hold of them and went mad trying to get out."

"A small animal?" I ask slowly.

"A pygmy shrew?" Jakob ventures with a straight face.

"Rabid muskrat?" Liljan asks.

"Marit, go! Fix them immediately. Before Mrs. Vestergaard takes notice," Nina says. She raises her voice to address the rest of the kitchen: "And the next person I catch with food anywhere outside the dining rooms will be rewarded with extra chamber pot duty." She pulls my arm to hurry me toward the corridor and mutters, "I'm setting traps. For *rats*."

Over her shoulder, Brock waves his shears at me sweetly.

I narrow my eyes. *Ah.* So it wasn't rats that got to the curtains. Just one rat in particular.

This work requires more than careful little drips of magic, and I imagine all the creative ways I might exact revenge on Brock the entire time I'm doing it. Eve is stretching in the ballroom, which Helene has turned into a makeshift studio. Eve dances in the mornings and meets with a tutor in the afternoons, drinking in lessons on mathematics, grammar, rhetoric, and Danish history. Helene herself sits with Eve to learn the history of the Danish West Indies—the 1848 slave rebellion led by a man named "General Buddhoe" Gottlieb and St. Croix's resulting emancipation. Some evenings Eve sends for Jakob, and he teaches her about the stars and planets, medicines, and the mines.

I smile, thinking about the secret message I found yesterday, tucked into the slip pocket of one of her dresses.

.. / . - - . - - - . . . . . / - . . - - - - - . . .

I love you

I sent her back directions in Morse. If she follows them, she'll find the lavender wisps of wisteria that lead to the greenhouse behind the servants' quarters.

Nina towers over me, inspecting my work with pursed lips when I'm putting the last stitches in place. I've taken a drape that looked like a limp, dirty mop and brought it back to a lush and patterned brocade.

"You've done it," Nina says begrudgingly. The color begins returning to her face and my opening appears, as neatly as a carpet rolling out in front of me.

"Yes," I say, following her back to the kitchen. "Now, about that day off . . ."

She quirks an eyebrow at me.

"Half day," she says with narrowed eyes. "And you and Liljan can do some household errands I need done in town."

"I'll drive them," Jakob quickly offers.

"Take the phaeton," Nina orders, and turns with a huff.

In the morning, Liljan's stockings have gone missing, as they seem to every other day.

"Go on. I'll be down in a moment," she promises, digging through her trunk on her knees.

Brock is in the kitchen, sifting through seeds and young plants Helene had sent from St. Croix: mint, coconuts, guavas, even pineapples. "How am I supposed to grow some of these when I've never even seen them before?" he mutters, examining their leaves.

"Better get them sprouting," Dorit says. "Mrs. Vestergaard gave me recipes that call for incorporating those ingredients into the Christmas dishes."

"Thank you, Brock, for helping me yesterday," I say with sweet sincerity as I fill a silver canister with hot chocolate. Relishing the look of confusion on his face, I pull my coat on, waggle my fingers in a wave, and follow Jakob outside.

He helps me up into the open phaeton, his hand on mine but careful not to touch my clothes, and then hoists himself into the driver's seat.

His breath feathers out into the air, and he fastens and unfastens the buttons on his gloves as if he's nervous. I unroll two thick furs over my lap. "I'm sending my inquiry to Dr. Holm today," he says. He pulls out a white envelope from his pocket. "I wrote it five times," he admits, laughing a little. He clears his throat and puts the letter back in his pocket, and it hits me again how handsome he is.

I ask shyly: "Do you really think there could be a cure for the Firn someday?"

"If anyone can find it, it's Dr. Holm," Jakob says, turning toward me in his seat, his eyes lighting. "When Dr. Holm published his initial research, it changed so much. It helped people to not be so afraid or suspicious of magic and made us more hirable in houses like this one. It was the first time anyone would provide a solid answer about what was really happening to us."

"Has anyone else tried to find a cure?" I ask. When I unscrew the silver canister, steam floods into the air like released spirits.

Jakob shrugs, thoughtfully stroking the reins in his hands. "The Firn isn't something contagious, like cholera, that threatens the greater population, so there isn't much urgency. It only affects those of us with magic—and almost solely the lower classes at that, because the rich never use magic enough for it to become truly dangerous—so a cure doesn't receive much attention. Perhaps some people even believe we deserve it, because we make the choice to use magic." I pour the hot chocolate into a tin cup, careful to keep my hand steady. It still feels unnerving, to discuss magic so openly. "But for some, magic means being employed, having a place to live, food to eat," he continues. His hand brushes mine when I give him the steaming cup, and the touch sets off a fluttering deep in my stomach. "The choice isn't always so straightforward."

"Stockings acquired," Liljan announces triumphantly, climbing with a bounce into the phaeton.

"Oh good," Jakob says. "So glad we are back to talking about undergarments."

Liljan laughs and unwraps a bundle of æbleskiver—round doughy treats stuffed with lingonberry preserves—and I hand her a cup of hot cocoa. "Helene sprinkles gold flakes in her cocoa for special occasions," Liljan says. I take a hot, rich sip of chocolate down my throat to cover the onslaught of sudden nerves as Jakob jolts the horses to a start. We are on our way. I've thought of little else for the past week, running over and over what Jakob said those nights in the library and under the stars.

Why would you murder half your work force and then cover it up?

You wouldn't.

Unless it was to hide something you wanted to make sure never, ever came to light.

"How shall we pass the time?" Liljan asks. "Gruesome trivia, of course!"

"Gruesome trivia is Liljan's favorite," Jakob says solemnly over his shoulder.

"Christian IV got peppered with shrapnel to the face in the Battle of Kolberger Heide," Liljan tells me as the phaeton plunges into the dark patch of forest. "It cost him an eye," she says, shuddering almost gleefully. "When the doctor removed it, Christian IV asked him to extract the shrapnel and then he *made it into earrings* for one of his lovers."

"No!" I swipe her with my napkin. "That cannot be true."

"It *is*," she insists. She snaps me back, sending several crumbs sprinkling into my hair. The air around us smells rich with pine and chocolate.

Though my stomach is tightening into larger and larger knots,

I smile. I've never done this before—had a cocoa on a day trip to Copenhagen, laughing with friends. It feels even more luxurious to me than a hundred nights spent going to the ballet.

"And the royal throne chair is made with unicorn horns," Liljan continues.

Jakob clears his throat. "Actually, those are narwhal tusks."

"You're such an insufferable know-it-all," she says affectionately, and gives him a hard flick on the ear. "Perhaps Dr. Holm will actually find it endearing."

"Don't get ahead of yourself. He hasn't accepted me yet," Jakob says stiffly.

His hands are gripped around the reins and I feel a twinge that I try to ignore. I never wanted to fall for anyone who could be taken by the Firn. Though, if someday he could actually cure it . . . I allow myself the barest flare of hope, then pull it back. Hoping for things in my future feels frightening, like sewing with a thread that will unravel at any moment. My resignation to a life at the Mill and at Thorsen's felt bleak and so much safer. Now I'm surrounded by Helene and Eve, by Philip and the royal family, by Jakob and Liljan—all people who have such high hopes for changing the future.

I swallow the final bit of cocoa, where all the bitterness has settled at the bottom. I'm the one still looking at the past.

When we arrive in town, Jakob ties up the horses and we part —he giving us a salute and turning toward the post office, Liljan and I hurrying away along the lamp-lined streets to the tailor's shop. But first, I take a detour to the Nationalbanken. If I'd been here a hundred times before, the memories would have all flowed together and perhaps been lost, as slippery as a thousand grains of sand. But since there was only that one day, it shines back at me as singular and clear as a penny dropped through water. I can see Ingrid twirling around that lamppost. Me dropping my sesame bun.

"Should we pop in and say hello to Ivy?" Liljan asks as we pass the glass shop. The windows are clear, like panes of fresh water running down the walls, except for the top strip, patterned with the red and gold of our national coat of arms. Three blue lions, nine crimson hearts, topped with King Christian V's crown.

"I —" I say, and the words die on my lips.

Just beyond the glass is a familiar figure.

I see his honey hair, the striking curve of his handsome nose. I grab Liljan's arm and duck out of the way just as he turns in profile.

"Is that Philip Vestergaard?" I ask, heart racing. Today of all days. I straighten and steal another glance.

He didn't seem to notice us. I see him turn back and smile at Ivy.

She gives him a sweet smile in return.

What is he doing here?

"Why do we have to hide?" Liljan hisses. "We're just going to the tailor shop."

"No," I say, and when I'm certain neither Philip nor Ivy is

looking, I hurry on toward the Nationalbanken on the corner. "I have to stop in here first," I say to Liljan. I take care to make sure my coat completely hides my Vestergaard uniform.

"What for?" Liljan looks at me. "I'll come too. Then we can go get the fabrics together. I'll need your help."

"All right," I say. She follows close behind me as I pull open the heavy doors and approach the counter. It is dimly lit inside, and I clear my throat at a man peering down at papers through a monocle.

"Yes?" he asks, looking up at me.

"I wish to access my account." I remove my gloves and try to speak with authority. "The name is Gerda Olsen, and the account was opened by Claus Olsen in 1856."

He looks into his files and then disappears. I can feel Liljan's eyes boring into me.

"Gerda?" she whispers. I shush her.

When he comes back, he says, "And what would you like to do with the account today, Ms. Olsen?"

I feel like throwing up. I'm trembling with excitement and dread. My father was here. He left something for me.

"I'd like to close it out, please," I say.

"Very well."

I fill out the paperwork with a shaking hand. The man hands over an envelope filled with a small bit of money—it's the combined amount my father meant for both Ingrid and me, and it's gained interest over ten years of sitting untouched. It's modest, but it still represents more than I've ever held in my life.

Perhaps even enough to help me bridge the gap if I ever need to leave the Vestergaards' in a hurry. *Thank you, Papa,* I think, and blink back sudden tears. It's the first time I've felt watched over or taken care of by someone else in so long. I almost forgot what it felt like.

Then the attendant says: "There's something else here." He examines a note in the files. "Unusual. We've held on to something additional. The account owner was supposed to come back to claim it, and it appears that he never did."

He holds out a small package that fits neatly into his palm.

It's as light as an egg when he hands it to me.

I exit the bank and stride past the glass shop. Philip appears to be gone. I find a tight, narrow alley, out of sight, and stand in the gently falling snow, with Liljan peering over my shoulder.

Inside the package is a small folded pocket hastily sewn out of muslin.

But the stitches aren't just stitches. To the untrained eye, they would just look like a messy job. But when I look at them, I see something different. A message.

"If you find this," the hem reads, *"it means you are both very clever, and I'm either imprisoned or dead."*

It was a series of bread crumbs that only we could have found.

Because Ingrid would have known that portions of my father's letter were a lie.

And I would have known how to read the Morse.

I turn the pocket all the way around. And when I do, a small red jewel drops into my hand.

I close my fingers around the stone and trace along the rest of the dots and dashes my father left.

They run around the length of the seam, and I have to squint to read them, even more so when tears prick my eyes and threaten to spill over. Discovering new, unread words from someone who has been in the ground for ten years is like finding the most precious kind of lost treasure.

The mines are costing Danish lives. I'm not sure how far up it goes. Find a way to get this message to King Frederick. Even if you have to use your magic. Be very careful, and anonymous if possible. Tell him to find these stones in the mines and not to stop until he has seen them with his own eyes. Or more people will die.

I hold up the jewel, darkly glittering in the sun.

-- --- ..- . / .-.. . --- .-.. .-.. . / .-- ..
.-.. .-.. / -.. .. .

More people will die.

Another tear falls on the muslin pocket. Did he mean himself? The miners who lost their lives in the landslide?

I scrunch the fabric in my hand.

Or could he have meant something else?

"What is that?" Liljan breathes.

I hold up the stone so she can get a better look. It's red, like a garnet. It's light, barely the size of a coin, but it feels so weighted with this horrible truth.

My father suspected something—enough to stop in

Copenhagen, close our accounts, and open a separate, hidden one for us to find. He was planning to come back and get it, and contact the king of Denmark himself.

But he must have written that letter to Ingrid in the mines when he realized he wasn't going to make it out. A hanging thread that I didn't manage to find until now.

Jakob was right. My father's death wasn't an accident.

More people will die.

He knew something—and whatever he knew got him killed.

I close my hand around the stone. What am I supposed to do now that all these people are dead? My father wanted us to contact King Frederick, but that was years ago. Now he's gone as well.

And . . . what if any parts of this message are actually a lie? My father expected Ingrid and me to find the note together. His words could all be backwards, the meanings flipped—the note could be telling me to do something when really it means the opposite. I clench my fists at my sides, like shells. Ingrid would have known.

"Let's go," I say to Liljan, tucking the stone away. "Or we'll be late to meet Jakob."

We walk through the curving lanes toward the tailor shop, but I pause in front of the glittering windows of a jeweler, thinking. Maybe this stone's meaning is lost, long gone with the dead, buried with my father, with King Frederick, with Aleks Vestergaard—but it could be valuable enough to get Eve and me away from here, start a new life somewhere.

I want to find out what the stone is and how much it's worth.

I pull it from my pocket. But Liljan swiftly yanks me back, and her face, for once, is deathly serious. "Not here," she says in a low voice. "The jewelry shops are all tied closely to the Vestergaards. I wouldn't let anyone know you have that."

I back away from the windows, feeling confused, frightened, and so alone. Liljan steps forward and laces her arm through mine. This time her touch doesn't spread color across the threads of my clothes. Instead it is the simplest touch of comfort, and it sends hope flooding through me.

"We'll help you, Marit," she whispers. And she stands with me there on a quiet street, with snowflakes falling around us and our breaths both faint with chocolate, and lets me cry.

CHAPTER FOURTEEN

"**I** ... DON'T KNOW WHAT THIS IS."

Jakob looks up from the lens of his microscope, his dark eyes deepening with thought behind his spectacles. We're sitting at the apex of the house, a nook nestled at the top of the servants' quarters that is packed with trunks of old paintings and china. It's where Jakob stores his books in tumbling stacks, where he's set a rickety desk beneath a skylight. He moves the candle closer and peers down again at my jewel through his acorn microscope—a small bronze tool with a rounded top that is compact enough to fit in his pocket. "I don't recognize it," he says, squinting. "It has all the markings of a real jewel, for certain: it has these tiny imperfections—scratches and pits on the outside—and little inclusions of feathers when you look close enough. But I can't tell which one it is."

I let out a deep exhale and set aside my sewing, which I've been working on in the corner without an ounce of magic. Jakob gestures me over, and when I bend to look into the microscope,

I feel the ends of my hair graze his arm. The jewel's red surface suddenly becomes a stained glass that bursts with color when magnified: fractals of opulent blues, vibrant pinks, golds. Among them are pockets of darkness flecked with deep, shimmering silver, like the night sky.

"Only a limited number of red-colored gemstones exist in the world," I say. "By process of elimination, we can narrow them down and then determine which one this is."

I take another look at the stone, this time without the microscope, and with a curious twinge remember the flash of red when Queen Louise peeked into the velvet box from Philip at the ballet.

"One problem," Jakob adds. "We can look up all the red stones in the library, sure—but my magic can only read words, not pictures. That's going to add to the amount of time we spend searching."

Time, I think, throat tightening. The one thing I don't have. I feel my fear of the Firn in the taut muscles beneath my shoulder blades, in the pit of my stomach. Every day I stay, the more magic I'm forfeiting.

Every night, I have to force away the images of Ingrid's cold body again, and I can't go to sleep until I've thoroughly examined my wrists.

"It will go faster with three of us," Jakob says kindly when he sees the look on my face, and all I can do is nod.

That night I hide the money my father left me in the straw of my mattress. Then I strike a match and watch it flare against the candlewick. I bring the gemstone into the light, clutching it between my fingers.

Touch the hasty threads my father sewed into the cloth.

More people will die.

I close my eyes, suddenly looking at my memories through a new lens. Through the lighted lens of this jewel.

Because the night she died, my sister was worried.

❧

I thought I understood why. She had a lot of things to worry about, after all. Losing the house, how we were going to pay for food. Dark circles had started to pool under her eyes from the nights she spent pacing the hallway when she was supposed to be sleeping. Most of all, she seemed worried that someone was going to come and take us away, possibly even separate us. She dropped her wooden spoon onto the stove with a clatter when the knock came on the door, and I knew that's what she was thinking when she told me to hide.

I stopped eating my porridge and froze. I just looked at her.

"Hide," she repeated. "Hide now, Marit, and don't come out until I say."

I ran into the next room and opened the storage box under the window, where it smelled musty, where I used to play with my doll. I heard Ingrid clean my dirty bowl and then take a deep breath before she opened the door. I realized then that I was still holding my spoon.

I wish we had just run. I wish I would have stayed with her. I wish I had wrapped my arms around her and told her how much I loved her.

I don't know how many men were there that night. At least three. I heard their heavy boots on the floor and their deep voices. I heard the way they questioned her, about Father's job at the mines, about his assets and accounts, where he would keep something he wanted to safeguard. If he had left anything for us to sell, in order to take care of ourselves in the event of his death. Their voices sounded concerned but also urgent, and when Ingrid told them she knew nothing, the men acted as if she had done something wrong. They moved from room to room. Almost as if they were looking for something.

The space where I hid myself was cramped, hot, and small, and I felt a choking in my throat and lungs that I soon recognized as fear. Growing. The longer they stayed. The closer their footsteps got to me. I heard my own heartbeat, thundering and warm in my ears. I sucked on the spoon, focused on the faint taste of wood, to drown it out.

"You have a sister," one of them said when they reached the room where I was hiding. I shifted in the box and hot, silent tears began to roll down my folded arms.

"She's not here," Ingrid said quickly.

"Where is she? We'd like to speak with her. Only a few questions." I couldn't see his face. He didn't sound as if he was smiling. "Listen, girl. We're not going to hurt you."

Through the slit of the box lid, I watched as Ingrid's fists tightened next to her sides. I saw them curl into shells, until her knuckles turned as white as chalk. Her tell. The way I always knew she was using her magic.

Her voice broke a little. "She's only six," Ingrid said softly.

And suddenly, it was as though the very air in the room changed. I took the spoon from my mouth and rested it gently next to me. I risked opening the chest just a little more so I could see her face. I always thought my sister was the most beautiful girl I had ever seen. I loved the way she squeezed her eyes so tight when she laughed, the small gap between her two front teeth, the way she would snap her fingers as a reward for a joke told well. But that night, for the briefest second, she looked so unbearably sad. Then she took a long, deep breath. Closed her eyes. And when she opened them again, they looked different. Fierce, determined.

Resigned.

"There is nothing here," she said in a voice that sounded strangely calm. Her tone was carefree and almost soothing. "We know nothing. You spoke to both of us and searched our house but didn't find anything. And you are leaving satisfied and never feel the need to come back."

Ingrid's magic always meant being able to tell when other people were lying.

But that night—she drew down from a deep, deep well. She used magic I never knew she had.

She got them to believe the lies she was telling.

They turned to leave, and I opened the lid enough to see that one of the men had a scar on his cheek in the shape of a fishhook. He looked almost dazed as he made his way to the door. Cramps spread through my limbs like fire in that box, as though I had been held under water for too long. I waited until I heard the door shutting behind them, the dead-bolting of the lock, before I emerged.

But when I finally climbed out from my hiding place, Ingrid was staring down at her wrists.

She looked up at me and my heart stopped in my chest. And I knew, even then, that moment was going to haunt me forever.

Something was terribly wrong.

"Marit," she said, her eyes shadowing with fear. "I think . . ." she whispered desperately, "I think I went too far."

I looked down and saw the blue. Knitting like lace just under her wrists.

"Ingrid!" I started to wail, knowing it was already too late, feeling my heart twist into a chain of spiked wire. I told my feet to run, hearing that garish nursery rhyme about ice and magic singing in my ears — and it made me hope that maybe if I could just start a fire, if I could get her warm, maybe it would be enough. My small fingers fumbled over the matches. I remember crashing toward our room, finding her favorite scarf, the one the color of violets. Wrapping it around her, and using all the blankets I could find, and lying down next to her. Pleading with her.

I remember what it felt like. That too-quiet moment. When I realized she couldn't hear me anymore.

I hug myself now in my bed. I always thought those men

came because they were trying to force us out. To sell the house for money, and put us in the orphanage. I thought that was why Ingrid sent them away, why she was so frightened.

But now a new thought circles in my mind. I don't let it land; I don't look right at it, because it's so sad that I can hardly bear it. But I can feel it, hovering nearby.

I realize now that those men might have come from the mines.

Maybe my father's actions killed Ingrid. He took the stone, without permission, and the people from the mines came for it. Maybe they suspected that he'd stolen it. Maybe they were willing to do anything to get it back.

My fingers falter over the stitch of his words. Maybe his choices actually got a lot of people killed.

So Ingrid persuaded them to leave us alone. She made them go away.

And then she died.

⁂

My heart cracks into tiny, delicate lines as I hold the jewel up to the light. What could possibly make this stone so important? Important enough that it caused so many deaths? Nothing I do is going to change the fact that my father and sister are dead. But this stone—what I do next with it—could put me in danger. It could hurt the Vestergaards—and as a result, every person in their employ. I glance across the flickering shadows toward Liljan, to the even beat of her breathing. Most of all, this stone could hurt Eve. And isn't that the very opposite of why I came here in the first place?

I think of my father, frantically trying to leave this message. I think of what it must have been like, to die in those mines. Did it happen quickly or did he suffer? Did he even have time to think of me? I swallow back a lump in my throat, my mind turning to Ingrid. I think of her fingers curled at her sides when those men came to our house. I think of the lengths she went to in order to protect my life.

I pull out my petticoats. The stone glitters, warming in my palm.

Who could have killed those miners, and why? Who would benefit from it?

My needle is sharp silver in the candlelight.

Aleks? · - · · · · · - · - · · ·

Philip? · - - - · · · · · · · - · · · · · - - ·

One of the other miners?

Jakob said that in ten years, there has been little turnover in the mines. The men who came to my house the night Ingrid died might still even work there *now*. My teeth grate in a sudden shiver. But why would only some of the miners have been murdered, and the others spared?

Almost all the other players have changed over the past ten years. King Frederick, Aleks Vestergaard, my father, and the other murdered miners are all dead. If there's any chance of knowing what truly happened that day, I'll have to find the people who overlap between then and now. Helene wouldn't marry into the family for at least another two years. One of the only living links left is Philip.

Nina's footsteps creak on the stairs. I look at the list of dots and dashes running across my petticoat like rain.

Was there anyone else who had something to gain that day? Or something to hide?

Find the pattern.

Connect the threads.

I'm the seamstress, I think, blowing out my candle with a *whoosh.*

Good thing that's exactly what I do.

CHAPTER FIFTEEN

THREE MORNINGS LATER, after coffee and toast slathered with raspberry jam, the letter comes.

Liljan finds Jakob and me, an envelope clutched in her hand. It's sealed with red wax that's as dark as crusted blood.

"For you!" she says, handing it to Jakob. "Already! Dr. Holm must be really eager for an apprentice."

"Or really *un*-eager for one," Jakob says, hesitating before he takes the letter between his long fingers.

"I've even bought us a few moments without Brock or Nina snooping," Liljan says.

"How?" I ask.

She wiggles her eyebrows. "I left Nina a trail of half-eaten candies that leads directly to his room." She holds up a single finger, tilting her head to listen.

"BROCK!" Nina shrieks a second later.

"Right on cue," Liljan says. "Now, what does it say?" She looks at Jakob's face and claps. "Oh—you've read it already, haven't you?"

Jakob clutches the letter and flushes scarlet. "It says he'll consider taking me on," he says, his hands betraying a tremble when Liljan takes the envelope from him and breaks the wax seal. "But first he wants to meet with me." His face is dawning with a grin. "To see if I have any promising ideas."

"Which, of course, you do," Liljan says, reading the letter.

"Now, how should I present those to him?" he murmurs to himself.

"A song and dance number might be best?" Liljan ventures, cocking an eyebrow.

"Or perhaps gruesome trivia," I deadpan. Now I take the letter. "Gruesome trivia is Liljan's favorite."

"I once knew of a woman who gave her own son smallpox," Jakob says, dropping his voice to an eerie pitch. "She rubbed the powdered scabs of it into scratches on his skin." He adds with an evil laugh: "On purpose."

"That's horrible!" I say, recoiling, at the exact moment Liljan claps.

"Ooh, yes!" she says gleefully, settling in. "I want more."

"Why would anyone ever do that?" I ask. I think of my father, how his large, worn mining hands looked holding my tiny doll teacup.

"It was a very good thing, in fact," Jakob says quickly. "It was variolation, the precursor to vaccines. People exposed themselves to deadened bits of smallpox through tiny scratches in their bodies, and it would eventually give them immunity. It made the body attack the smallpox instead of the smallpox attacking the body." He looks at me and adds gently, "It actually saved her son's life that way, and eventually many others."

He tells us of his other theories, of plants, poultices, and disinfectants, of blood transfusions and hot sulfuric springs, as we pilfer Nina's key again. We climb the back stairs to the library and he tells us how the Firn was named—for the snow on top of mountains that melts only a little before freezing again, building up into a denser and denser ice. It reminded Dr. Holm of what magic does in our veins.

Then we turn our attention to tucking the jewel books beneath our uniforms and squirrel them away, one at a time, to Jakob's attic nook to pore over after our chores are finished.

There are so many red stones. My fingers flip through the pages: ruby and carnelian, garnet and sunstone, bixbite and cinnabar. There are encyclopedic entries about them, but Jakob is also combing through the library for other things that could help us: legends or ancient folklore, medicinal purposes, anything that could explain why a red stone might be worth killing people to keep secret. Liljan turns from a page on Viking sunstones to flip through the notebooks Jakob has piled next to his desk. "Jakob, is one of your ideas being bled by leeches? Oh, for the love of figs, please don't let that be the cure. Can't you just invent some nice-flavored medicine for us?"

"Oh, yes, Liljan, while I'm saving your life, I'll try to make sure it tastes good," Jakob says sarcastically. He runs a hand through his hair and adjusts his spectacles.

"Listen, I'll help you put these ghastly notebooks together

into a beautiful, professional-looking volume of all your ideas," Liljan says. "Marit can bind it"—I nod—"and you can bring it to your interview."

"And I'll help you with your suit," I offer. He gives me a pained look. "What?" I ask. "Your sleeves are far too short and the fabric is worn at the collar."

He rolls his eyes. "Thank you," he says dryly.

"Thank us by curing the Firn," Liljan says. I nod in agreement.

"And Jakob," she says, batting her eyelashes. "When the time comes . . . my favorite flavor is licorice."

❧

Late in the afternoon, I part the strands of wisteria and walk through the coolness of the shaded corridor, the shadows inside turning from faint lavender to blackberry. When I reach the greenhouse door, I pause when I hear someone whispering. There's the scuffle of a shoe and the sound of someone falling. Then a muttered curse.

I silently open the door to find Eve practicing alone near the potted orange trees. I'm quiet enough that she doesn't see me at first, trying a new step. She falls again, and then again. This time, when she picks herself up, she notices me.

"Did you come for the plums?" I ask solemnly.

Her face breaks into a grin. "It's warm in here. And I like the way it smells. I mean, I suppose it's not wool and mothballs," she says, executing a tart spin, and I laugh.

"Do you want to see what I've been working on?" She giggles, almost shy as she shows me what Helene's been teaching her. I can see a difference already. There's a new grace to the way she holds her hands and uncurls her spine, a power trembling in her muscles when she slowly extends her leg. She moves carefully amid the glass orbs, amid the smell of a fruit garden, the light filtering through the leaves as if we're under water.

I lean against the part of the wall not covered with moss. *What will it do to us,* I think painfully, *if my father tried to bring down the Vestergaards?* If he really was murdered—and if the Vestergaards really were somehow involved—then I want to take Eve and run as far away from here as we can.

But what if that isn't her choice? I ask myself. *What if* this *is what she chooses?*

What would it do to us—to me—if she knew these people had murdered my father and she decided to stay with them anyway?

Eve ever so briefly ascends to her toe and comes back down, and she beams at me.

I clap. "You've gotten so good," I say with delight. "Already." I take a step toward her and embrace her in my servant's uniform. "And you're taller, I think."

"I'm pretty sure I stopped growing the day I turned eight." She laughs, and the sound of it makes me feel guilty about the stone I have hidden in my pocket. That by keeping yet another thing from her, I'm doing something wrong.

"Are you enjoying your lessons?" I ask, releasing her. "Learning the things you always wondered about where your mother is from?"

"Yes," Eve says. She brings her arms into an effortless arc over her head. "I am. But part of it feels strange to have to be *taught* things about her, and me. At the Mill, I often wondered, of course, but . . . is it strange that it feels a little scary now, to look?" She twirls, musing. "What if it changes how I feel? About myself?" Her body revolves so slowly, in such a tight, controlled circle, that it's hard to believe. "Or who I thought I was."

My hand brushes against the jewel and I swallow.

We say that the past anchors us, gives us roots and a foundation—all things that hold us down. *But maybe that isn't always a bad thing,* I think. Maybe, sometimes, the past provides just enough substance to push off from and reach higher.

Eve makes one last attempt at the complicated spin she's learning, but instead of finishing she falls on one knee.

"Careful," I say, pulling her to her feet.

"I *am* careful," she insists, dusting herself off.

"No," I say delicately. "Just . . . be careful. Keep an eye out for Philip. All right?"

There's the first flicker of something in her eyes. "Why?"

"I just don't get a good feeling about him," I say.

There's a flash of movement in the corner of my eye, and Brock emerges from a patch of growing bay leaves. I wonder how long he's been standing there, listening. I turn toward him, heart pounding. He stands upright and at attention, his arms tucked behind his back.

"Excuse me, Miss Vestergaard. Is this servant bothering you?" Brock asks.

Eve whirls around. "Excuse me, Marit, is this servant bothering *you?*" she retorts, eyes flashing, her chest heaving with indignation. Brock takes a half step back, trying to mask the shock on his face, and it's all I can do not to burst out laughing. Eve and I have always looked out for each other — us against everyone else. Once, when Sare made fun of some poppy seeds caught in Eve's teeth, I ran my fingers along the thread of Sare's buttons so that her dress popped open as soon as I stepped into the next room.

Then no one was laughing at Eve's teeth anymore.

"No, Miss Eve. There's no problem here," I say deferentially. Brock bows an apology at her, and when his head is bent, she shoots him a dirty look and an extra gesture I didn't even know she knew.

"Do let me know if that changes, Marit," she says, floating regally through the door and into the wisteria curtain, the ends of her ribbons trailing behind her.

For the first time, I realize that maybe she doesn't need me as much as I believed.

And as soon as she's gone, Brock steps to block the door, trapping me.

"That little trick with the candies in my room," he says. "Was that you?"

"No," I say honestly.

I try to push past him, but he's as solid as a brick wall.

"You know, Marit, I've been watching you," he says, crossing his arms in a slow, menacing way. "Sneaking around. Visiting the Vestergaards' library, and that space of Jakob's in the attic. You're up to something. And all those infractions," he says, ticking off his fingers, "are ones that Nina should likely be informed of." He straightens, rising up to his full height.

"You can't force me out," I say in a low voice. I take a step toward him. Now that he's discovered my connection to Eve, I'll press it to my full advantage instead of trying to hide it. "When it comes down to it, *I* have a bigger in with the Vestergaards than *you* do. But"—I take another step toward him and pluck a golden pink grapefruit from one of his trees—"if you'd like to risk it, go ahead. Just know I've got someone pulling for me on the inside. And maybe Mrs. Vestergaard would like to know exactly who is responsible for her wasting time having to find a new seamstress over and over again. Or ruining her curtains."

He steps aside just enough for me to shove past him and out the door.

But then he follows me into the corridor. "Do you know what else I've discovered?" he asks, trying to keep step with me. I bristle and quicken my pace. "You stay up late at night so you can do your jobs without magic." While he walks, he pulls a silver coin from his pocket. It's the talisman he always carries, the charm that he superstitiously flips whenever he uses magic. "You don't like to use it, do you? You *hoard* it."

"So?" I ask, throwing open the kitchen door. Wondering if

I should make good on my promise to actually tie him to the banister. "What does it matter to you?"

I don't even hear Liljan approach. Brock's face registers her sliding down the railing toward us at the last moment, but he's not quick enough to stop her from landing and plucking the coin from right between his fingers.

"Keep away!" she sings.

He swears. "Liljan, you're such a royal pain in the—"

She holds the coin out tauntingly to him, then turns and flies into the kitchen, where everyone is gathering for dinner.

"Liljan!" Brock lunges after her, but she manages to toss the talisman over his head to Lara, who giggles and immediately throws it on to Oliver. Brock attempts to grab it but just misses as Liljan leaps and snatches it back again.

"Just how will you keep the Firn away now?" she teases him.

"Do what I do," Signe calls out as Liljan tosses the coin to her. She passes it to Oliver and says, shrugging: "Pray."

"Or only use magic when you sit by a fire," Oliver adds. He throws the talisman to Declan.

"Pour it out all at once, then take a week to rest," Declan advises. The coin arcs through the air, gleaming in the firelight.

"No, just use a little each day," says Jakob, reaching up to catch the talisman. He flips it into one of Dorit's measuring cups.

"Use the right recipe," Dorit says. "And it will taste like you used magic anyway."

"Find ways to cut corners. Save and stretch your own magic,"

Rae says dreamily. She plucks the coin from the measuring cup and looks at Brock, of all people, with stars in her eyes. She hands it back to him. "And each other's."

So they do care. Carrying their talismans and old wives' tales like armor. Spilling out magic, tending to one another, and hoping for the best. I think of Ivy's glass orbs hanging in the greenhouse and wonder if they help Brock's plants grow better, somehow—if, like Ingrid did for me, Ivy poured out some of her magic to help someone she loves.

"Marit's up to something," Brock announces. His chest is heaving and his eyes are spitting fire, and I suddenly try to make myself invisible in the corner of the kitchen. "And I don't trust her in the least. I think she's spying on us."

"What?" I cry.

"She's snooping around the Vestergaards. She isn't being entirely honest about why she's here. Don't you think you should have told us all a certain critical little piece of information?" he asks. "That you knew Eve before you both came to this house?"

"Is that true?" Rae asks. She comes to stand next to Brock, folding her arms over her chest. "Did you know her from before?"

"Y-yes," I stammer. "But, for fig's sake, I'm not spying on you."

Dorit sidles up next to Brock, still holding her wooden spoon from the stove. Jakob and Liljan take a step closer to me, as if we are a seam that is splitting down the middle. In a move that mirrors it, Brock takes off his jacket and methodically tears the fabric with a loud ripping sound. I gape at him.

"Mm," he says, grimacing. "Seems as though this is going to need mending." He waits a beat, then holds it out to me. "Would you like to borrow my talisman?" he asks wickedly.

Jakob bristles. He's moving before I can react, taking the coat and throwing it back at Brock.

"Fix it yourself."

Jakob's body is tightened into a protective stance in front of me, and I try not to notice the curves of his muscles under his shirt.

"It's all right," I say to him quietly. I step forward, looking between the two sides of the staff. "It's true. I did know Eve from before. But I'm not spying—I'm only trying to look out for her. We grew up together. She's like my sister." I extend my hand, offering to take Brock's ripped jacket. "After all," I say softly, "who's to say what lengths we would go to for a sister?"

To his credit, Brock looks the slightest bit sheepish when he hands over the jacket.

"I'm still going to stitch it together using some horrible dirty word," I inform him.

"Well, first start with this," Nina says, barging into the kitchen. "A warm evening dress for Eve. Mr. Vestergaard is taking Mrs. Vestergaard and Eve to Tivoli Gardens."

Philip Vestergaard. Seeking out private time with Eve and Helene.

Again.

It's just kindness, I tell myself. And it's in Tivoli Gardens, a public place surrounded by crowds. He's taking care of his brother's widow and the only family he has left around the holidays.

Yet I still feel a stirring sense of unease.

It's hard to hide, even while I feel Brock's eyes search my face for a reaction.

"You're up to something," he repeats. He smiles wolfishly and pockets his talisman. "And I'm going to find out what it is."

I pluck out a knife and hold it up until he saunters away, then slice clean through my grapefruit.

"Any way I could get a ticket to Tivoli?" I murmur to Liljan and Jakob.

"Perhaps we should all go," Liljan suggests cheerfully. "Listen, you got us into the ballet," she says, licking jam off her fingers. "Now, leave this one to me."

CHAPTER SIXTEEN

Philip
November 25, 1866
Tivoli and Vauxhall Pleasure Gardens

TIVOLI SHIMMERS WITH LIGHTS.

I follow Helene and Eve through the darkening night to the wooden gate with its ticket houses on each side. Beyond the gate are twining strands of canals and moats, spilling out from the lake, looping around the gardens. The reflections from the gaslights gleam in water that's as black as ink. I recoil at the sound of a shattering scream, taking me instantly back to the war. But the shriek is merely carrying through the night from the roller coaster. I hear the creaking of its joints; more screams as the carriages fall, mingling with laughter. There's a crackle of fireworks.

I take a breath and feel a deep sense of pleasure. Beautiful Denmark.

Beside me, Eve's eyes are wide and alight with wonder.

But Helene is irritable. She's even stiffer than usual around me, as though a sheen of ice covers her every move. She wears that coat with the embroidered flowers on it, but as usual, she wears no jewels. She never has. It rankles me, as if it's a personal affront.

Aleks may have saved the mines the first time, but I was the one to find the jewels and save us the second time.

Not him.

Me.

Tonight, I follow the smell of sugar-glazed almonds and mulled gløgg through the gate, gravel crunching under my boots. We round the corner to come face-to-face with an advancing wall of the Tivoli Boys' Guard, thirty-odd children in uniform, known as the Lilliputian Military. Helene leans forward to buy Eve a bag of hazelnuts and marzipan. She cocks her head at me with an unspoken question and, at my nod, buys two gløggs that wisp with steam.

Her hand is naked when she hands me the cup.

Aleks loved her even more for it, that she didn't cover herself in the jewels from our mines. She has always preferred simple pieces of glass to our gorgeous rubies, thick and fat, or the dark sapphires that lick and spit light like a fire. But even if she doesn't want to wear our jewels, she is housed by them, clothed by them, fed by them. Aleks used our newfound riches to buy the Vestergaard estate in Hørsholm. We replaced the necklaces and earrings my mother sold off during the war. We sat in the prime boxes at the ballet house, watching Helene dance. And at Aleks and Helene's wedding, Vestergaard gemstones twinkled across my mother's hair like a universe of dark stars.

Helene didn't wear any.

"Can you stop that?" Helene suddenly asks me, her voice slicing through the air like fresh-cut steel. I must have started to hum "The Brave Foot Soldier" without even realizing it. I sip my gløgg. The fireworks crackle over our heads, leaving glittering trails of fire and smoke in the sky.

"Is it magic?" Eve breathes, looking up. Her voice is so reverent that it almost sounds fearful. I examine her, this small girl Helene plucked from a southern orphanage.

"No," I say. "It's gunpowder." At that answer, Eve seems to relax.

"You don't like magic?" I ask, eyeing her.

She shakes her head. "No one should use magic." Her voice turns to disgust. "It's cruel."

I laugh in surprise before I can help it. She flinches.

"You do know that you have magical people working all around you," I inform her. "Working for you. Every day."

"What?" She looks horrified. "That's not true."

"I assure you, it's very true," I say.

"But—but doesn't it *kill* them?"

She looks to Helene, as if Helene will explain it all, give her an answer to assuage her horror, and I chuckle again, immensely amused.

"Yes, Helene, do you ever feel bad?" I ask, and take a deep sip of gløgg. "That you ask people to pour out so much magic for you?"

The sound of the boys' guard grows distant, and the lights shimmer in the lake. Helene's silence grows so stony that the air around her practically crystallizes.

"Everyone makes their choices," she finally says to Eve. "If it's worth it to them or not. I pay them well."

Eve swallows. "But not . . . *everyone* who works in the house has magic?" She looks at Helene with a touch of suspicion. "It's not a *prerequisite?*"

But Helene isn't listening. She's radiating fury at the smirk I'm not even trying to hide. "Don't look at me like that, Philip," she snaps. "You think I don't know what it's like to pay a price, to give up part of my life for something? What do you think ballet is? It took years of my life that I spent practicing and rehearsing, all for those few moments a night on stage. It weakened my body, cost me in injury. And now it's gone. It might not have taken years from the end of my life, but it cost me part of my life all the same." She tosses the rest of her gløgg into the street. "Everyone makes their own choices."

"Irritable tonight, are we?" I ask. I lean on a wooden railing. "Even more than usual."

"Well, you're irritating," she retorts.

There's a sudden rippling in the crowd as the royal guards spill through the front gate. I turn toward them with heightened interest. So the king must be coming tonight.

Eve steps forward to examine the carvings of the merry-go-round, and then, so only I can hear, Helene begrudgingly admits, "Bournonville and I are disagreeing. He disapproves of the vision I have for the future of the ballet, for dancers. He's grooming someone else to take over the company when he's gone." She swallows and looks away. "I'm not certain they will even allow Eve to audition."

"So start your own company," I say breezily, but Helene catches me off-guard when she says, "That's exactly what I plan to do. Perhaps Eve and I will do a series of salons," she muses. "Experimental." She looks away, into the distance. "Perhaps if Denmark won't have us, we could travel to Paris, St. Petersburg."

King Christian IX enters Tivoli through the front gate, trailed by an entourage of guards.

"Either that, or perhaps it's time to shift my attentions." Helene's fingers graze her lips in thought. "Maybe it's time I learned the business of the mines."

My head snaps up and I try to mask my panic. No, that cannot happen. Helene needs to stay far away from the mines, in the tenuous arrangement we've struck—where she allows me to manage the ownership Aleks left her and never, ever interferes.

"And deny the world of what you can do?" I ask. "I never knew you as one to give up so quickly, Helene."

An idea of my own is starting to form.

"Eve," I call. "Come with me."

I take Eve's elbow and stride toward the king, with Helene following close behind.

My thoughts turn like gears. King Christian IX may be the father-in-law of Europe, but he's also deeply unpopular. He gained the crown and immediately lost the Second Schleswig War, forfeiting our duchies—our vital trading veins, the ones my father died for — to Prussia. The king is on shaky ground, in dire financial straits, and desperately trying to strike a new balance between his sovereignty and parliament. There are rumors whispered that he'd even consider handing over Denmark's very independence.

Something hardens in my chest like a fist. We will not be like that little boy, standing powerless in the cold, on the brink of losing everything, looking with longing at power and magic in an alley.

If we play our cards right, we all have the chance to gain something here.

The head of the king's royal guard recognizes us from the night at the ballet and lets us through.

"Your Royal Highness," I say in greeting. "It is a pleasure to see you again."

"Philip," the king says. "My daughter Dagmar thanks you for the exquisite wedding gift you sent."

"And a scepter to follow shortly, for your son King George I," I say smoothly. "How fortuitous that we should see you here, as we were just discussing an invitation. We would be honored by your presence in Hørsholm in the new year. Perhaps my niece, Eve, could even perform for you and the queen."

Helene stiffens beside me. She subtly clutches my arm and squeezes it in a viselike grip but doesn't correct me. How can she? I've put the plan in motion already.

Just behind me, Eve sways.

The king smiles with polite, but reserved, interest. "Oh?"

I draw closer to him. "I have business of great importance that I wish to discuss," I say quietly, so that only he can hear. "Something to help your children, and all of Denmark."

He looks at me with renewed curiosity. Now I have his attention.

I step back. "I'll send the formal invitation to your courtier," I say.

"Excellent," the king says.

"What are you doing?" Helene whispers through gritted teeth as soon as we are out of earshot. Her grip on my arm threatens to leave a bruise.

I shake loose of her. "Giving you a chance to make Bournonville reconsider," I say. "What can he do if you've captured the king's imagination and seal of approval? Make it spectacular. Use magic if you have to. With the king's backing, you can change the face of ballet and improve the Vestergaard name at the same time."

And stay far, far away from the mines.

I look at Eve, her hesitant face lit by another exploding firework. "You're welcome," I prompt, giving Helene's shoulder the slightest nudge.

"Thank you," she says begrudgingly. She looks at me with unmasked suspicion, but for the first time, she almost looks beautiful to me. For once, I don't see her as a threat. I light my cigar and lead them on through the looping lanes of Tivoli.

❧

Later, in the carriage, Eve's head lolls heavily with sleep. Helene covers her with a second blanket and a thick silence fills the cabin.

I catch myself humming again and stop. I think Helene is sleeping too, but then she asks softly, "Why are you giving all those jewels as gifts to the royal family, Philip? What are you playing at?"

I inhale deeply. She still owns the largest share of the mines, thanks to Aleks, and if my plan is going to work, she'll have to support at least some of it.

"I'm finding a way into their circle of influence."

"Yes. You're buying our way into a relationship with them. But ... why? To what end? Is it going to benefit the mines, somehow?"

"Do you know why Denmark won the first war and lost the second?"

She hesitates, eyes narrowing. She thinks I'm changing the subject, refusing to answer her question.

But I'm not.

"People say we never should have entered the second war in the first place ..." she begins.

"Perhaps not. There was a crucial difference between the two wars. In the first, when my father and brother fought, Britain came to our aid. In the second, they didn't."

"What does that have to do with the jewels, Philip?"

I close my eyes.

I think of the birds, when they suddenly stopped singing.

War.

I think of the bodies.

There was a man in the trenches next to me who had magic. He reminded me of that little boy in the alley. Flicking his fingers.

A shudder rips through me.

I think of the first dead body I ever saw. In the morgue that night with Tønnes.

"Was it terrible for you?" Helene asks softly. "The war?"

"Have you ever known fear, Helene?" I ask. "Did you know that it has a taste?" I thought I knew what fear was when I was a little boy, worrying about my mother, my brother, worrying about going hungry. But this—this was utter destruction and humiliation. Palpable fear was like dank mildew in my mouth the first time I tasted it. Cannons loaded with case shot, shells hissing by, men with shredded faces. I still dream of it some nights. Ambulance carts filled with straw you could wring blood from.

"Philip—" Helene begins.

I hardly hear her now. I'm halfway back there again. I didn't pay for some poor farmer to take my place on the battlefield in that second war, like so many other people as rich as I was did.

Maybe I was trying to live up to my father's memory, still walking in my brother's shadow. Maybe I felt as though I deserved it, after what had happened in the mines. There was human waste everywhere in Dybbøl, after bombs destroyed the latrines, waste mingling with decaying body parts and giving rise to typhoid fever. Sludge, mud, and brain matter.

I remember the moment when the birds stopped singing.

In mines and in wartime, that's a sure sign that death is near.

I open my eyes. "Do you know why the British didn't come to our aid the second time? Because of Queen Victoria. Bloody Queen Victoria." I blink toward the stars. "The British public wanted to help us. We were the underdogs. But her eldest daughter had married the crown prince of Prussia. So she sided with them. These seemingly little events, they shape the destinies of thousands upon thousands. That one marriage changed the fortune of a whole country. Sealed Denmark's fate, cost us a quarter of our land, our dignity, generations of Danish lives. No one was singing 'The Brave Foot Soldier' when we marched home. Half of us never left there at all."

I swallow, my mouth dry as bone. I look at the red stone on my finger.

"If you could prevent that from happening ever again, would you? If there was something you could do to change that, you would do it, wouldn't you? If it were in your power?"

"Is it?" she asks, her voice crystal clear and strong.

I swallow back the taste of mildew. "You think we're so different, Helene, but we're the same. We both clawed our way up from the hands we were dealt. Now we're putting our pieces in place. Both of us are playing the long game, aren't we?"

And if we do it right, we won't just win.

We're going to change the whole damn board.

CHAPTER SEVENTEEN

Marit
November 25, 1866
Tivoli and Vauxhall Pleasure Gardens

O N THE NIGHT THE VESTERGAARDS visit Tivoli,
Liljan wrangles us a holiday outing for the staff. We
invite Ivy, as well. Walking as a group through the looping,
pruned boxwood hedges of Tivoli's grounds, I subtly set the
pace near the front, keeping us within a calculated distance of
the Vestergaards.

Colored lamps float on strings above us and adorn the walking gardens like a necklace of beads. The moon is a bright pearl
sliding among them. There's a heady scent of sugar and alcohol
as concessioners dot the dirt lanes, selling dried figs, raisins, sug-
ared apples on a stick. I've never been to Tivoli before, but my
father always talked of a time he came here with my mother right
after they were married. My father said my mother screamed
bloody murder on the roller coaster, clutching his hand so tightly
she threatened to break his fingers—then promptly asked to
ride again. I don't remember what she looked like, because she
died when I was three. I never had a photograph of her, but

I've invented an image of her in my head, dark haired and rosy cheeked and quick to laugh, always clutching my father's hand.

Her name was Johanne.

It's actually a lovely evening, and I am wrapped tightly in a wool coat and gloves I lined with lush scraps of sable. When I shiver a little, Jakob lends me his scarf, and I pretend as if I'm tucking my nose deep into the wool because I'm cold. Not to breathe in his scent.

"My feet are cold," Liljan announces, stomping.

"More gløgg!" Rae suggests gleefully.

"Look, Vee," Brock says, pausing at a candy stand. "They have lemon flavor. Your favorite."

I use the moment to slip away and draw nearer to Eve and Philip. They seem deep in conversation, and Eve flinches at the sputtering fireworks above our heads. The explosives crackle and smoke, and when I'm almost within hearing distance, the crowd suddenly starts to stir. Whispers rustle and rise into the air around me like dragonfly wings taking flight. *Royal guards. The king is here.* I steal a final glance at Eve but lose all hope of keeping track of her in the moving crowds and reluctantly turn back.

I didn't think anyone noticed I'd slipped away. But of course, I couldn't be that lucky.

On the carriage ride home, Brock pulls out the handful of hard candies he bought, wrapped in a little package. He pours them into his sister's hand like a trickle of crystallized tourmaline. "You know, Vee, you could make a mean hard candy out of glass," he says. "It would look just like these do. But it would break someone's tooth."

Ivy examines the lemon candies in her palm. "You're not nearly as unkind as you like to think you are," she says to him, which makes me promptly choke on my gløgg.

"Have you always gotten on so well?" Liljan asks them. She throws Jakob a smirk. "Our mother used to lace us together in one of her old corsets."

"I can hardly picture that," I say.

"He would read my diary," Liljan says indignantly, as though she's still put out by it.

"The musings of a nine-year-old," Jakob says. "Scintillating. And mostly full of complaints about me."

"It's not as if I could even lock it. You were so infuriating."

"And then you retaliated. *You* . . ." Jakob says, his cheeks flushing.

"Yes! Turned the back of your trousers brown," Liljan says, suddenly shrieking with laughter. "As if you'd soiled them!"

"For the record," he says dryly, straightening his collar, "I didn't."

"Stop," Liljan gasps, clutching herself, tears rolling down her face, "or *I* might."

He gives her braid a tug with such a simple affection that it makes me suddenly yearn for either Ingrid or Eve, or both. Liljan pushes his hand away and initiates a game in the frosted windowpane of the carriage.

"What were you doing tonight when you snuck off from us,

Marit?" Brock says, leaning over to whisper low in my ear, and I bite back a surprised yelp. "What? You didn't think I'd notice?"

"Why are you always spying on me?" I whisper. I grind the heel of my boot warningly on his toe. "Cur."

"Hi, Pot," he says, kicking me off. "I'm Kettle. Why does my spying make me a cur but yours is somehow fine? I know you were following the Vestergaards again."

"It's different because I'm doing *mine* out of good intentions," I say.

"Everyone's intentions seem good to them," Brock says. "You better learn that right quick, little seamstress."

Ivy dips her head toward us. "What are we whispering about over here?"

"Just making sure Marit doesn't wander off and get lost forever," he says menacingly, and I shift to crack the growing tension in my neck. Ivy twists her hands together and plays with the end of her long white braid.

"Brock, listen," she says, and her voice is no longer teasing. "Stop torturing poor Marit." She takes a deep breath, as if steeling herself, and says: "There's something I have to tell you."

Brock stiffens a little at her serious tone. "Go on, then. What is it?"

She looks out at the sky of ink beyond our window, exhaling a weight from her shoulders. "I'm never coming back to work for the Vestergaards, even if they ask me to," she says simply. Her breath carries the tart and sweet from the lemon candy. "Because I've stopped using magic. And I think perhaps you should too."

She draws Jakob's and Liljan's attention. "All of you—really. I'm sure there are other jobs for each of you that won't require so much of yourself. You know, I've learned that in most other estates, the servants don't stay past two, maybe three, years at most."

"Vee—" Brock says, paling. "You know this is the best thing out there for us. The Vestergaards pay the highest wage. They're never cruel. We're free to leave anytime."

"It's true," Liljan agrees reluctantly, pulling her blanket tight up around her neck. "I'm so free to leave that I actually want to less."

"It's a good life, for now," Brock insists. "We know how to cut corners, how to siphon and spare magic. We help each other. Look out for each other." He lowers his voice. "You know I don't believe Aunt Dorit has *actually* used magic in years."

"I know that was true before," Ivy says. She hesitates. "But . . . it seems as though Helene is asking for more magic than before. Ever since Eve arrived."

"It's not Eve's fault," I say too quickly, instantly defensive. "She doesn't have any idea about the magic. She wouldn't even want it, if she knew."

"Well, then," Brock says after a beat filled with meaning, "maybe she should find out."

I shrug, trying to pretend as though it doesn't matter to me, because if he discovers that it does, our balance of power will shift again. And I'm not giving him one more thing to use as leverage over me.

"I can't leave yet, Ivy," Brock says, and he almost sounds bitter. "I'm not going to be like Father. I've been careful, saving up. If I stay two more years making a Vestergaard salary, you and Mother won't ever have to worry about money again."

"You are nothing like him," Ivy says kindly. She plays with the end of her braid again. Puts her hand on his. Her fingers are small, her nails bitten.

And then the carriage stops so abruptly that Liljan and I are practically thrown out of our seats.

I land halfway onto Jakob's lap.

"I'm sorry," I start to say, flushing madly at the curve of his body against mine, when there's an insistent pounding on the carriage door.

"This is the Danish Police Corps," a voice bellows from beyond it. "We need to search your carriage."

The door swings open.

"Good evening," a man says, holding a lantern up to peer at each of our faces. He has a thick mustache and is dressed in a navy blue uniform. Behind him are three other uniformed men, the firelight flickering in shadows across their faces. My stomach instantly knots, and for half a second, I see the men who came to our house that night Ingrid died. I look for a scar shaped like a fishhook.

But then I blink, and they are back to being regular policemen.

"Apologies for the disturbance, but we are looking for someone," the first man says gruffly. "A woman has gone missing from a house in the area."

"Missing?" Jakob asks.

"A house servant. Female." He scans our faces carefully. Double-checks a paper in his hand. "Have you seen anything unusual tonight? An older woman traveling alone on this road? She would have been sixty-five years old, with graying hair."

We shake our heads no.

"Godspeed to find her," Jakob murmurs. "It's cold out there tonight."

The policeman nods dismissively. "Take care and keep your eyes open."

He closes the door.

"Oh, dear. I hope they find her soon," Liljan says, peering out the window. The carriage jostles to a start again.

"Unless she doesn't want to be found," Ivy says. "She's a house servant. She might have run away."

"Ivy—" Brock says, and his face hardens. "What's gotten into you? I can tell something is wrong. You've seemed off the whole night. Did something happen at the glass shop?" His voice drops to almost a whisper when he adds: "You can tell me."

She watches the first falling snowflakes through the dark glass of the window. And then a sudden shudder rips through her.

"I saw someone get the Firn," she says softly, as if she's far away. "A little boy." She squeezes her eyes closed. Swallows. "He was so young. He sort of looked like you, Brock, and his mother always came in the shop with him, and then—last week—out in the street." Her voice wavers. "She must not have realized that he was using it all the time, to keep her out of the rain. His mother screamed. I saw the way it went through him," she says, the air in the carriage suddenly turning taut and too warm, "like dark branches. His body looked so unnatural, lying there in the street. I saw the way his mother tried to shield him, so no one would look at him with that expression—with disgust, or fear, or like he was something not human—when he was just this sweet little boy." Ivy has a look in her eyes, a haunted one, of a nightmare suddenly becoming real in front of her. "How stupid we are," she whispers, "to even risk it."

A feeling of heaviness and foreboding settles over each of us, as thick as a blanket. She has broken the unspoken rule, the same one we had at the Mill—that we never acknowledge the dark future that potentially awaits all of us. And I realize that Ivy doesn't have to make fake hard candies for anyone to be fooled. I've been doing it to myself. I can't forget that even though there is sweetness in my life at the Vestergaards', I'm really sucking on a piece of glass.

"Ivy—" Brock says.

"I'm done using magic," she declares. "I wish you would be too."

Ivy's hands tangle in her braid as the carriage stops at a streetlight at the glass shop and she climbs out. She's choosing life at the expense of her home, and her family.

But she's had all those things for years.

Now that I've had the faintest taste of what a home, what belonging, can feel like—perhaps going back to safety, and loneliness, is actually worse.

We arrive back at the Vestergaards' just in time to see Eve disappear through the front door. I breathe a sigh of relief. Philip is returning to his carriage when we climb out.

He gives us a nod of acknowledgment, even raises his hand in farewell, which surprises me as a kind gesture. Many people of his stature would not acknowledge a group of servants at all.

And that's when I see it. The ring he wears.

My stomach tightens and my fingers suddenly feel like ice.

I noticed it offhandedly at the theater, but of course it didn't have any significance to me then.

I don't bother to hide my stare as he gets into his own carriage, his hand on the door, the driver holding out the lantern in such a way that I can clearly make out the glinting shade of red.

The stone he wears looks exactly like the one my father hid as a clue for me.

CHAPTER EIGHTEEN

"JAKOB," LILJAN WHISPERS THE NEXT MORNING.
She grabs his sleeve as he passes by our room on his way downstairs and then furtively shuts the door behind him.

"Um, hello, Marit," he says, glancing awkwardly around our little bedroom.

He seems to be avoiding looking at me sitting on my bed.

I abruptly stand.

"I need some help. I want all the records on the Vestergaard jewels we can find," I say. "Sales, inventories, types of jewels they mine. Every scrap you can possibly turn up. Do you think you and Liljan could help me?"

"All right . . ." he says, weighing the request, and he seems better able to focus now. "You find a new lead to follow?"

"I know it's a lot to ask," I say, hedging. Risking their jobs. Thrusting them deeper into this mystery. I pull out my father's hidden stone from my pocket. "I think Philip was wearing this same strange jewel last night."

Jakob turns to Liljan. "Are you up for it?"

"Espionage!" she begins with enthusiasm, but then she suddenly freezes.

Nina's footfalls are on the stairs, and they are rising rapidly toward us.

"Hide," Liljan whispers urgently, and I point Jakob to the narrow space between the wall and my straw mattress. I kneel and pretend to fold my uniforms in the trunk to block Nina's view.

Just in time. She knocks once on our door and then barges in without waiting for a response.

"Marit," she barks. "Eve says she needs this mended. Immediately."

She's holding Eve's dress from Tivoli last night.

"Yes, ma'am," I say, and snatch it from her as quickly as I can. When I step back, I can feel the faint warmth of Jakob's breath on my leg.

She gives us each a half-long look, squinting as if she can sense our nervousness but can't quite pinpoint why. Then, after an eternal moment, she abruptly turns and moves on.

I clutch Eve's Tivoli dress, with its lush rose-pink color I chose just for her. Run my hand along the satin until I find a tiny, clean rip in it. Almost as if someone cut it intentionally, with scissors.

With my heart in my throat, I turn over the hem and discreetly thumb into the secret pocket.

Inside is a scrap of paper inscribed with a line of dots and dashes.

SOS

"Excuse me," I say, and I practically fly down the stairs and through the underground corridor to the main house and then up to Eve's room.

As soon as she opens the door, I blurt, "Are you all right?" I step into her room and promptly close the door behind me, shutting out a curious gaze from Lara, who is dusting in the hallway. "Did something happen last night at Tivoli?"

"Marit," Eve says. She tosses me a pair of satin shoes and sits to pull on her stockings. "Can you help sew ribbons on those? We can talk while I dress. I have so much to tell you and barely any time."

I move Wubbins to sit on the bed.

"I have big news," she says, rolling her stockings up her legs, buzzing with an energy that seems to be some blend of terror and excitement. "Enormous, stupendous. The biggest news ever. But first—Marit—did you know that some of the staff here have magic?" she asks breathlessly.

My heart sinks.

"I don't know how to feel. It seems wrong. I don't want them to use it," she says, brow knitting, "especially for me. Can you find out which ones have it? Do you know?" She looks up at me with her big brown eyes.

I look back. I have to tell her. I cannot lie to her again. I scramble for the right words, the way to frame it. I set down the shoes.

"Eve, I—"

But she grabs a new pair with fresh laces and begins to put

them on. "And there's more, Marit. It's Philip," she says, tightening the laces. "He has something planned. We saw the king at Tivoli last night and Philip invited him here. The *king*, Marit," she cries, "is coming *here!* To watch me dance!"

A sudden thrill runs through me. I think of my father's letter, of his secret red stone hidden in my pocket. Of him wanting us to find an audience with the king, no matter the cost.

Do I dare tell Eve the truth now? Risk her anger, risk losing the relationship that matters most to me, risk being kicked out of my employ — right before the king is, impossibly, coming to me? This could be the one opportunity I ever get.

"I don't know if I can do it," Eve says. She reaches across the bed and takes my hand. The waver in her voice finds all those tiny little cracks in my heart and threatens to shatter them.

"I'll help you," I tell her, echoing Liljan's voice from that cold day in Copenhagen. I close my hand around hers. "I'm going to be right here with you."

Lara knocks on the door and calls, "Miss Eve? The choreographer is here."

"I have to go," Eve whispers. She kisses my temple. And then as quickly as a snowflake melting, she and the moment are gone.

♨

"Hygge," my sister once said when I was six years old, "is hard to explain because it's a feeling. It's like trying to describe a color."

She tugged my hair into a plait, sending a delicate tingle along my scalp, and gestured around the room: to the fire blazing in the hearth, the snow falling white outside the window. My father stood over the coal stove, the kettle starting to whistle beneath his big, worn hands. "For me, it's honey tea and cinnamon sugar æbleskivers, a deep chair and a good book and a blanket. It's being cozy and content with you and Far." She closed her eyes and smiled. "It's being warm here"—she touched her heart— "even when the world is cold."

Hygge. The very mention of it calls up a heady mix of clove and citrus peel and smoke wisping from candlewicks, warm coals burning cobalt and orange. Ingrid crafted a crown from wire that year and made it bloom with felt flowers and glass birds. I remember following the lace of her white nightgown to line the mantels with candles; the way she made custard cream from one of Mother's old recipes and whipped it with egg whites and orange zest.

That warm sense of contentment, of rightness, of home, even when the rest of the world is cold—that is what I want the king to feel when he watches Eve dance. I want him to wish that he could sit and watch her forever.

I spent the early weeks of December feverishly making holiday dresses and sewing plump satin ribbons onto fragrant fir wreathes that hang on all the windows and doors. But tonight, it's Christmas Eve, and the staff is off. I put on the blue-green dress I wore to the ballet. We hold hands and sing hymns around the Christmas tree, which is draped with Danish flag garlands and lit with wax candles. Nina's voice is surprisingly rich when she sings "Dejlig er den himmel blå."

For the staff dinner, Dorit created a hot buttered rum with maple syrup, butter, red pepper, and cinnamon that makes my lips tingle. Candles are lit in the windows. Serving dishes are piled high with pork roast stuffed with prunes, pickled red cabbage dyed dark crimson with currant juice, thickened gravy, and fried brown-sugar potatoes. We each sample the Danish-Crucian dish Dorit created for tonight at Helene's request: rødgrød, red pudding usually made with berries and cream but tonight made with delicious pink guava instead.

"How is life at the glass shop, Ivy?" Lara asks, pulling up a chair after we've said grace. And whether because it's Christmas Eve or Ivy's here again, Dorit even gives me a full portion of roast.

"Fine," Ivy says, "although I miss Dorit's cooking and do feel as though I always smell of glass paste."

"That's not your perfume?" Brock teases.

"I heard the king is coming here," she says. She lets her comment hang in the balance among us, and her meaning is clear. "How exciting."

I swallow, thinking of the work Helene expects me to do on Eve's costumes. Ivy was right. These events to help secure Eve's future are requiring more and more magic. Everything meant to help Eve make a home here is making home here harder for the rest of us.

"Well, His Royal Highness hasn't officially accepted yet,"

Brock says. He gives a tight smile, which sends Ivy dipping into a large burlap bag at her feet.

"I'm sorry for the last time we were all together, at Tivoli," she says. "I felt as though I left on bad terms. So . . . I've brought gifts!" She rises with her arms full of small lumps wrapped in brown paper and makes her way around the table, distributing them by name.

"You've changed your mind, then, about the magic?" Brock asks.

"No," she says proudly. "I made these months ago, and the rest I finished by hand."

When she reaches me, I keep my head down. I concentrate very hard on cutting my meat, expecting her to walk right past me to Liljan. But instead she places a wrapped gift in front of my plate and says, "Merry Christmas, Marit."

I look up at her with an unexpected pricking in my eyes. "Merry Christmas, Ivy."

Inside each package is a cube of glass. They're gorgeous and heavy and clear, like pieces of ice. Mine has edges that look sewn, like embroidery. "They're paperweights," Ivy explains, "but I made a little divot that also holds a tea candle."

Dorit beams at her. "Look at you, dearie, always bringing a bit of light."

"I love it, Vee," Brock says. And I will admit that though he's a miserable little sod, he looks like a different person whenever he's looking at her.

"The nisse is certainly going to *love* this risalamande," Liljan says, tucking into rice porridge with whipped cream and an almond hiding in it. She winks at me wickedly and I lick the warm cherry sauce off my spoon. I used to read Eve Danish folktales on Christmas Eve in the Mill, when she had just begun methodically eating her chocolate biscuit from Mathies.

"The nisse wears a pointed red cap," I would tell Eve. "He is roughly the same size that you are, and he will cause all sorts of trouble if we don't leave him a treat in the attic."

"We're not doing any of that nonsense," Nina announces tartly now. "Nisse is legend, but you know what isn't?" She pauses and drinks her buttered rum. "Rats."

Undeterred, Liljan pushes open the door to Jakob's secret nook later that night, carrying a tray full of forbidden hot cocoa and second helpings of risalamande. Some of the whipped cream sloshes over the side to the floorboards. "Nina will serve my head on a platter of fine Vestergaard china for this," she says, setting the tray down on the floor.

"She'll chop us like almonds," I agree, handing Jakob a cup. "Hide us in risalamande."

"She'll dip us in hot wax and make us into candles," Jakob says. "Especially if she knew that I stashed these here yesterday." He pulls a tin of butter cookies out from behind a vase.

I eagerly take a cookie and dip it into the whipped topping, watching the butter crumble against the cocoa and chilled cream, and curl into my blanket.

"For you, Lil," Jakob says, reaching under a pillow and

handing Liljan a package. She muffles a shriek when she rips open the paper to find a book about grotesque history. On the front there's a painting of a rotting head and a helmet covered with spikes. "Thank you!" Liljan says, gleefully embracing the book to her chest.

"You're such an odd little duck," Jakob says with fondness.

"Quack, quack," Liljan says.

"And for Marit," Jakob says, and they turn to present a gift to me together.

"The copies of what you wanted," Liljan says formally, taking them and handing them over to me with great ceremony. "You'll need to destroy them completely when you're done."

Jakob has found everything I asked for, and Liljan made exact copies for me—down to every unique jot and tittle of handwriting. I comb through the sheaf of paper, scanning the statements. There are payments to the miners, registers and dates of gemstones selling through a network of four jewelry shops based out of a flagship store in Copenhagen. It's going to take hours to sort through. The stack of paper is as thick as my hand is wide.

Jakob clears his throat. "One more thing that might help," he says, and hands me a heavy package. I unwrap the paper to find a tome on gemstones, minerals, and metals. "It's the most detailed one I could find," he says. I crack it open, feeling its weight on my lap. It must have cost a small fortune.

"Thank you," I breathe, and Liljan and I sit together, clutching our books to ourselves with unmasked delight.

"My turn," I say. I knit Liljan three new pairs of stockings, since she's always losing hers, and made Jakob thick gloves for skating. When he pulls them on, there is a gap of skin at his wrists between the gloves and his shirt, because his sleeves always fall an inch too short for his arms.

"Thank you," he says. His hair is more mussed than usual, and when he brings his hands down to rest on his knees, his bare wrist suddenly grazes mine.

He doesn't move it. The very ridges of our wrist bones are touching, and that slightest touch sets my skin tingling. I keep waiting for him to move, but he doesn't. Maybe it's so inconsequential to him that he doesn't even realize it's happening.

Or maybe he actually wants to keep touching me.

The thought makes me so nervous I blurt out: "I have an idea!"

"Mm?" Liljan asks, glancing up from an illustration of a cannon, a half-eaten candy cane hanging from her mouth.

"What if we asked Helene for Vestergaard jewels to weave into the costumes? We could tell her we want to make it special for Eve—use jewels only found in Vestergaard mines. And we want them all to be red."

"You're a genius," Liljan says triumphantly around the candy cane. "That's perfect!" She stands and does a little jig in her socks. Jakob finally moves, stripping off the gloves I made to light a small coal stove in the corner, and though the flames curl and dance, the space next to me suddenly feels cold.

"Let's stay here forever," Liljan whispers. She sends color

flooding across the walls around us, turning them from faded white to a lush grove of fir trees, covered with snow. When Jakob sits back down, she yawns and leans her head against his shoulder.

After a moment she's fallen asleep, and it's as if she's left for a different room. Jakob gently slides her head onto one of the oversize pillows and covers her with a blanket. Then he looks up at me for a beat too long. Like something is going to happen.

I hesitate. Then I reach across the space between us and take his wrist in my hand.

I feel his pulse quicken beneath my fingers.

"Here," I say, touching the end of his sleeve, my heart pounding as I loosen each thread. "The cuffs should hit you here," I explain, delicately sweeping my fingers over the bones of his wrist. There's a flush of something swirling across my skin, little zings curling up my arm, and I'm conscious of how still he's gone, how close we are, how his breath grows shallow at my touch. It suddenly feels warm in here, like spring coming for winter, the electric hum of bees and unfurling of flowers. Like things coming alive.

"There," I say when I finish lengthening his sleeves and shifting the buttons. I let go of him and add, "How handsome."

He flushes. "Thank you," he says hoarsely, absently feeling the place my fingers just were.

There's a tug in my belly and I sink deeper into the softness of my blanket, with Liljan breathing next to me. The fire crackles from the corner.

"Maybe *this* is the way you cure the Firn," I murmur.

"With what?" Jakob asks, a smile playing on his lips. The three of us lie under the skylight, beneath snow and stars, and even though there are a hundred reasons why we shouldn't, what I really want is for him to lean over Liljan and kiss me right now.

"Hygge," I answer softly, and think of Ingrid. How she tapped her chest with her eyes closed, smiling at the moment when warm contentment started flowing through her from the inside out.

⁂

Three days before New Year's, Jakob heads to the capital to meet with Dr. Holm. Liljan climbs into the carriage with him to run errands for Nina in town. Jakob raises his hand to me, the other holding the book of ideas I bound for him this morning. Liljan pauses when she looks over her shoulder and I feel a sort of shimmer in the air. I sense that something is about to change with what we are setting in motion.

And then they are both gone.

The house is emptying after the holiday—Philip leaves to return south, and though he's due back one more time for the new year, I hope that soon we won't see him again for months on end. It feels like letting out a stale breath, to watch his carriage pull away, snow sticking in the wheels. Ivy is the last to leave that morning. She borrows one of the Vestergaard horses, saddling it in the stables. She'll return in a few days, to ring in the new year here. I tighten my apron, unable to shake this unsettled feeling that is forming like cobwebs in my chest.

Time to approach Helene about the red stones.

I advance toward her bedroom with Liljan's sketches tucked into a leather folder. "It's all about presentation and confidence," Liljan said to me last night, pouring out red on the paper in splashes of scarlet and crimson.

"I wish you'd do it," I told her. "You're better at it than me."

"You can do it, Marit," she insisted.

I hesitate in front of Helene's door, smooth my apron, and then raise my hand to knock. "Mrs. Vestergaard?" I ask softly.

There is nothing but silence in return.

Then the door opens abruptly, sending me jumping back.

"She went out," Lara says, covered in soot from dusting out Helene's grate. "Early this morning." There's a smudge on her cheek, and she's holding a feather duster.

"Has Eve gone too?" I ask. I turn toward her room, my heart lifting at the thought of a few moments alone with her.

"I'm not sure," Lara says, and then below us, the front door bursts open with a violent scrape.

Someone staggers in, the snow swirling into the room with their steps.

"Who's there?" Lara calls, peering over the banister.

I can feel the cold seeping in from outside.

"Help me," a woman's voice says. "Help. In the road." She

takes in a jagged breath and it almost sounds like a sob. "I think they're both dead."

Lara drops her feather duster and screams.

Because Helene Vestergaard is standing in the foyer.

And the front of her coat is soaked through with dark red blood.

CHAPTER NINETEEN

HELENE CHOKES OUT, "In the carriage." She shudders. "Help."

I start to move toward the foyer and, as if through water, I hear someone ask, "What's happened?"

I walk forward. Dread and stillness are settling deep within me, icy cold and crystallizing with a thousand different threading branches. I hear no sound at all.

And then it all comes rushing in.

Panic, loud voices, my own heart beating wet and hot in my ears.

"Is that your blood, Helene?"

She shakes her head, dazed.

"Then whose is it?"

Liljan?

Jakob?

. . .

Eve.

The others would break my heart enough, but she—oh, she —she would be the worst.

I fly downstairs, out the gaping front door, into the wall of frigid air, as Nina flings the carriage doors open. Declan is trying to grasp hold of the first bundle, hauling it to the servants' delivery door. I feel bile rise in my throat. He struggles under the limp weight of it.

A human weight.

Nina gasps.

"Brock, help!" she yells over her shoulder.

"What's happened?" Brock appears in the kitchen doorway and springs into action.

"Clear the table inside," Nina says. "Boil water and get bandages."

"And fetch Jakob," Helene orders.

"He isn't here," Lara says, paling. "He's in town. With Dr. Holm."

Helene swears as the bundle lurches between Brock's and Declan's hands. Blood drips onto the white snow. A man groans, and when the blanket falls open, I realize, with dread:

It's Philip.

Brock and Declan drag Philip into the kitchen, and we follow behind, jumping to clear the table, to find linens to staunch the bleeding.

"Go get Dr. Holm," Helene barks at Declan. "Go!"

"That girl," Philip says sluggishly as they lay him on the table.

"Was being attacked—I tried—" he says. "To fight him off." He winces, and blood pours out from a slash in his side.

The air around me stops, as if the very dust hangs suspended.

What girl?

Where is Eve?

Why isn't she with Helene?

I am so afraid. Too afraid to ask. Fear is icy fingers, climbing up my spine one by one, reaching with its dark, frozen grasp to wrap around my heart.

"What girl?" Brock says urgently, looking up from Philip, his voice rough. "What does he mean, *that girl?*"

Helene takes a deep breath and a step forward. The look on her face, of aching sorrow, of sympathy, says it all. She seeks out Dorit's eyes, placing a bloody, wordless hand on the cook's, and then Brock's.

"I managed to get her into the carriage," Helene says quietly. "But I'm sorry. It was too late."

"Oh, Ivy," Nina says. "Oh—no," and Dorit's legs give out from beneath her as she sinks into a chair.

The sounds of panic have drawn out every servant in the house, but suddenly we are all still. Frozen in horror. Brock turns and sprints back out to the carriage, with Dorit trying to rise and limp to follow, but Nina holds her back, saying, "No, Dorit. Stay here."

"What's happened?" a voice says behind me. A small voice, frightened. Familiar.

I whirl around and it is her.

Eve.

Terrified and so small, her muscles tense instead of the gentle way she usually carries herself. I bite back a cry and move through the throng of servants. Discreetly reach out and touch her wrist when no one is looking. Breathe in the scent of her hair oil, of the cream she works into the leather soles of her ballet shoes. Feel her pulse, beating strong and quick with fear.

"What happened to him?" she whispers to me, her eyes fixed on the table as Philip yells out.

I whisper, "Don't look," and pull her closer to me. Blood is beginning to spill out from the table and pool on the floor. The kitchen smells like iron. Something on the stove is starting to burn.

"Find towels," Helene orders Nina. "And Eve—can someone take Eve to the main house?"

"I will," I quickly volunteer. I'm starting to feel ill.

"No, Marit. I need you here." Helene meets my eyes and I try not to see the dark, crusted blood in her hair. "You're going to have to sew him up."

What?

No.

I let go of Eve's wrist and she slides down the wall to crouch in the shadows. Watching.

"But I'm not medically trained," I say. I look around desperately.

"No one here is. But we have to stop that bleeding or he's

going to die, Marit." Helene grabs my shoulders and looks into my eyes. "You must try."

I wring my hands and focus on the scent of her, the faint hint that remains of paper whites, of life. Rae and Declan bring towels, and the kettle starts to shrilly scream on the stove. With roiling nausea, I approach the table. Philip is writhing in pain. He seems only half-conscious. "Be still," Helene says. "You're losing too much blood."

"Some laudanum, ma'am," Nina says, her hands shaking as she pours some for Philip and then pushes a spoonful toward Dorit. He chokes it down as I peel back the clothes on his torso, trying not to be sick. There is blood, and a mess of flesh. Several gashes go deep enough to expose what I guess must be muscle.

I rip more of his clothes out of the way and, as I do, find a patchwork field of raised skin. Scars and scratches. Some of them look like burns and cuts. Some are fresh and barely scarred over, but some are old and faded.

So many scars. I don't have time to stop and wonder from what.

"You can do it, Marit," Helene says firmly. She comes and stands next to me. Lara hands me a needle and black thread. But I don't know what I'm doing, don't have any idea how to mend the mess in front of me. I blink and try a few tentative stitches, but there is so much blood pouring from his side that I can't see anything at all.

Philip groans and passes out.

I don't know how much blood a human body can lose and still survive, but I can't imagine it's much more than this.

If I don't do something quickly, he's going to die. All my grudging suspicions about his mines, the Vestergaards' hand in ruining my life, my distrust of him for Eve, come swirling to the surface. But enough to let him die in front of me? When I could at least try to prevent it?

I set the needle down on the table and summon my magic, feeling its chill tingle through my fingers. I don't let myself think about anything—not that I'm plunging my hand across skin that's separated too widely, or into the deeper layers below it. I close my eyes and pretend the wound is just an awning, or the curtains Brock shredded. I remember running my fingertips over Mathies's canvas, wishing to heal the rips in people. I need to bring Philip's wound back together, create a seam, and as soon as I think of it like that, I feel the gash begin to gather and pull, to knot beneath my fingers.

I'm swimming in my magic, pouring it out as I finish the deepest cut and move on. There are several more gashes, as if he was slashed and stabbed with a knife. I tend to the three deepest ones, and when I'm finishing the last one, my gaze happens to fall on Philip's hand. To the ring with the red stone in it.

And then I feel something between my fingers. Something small and sharp.

I scrape the little object out of Philip's side.

What is it?

A bullet?

A piece of shrapnel?

No, that doesn't make any sense. These are stab wounds.

I set the little object aside, then double my focus on bringing the wound together and healing it.

When I finish, I sit back with a gasp.

"You've done it, Marit," Helene says. Her hand grazes my shoulder. "Thank you." She suddenly looks exhausted. Nina pushes her way toward us with bandages and begins to wrap them across Philip's fresh wounds. "Prepare the guest suite for him," Helene announces to the rest of us. "He'll stay with us to recover. And—" Her voice cracks, her jaw working, tensing. Her eyes are dark pools of sadness. "Someone should fetch the coroner."

Brock is backlit against the white snow, a dark shadow in the doorway. He staggers into the room, his arms full, holding his sister to his chest.

Ivy is also covered in blood. Her hands and pale blond plait hang limply, her fingers lifeless and bone white.

Those fingers that made the paperweights, the eyes that saw me, the kindness that bloomed under pressure, all snuffed out like a candle.

I lean back, breathless, and Lara crouches next to me with a basin of warmed water. I scrub Philip's blood off my hands, violently, until the skin is red and raw and the feeling of my magic is fading away. I quickly turn over my wrists and inspect the skin there out of habit.

No sign of the Firn. I breathe a deep, shaking sigh of relief.

But when I look up, Eve is staring at me.

I almost forgot she was there. That she was crouched along the wall, watching me pour out the magic I swore to her I didn't have. Her face is like the sun moving behind a cloud as understanding sets in, and I see a hundred variations of shadows — horror, anger, disappointment, disbelief. But the final look that settles on her is simply sadness.

The kind that sets in like a deep stain and ruins something precious, until it can be remembered only for what it once was, and thrown away.

※

Dr. Holm, Liljan, and Jakob arrived a little more than an hour later, a thin sheen of sweat covering them despite the cold, their horses frothing at the mouth with exertion. Jakob had just finished his interview with Dr. Holm when Declan reached them, and they came bursting into the house together. Now the foyer and front sitting rooms swarm with policemen and the cremator from the morgue and curious neighbors from the nearest estate a quarter mile away. Philip is moved, on an improvised stretcher of sheets and boards, upstairs to one of the spare bedrooms. He has fallen into a coma.

"And you, Mrs. Vestergaard," the chief of police says, crowded into the sitting room off the foyer. I recognize two of the policemen from the night when they stopped us in the carriage on the way back from Tivoli. "You didn't see anything?"

I've changed into a clean uniform and we are all scrambling to handle the tasks that would normally fall to Dorit and Brock. The orchids can't mask the smell of burned coffee. I set a fresh silver teapot onto the serving table, positioning myself to hear as much as possible.

"By the time I found them, the attacker was gone," Helene answers. She has also changed into a clean dress, and Liljan took the blood-covered one to destroy. "He must have fled. Perhaps you should check the hospitals and infirmaries. See if anyone came in with injuries consistent with a struggle."

"We're combing the entire area thoroughly," the police chief says, putting away his notepad. "But allow me to suggest, Mrs. Vestergaard, that you refrain from traveling the roads alone until we have apprehended the culprit. We've had two missing persons reported between here and Copenhagen in the last month, and neither of them have been found. I don't mean to frighten you, but it might be related."

"Thank you, gentlemen," she says. When the foyer finally empties, Helene closes the door and double-latches the lock.

I see Eve hiding in the shadows to eavesdrop, the way we used to at the Mill when Ness was speaking late into the night to prospective parents or her occasional gentlemen callers. I remember kneeling next to Eve on the staircase, the ends of her hair tickling my leg. Some nights I had to cover her mouth to prevent a giggle from giving us away. I won't give her up now, either, and I offer her a discreet, tentative smile, but she abruptly turns away.

Liljan and I light more candles than normal in the servants' quarters, trying to keep the darkness from gathering in the corners and crevices of the house. Everyone is wearing that stunned expression of grief, the same one orphans always wore on their first days at the Mill, as though they are peering at life through a newly shattered window. Trying to make sense of the distortions, even though nothing looks quite right anymore.

All I can think of is the way Eve looked at me as though I had utterly betrayed her.

Every time I close my eyes, I see her face again, the slump of her shoulders, the rapid blinking of her eyes. A complicated knot forms deep in my stomach. Is there a word for when you devastate someone you love? It feels like the heaviest weight, a terrible, creeping coldness.

It feels the exact opposite of the way hygge does.

We're finishing up with the last of the mess in the kitchen, and I gather a pile of bloody towels to be burned. But something falls out of them and hits the floor with a tiny clatter. I bend to retrieve it.

What I find is small, sharp, and encrusted with blood: the object I pulled from Philip's wound.

I almost throw it in with the towels—just another part of today's horrific mess that needs to be burned and forgotten.

Instead, I walk to the sink. Hold what I found beneath the water, and begin to scrub and wash it. The red blood flows down the drain.

Carefully, I turn the object over in my fingers. Now that it's clean, it's almost clear.

I hold it up to the light before I realize what I'm looking at.

It's a tiny fractured piece of glass.

CHAPTER TWENTY

I SLIDE INTO BED THAT NIGHT, and when Liljan blows out the candle, I stare into the dark.

"Liljan," I whisper. "Something happened when I was sewing up Philip."

She instantly rolls over. "What?"

"There was a piece of glass."

"Glass?" she whispers.

"Yes."

"Where?"

"Inside his wound."

She sits up.

"What I haven't been able to reconcile is," I say, "how . . . did it get there?"

Death seems to follow this family at every turn. First, my father and the other miners. Then Ingrid, after those men came possibly looking for the stone. Aleks Vestergaard. Ivy. And now Philip has been left gravely wounded, close to death himself.

Surely this much violence and misfortune can't be coincidence?

Philip was the person I've suspected most up until now, but this time, he was a victim. And if his story is to be believed, he almost gave his life trying to do something heroic. For a servant, like me.

. . . Except for that tiny piece of glass.

Liljan's voice drops to a whisper. "Glass? Do you think it could have been Ivy?"

"That's what I was thinking. But he said he was trying to help her."

"Could he have been lying?"

"But why? Why on earth would he want to hurt Ivy? It doesn't make any sense."

I look up at the ceiling and am quiet for a long moment.

"There's something else that's bothering me," I say, shifting with unease. "The timeline from the story Philip gave doesn't add up. He left before Ivy. So how did he come across her being attacked?"

"Not sure. And Helene didn't see the attacker either?"

Eve was here, safely sleeping, when Helene came upon the scene.

Which means that no one knows what really happened today but the two of them.

Helene and Philip — their word and no other witnesses.

And someone else wound up dead.

Liljan suddenly goes still at a noise just outside our room.

I heard it too.

The sound of a footstep, creaking on the old wooden floorboards.

I bolt upright at a sharp knock on our door. Liljan leaps to her feet. Pulling her robe on, she opens our door a crack.

There's enough moonlight for me to glimpse the hem of Eve's nightgown peeking out from under her coat as she pushes into the room.

"Eve?" I ask, blinking, pulling free of the covers.

"I need to talk to Marit," Eve says to Liljan, her quiet voice prickling.

Eve glares first at Liljan and then turns it full-force on me, sparing a brief glance around the room as I find a match and light a candle. "Eve, come here," I say. I set the candle next to my bed and sit cross-legged, patting the spot on the quilt beside me. She stays standing, keeping me at arm's length. Liljan scrunches down under her comforter, trying to make herself as small as possible.

"No," Eve says. Her brown eyes lick with fire. There's a troubled crease in her forehead. "You *lied* to me, Marit."

"I'm sorry, Eve," I say. "I—"

"So *she* knows?" Eve asks, throwing a glance toward Liljan, who has become a small quilted ball. Her blanket is steadily turning to the pattern of our walls. "You've known her for barely a month and you told her that you have magic?"

"Eve," I try to explain. "It isn't like that. She has magic too. Everyone who works here does—"

Eve chokes on a laugh in disbelief. "So *everyone* here knew about it? Except for me?"

"Well, yes, but—"

"You've lied to me my entire life." Her lips purse in that way they do when she's so furious that she's about to cry.

I fall silent. I did lie. Right to her face, back at the Mill. And every day, the lie of omission. I am ashamed, and my excuses suddenly seem weak and not enough—that I lied, over and over again, simply because I didn't want her to worry about me.

"Marit," she says. She takes a shaky breath and the words come tumbling out. "I know you think that everything must be perfect for me now, because I have a new family and more money than I ever dreamed of and I get to dance, but"—her throat bobs, her voice getting higher with the threat of tears—"the truth is, this is when I needed you the most. You're the only thing I have left from my life before. Everything is different—*everything*—and I just wanted one thing to be the same."

It's as if a thread is pulling out too fast from the fabric, and if the end sails right through the needle before I can catch it, I'll lose the strand forever. At the Mill, I always thought the future would be what tore Eve and me apart—other people's decisions that I couldn't control. Instead, it will be the past. It will be my own decisions that undo us.

"But you lied to me, my whole life. So that other part before doesn't even seem real now. It's like you made me lose that, too," Eve says. Her eyes well with angry tears. The hurt that carves into her voice makes my heart curl up in a ball tighter than Liljan. "I used to know you loved me. In fact, it was one of the truest things I ever knew. Now . . ." She trails off with a sharp shrug.

I suck in a breath. "It *is* true, Eve," I say, trying to keep the edge of frustration out of my voice. "I know I lied, and I am very, very sorry. But you have to believe that every choice I've made has been because of how much I care for you." *Sometimes at the risk of my own life,* I think, but don't say.

Her fingers are tapping absently along her coat, the way they do when she is anxious or upset, and I know I've hurt her deeply. "I always thought of you more as a sister than a friend," she says, her voice shaking. "But now, Marit—you really aren't either to me. So . . . maybe you should find somewhere else to work with your magic."

She draws her small body into that commanding ballerina presence and strides right out the door. Years of trust, of love, of relationship, broken and gone, just like that. It always struck me as unfair—how easily trust can be broken. How long it takes to knit together. How it's ruined now, like a blade slashing through a gown. Like Ivy's very life is gone. One moment here, then lost forever.

Liljan finally peeks out from her blanket. "I didn't know so much fierceness could come out of such a small person." Then she sees my face and sits up and hugs her knees, her voice softening. "You know how young people are when they're upset. She doesn't really mean it."

Hot tears spill onto my clenched fists. I never wanted Eve to worry about me. To fear that the Firn might one day come and take me, just like it took her mother. I know what it's like to live with the fear that magic could kill someone you love. All this time, I believed I was protecting her. Instead, I somehow turned the shield around and wounded her with it.

I pull the covers up to my chin and barely sleep that night.

From the windowsill, Ivy's paperweight almost seems to glint at me.

❧

The next morning, I make a purposeful detour past Philip's room. The door is ajar and I steal the briefest look inside. His valet sits at his bedside—a slip of a man with a small mustache and thin, nervous fingers that look like spiders. Weak sunlight pours through the window, casting Philip's skin in a sick gray tinge. His chest barely seems to rise. For the first time, he doesn't give me the chill of something wrong.

I actually feel sorry for him.

I hurry on to fetch a corset Helene asked me to mend. But Dr. Holm is discussing something with her in the foyer on my way back, and he stops when he sees me. "This is the seamstress that helped to stitch Philip?"

Helene nods.

"She did a good job." He cocks his head. "I'd never thought to use magic on sutures. Perhaps you'll let me know if you're ever done with her services here?"

I turn away before I hear her answer, bristling at how he spoke of me like a pair of scissors or a scalpel to be wielded. Tucking the corset beneath my arm, I take the underground corridor and then slip out the back door. I need a moment of fresh air — of life and color. I unlock the latch to the greenhouse and wander through the aisles, through the murky filtered light and the orbs of glass, breathing in the moist scent of things that are living and blooming.

If Ingrid were here, would she have already solved what my father wanted us to know? Would there have been an easier way forward, a better trail to follow, if only I'd figured out the bank clue earlier? Ten years passed, ten years' worth of bread crumbs to blow away, to shift the path. For people to die, for rulers and landscapes to change. Maybe I missed my chance and now it's too late. Because I was so focused on the fact that my father wrote the letter to Ingrid and not to me, I couldn't see what was right in front of my face.

I find old glass bottles meant for jam and push lavender ranunculus stems inside, tucking soil around a few new seeds as if I'm making a bed. *Life, life, life.* The smallest act of resistance, when everything around me seems to be ruined or dying.

I return to the house and line my bedroom windowsill with the blossoms, surrounding Ivy's glass paperweight.

When I descend the stairs again, I pause at the sound of strange voices. Male voices—two of them, coming from the kitchen, and I don't recognize either one.

I come around the corner cautiously, still wiping the soil from my hands. A man sits at the kitchen table loudly slurping his oatmeal, his hair glistening with pomade. Muscles strain through his shirt, his face is as red as a roast, and there's a large revolver in a holster at his pocket.

"Helene's hired a guard," Nina explains. "This is Peder."

He slurps loudly in response.

I eye him and slide into the place next to Rae, who is jittery, jumping at the slightest sounds.

"Why are you still here, Malthe?" Brock asks the second man, whom I now recognize as Philip's valet. Brock glares over the rim of his coffee cup, but the gesture almost seems defeated. There's no point in trying to bully someone out of a spot anymore. Not now that Ivy isn't here to fill it.

The small man clears his throat. "I'm tending to any needs Mr. Vestergaard has while he is . . . incapacitated."

"Yes, because people who are incapacitated have so much need for a valet," Brock says witheringly. "Rae, this has gone cold." He taps his coffee cup. "Heat it for me?"

Rae jumps up, and the moment she lays her palm along the ceramic cup, steam wisps from its top.

The valet starts violently.

"Was that . . . magic?" he asks, looking at Rae with awe. "You use magic?"

"You don't?" Rae retorts.

"No," Malthe says. "Mr. Vestergaard doesn't employ any people with magic."

Interesting, I think. Philip continues to surprise me.

"Does anyone know what happened? I heard he was injured trying to help a young girl," Malthe says, fishing for information while he twirls his coffee with his finger.

Brock growls, "Don't speak of her here." He shoves away from the table hard enough to send his chair clattering and slams the back door on his way out.

Malthe's altogether unwanted infiltration of the kitchen area and his shock at seeing magic do nothing to endear him to the staff. They shift to put a small but definite space between him and the rest of them.

Good luck, Malthe, I think dryly. "Stiff stuff," I whisper as I walk past him. Then I take my own advice, gather every last dreg of my courage, and follow Brock outside.

He is crouched at the end of the pergola, near the entrance to the greenhouse. His back curves away from me. His face is turned down toward the dirt.

I walk toward him, through the corridor. The purple-tinged ends of wisteria blow in the breeze, light as lace. But then the ends begin to darken, from lavender into the ugly color of a bruise.

And then, bough by bough, the wisteria begins to dissolve.

Brock's shoulders shake, and the tunnel withers and disintegrates around me with each step forward, the vines curling and shriveling up, the flowers shedding into a spray of ash.

When I reach him, I kneel and join him in the cold dirt. This magical place is gone now. The outside world has flooded in, with its gray sky and all its beauty reduced to decay and ruin.

"I am sorry, Brock," I say, the cold wetness from the dirt spreading up to my knees. "I'm so sorry." I shudder under the weight of the guilt I feel—the heaviest weight there is. "I took Ivy's place," I admit. I whisper the thought that has been haunting me, keeping me from sleep. Making me wish I never came here. "If I had given up the spot like you wanted, she might still be alive."

The last remaining purple petals are being crushed beneath the toe of Brock's boot.

He takes deep, heaving breaths, and then he looks up at me, his face contorted with anger and despair. The door to the greenhouse silently opens, and Dorit slips from the shadows.

As if on cue, Rae comes out from the kitchen. She saunters down the corridor and stands behind me. And suddenly I realize I am trapped. Rae hands Brock an enormous pair of shears, and a chilled wind whips my hair into my eyes and makes them sting.

Brock takes the shears. He squints up at me, his eyes bloodshot.

"Leave us alone, Marit," he says.

I clear my throat. It feels tight and dry. "There's something I think you should know." Brock's jaw twitches.

"I saw Philip at Ivy's shop about a month ago."

He narrows his eyes at me.

"Perhaps it was nothing. But then they ended up—she ended up—well, they were together, when it happened," I say. I swallow hard. "And then I found this in Philip's wound." When I hand Brock the tiny piece of glass, his face flushes an angry red.

Dorit covers her mouth.

"You don't trust Philip," Brock says. He lifts the shears and points them at me. "I heard you say that to Eve in the greenhouse one time. You're always snooping around, watching him. Why?"

I purse my lips, feel the ash of the flowers in my hair. I don't know what the truth is. If Philip is a victim, a hero, or a murderer. "Nothing definite. It's just . . . that bad things seem to happen whenever he is around."

The rumors surrounding Aleks's death, those miners, Ivy. Philip wearing the same stone as the one my father left behind. What do all these deaths and horrors have in common?

Just one person.

"I think there are some questions about the Vestergaards that still need answers," I say carefully.

Brock looks up at the second-floor window, to the room where Philip is in his coma.

"These were Ivy's favorite flowers," Dorit says softly, her arms full of vibrant pink dahlias. "We'll bury them with her."

Brock plunges his shears into the half-frozen ground with such force that I flinch. And then he extends a trembling hand to me.

"When we return," he says, offering the most unexpected truce I could imagine, "we're going to help you get those answers."

CHAPTER TWENTY-ONE

BROCK AND DORIT LEAVE the next morning to bury Ivy. Their home is thirty miles west of here. A heavy cloud settles in my chest as their carriage pulls away. We made secret arrangements to meet in Copenhagen in three days.

I watch their carriage until I can't see it anymore.

Then I pour myself a cup of coffee and set to work.

Tucked between the satin layers of one of Helene's gowns are the pages of information Jakob and Liljan gave me on Christmas Eve, right before everything went nightmarish and sideways.

I take a sip of coffee and begin sifting through the pages. According to the records, there are five types of gemstones sourced from the Vestergaard mines: diamonds, rubies, emeralds, quartzes, and sapphires. They are distributed in four jewelry stores across Denmark, all owned by a single jeweling family named the Jeppesens. Their flagship store is in Copenhagen.

These Vestergaard jewels are the only gemstones known to be sourced in Denmark.

I reach into the depths of my petticoats and run my fingertips over the smooth facets of my father's stone. It's a brilliant dark red in the sunlight, almost black when it's in the shadows. Clearly it isn't a diamond, emerald, or sapphire. It doesn't look like quartz to me, and Jakob didn't think it was a ruby.

Where did it come from, if not from the Vestergaard mines?

I turn the page to see if I've missed anything.

Could there be more stones growing in the mines than the Vestergaards let on?

Or—if this stone didn't come from the Vestergaard mines—where *did* it come from?

I chew on my lip, considering, and then turn to the financial records. It always makes sense to follow the money.

The numbers in the financial statements are neat and ordered, spanning years and alternating between two sets of male handwriting. In recent years, I notice, the writing steadily turned to just one. That must have been when Philip Vestergaard took over complete management of the mines.

When I come across the salaries for the miners, I look twice—what's listed there is *far* beyond anything my father would have ever taken home. There are equally generous and regular payments to the Jeppesens, the family handling the jewel trade throughout Denmark. I whistle under my breath when I calculate the numbers, and make note of them in my petticoats.

I saw Thorsen's accounting books. I know how much he would take from the farmers and tradesmen for selling their buttons and wool and beads. A cut of the profits. Nothing like this—exorbitant additional payments on top of that.

Why would you pay jewelers a significant amount of money to sell your jewels? Don't the jewelers need the Vestergaards more than the Vestergaards need them?

"Marit?" Nina's voice calls from downstairs. It's tinged with slight annoyance, so I estimate I have approximately three and a half more minutes before her irritation escalates into something more serious. I want to get through these papers and destroy the evidence. I've already had them floating around for too long.

And then I come across the gifts for members of the royal family.

I run my fingertips down the descriptions, imagining the twining crown of diamonds and rubies for King Christian IX and the matching tiara described for Queen Louise.

I see the necklace of rubies meant for Princess Dagmar— now Maria Feodorovna, the future empress of Russia. That was the flash of red when Queen Louise opened the velvet case the night of the ballet.

But the list continues.

"Marit!" Nina sounds slightly more perturbed this time, and closer. I wedge my chair under the doorknob of my workroom and quickly sew a record of the gifts into my petticoats:

Diamond and emerald necklace, for Princess Alexandra, married to English royalty.

Emerald scepter, for the king's son George I of the Hellenes.

Ruby ring, for another son, Crown Prince Frederick, rumored to be considering an engagement to the princess of Sweden.

Extraordinary, valuable gifts. *Why?*

"Marit!" Nina is standing right outside my door.

Perhaps the Vestergaards are very generous people.

But a more cynical person might look at these records and say: *Everyone, from the bottom to the top, is getting a piece of the pot.*

Nina jiggles the doorknob. "Why is this locked?"

"Coming!" I say. I hurriedly feed the Vestergaards' records into my stove.

"What are you doing in here?" Nina asks sharply when I open the door. My face feels flushed with guilt.

"Just mending Mrs. Vestergaard's dress," I say. "Like I was asked to."

Nina narrows her eyes, because she isn't a fool. "Dorit says you need a spot of time off on Thursday," she says. "She asked for it, for you. Personally." She purses her lips, and we both wait each other out. I cock an eyebrow.

"Make certain that dress is ready before you go," she says. She gives me a long look before she closes the door.

By the time I return to my worktable, the Vestergaards' records are nothing but ash.

I feel a scratch at the back of my throat. None of the red stones in Jakob's book appear to match the one my father left or Philip wears. The Vestergaards' financial records shed no light either.

There's one place where I could find out for certain what my father's stone is, but I can't waltz into the Jeppesens' jewelry store and ask . . .

Not as myself, anyway.

My eyes fall to the sumptuous layers of Helene's dress.

I'm meeting Brock and Dorit in Copenhagen to seek out answers about Ivy. But . . . who's to say while I'm there, I can't uncover a few more?

❧

Our New Year's celebration at the house is quiet and subdued, and when I slip into the carriage bound for Copenhagen on January third, I do it with Helene's dress stashed in a trunk at my feet.

Nina gave me a sniff this morning, narrowing her eyes slightly at my trunk, but then bit her tongue.

"Be back this evening" is all she said, and I hurried out the door before she — or I — could reconsider.

Right on schedule, Liljan darts out the door just as the carriage wheels start turning. She runs her hands over my hair and face until I feel the bridge of my nose and the hair on my scalp faintly tingle. She inspects her work, gives me a peck on the cheek, and jumps back out of the carriage. I cover my changed hair with a hat, tighten its ribbons under my chin. Every time we hit a stone, the trunk knocks against my foot, reminding me just how many things could go wrong today.

And all the terrible things that will happen if they do.

I instruct Declan to drop me off with my trunk at the corner of the Nationalbanken. I make sure the hat is completely covering my hair and confirm details with him for the return home. Then, as the horses amble back onto the cobblestone street, I take a sharp turn and head straight into the crowd.

The sky is gray and thick with pillowing clouds this morning. It's lightly drizzling, and the snow left in the street gutters looks more like soot. Dorit and Brock are standing in the midst of a bustling center, near a fountain with stone doves taking flight. Neither of them has an umbrella, and I spot Dorit's faded mauve hat first, then Brock next to her. Both of them look haggard, and neither is smiling.

I tighten my grip on the trunk and go to meet them.

"What's that?" Brock asks gruffly. He nods at my trunk, which is good because it means he isn't looking too closely at my face.

I purse my lips. "We all have answers we want to get today."

"Has Philip woken up yet?" Brock asks.

I shake my head. "And the police want to speak with him, but they told Helene he's not a suspect. They think Ivy was just in the wrong place at the wrong time."

I passed a few policemen on horseback this morning, patrolling the area at Helene's insistence, but their working theory is that the culprit was a troubled vagrant who is likely long gone by now.

Brock's jaw tightens. He wants to ask some more questions of his own. And so do I.

"The glass shop first" is all Brock says abruptly to me, and I give him a curt nod. We hardly trust each other in normal circumstances, and the tension of this situation only makes it worse.

I walk several paces behind him and Dorit, fixing my eyes on Dorit's heels and the small chip of leather that flaps with every step on the wet cobblestones. The air smells like smoke and salted fish, and we enter the glass shop where I saw Philip standing with Ivy all those weeks ago. A small bell tings, and a young girl with enormous, haunted eyes steps forward and says, "May I help you?"

"Yes. We're here to see a girl named Hanne," Brock says, taking off his hat. "Does she work here?"

The girl pales. "I am Hanne. What is this about?"

Brock reaches out his hand and says, "I'm Ivy's brother." He gestures to Dorit. "This is her aunt."

"And I'm her cousin," I say quickly.

"Oh," Hanne breathes. "I'm sorry for your loss." Her large eyes get even wider. She peers out the door, checking the street both ways. Then she locks the door behind us and says, "Come with me."

The stairs creak beneath our feet as she leads us up to the second floor, then pulls open the door to a small room with two round stained-glass windows set in the walls like portholes. The room smells faintly of soap, and though it's little bigger than a closet and the wallpaper is faded, it is neat and clean. "We have only a few minutes before the shop owner comes back," Hanne says. "He probably wouldn't want all of you up here. But you can fetch her things."

I turn around and survey the room. This is where Ivy lived.

Her bed has been stripped down to the bare straw mattress, and the sight of it makes me unbearably sad. As Dorit begins to collect a few of Ivy's clothes still folded in the closet, I notice that Hanne has a glass paperweight on her nightstand too.

"We were actually hoping to ask you some questions," I say. "Do you recognize this person?" I quickly unroll a thin tube of paper I hid in my petticoats to reveal a small, very lifelike portrait Liljan made of Philip.

Hanne takes the paper from my fingers and gives it a long look. She squints, then finally shakes her head and hands it back. "No. I mean, we have a lot of customers, so I can't be certain I've never seen him."

I let out a breath. "But this man wasn't here frequently?" I press.

"No. What is his name?"

I hesitate, my eyes flicking to Brock briefly before answering. "Philip Vestergaard."

Hanne shakes her head again. "Philip Vestergaard, as in the Vestergaard mines? No, he hasn't ordered anything here in recent months. Why?" she asks, turning her haunted eyes on me. "Is he the suspect? Have they found any of the others, too?"

I pause while rolling up Philip's picture.

"No, he isn't a suspect," I say carefully. "He was also injured in the attack. What do you mean, 'any of the others'?"

"I tried to tell the police. About all the other servants and workmen, just like Ivy, who have gone missing. People have sought me out here at the shop, at least two a day since it happened—some about a cousin they had, an aunt, or a brother. They want to hear about what happened to Ivy, wondering if their loved one might have met the same fate. I tried to tell the police that she's the latest in a long line. But she's the only"—she swallows—"the only . . ."

"The only what?" Brock asks.

"The only one to be, um, found so far. A body, I mean."

Dorit closes her eyes and sags against the wall.

"So the police know? That other people in this area have gone missing?" I press.

Hanne turns her enormous eyes on me again. "The more important question is, do the police *care?*"

Her chin quivers.

I think of Ivy, begging us all to stop using magic on the night that servant woman went missing. I wonder how long the police looked for her before giving up. We'd never know if anything happened to her. The papers don't usually spend ink on news involving servants. Sometimes Firn deaths are splashed across the pennies, but more as garish entertainment than news.

"But, perhaps," Hanne ventures to us hopefully, "now that a Vestergaard—someone prominent, someone they find *important*—has been injured . . . perhaps they will start to pay more attention? Find out what happened to all those other people?"

I turn abruptly. "May I use your washroom?" I ask. I feel more confused than ever. If other servants have been disappearing or

going missing, then perhaps Philip's story about an attacker actually *is* the truth. After all, he was there with us at Tivoli on the
night that other servant went missing. I saw him with my own
eyes.

"It's in the hallway," Hanne says, and I find it and lock myself
in. I didn't know if I'd have the courage to go through with
my plan for Helene's dress today. But I'm not going back to the
Vestergaards' empty-handed, not without some sort of new lead.

My fingers are trembling as I unclasp the pearled buttons on
Helene's dress and step into it. The length is much too long for
my legs and the fit is a little too snug in the waist. I say a quick
prayer under my breath and close my eyes, and as magic sings
through me with its chilling prickle, I tailor the dress to fit my
own body like a glove.

I open my eyes and startle as I catch my reflection in the mirror. For one half second, I almost think I am seeing someone else.
Just before the carriage pulled away this morning, Liljan dyed my
hair a dark crimson and covered all my freckles.

And in Helene's gown I look, and feel, rich.

I stuff my maid uniform into the trunk, and when I sweep
into Hanne's room wearing Helene's dress, Brock's and Dorit's
jaws almost hit the floor.

"Um, what are you *doing?*" Brock demands.

"Quickly," Hanne says, giving me a doubtful look and ush-
ering us out the door. "I'd rather you were gone from up here
before my boss returns."

"Thank you," I say to her, and I go down first, with Brock and Dorit leaving the shop on my heels.

"What happened to your hair, Marit? Is that *Mrs. Vestergaard's dress?*" Brock asks as we walk down the street. "What are you trying to pull?"

Dorit says wearily, "Marit, this wasn't part of the plan."

"I'm sorry, Dorit. I have a chance to do something today, and I'm taking it," I say. I shove the trunk into Brock's chest. "And . . . I need Brock to watch my trunk."

Brock makes a growling sound deep in his throat, clutching the trunk, and I am careful to pick up the hem of the gown and keep going. I can hear Brock and Dorit follow me as I head up the cobblestone street. I channel Helene as I walk. Chin in the air. Graceful strides, head raised, confident. I will not step in a puddle of mud or pile of horse dung and get incriminating evidence of this excursion on this gown. Just in case, I go over my backstory in my head. My name is Johanne Ibsen — my mother's name. I age myself up to twenty. Without my freckles, it is passable. I'm from the village two towns over from Karlslunde, the one where the Madsens live.

I wish, for perhaps the hundredth time, that they had just adopted Eve that day instead.

The jewelry shop appears in front of me. Its wood is painted a dark, lush black, and it says *Jeppesen* in swirling gold-plated lettering in the window. Beyond the glass is a display of a model wooden boat, sailing on a sea of diamonds and sapphires.

This is the Jeppesens' flagship shop. The one that sells the most jewels and gets a tremendous annual payoff from the Vestergaards.

"You asked the questions you wanted. Now it's my turn," I say to Brock. "As far as you're concerned, today my name is Mrs. Ibsen. And if you don't want to be involved, you should probably get away from me now."

This is the riskiest thing I've ever done.

Inquiring about jewels right under the Vestergaards' nose, wearing a dress I borrowed without permission from Helene herself.

If I get caught, I'm fired, of course.

But—I try to laugh at myself for even thinking it—could someone *kill* me for this?

I pass the street where Liljan let me cry and then I gather my nerve.

Brock has my trunk in hand as he settles Dorit into the window seat of a café across the street. They will keep watch on me from a careful distance. I was counting on Hanne pointing more of an incriminating finger at Philip Vestergaard, so they wouldn't tell on me for what I'm about to do now.

If they side with the Vestergaards and give me up in this, I'm in big trouble.

"Watch over me, Papa," I say under my breath, and step through the door.

◦~

"Hello," I say, entering into the warm dimness of the shop.

This dress is heavier than I thought. I can smell the faintest whiff of Helene's narcissus perfume when I move.

"Hello," the jeweler says, his voice even and smooth. He promptly rises from behind his black wood counter and glides toward me, the way Thorsen would act when a wealthy client came in. We all learned the signs, of course, even without the obvious jewels or furs. It was the aura of assurance. The sheen of fabric, the very slight wear of the shoes.

The wealthy men were often in a hurry, because they were very busy and important.

The wealthy women were never in any hurry at all.

So I take my time, surveying the shop as if I have all the moments in the world. As if my heart isn't hammering inside my chest. *It is not a crime to be in this store,* I tell myself.

Although perhaps it is while wearing a dress that doesn't really belong to me.

"Can I help you with something, miss?" the shopkeeper prompts.

He is sizing me up. I can feel his ticking glance, taking in my youth — wondering, perhaps, if I could possibly have enough money to be worth his while. Perhaps hoping that my immaturity, combined with a lack of companion, might make me spend more than I should. His countenance warms slightly when he takes in the meticulous handiwork — *my* handiwork — on Helene's dress.

Well, that's fine. I am sizing him up, too.

And he has no idea that the intimate details of this shop's financials are recorded along the insides of my petticoats.

"I must confess I don't usually wear much jewelry," I hear myself say. I tuck my workers' hands behind my back, so he can't see my ragged nails. I could angle this approach in so many ways: naive, shrewd, haughty, friendly. "But my husband would like to get me something I genuinely enjoy." I am looking at the twitch of the jeweler's mouth, the way he responds to the information I drop like crumbs.

The jewels of the shop glitter like a colorful frozen garden around me.

"Where do these stones come from?" I ask, and when I turn to survey them, it's like being at the center of a kaleidoscope. "Russia? Germany?"

"Right here in Denmark, madam."

"All?" I ask, feigning incredulity.

He gives a slight nod.

All of these are Vestergaard jewels. The numbers I saw on the Vestergaards' financial documents, the sheer profits they reap, are astonishing. *Millions* of rigsdalers. Vestergaard jewels branch out to flood through Denmark's economy like arteries, touching royalty, touching commerce, elevating our entire national worth. I take a step toward a stone that's a unique shade of aquamarine and set with two flanking diamonds. What did my father know about those mines?

I wrinkle my nose as I pretend to look around the shop. I've always believed that you catch more flies with honey, but there are some people who just seem naturally drawn to vinegar. Like Brock. Thorsen was one of those people, and—judging by the gleam in his eye—I'm betting this man is, too.

"I like the idea of wearing a Danish stone. But . . ." I turn my voice haughty, like the worst women who visited Thorsen's used to do. "I want something special. Something that not everyone else has. Something . . . different."

"Different?"

My eyes trail over the jewels, trying to catch the price of the smallest one. I brought all the money my father left with me, just in case I had enough to buy the most modest stone and could take it home. I wanted to look at it—compare its facets and makeup to the one my father left me.

I glimpse the numbers on its price tag and my heart sinks.

Everything I have still isn't enough.

"I'm drawn to a deep red color. But—" I sniff. "Not a ruby," I say. I take a disdainful look around the shop and sigh. "I don't think you have what I'm looking for . . ."

The more uninterested I seem, the more his interest in me grows.

He moves closer. Fixes his eyes on me. We are doing a dance, and I am playing my part, and now he will play his.

"Of course this isn't our entire inventory," he says, almost coyly.

My interest piques, but I blink at him, as though I'm bored.

He leans closer, the way one does to share a secret.

"With enough notice," he says, "I could get a stone in almost any shade you wish."

I narrow my eyes. The Vestergaards own the only known jewel mines in Denmark. They list five official stones in their accounts. Don't miners coax stones out of the earth, and they simply *are* the color they are?

"I could take down your information, Mrs. . . . ?"

"Ibsen."

"And then I could contact you once we have some additional options to consider, Mrs. Ibsen."

My curiosity is like a growing hunger, but of course his offer won't do. I can't give him my address at the Vestergaards'.

"Mm," I say noncommittally. I want some answers, and I want them today. I feel a sense of foreboding as my fingers are drawn toward the stone hidden in my pocket.

I could find out what it is, right now.

Should I take the risk?

I close my fingers around the stone.

I wouldn't let anyone know you have that, Liljan said the day we visited Copenhagen. Liljan, the risk taker. Warning me not to take a risk.

But today I'm not Marit Olsen, servant girl to the Vestergaards. Today I am little more than a phantom, wearing the name of my dead mother and a dress that doesn't belong to me, and the question is dancing on my lips.

Finally, an answer to the riddle my father left me.

Could you tell me about this one?

I've got the stone in my grasp, pulling it from the shadows of my pocket, when Brock suddenly bursts in the door, his boots caked with sludge and his face mostly obscured by a bouquet of lush, light pink roses.

"Mrs. Ibsen?" he says to me. "A gift, for you. From your husband. He'd like to meet you now for lunch."

"How thoughtful of him," I say. I drop the stone back out of sight in my pocket and take the armful of roses from Brock. One of the thorns grazes my arm. "These are lovely. I suppose I'd better return to discuss this more another time."

The shopkeeper gives me a slight bow. "Mrs. Ibsen," he says.

Brock holds the door open for me and ushers me outside, whispering under his breath as I pass, "Keep the flowers up. Malthe is coming down the street. I don't know if he would recognize you. But I didn't want to take the chance."

Brock swiftly leads me by the elbow and pulls his hat down low as Malthe walks right past us. I sneak a quick glance back as Malthe strides up the stairs to the jewelry store. He carries a Vestergaard briefcase, imprinted with the hammer and pick. Then he steps into the shop, and Brock and I disappear into the crowd.

Four blocks later, the carriage is waiting for us with Dorit inside.

"Marit," she says crossly as the door shuts behind me. She closes her eyes. "Don't ever pull something like that around me again, or I'll take a switch to your hide until it's raw."

"I'm sorry, Dorit," I say, setting the flowers down by my ankles.

"Don't you think she's been through enough already this week without your little stunt?" Brock snaps. "You put us both in a terrible position." He covers Dorit with a blanket. And he's right. I suddenly feel ashamed.

"I'm sorry," I say softly. The flowers at my feet are so pungent they're making me heady.

"Maybe next time you want to steal an outfit and play dress-up, you could be a police officer and interrogate Philip instead," Brock says.

"Excuse me, I didn't *steal* this dress," I say. "I borrowed it."

"Semantics," he says, chuffing.

But it isn't. I'm not a thief. There's a line between a little mischief and crime, and I won't fully cross it. I couldn't afford any of the stones in that jewelry store, but I wouldn't stoop to stealing one. When I take something—like Thorsen's fabric and beads—I either pay for it or give it back.

Borrowing isn't the same as stealing.

Which makes a light suddenly go off in my head.

"Actually," I say, "thank you. You just gave me an idea for the next thing I'm going to borrow."

I might not be able to steal a stone. But maybe—just like this dress, and Eve's beads—I can *borrow* one. And then put it back before Philip knows it's gone.

"You're welcome, by the way," Brock says curtly. "For helping you back there."

"Thank you," I say, softening. Did he use magic to grow these flowers? He must have. If someone told me even last week that

Brock would risk magic in order to help *me,* I never would have believed it. "I owe you a favor."

"Let's just say you *borrowed* it." Brock leans his head against the seat and closes his eyes. "Which means you have to pay it back at some point."

I steal a glance at Dorit to make sure she isn't listening. Her chest is rising—she has fallen asleep. I pull my uniform from the trunk. It feels scratchy after the lush fabric of Helene's gown against my skin.

"I, um, need to change back," I say. I pull the enormous bouquet of flowers to my lap to block Brock's view and begin to unbutton Helene's dress. "Don't you dare look this way," I threaten.

"Are you joking?" he says. "Jakob would pummel me."

"*I'd* pummel you first. And, um—I don't know what you're talking about," I say, cheeks lighting on fire.

"Right. You're both as subtle as a hand grenade," he says sullenly. But I notice he is careful to fix his eyes out the window, and after a moment of silence he surprises me further by saying, "If you're doing more borrowing, I want in on it."

I am back in my servant clothes, with my hat on and Mrs. Vestergaard's dress stashed in the trunk again, by the time we pull down the lane to the house.

"I have one more plan before I have to resort to borrowing," I say, tightening my hat strings beneath my chin. "I'm hoping it doesn't come to that."

"I can't decide if you're incredibly smart or the most foolish little ninny."

"And I can't decide whether I dislike you or not. You make it difficult to pick a side. Here," I say. I open the trunk, pull out his mended jacket, and throw it at him.

He runs his fingers over the place where the rip was. It looks as though it never was there.

"Did you use a dirty word in your stitches?" he asks.

I purse my lips.

Actually, I sewed his rip with Ivy's name and birth and death dates.

Just like I sewed my family's names into my own seams.

"Don't you wish you knew," I say tartly as we climb down from the carriage.

He gives me a sharp jab with his elbow, and I stick out my foot to trip him a little. But then we turn to help Dorit between us, and by the time we step inside the Vestergaards', we could almost be standing side by side.

CHAPTER TWENTY-TWO

Philip
January 3, 1867
Vestergaard Manor

I N MY NIGHTMARES, I am plunged back into war.

I am back in the same place, fighting for the duchies again. This endless cycle, like a garish hallway of mirrors that keep reflecting. I was proud to carry the Vestergaard name. Proud to fight for Denmark. Those duchies cost my father his life, and I was not about to let that go to waste if I could help it. It would be like trading the rest of the life I could have had with him, all for land we barely managed to hold on to for a few more meaningless years. So I strapped on my uniform and latched up the leather of my boots, and I marched into war with the rest of them.

There was gray rain, turning everything cold and wet. Turning mud slick, turning solid ground treacherous. The war is feeling this way too. Firm ground becoming less and less sure.

And turning my matches soggy. I futilely try to light a cigarette. Then the man standing next to me bends and I hear the snap of his fingers. His cigarette comes alive with flame.

I turn toward it instinctively. I think of the little boy snapping his fingers in the alley, of the little boy I was, snapping useless fingers in the cold darkness.

"You know, when I was younger, I used to wish for that," I say carefully. *Magic.*

"Brutal thing to wish for . . ." he says, his lips curling the words around his cigarette. "I'd wish for money, treasure, gold, safe passage home, if I had a wish. A girl to love, perhaps. Or at the very least, an umbrella."

I'd wish for my father back. Or my brother. I'd wish I could make my father proud. Make his life sacrifice not worthless.

"Love," I say, chuffing. He lights my cigarette with the end of his. "Is that what you're wishing for?"

"Nah. I want to be a cartographer. I don't want to be here, shooting a gun. I want to see Antarctica." He sticks his hand out. "I'm Jasper."

I look at his hand for a beat too long. The only friends I've really ever had are Aleks and Tønnes.

"I'm Philip," I say quickly, shaking his hand. I gesture to his fingers. "You'll be glad you can do that—light yourself a fire. When you're surrounded by hunks of ice in Antarctica."

He grins, with gallows humor. "Ice seems to be my destiny. One way or the other," he says dryly. "What would you wish for now? If not love, magic, or the arctic tundra?"

The cannons have gone silent. The night cold is brutal, the stench of bodies and sewage awful. I remember the handkerchief I pressed to my face that night in the morgue. Would I have gone along with Tønnes's idea if I had understood what it meant, to see a man die in front of me?

I don't know.

"Perhaps I'd wish to go back in time," I say quietly. "Maybe change one decision. One I didn't realize at the time would be so monumental."

"Never too late," Jasper says, and sucks on his cigarette. "Unless you don't make it out of here, of course. Then you're too late, you unlucky bastard."

I swallow hard and take a deep breath of smoke. "Can't go back now. Only go forward and make something out of the wreckage."

"That's a big wish," he says. "I'd wish for a pound of smoked salmon and butter open-faced on rye. And for the bloody British to get here quicker." He stamps his feet in his boots. "I thought they'd be here by now."

We share a cigarette the next night, and the next. The Prussians are better armed than we are, with a new gun they can reload while lying down. We have to stay standing to load our rifles. As the barrage of cannons continues like pulsing thunder, days bleed to night and the mornings show more and more bodies littering the ground, the trenches, weighing down ambulance carts stuffed with soaked straw. Until we steadily realize.

"No one is coming to help us," Jasper says on the fourth night. He leans against the butt of his rifle, dazed.

He pulls out a cigarette.

He's right. The British aren't coming this time, like they

did in my father and brother's version of this war. Queen Victoria's already sided with the Prussians. Because of her daughter's marriage.

Jasper snaps his fingers, and I see the flame flicking between them, just for a second.

I'm not the only one who sees it.

"Want a—"

The question dies as instantly as he does.

One cracking shot, and there is brain on my face.

I'd always thought that magic was power. But magic couldn't help him, not this far downstream. I look at Jasper's limp hands, the cigarette he dropped with its magic flame extinguished in the mud. Power has to start much earlier, not on the battlefield, not with magic or tanks or guns, but in the strategizing. In the beautiful gilded state rooms, where words have more potent power than bullets. When it's still possible to change people's minds. By the time we're here, it's too late.

I make sure that Jasper gets properly buried. I pay for his cremation, his funeral. I don't know why he mattered so much to me, when I didn't know him but for a handful of days. When there have been so many others before him, and will be after him.

And then I begin to plan.

What do I wish for now that the war is over and Denmark has accepted defeat?

I don't wish for magic anymore. Now I'm going to make sure that Denmark is never abandoned or even threatened again. And that starts with the royals. Playing the games, making strategic and calculated moves, and flexing a powerful influence in those state rooms.

Yes, more people will die to get there. People like Jasper. But his sacrifice was for the greater good, and theirs will be too. If some people die now, perhaps fewer will die later.

There's still a way I can pull something good from all the wreckage.

That's why when I wake up from my coma and Helene pays me a visit, I know what I have to do.

She looks gaunt but strong. Her arms are crossed, her hair pulled back tight, and she's in a dress that streams down to the floor. She always had a presence that turned every room into a stage. She was the only one who could make gems look dim.

"Philip," she says softly. She is holding a gilded envelope in her fingers. "The king has accepted our invitation. But I'm no longer convinced this is the appropriate time for Eve to perform for him," Helene says. "Perhaps we should cancel. Or at the very least, postpone—"

"Do you want to get Eve into the royal academy?" I interrupt.

"Well, yes, of course. If she's going to be a Danish dancer, on the Danish stage, she needs to be in the academy. Otherwise I'll need to start exploring other options. Perhaps even in other countries."

That does actually sound rather appealing. But I can't throw away this opportunity with the king. Not after the humiliation of Schleswig and Holstein and how badly we overestimated the support of our allies. We may have lost land and power for the past hundred years, but we hold firm here.

"We'll downplay the attack and my injuries. I don't want to jeopardize anything with the royals or sacrifice Eve's chance at the academy," I say smoothly. I sit up and don't allow myself to wince at the shooting pain across my abdomen. "Yes, we proceed. There are things we need from King Christian."

And things he is going to need from us, too.

Yes. Bring the king to me.

And together, we'll make the Vestergaards, and Denmark, invincible.

CHAPTER TWENTY-THREE

Marit
January 4, 1867
Vestergaard Manor

"**P**HILIP'S AWAKE," LARA ANNOUNCES when I step into the kitchen first thing the next morning.

Liljan and I stayed up late into the night. She dyed my hair back to its original color and returned a smattering of freckles to my face. Then we sat between the beds, secretly eating licorice and putting together a plan with two prongs.

The first depends on whether or not the ballet salon is still happening and whether or not I can procure some Vestergaard stones under the guise of embellishing a costume. If that plan fails, we'll move on to the second, trickier one—a plan infinitely more tricky now that Philip is awake. I straighten out my apron. The first prong better work, and it starts with me.

Rae, Peder the guard, and Philip's valet, Malthe, are sitting around the kitchen table with coffee. Everything is a shade duller and quieter now. The clanking of pots is subdued. No one is whispering or laughing or whipping towels at one another. Dorit slept in, and the bread Rae baked is half-burned and sunken.

"Did Mr. Vestergaard get a good look at his assailant?" Peder asks the valet. I can see the guard's revolver. He keeps reaching down and touching it.

"No. Only that he seemed like some vagrant. Medium build, light hair and eyes. Philip says he smelled tangy, like alcohol."

A vague description that in Denmark could have been anyone. Helene says she saw nothing; Philip's information is unhelpful. They could be telling the truth.

Or they could be covering something for each other.

"I'll take that," I say to Lara, and load a tray with coffee, cream, and, at the last moment, a sprig of violets in a crystal vase. The corridor to the main house is freezing; my steps echo, and the enormous vase on the table in the foyer is empty of flowers and smells slightly of decay. I knock quietly at Helene's door. The hallway is as still as death.

"Mrs. Vestergaard?"

Helene opens the door.

"I don't mean to pry," I say, holding out the tray, "but I wasn't certain if I should proceed with the salon costumes . . . ?" I trail off at her piercing stare. Surely, after all that's happened, the event will be postponed or even canceled altogether.

Helene takes the coffee from me and sips it black.

She says coolly, "We proceed as planned."

Then so, I think, *will we.* I clear my throat and step into her room to unload the tray. "Then I'd like to propose an idea for the costumes," I venture. "I'm envisioning Vestergaard stones. I'll embroider them right onto Eve's costume, into the fabric." I lay out the vase of violets and pitcher of cream on the vanity. "Her very tutu will be a piece of jewelry."

Helene hesitates, narrowing her eyes. "I do like the idea," she hedges. Her eyes fix on a portrait of Aleks as she considers. "But I'd like to pursue something else. I don't want to bother Philip with it now, and I'm not convinced we could get the stones in time. Maybe for another show, in the future."

But *this* salon is the one with the king in attendance. I'm battling my suspicions, wanting to press her, when Eve suddenly slips in through the open door. Her hair is plaited up around her head and she makes a point not to look at me. It makes me feel like a piece of furniture in the room. One that she's planning to give away.

"I've lost another week of practicing, Helene," she says tentatively. "You still want to continue with the salon? I'm . . . not sure I'm ready to perform for the king. Perhaps I should simply work on my audition for the royal ballet academy?"

Helene hesitates and sets down her coffee.

She turns to look Eve straight in the eye and says, "Eve, I'm not certain that's going to be possible."

"Why not?"

"As it turns out, after speaking with my contacts at the Royal Danish Ballet about your audition, they feel that perhaps Denmark isn't quite ready for ballet to . . . change. For the *ballerinas* to change," she says bitterly. "As much as we are."

Eve stills. "Oh," she says, as if she can't quite catch her breath.

"But if the king enjoys your dancing, then we will force their hand." Helene's jaw twitches. "And oh, how I long to force their hand."

At the crushed look on Eve's face, a licking, burning rage ignites within me and drowns out everything else. I'm furious at myself that I managed to hurt her. Furious at these nameless people who would dare take away this chance from her, when she has come so miraculously close to it. There's a lump in my throat, growing so large that I'm choking on it. The people who love her, and the thing that she's good at — they aren't supposed to hurt her. They're supposed to be what gives her a future. I can't pretend to understand all the facets of what she feels, but I feel her hurt so keenly within me, like light refracting. Hurting for her is entirely different than hurting for myself. It goes to a separate place and slices deeply and tenderly there. And so I turn the hurt to anger, almost without thinking. It is easier to take a broken heart's edges and bend them to face outward instead of in. It provides a little relief from their piercing, to turn the jagged parts around and wield them instead as a weapon.

"So we'll do the salon," Helene says firmly. "Marit, let's plan to discuss other ideas for the costumes."

"Shall we practice today, then?" Eve asks quietly. The gracefulness and joy she usually exudes are gone. She moves like rusted tin — hunched and stiff, as if she were trying to protect something soft. I sense her gathering herself as though she's been shoved over, and she's mustering the strength to get back up again.

"I do think we should spend today practicing. But, Eve," Helene says softly, "before that—have you ever tasted sugar cakes?"

Eve frowns slightly, then shakes her head.

"Oh, that won't do," Helene says with mock gravity. She hesitates, then reaches out for Eve's hand, covering it like a glove. "We must fix that immediately."

I'm slightly confused at this turn of events, at the suggestion of two ballerinas eating sugar cakes just after breakfast, but I follow along two paces behind them, through the too-quiet house. Helene descends the stairs to the corridor that connects to the servants' quarters and walks briskly through it, but she pauses at the entrance to the kitchen.

"Hello?" she calls ahead, as if to announce herself.

There is such a complicated dance always going on between their upstairs and our downstairs. Part of service is learning the steps quickly and understanding how to navigate all the tricky lines that are both unspoken and uncrossable.

"I don't mean to interrupt," she says, crossing over the invisible line into the kitchen.

Dorit is flattening dough over and over with a rolling pin. She looks up without expression. "This is your home, my lady," she responds dully.

Helene hesitates. "It is my house," she corrects. "But this is your space. I've hardly stepped foot here in years . . ." The unsaid words hang painfully in the air: . . . *other than the bloody day that Ivy died.* "Are you certain you're ready to be back?" she asks, and she slips into her authority again like it's a garment, her voice becoming gentler still.

"I need something to keep my mind and hands busy, Mrs. Vestergaard," Dorit says, pushing the rolling pin firmly against the dough. "Sitting with my thoughts is too hard yet."

Helene touches the edge of a towel, straightening its wrinkles. "I know the sting of grief," she says gently. "It will get better."

"Please." Dorit gestures to the table. I sense Eve tensing for the briefest second, as if she expects to see traces of Philip's and Ivy's blood there. "May I fix you something?" Dorit asks, roughly wiping her eyes with a dishtowel. "A cup of tea? A scone?"

Helene stops her from rummaging through the cupboards. "Actually," she says, "I was hoping I could cook something. With Miss Eve."

Dorit barely masks her surprise. "Oh—well, yes, of course, my lady."

"I'll need sugar, coconut, bay leaves, and fresh ginger."

As we spring into action and gather the ingredients, Helene dons an apron and gestures for Eve to put one on over her dress. Eve glances at me out of the corner of her eye, as if she can't help it. When our eyes meet, she scowls.

Helene turns to Eve. "You told me, that first day in the carriage, that 'The Nightingale' was your favorite Hans Christian Andersen story. Well, 'The Snow Queen' is mine."

Just like me. Rae instantly sets a saucepan of water to boil, and Helene adds sugar, bay leaves, and ginger to it as she tells Eve the story of Gerda and Kai, of the devil who makes a magic mirror to reflect the world with pointed ugliness and distortion. "When it shatters, splinters of it—some as small as a grain of sand—lodge into people's eyes, so that all they can see is the worst of everything around them," Helene says, stirring in the coconut. "It gets into their hearts; it freezes them to ice. But our heroine, young Gerda, follows her childhood friend Kai after he gets one of those splinters in his eye. She follows him to the palace of the Snow Queen and cries hot tears that penetrate into his chest and thaw his frozen heart."

I can't help but wonder, as I always do when I hear this story, if it was inspired somehow by magic. Maybe Hans Christian Andersen heard about the Firn and made this story, writing a happy ending for us even if we can't have it in real life.

"The best stories are always spun around a kernel of truth," Helene says. "Sometimes it seems like the world has all sorts of glass splinters in its eye. And I want to change that."

Helene plucks out the bay leaves and ginger and carefully measures the steaming coconut sugar into small round lumps on a tray. "Sugar cakes, like my mother used to make in St. Croix," Helene says. "We'll let these cool, and in the meantime—I'll need a pencil, please. And some string." She sets another pot of water to boil. Measures out more sugar.

"Aleks taught me this trick, to help me understand the way crystals and stalactites form, in the caves of the mines," Helene says, and I listen with heightened interest. "But it reminds me of 'The Snow Queen,' as well." Helene sends the sugar to swirl like a blizzard into the water. She stirs the mixture until the sugar has dissolved, then pours it into a glass jar.

"The sugar will crystallize here on the string, and then it will begin to build on itself, little by little. And I think people can let hatred grow, just like this. Letting it build up and harden, forming inside of them." She ties the string to the pencil, then balances the pencil over the jar so that the string dangles down into the mixture. "But here is the difficult part for us, Eve," Helene continues. "It's not letting hatred form in response to hatred. Because what builds isn't lovely or valuable. Instead, it's like poison—hollowing out and destroying." She swallows. "We both know well how concerned some people can be with what we look like on the outside. But we have to make sure we don't start to look like them on the inside."

"But they started it," Eve mutters.

"You're right. And we rarely succeed in removing those slivers of glass through the use of force or even arguments of sense or rationality. But sometimes with beauty and awe—with art, with books, even perhaps with dancing—we can gain access to hearts as hard as rocks. We can make them cry and think, and sometimes that's enough to get the splinter out. Sometimes, through the door of beauty, they might let us slip in deep enough to change their own minds."

Eve is quiet for a moment before she says softly, "That sounds hard."

"Hard? Terribly. Is it a burden that should fall on you to carry?

No, Eve, nothing about this is just or fair. But is it *possible?* Yes, I believe it is." Helene reaches for Eve's downturned face. Cups her cheek.

The first microscopic crystals are beginning to form along the string. Eve stares at them, her forehead creasing in thought. I picture my heart, its broken edges turned out to form spikes. Perhaps I pay a price for turning sadness to anger. Maybe the cost is a heart that becomes a little bit harder each time.

"You don't ever wear jewels," Eve comments to Helene. She touches the Vestergaard crest on her necklace.

Helene shakes her head. "I like glass best," she says simply, and I watch her from the shadows. She gestures toward the window. "Glass is fragile but strong. It allows us to see through the walls we've built around us." She pulls out a small silver pendant from her pocket. "It never calls attention to itself but always to what's beyond it." The pendant opens to reveal an image of Aleks resting behind the glass. She gently touches his face. "It can protect things from damage. And yet, when you aren't careful with it," she says, smiling ruefully and picking up the crest around Eve's neck, "watch out."

Her words seem so genuine that I no longer know what to believe. Seeing the way Helene acts with Eve, that delicate balance of challenge, belief, and encouragement, makes the realization slice through me like a paring knife.

Helene Vestergaard is actually a good mother.

The kind I would want for Eve, if I could pick.

"I think these are ready now," Helene says, handing her one of the sugar cakes. Eve sinks her teeth into it. She smiles and licks her lips. "Thank you," she says shyly.

Helene smiles and picks up a cake for herself. "Perhaps our favorite dishes will be a combination of something West Indian with something Danish. Like we are."

"I am ready to practice now," Eve says, standing. She juts out her chin, and that flowing ease has returned to her muscles. She looks graceful, but more than that, she looks as though there is pure power flowing through her. "Would you like to see what I've been working on?" she asks, with kindness layering into her voice, and I look up with sudden hope that she has decided to forgive me, after all.

But she isn't speaking to me, or to Helene. She's reaching out her hand to the cook.

Dorit looks surprised, but after an uncertain glance at Helene, she nods and moves to take off her apron. Eve leads her toward the ballroom, and for the first time since Ivy died, Dorit's weathered face turns up into a smile.

"Go to work on the costumes, Marit," Helene says. "Do whatever it takes to make her shine."

I clear my throat. "Yes, ma'am," I say, and Helene's skirts swish out the closing door.

It stings to be left alone here in the kitchen.

I walk to the glass jar. To the crystals forming in a small crust on the string.

A Vestergaard loves Eve. And—the thought is like a dagger to my heart—is doing a better job of it than I have done.

I turn the glass jar in the light and suddenly, though my heart is aching, I know how we're going to borrow Philip's ring and compare it to my father's stone.

All without Philip ever even realizing it's gone.

CHAPTER TWENTY-FOUR

THAT NIGHT, I PAUSE in front of Brock's door, hand raised to knock. Hesitating.

When he opens the door, his face registers surprise to see me standing there. I bring a finger to my lips to keep him quiet. Then I shove my heavy books of jewels into his arms and begrudgingly gesture for him to follow me up the stairs.

"Our party is growing," I announce without enthusiasm as I lead Brock into Jakob's attic nook. Jakob extends a handshake to Brock as I sink into a large pillow beneath the skylight, carefully balancing the glass jar with Eve's sugar crystal in my hand.

Liljan pours hot chocolate into chipped china cups.

"Helene didn't accept my idea about the costume stones," I say, settling into my oversize pillow. I set Eve's crystal jar on the floor. The glass paperweight Ivy gave to Jakob is perched on his desk, and Brock's gaze keeps drawing toward it.

"Disappointing," Liljan says, "but not altogether unexpected." She stirs her hot chocolate with a long, thin pretzel stick studded with salt. "So we move on to the secondary plan, then."

"I've volunteered to take over Philip's care once Dr. Holm leaves," Jakob says. "Perhaps I can make some excuse to get us in there."

"But simply looking at the ring won't be enough, of course," Liljan says grimly, handing us each a hot chocolate. "How else can you tell what type of jewel it is unless you look at it under the microscope?"

"Right," I say. "Which is why we're going to borrow it."

Jakob chuffs in disbelief. "Wait. You want to steal a ring off Philip Vestergaard's finger?"

"Not *steal*," I correct him. I shoot a meaningful look at Brock. *"Borrow."*

Brock bites into his pretzel with a crack. "She wouldn't want to get rusty."

"I plan to put it back," I insist. "And for him to never even realize it's missing."

"Ooh," Liljan says, rubbing her hands together and crossing her legs. "Do go on, little Marit."

I hold up Eve's crystal.

"Do you think between the four of us, we could make a convincing imitation? Something like this, to buy us a brief amount of time while we look at Philip's?"

"I don't know," Jakob says skeptically. "Gemstones are notoriously difficult to falsify."

I take the jewel dictionary from Brock. "That's what this book says, too. Mostly because we don't have the tools to do it. The closest anyone has come is with Venetian glass, but clearly no one would mistake that for an emerald or a ruby. It's too dull; the colors aren't accurate. Unless . . ." I turn winsomely to Liljan. "You had the *magic* to do it just right."

Brock looks at the crystal growing in the jar at my ankle. "Are you saying you want us to make a convincing imitation of a gemstone—to trick a gentleman who handles gemstones for a living—out of *table sugar?*" he asks in disbelief.

"No." I stand and reach for Ivy's paperweight on the desk. "I thought maybe we could make an imitation jewel out of glass," I say.

And as my fingers close around it, an idea hits me like a gust, so powerful that I almost sink to my knees.

I lower the paperweight slowly.

An imitation jewel, made out of glass.

I suddenly remember that day we saw Philip Vestergaard in the glass shop.

Why did he pay a visit to Ivy and then never order anything?

Why was he there with her on the road that day she died?

"Marit?" Jakob says. "Are you okay? You look as though you're about to faint."

I can smell the rich chocolate wisping from my untouched cup.

"I just had a terrible thought," I whisper.

So terrible. But it would explain so many things.

"What if . . ." I say, my heart thundering in my ears. "What if the jewels that come from the Vestergaard mines aren't really jewels at all?"

My thoughts come spilling out into the stunned silence.

Oh, hell's bells, it all makes so much sense.

"The Vestergaards haven't always had gemstones in their mines," I say. "They were discovered little more than a decade ago." I drop to a kneel and set the paperweight on the floor next to me. "We've thought all along that those miners might have been murdered," I say, turning to Jakob. "To cover something up—to keep something terribly important a secret. What if they were trying to expose that the jewels aren't real jewels?"

"Wait," says Jakob. He runs his hand through his hair, pulling it in thought. "How could that be true? It's almost impossible to make a false gemstone. We don't have the tools. You just said so yourself."

"But people with magic *do*. Think about it. It could be possible to forge a passable gemstone if, say, you had a very special ability to manipulate glass." I hold up Ivy's paperweight. An intense, murderous look is gathering across Brock's face like a storm. "And a very special ability to dye it any shade you wanted."

"A combination," Jakob says slowly, "of what Liljan and Ivy could do, you mean."

Liljan is silent. Her hands have turned bone white around her teacup.

"What if . . ." I say, and swallow, "the stones that have made the Vestergaard fortune aren't made in the mines, but by magic? The average person—even royalty—would never be able to guess. The only people who could tell the difference would be jewelers. And you should *see* all the payments the Vestergaards make to the single jeweling family in Denmark. Maybe they pay them off to confirm the jewels as genuine and look the other way."

Yes. I remember the eagerness on the shopkeeper's face when he offered to get me a stone in any shade I wanted. How could you promise that—unless you had the ability to control exactly what shade a stone would turn out to be?

"But if that's true, then attacking Ivy makes even less sense," Brock says, with barely contained fury. He stands. "Why would they kill Ivy? They wouldn't want her dead. They would want her very much alive."

I hesitate. "Perhaps she refused. Perhaps . . . this isn't a job you take voluntarily. Except . . ." My breath shortens. "Perhaps they underestimated her."

What made her useful to them also made her dangerous. "Maybe they approached her on the road, when she was alone. To get her into the carriage and take her to the mines."

Brock's eyes are sharp and bright. He pulls out the small fragment of glass. "But she fought back."

Jakob swears under his breath.

It would provide a motive for killing any miners who were threatening to expose the system. Miners like my father.

It could explain why my father wanted the king to investigate what was going on.

It could be why Ivy wound up dead and the last people who saw her alive were the Vestergaards.

My heart pounds like a storm in my chest. Is this the secret my father wanted us to find ten years ago? Could we have stumbled upon a massive cover-up scandal that starts right in the Vestergaard house and reverberates throughout all of Denmark?

"So what do we do next?" Liljan whispers. Her eyes are like shining stones in the dark. "How would we ever go about proving it?"

"We get a jewel we *know* to be from the Vestergaard mines," I say. "Helene doesn't really wear jewelry. The only one we can realistically get our hands on is the one Philip wears. And Jakob can determine whether it's glass."

A thought suddenly occurs to me: Maybe that's why my father left me that jewel in the bank. He gave me a real jewel, possibly one of the only real ones in Denmark, to give us something to compare the false ones to.

Maybe that's what those men were coming to find the night Ingrid died.

I close my eyes.

"But how are we supposed to make the switch on Philip's finger without him waking up and catching us?" Liljan asks.

I hesitate. "I don't know."

"We'll drug him," Brock says at the same time.

Jakob winces. "All right — wait — just a moment," he says, tugging harder through his hair. "If what Marit is saying winds up being true, then it's horrendous, possibly even evil, and Philip deserves whatever's coming to him. But I'm supposed to be taking care of the man. He could be innocent. And drugging and robbing him seems to go *somewhat* against the medical code of honor."

"So close your ears and look the other way," Brock says. "Dorit will slip the drugs into his food." He gives his knuckles a loud crack. *"With pleasure."*

I hesitate. "I'll be the one to take the ring," I volunteer. "Your hands can stay clean."

"And I can grow anything you want for a sedative. You'll be doing him a service. Otherwise I can give it my best guess," Brock says, his face darkening further, "but I can't guarantee I won't kill him."

Though my theory is thrumming through me at full tilt, I feel the briefest tug of warning. What we do next could hurt the Vestergaards—and Eve. It could destroy every single one of our futures, cost us our employment and livelihoods. It could make a lot of people very mad.

Powerful, dangerous people with much at stake. People who have killed before.

And if Eve thinks I betrayed her once already, could she ever forgive me for my involvement in this?

The cloud of doubt recedes slightly when I think back to the records I saw, the rows and rows of Vestergaard jewels that filled the profit margins over the past ten years. How much glass magic would it take to make that many jewels, after all?

Certainly much more than a single person could manage.

The magic of ten people?

Twenty?

More?

And . . . are they there of their own accord, like we are here in the house?

Or could something even worse be happening in those mines?

"If they hurt Ivy," Brock says, running his finger dangerously over the raw edge of his cracked china cup, "they are going to wish they had never met me."

Our candles flicker along the walls as we slip back to our rooms, through dark corridors that run like veins deep into the house. If a Vestergaard scandal really starts here, with these people, in this home — then its end is going to come from the last place they would ever expect.

From inside their very own walls.

CHAPTER TWENTY-FIVE

THE HOUSE EXPLODES WITH ACTIVITY. The salon is still moving forward, and the royal family is coming here in less than four weeks. I tell Nina that Brock and I are meeting about designing stage curtains and flowers, and instead we join Liljan and Jakob in the attic and map out our plan.

I am going to find out Philip's exact schedule and make our strategy.

Jakob will research the sedative that Brock will grow.

Liljan will make the decoy stone using glass from Ivy's paperweight. Jakob unearths instructions about ways to cut and shape glass using ground-up stones and oils instead of modern tools we can't easily secure.

Brock will approach servant networks in the neighboring houses and shops in Copenhagen, sending out questions like droplets of dew to slide through the web and collect more information. At the glass shop that day in Copenhagen, Hanne said other servants have gone missing. If we're right, there should be some sort of pattern as to who they are: servants with glass magic, color magic, metalwork, gold—anything that could be used to help create realistic-looking gemstones.

Philip is growing stronger, though, even walking around. I glimpsed him through the twining flowers in the foyer, leaning on his cane with strain on his face as he contemplated attempting the stairs back to his room.

I keep the glass jar on my windowsill. Every time I see the sugar growing inside, assembling bit by crystalline bit, it makes me think of Eve.

Because our relationship was that way, something that formed over time, with each moment and memory building on the last. My lie shattered it all, like taking a sledgehammer to something precious and delicate.

It makes me want to win her back.

I watch her in the ballroom, in the makeshift studio. The parquet floors gleam with winter sunshine. Eve dances next to an older girl with light brown skin who speaks Italian and teaches her how to spot an object so she won't get dizzy in the midst of her turns. Helene is calling in all the favors she has. The ballet contacts she's made over the course of her career arrive for over-lapping visits with their trunks packed to stay for four or five days at a time. They teach Eve fouettés, with accents that fly off their tongues and their ideas about what ballet could become bouncing off the walls, arguing and rising and falling and blend-ing like music. But Eve remains distant with me when I fit a potential costume on her. Her thank-yous are perfunctory; she looks at my forehead instead of my eyes.

Dorit throws herself into deciding the menu for the salon as though she can channel her grief into something of beauty. For two weeks, she lets the rest of us taste the leftovers after Helene has cast her vote: Edible flowers, rum custard, and lemon tarts that practically fizz on my tongue. Sirloin packed with pepper and flaked with gold leaf, pies heated to golden brown with real violets encrusted with sugar on top. Wreathed layers of kransekage, this time tinged with the essences of mango and coconut. And these are the dishes she hasn't even used magic on yet. "I'm getting too old to spend magic on practice," she says. She adds dashes of syrup and berries while I dot corsets and shoes with beads and branches and jewels. "I'll save that for the day of the king."

I walk beneath the barren trellises of the old wisteria corridor each afternoon, watching for when Philip's curtains are closed and opened, timing the length of his rests. I steal glances up at Eve's window, too, remembering the time I was eleven years old and I secretly made an embroidered piece by hand at the Mill. It was a portrait of my family. I gave Ingrid a flower crown and my father a book, and I did the whole piece without relying on any magic at all. I was actually proud of it until Sare dredged it up out of my things one day and said the faces looked like boiled eggs wearing wigs, and after that I couldn't see my work any other way. I threw it in the garbage. But Eve fished it out and kept it for herself.

I didn't know until I found it tucked into her pillowcase more than a year later.

The thin crust of snow crunches beneath my boots, and I shiver, suddenly realizing how much loneliness can feel like cold. Like wondering if you'll ever know what it feels like to be warm again.

I miss her.

I rush back up to my workroom and begin to put messages in everything my hands make for her. There must be a way to show her that it was real, all of it. That I will fight for her and for that relationship I unwillingly shattered, no matter how long it takes and how hard it is to put those pieces back together again. I begin to cover her dresses, her costumes, her shoes, with words. Not with messages of warning or fear, but with love.

When the salon is a little less than three weeks away, Helene and Eve decide on the final design for Eve's costume. I start it from scratch and I lace our memories into every part of it. Memories are like a duet, with layered perspectives and harmonies knitting together, shared between two people. These are mine. I'm singing to her the parts she forgot or she never knew.

In the fabric lining the corset, I write: *When you were five, you once made earrings from torn strips of penny papers and dyed them with old coffee. They hung from your ears like limp brown seaweed but you said they made you feel like a princess or a famous dancer.*

On the inside of her satin laces: *I have always loved your laugh that starts in a low roar and builds higher and higher until you get this dimple in your cheek. It is like a punctuation mark to the best sound in the world.*

When she came to the Mill, she made me laugh for the first time in three years.

In the length of her hair ribbons, I write: *I read Hans Christian Andersen stories to you when you were six. I was nervous to share them with you, this special part of me I shared only with my father, and if you'd rejected it or thought it was silly or boring, it would have spoiled something precious to me a little bit. But instead your eyes lit up and it made those stories even better and dearer because I got to share them with him and with you and it felt like making something grow again from an old seed.*

Each fold of her tutu fabric holds a memory. *When you were five and learning to write, you got so mad at me for making you hold your pen the right way that you threw the pen and stomped your boot hard on my foot.*

When you were three, you used to say "lemomade" and "upslide down," and it was so endearing that I didn't correct you and I was almost a little sad when you grew up enough to start saying those words the right way.

When I start, I don't want to stop. She can dance in front of the king draped in love. I smile whenever I touch the layers of fabric, holding memories that will lift and fall around her like snow-covered boughs in the wind. No matter what happens, she'll have these memories. She'll know that even during those years she spent as an orphan, there was someone who desperately loved her.

"Knock, knock." Jakob gently cracks open my door. His dark hair is mussed, his lips soft and pink. "Liljan wants to meet," he says, gesturing toward the attic nook. I set down my sewing needle, glimpsing the books about medicine and astronomy half tucked under the crook of his arm.

"You've been with Eve?" I guess. I hesitate, biting my cheek. "How is she?"

"She's well, Marit. She picks things up quick. I just teach her whatever she wants to learn. And lately," he says, "what she wants to learn about is the Firn."

"The Firn?" I ask. I hear my own voice falter.

"She wants to know how it kills people. If there's a cure. If it can ever be helped."

"Yes. Well. Her mother died of the Firn," I say softly.

"And yet, if she's this interested in finding a cure . . ." he says. He turns at the landing and gives me a small smile. "My guess is that she's thinking of someone who is still alive."

I concentrate on his shoes, but I feel the tiniest lift in my heart as I follow him up to the attic.

Brock and Liljan are already there.

Liljan bars the door behind us before she pulls something out of her pocket. She presents it to us on a plump pillow, flashing the impish grin that Nina always calls downright terrifying.

"You're doing that grin that Nina says makes you look like a rabid vole," Brock informs her.

Liljan just smirks more triumphantly.

"Well? Does it pass?" she asks. Her eyes sparkle because she already knows the answer.

If I'm honest, a small part of me hoped Liljan wouldn't be able to create a convincing double. Because if she can, it means my theory might be right — and the next part of the plan makes my stomach turn with nerves.

I breathe out and pick up the ring in my fingers. "I had to make my best guess for the size of the band," Liljan says. "It's just gold leaf, but it'll work for now."

I hold Liljan's stone up to a candle flame and watch the light refract through the jewel. It's an exact replica. Could the Vestergaard jewel business really be one massive, intricate network of deceit? I didn't truly dare believe it until seeing what Liljan can do with glass and color. I pull out my father's stone and compare the two, side by side.

"It's a perfect match," I say.

"So are we doing this, then?" Brock asks, chafing his hands together.

Jakob removes his spectacles, sighing heavily. "Everything about this is foolhardy," he says.

"Just think of what Nina will do if she finds out!" Liljan says gleefully. She takes the replica-stone back.

Jakob looks at me through his dark eyelashes, as if he's asking me an unspoken question, and I get a sudden heady rush from all the danger I'm flirting with right now. The danger of magic and the mystery of the mines and, maybe most of all, him. It feels just like all those futile times I tried to keep my heart from Eve. *Don't get too close. Don't care too much. Don't use magic. Don't hope too much for the future.* But I'm not listening to any of those cautions right now.

I move my hand in the shadows to graze his, and the touch shoots giddy sparks across my skin.

"You're up, little birds," Liljan says, rolling the stone between her fingers so it flares in the light. "Let's see just how deep this deception lies."

CHAPTER TWENTY-SIX

I SHOULD KNOW WE AREN'T off to an auspicious start when Malthe, Philip's valet, appears at the breakfast table in the morning.

I swallow and meet Liljan's eyes over a dish of Dorit's øllebrød, porridge made with scraps of rye bread soaked in sugar and beer.

"Back so soon, Malthe?" Liljan asks sweetly, twirling her spoon in the dense porridge.

"Had to bring some things for the salon at the master's request," he says.

I play with the false gem tucked in the scratchy fabric of my pocket folds. We already knew there would be more policemen in the area than usual, because they've been patrolling the roads nearby ever since Ivy was killed. But then, barely an hour later, the front door opens. Liljan's face mirrors my own when the captain of the king's guard is announced. Eight armed men trickle in after him and branch off through the house, inspecting the entrances and exits, the dining room, kitchen, and ballroom, in advance of the king's visit.

Dorit hums while she chops baked hazelnuts for the Mazarin cake, but sweat trickles down her back. She keeps glancing at the small, empty glass jar that, up until this morning, held an herb Brock grew that is similar to a poppy. The salt and spices in today's lunch—a stew—will mask the herb's taste and smell. It should make Philip sleep deeply for several hours.

"Smells good," one of the guards notes to Dorit. She swallows hard and adds another handful of crushed pepper to the simmering stew.

I follow Brock to the ballroom, where we pretend to devise a way for heavy velvet curtains to work with the pulley system he's constructing. Declan is building an elaborate stage for Eve. The wood responds to his touch, the designs etching beneath his fingertips into whittled legs and swirled impressions plated with gold leaf. Around the stage, Brock morphs the ballroom into a living garden. Each day it spills over a little more with fruit trees, with vines and walls of buds. Between the branches of an orange blossom tree, I watch as Eve's feet suddenly go out from beneath her, tangling together like hooks catching, and she goes down hard on her hip. She kicks at the floor in frustration, her freckles darkening on her flushed cheeks.

"Again," Helene says, and Eve pulls herself up and gets back in position, even though I'm sure the fall will leave a bruise.

Philip leans on a cane, his arm in a sling and his shirt tight against the bandaging around his middle, observing with an unreadable expression. We've timed his schedule. He tires after he takes his turn around the house and sleeps heavily after lunch, so a slightly deeper or longer rest won't attract notice. I see the ring, gleaming dark red and heavy on his finger.

"What's he doing?" Brock whispers to me, hoisting the curtains along the rods.

Malthe appears with a leather case stained coffee brown — the same one he was carrying when we saw him that day in Copenhagen. He says something to Philip under his breath, and then the two of them turn together and climb the stairs.

"Today's no good. The house is crawling with guards," I whisper to Brock, my fingers playing with the heavy curtain folds.

"Jakob only made one batch of sedative. And we really can't afford to lose another day," Brock whispers. He tugs on the cords to test the curtains and they successfully pull open along the rings. By the time Malthe returns, he's alone — and the case is gone.

Stones. It has to be . . . Philip is going to make some sort of presentation to the king and it involves the jewels. I pin the curtains back to hold their place and think again about the entries in the records of jeweled gifts meant for all of the royal family. What is the point of outfitting the royal family with worthless glass?

I want to see what's in that leather case.

My nerves are wound so tight that I barely touch my lunch.

Dorit nods at me when she hands Philip's tray to Brock, who brings it through the main house to Jakob. Peder is patrolling the hall.

Our countdown begins now.

Dorit moves into position. "Shall we discuss the settings and timing for the final proposed menu?" she asks, and unfurls a paper across the entire length of the table to distract Nina. Liljan, Brock, and I make our way to Philip's room through the back channels of the house. My stomach feels as if it's been replaced with coiled, rusted springs, and they tighten when I glimpse Eve farther down the hallway. She catches sight of the three of us and pauses. Then she turns her head and moves on, as if she's seen nothing.

Liljan stations herself at the front hallway and Brock hangs back to guard the servants' staircase.

I knock quietly on Philip's door, five times, just like I would with Eve, and Jakob opens it without a sound.

I step inside and my heart beats a hair faster. The room smells like soap, flowers, and laudanum. Philip is sleeping, his breathing heavy and slow, and I feel the first twinge of guilt.

Is this wrong?

But I risked my life for him, to save his. A little laudanum and a harmless switch should be fair game.

"There's a problem," Jakob whispers.

"Please tell me you're joking," I say as my eyes adjust to the darkened room.

"He didn't finish it," Jakob says, nodding to a half-eaten plate of stew. "I tried to get him to, but he said he wasn't hungry. I gave him a little extra laudanum to help but I didn't dare give him any more. I couldn't risk it. But our timing is all off now—I can't know for certain how much is in his system or how long he'll stay under."

My eyes fall on the ring. Philip's still hands lie on top of the blanket.

"Let's move quickly, then," I say with a deep inhale. But when I approach Philip's bedside, I swear under my breath.

"Get Liljan," I say immediately to Jakob. I hold up the decoy to be sure. "The stones don't match each other."

I know it isn't just my memory failing me—the stone on Philip's finger has changed color. I examine it while Jakob summons his sister. It's a deeper red now, darkened to almost black. Like crusted blood instead of fresh.

Is it a different ring altogether? Or is it . . . darkening?

"Could it be losing its color because it's been dyed with magic?" I whisper when Liljan appears next to me.

"Perhaps if it was from a long time ago, magic could start to fade?" Liljan murmurs uncertainly. "I don't know. None of my colors have ever faded before." She touches the false stone and the color settles into a deeper, richer red. She hands it back to me.

And I hesitate.

She watches my face. "Do you want me to do it?" she finally asks.

Yes, I think.

"I can do it," I say. I feel Jakob's eyes on me as I gently take

Philip's hand in mine and work the ring from his finger. He stirs, shifting with a soft groan when I push the replacement onto his finger, and then settles again.

"Go," I say to Jakob, and slip the real ring into his waiting hand. He gives me one long, silent look, his throat bobbing, and then he's gone to examine the stone under the microscope in his attic nook.

"Buy me three more minutes?" I plead with Liljan. She nods, without question, and returns to the hallway.

I take one more glance at Philip to make sure he's still asleep, and then I begin to creep around the room. I have to find that case. I've been on my hands and knees for no longer than a minute when Brock appears. He lifts his finger to his lips in silent warning. Slips behind the open door to hide himself.

I hear Peder's voice. I freeze and move behind the bed.

Liljan's voice is full of forced cheerfulness in the hallway. I can practically see her bounding to block Peder in his path. "I was thinking," she chirps. "Perhaps we should discuss the entrance to the servants' wing with the king's guards — I have an idea I'd like to show you."

There's a pause when all I can hear is the thudding of my own heartbeat.

Then their footsteps begin to fade in the opposite direction and I let out a breath.

"What are you doing?" Brock whispers urgently. "Time's up. We'll find a way to get that stone back onto his finger later."

"That case we saw," I insist. "I have to find it first."

Brock hesitates, deliberating. "Hurry up," he relents. "I'll keep watch."

I search the room, my fingers sifting through the drawers and closets, and my doubts rise to plague me anew. What if the ring on Philip's finger is a mere glass fake? What, then? Will it end the Vestergaards? Is my loyalty to the truth, to Eve, to my father and those dead miners? To magical people I don't know who might be losing their lives? Are strangers' lives worth my relationship with the only person I love?

I open the closet and see two cases there, next to Philip's polished boots. I kneel, breathing hard.

"Hurry," Brock says from the doorway. "I barred the door to the servant staircase. No one is coming in that way. But Liljan can only hold Peder off for so long."

"Help me get this open."

I grab the coffee-colored case I saw in Malthe's hands this morning. We play with the lock and jiggle it with one of my sewing pins until we get the case to fall open.

But it's empty. Whatever Malthe brought for Philip is already gone.

I swear under my breath.

"Now the other one," I insist. I can already tell it has something inside it by the weight when I pull it out.

"Hurry," Brock says again. This lock is harder to open, and another precious minute ticks by before the latch finally clicks. I raise the top.

Inside is a tangled handful of rings, all jumbled together.

But these don't look like the other jewels.

They are all black. Smooth.

I hold one up to the light. It looks damaged. Charred or something, as if someone wanted to destroy it.

"We should go," Brock whispers, looking toward the door.

"Do you think he would miss it if we took just one?" I ask anxiously.

Brock swallows. He can see the hesitation, the fear, in me. I don't know if I'm brave enough to take the ring. To risk everything, to find out the truth.

He closes the case with a click. "I'll take the fall. If it comes to it."

Before I can speak, he snatches the blackened ring from my fingers and thrusts it in his pocket.

I freeze when I hear the softest sound of sheets rustling.

"What are you doing in here?"

Philip is sitting up in bed. His voice is eerily quiet and cold as steel.

And he is looking right at us.

CHAPTER TWENTY-SEVEN

B ROCK STANDS SLOWLY and kicks the case back into the closet.

Crimson color is swirling up his neck, but his jaw clenches and he remains standing still. I know what we're both thinking. People have died to make sure this secret stays buried. We might lose more than our jobs if Philip realizes what we are doing.

And then Philip yells for the guard.

Peder appears in half a moment with a panicked-looking Liljan on his heels.

"Get Helene," Philip orders. "The rest of you, stay put."

"Can I help you, sir?" Peder asks.

"I think these two were attempting to steal from me."

Peder returns quickly with Helene, and Eve on her heels. They crowd into the room. I can hardly look at Eve. My cheeks feel like flames.

"I'll ask you one last time," Philip says. He makes a show of pulling free from his blankets. He takes his cane and stands menacingly. "What are you doing in here?"

I meet Eve's eyes, only briefly. Then she breaks her gaze, and discreetly pulls the delicate Vestergaard crest from her neck. She slips it into her pocket.

"Oh," she says, letting out a nervous giggle. "I'm sorry. They came here for me."

I look sharply at her.

Don't do this, Eve, I think. *I don't deserve it.* I bite back tears, and my heart swells to bursting. I can't believe she is still willing to risk a lie for me.

"I lost my necklace just before the . . . accident," she says. "I've looked for it everywhere. I was too scared to come in here myself."

"Why didn't you tell me?" Helene asks. "I would have helped you."

"I was ashamed that I'd lost it. I'm sorry." Eve's face crumples. She's laying it on thick, with just enough fear and misery to be believable. "I was hoping I would find it and you would never have to know I'd been so careless."

I swallow hard and stay very, very still.

"Of course, I'll help you look for it now," Helene says. "It can't have gone far." She draws Eve close to her elbow and looks at both Brock and me. "You may go," she says.

I nod at her and take a quick step toward the door. Thanks to Eve, we've almost made it.

"Wait," Philip says. "I want to make sure that's the truth."

"Why?" Helene asks, her voice sharp. "I take my daughter at her word." Her eyes flicker brightly with warning.

"It isn't your *daughter* I distrust," Philip says coolly. He looks to me and Brock. "Please turn out your pockets."

Brock blinks rapidly, his pupils dilating. He takes a deep breath as Peder steps toward us.

There is a long pause between us.

"Yes. All right," I say stiffly.

I step forward first, putting myself between Brock and the others. Slowly, stalling, I reach into my pockets. I clutch the fabric inside and turn it out.

The only thing that falls out is one of Liljan's candies. It hits the rug at my feet and rolls toward Eve.

The guard grunts.

"Now you," Philip says, pointing at Brock.

I swivel to look at Brock. There is a haunting fear in his eyes. The look of someone who is about to lose the very last thing he has.

There's nothing I can do, and I'm standing nearly close enough to reach out and touch him.

Brock slowly puts his hand in each of his pockets and turns them out, one by one. Vest. Jacket. Pants. When he gets to the final pocket, the one where he tucked the ring, he pauses.

I have to do something.

I close my eyes.

I have to.

I picture the ring in his pocket, the hem of his sleeve where it hits along his wrist. I've never used magic on anything without physically touching it before.

There's no time. I can't let him get caught.

I call to my magic with desperate urgency, feel it lighting through my veins as if I've left a trail of kerosene, followed by a prickling of cold. I can almost sense the stitches in Brock's shirt, like feeling along a banister in the dark. I concentrate as though I'm filling my lungs with as much air as they can hold, as if I'm preparing to dive into deep, deep water. I think of Ingrid. How deep she must have dived that night she convinced the men of a lie, to get her magic to do something it had never done before.

I try not to think of what it cost her.

"Well?" Peder urges. "Get on with it."

I'm flirting with a magic I've never gone near before, going deeper and deeper into freezing, dark water, hoping I won't go so far that I can't find my way back to the surface. I swiftly unknot the threads of Brock's shirt and swoop them down to stitch around the ring. It's an unearthly feeling of ice and fire at the same time—of lungs bursting and burning within me while my skin feels the outer icy cold of the deep.

I'm kicking toward the surface, hoping I'm going to make it in time. With one last burst, I pull the stitches tight to hide the ring up in the hem of his sleeve. A ripple of seams, concealing treasure.

Then I force my eyes open and it's like breaking the surface and taking a gasping breath of air again. My veins suddenly ache with an icy cold that throbs and hurts, the way my head and the roof of my mouth do when I eat ice cream too quickly.

Brock pulls out his hand and shows the empty fabric of his last pocket.

I did it.

Philip twitches his fingers with irritation toward the door, and the false ring I planted on him shifts to turn its jeweled face downward. He looks at the ring for half a moment, and I hope he merely attributes its loose fit to the weight he's lost since the attack.

Everyone standing in the room parts for us like a curtain.

I'm shaking when I take my first step toward freedom, and my leg starts to buckle beneath me. Liljan's hand bolts out to steady my elbow before I can fall.

"Wait," Eve says. She draws herself up and looks unflinchingly at Philip. "I think you owe them an apology. Did you know that this is the very servant who saved your life?"

The room stills and I force myself to meet Philip's gaze. His skin is sallow, but his eyes and mind look strong. "Please forgive the accusation," he says quietly. "You can understand, after my recent attack why my suspicions might be heightened."

I nod and Brock, looking shaken, mutters something vaguely unintelligible. The guard, Eve, and Liljan leave the room. But Helene holds up her hand, blocking my way out the door.

"Philip, you'll remember that you are a guest in this house. I'll handle my own staff from now on," Helene says, and her voice cuts like steel.

He gives her a smile and nod that teeter on patronizing and

she leaves. But when I follow Brock out the door, Philip lashes out and catches my wrist to stop me.

"I don't know what the two of you were playing at," he says. The fake ring slides down his finger again. Beneath it, I see another scar left from an old burn. "But I am watching you."

I wrench my wrist away and try not to run. Shaking, I keep my head lowered and hurry down the maze of stairs, careful to keep distance from Brock and Liljan so I can have a moment alone.

I pause in the chill of the stairwell to the servants' quarters, gathering my courage. My heart pounds as I count to three and peek under the sleeve of my uniform.

The skin there is smooth and clear as a blank sheet of paper.

I let my sleeve fall and breathe out a shocked exhale and a prayer of thanks. That was a fool's errand, too close for comfort from every angle.

I fumble with the latch into the kitchen, trip over my feet, and collapse onto the bench. My muscles begin to tremble with shivers. "You're meant to meet the rest of them upstairs," Dorit says in a low voice. "But you look positively ashen, dearie. Tea?"

"Water," I croak.

"Damned stew," Dorit says. "I should have made him a pie instead. If he'd eaten the whole thing, this never would have happened."

"It's my own fault, Dorit," I say, my teeth chattering.

I fumble with the glass and knock it over. Dorit hurriedly rights it and pours a drink for me. I need to eat something. I don't feel right. I focus on drinking down the cool, clear water, one gulp at a time.

Brock suddenly appears at my elbow. "How the hell did you do that, up there?" he says, taking the seat beside me. "Are you all right?" His eyes are soft with concern. He looks at me with sincere tenderness, the way you might look at a younger sister.

The way he once looked at Ivy.

"I owed you a favor," I rasp. "And I always return what I borrow."

"Thank you," he says. He gently touches my elbow before tucking his fingers into the hidden folds of his sleeve.

He rips the blackened ring from the stitches and holds it out to me.

I'm reaching for it when Liljan appears in the doorway. My stomach turns at the look on her face.

"I'm sorry, Marit," Jakob says behind her, pushing his spectacles up.

"That stone isn't glass," Liljan says softly. She comes and puts her hand on mine. "We were wrong."

I was wrong. But I can't be. It made so much sense. It tied all the threads together. My thoughts set off like an avalanche. "You're sure?" I ask, my head suddenly splitting.

"It does look *exactly* like the one from your father," Liljan says. "Just darker. It has a similar crystalline structure under the microscope. But it's not glass, and it's not a ruby."

Then . . . what now?

My vision is doubling, and the disappointment is so weighted it's crushing. The king is coming in less than a week, and I have nothing for him. No proof of wrongdoing. Maybe because there wasn't any to begin with. Maybe I was just wrong. Maybe I've been wrong since the very beginning.

"I need a moment," I say. The greenhouse is where I want to go, where it is warm and feels like life and hope and safety. I stumble down the withered corridor and push open the door. The light is warm and golden-green, like being beneath the surface of water when the sunlight hits it. I close my eyes and breathe in the scent, trying to calm my heart, my thoughts. I was so sure I was right.

Jakob comes in behind me.

"Marit, are you okay?" He is beside me in two steps. He touches my elbow, and it sends that glittering spark up my arm. But when I turn toward him, his hand pulls at my sleeve, brushing it back just slightly.

My heart freezes.

Did I see something there now?

Magic flows like water.

"I was so worried," he says, and he gathers me into his arms as if to make sure I'm really there, and I can feel his heart beating so hard inside his chest. "And it made me realize that I have to tell you something."

Magic freezes like ice.

I smell the snow-fir scent of his breath, his skin. I'm so close to tasting him, what I've wanted for so long.

Use too much and it costs . . .

He bends to brush his lips against my cheek.

. . . a pretty price.

With a shy, sweet smile, Jakob hesitates, then leans to kiss me again, just at the corner of my mouth.

Marit, Ingrid says clearly in my ear . . . *I think I went too far.*

And instead of kissing Jakob, I flinch.

He tenses and draws back from me as swiftly as if I've burned him. "Sorry," he breathes immediately. "I thought—I'm sorry." He takes another step away to give me space, a mortified flush flooding his face.

I want to explain myself, to tell him he wasn't wrong, he didn't misread the signals, but all I can think about right now is what I might have seen at the hint of my wrist.

"Here. Take this," I say. I fumble with the blackened ring in my pocket and shove it into his hands without looking at him.

"Marit," he says gently, and when I glance into his eyes, I can see how much I've hurt him. "Please forgive me." He takes a deep look at my face. "I just—are you certain you're all right?"

"I'm fine," I insist, careful to keep my arms covered and the tears from falling. "Will you look at that ring, please?"

Please tell me that all of this, everything I've just done and given up, hasn't been for nothing.

Brock and Liljan have followed us. They stop, hesitantly, just inside the greenhouse door.

"Is . . . everything all right?" Brock asks, sensing the tension. "Did something happen in here?"

"Why don't you tell me what happened in *there?*" Jakob growls at Brock, taking a step toward him, and his voice has an edge I've never heard before.

I turn my back to them and look up toward the suspended bulbs of glass, the cascading green that swings above our heads, and blink back tears. Because I know what I saw.

When I hear the door finally close behind them, I bite hard on my lip and summon all my courage to look down.

I gently pull back the fabric of my uniform to reveal it. A crystal-blue lace, etched in a delicate pattern beneath my wrists.

The Firn.

CHAPTER TWENTY-EIGHT

I EXAMINE THE WAY MY VEINS have turned a silvery blue beneath my skin. It's advanced Firn, but it hasn't killed me on the spot like it did with Ingrid. Perhaps I stopped just in time. My breathing quickens. It feels like I am seeing my own grave, but someone stopped midway through carving my name on the headstone.

My throat grows tight and thick with tears. I can never use magic again. Not as long as I want to live to see the next morning. That part of me, of my identity, is suddenly and completely lost forever, and its consequences ripple outward beyond what I can even see. I'll have to give up my job at the Vestergaards'. Find another without relying at all on magic to set me apart. I wince anew when I think of Jakob, of Liljan, of Eve ripping the crest from her neck and slipping it into her pocket. Everything I've ever wanted is right here, and I have to leave it all behind.

In the privacy of my workroom, I cover the telltale blue markings by making little pincushion bracelets out of satin and carefully fixing them around my wrists like cuffs. I should go now, tell Jakob and Liljan. But I don't want to voice the horror out loud. Instead I want to curl in on myself, pretend the Firn isn't happening.

"You know, you didn't have to lead him on like that, Marit," Liljan says frostily when I'm changing out of my uniform that night. She pulls a brush down the long, shimmering sheet of her hair.

I pause. "I'm sorry?"

She purses her lips. "My brother. Or is there something happening with you and Brock now?"

"Wh-what?" I sputter. I fight an almost hysterical urge to laugh. *"No."*

"I saw the way you acted with Jakob, and you could have fooled me," she says, tugging her brush through a knot. "I thought you fancied him. He did too." She fixes her eyes on me. For once, they aren't light with mirth. They are set hard, like cooled marble. "You should be more careful, and don't play games with people's hearts next time. Especially my sweet, stupid brother's."

"I—" I begin. "I do care for him." My eyes well up. "Liljan."

With a deep breath, I unpin the satin cuffs and turn my inner wrists toward her.

The noise she makes is a swift cut to the softest parts of me. Her hand flies to her mouth, and the look of anguish on her face makes all my own fear come surging up again. I smother it back down, herd it into place, lock it up.

"You can't tell anyone," I whisper.

"Oh, Marit," she says. She carefully wipes the horror from her face and sets the brush down as if it might shatter.

"Promise you won't say anything," I say, buttoning my cuffs back up and climbing into bed. "I want to be the one to tell Jakob."

She nods. "I'm horrible for yelling at you. Horrid. I really am a vole." She comes and gets into bed with me. I snuggle down into the warmth of the covers, suddenly shivering uncontrollably. She wraps her arms around my shoulders and hugs me.

"What are you going to do?" she whispers. She gently strokes the back of my hair, pulling it out like spun silk. It tugs pleasantly, sending a prickle across my scalp.

"I have to leave," I whisper into my pillow. A wild part of me wants to ask Eve to come with me. I have the money from my father hidden in the straw, enough for a place to live and food for at least a month, until I could find some job that wouldn't require magic. What I could offer wouldn't be anything grand. It wouldn't come close to this house. She'd have to give up ballet, and Helene. All I could offer is me.

I'm never going to ask Eve to make that choice. But in my heart, I wish I could go back to the time when she would still pick me without a second thought.

Later that night, when silvery moonlight shifts along the walls like scales and Liljan has returned to her own bed, I throw on a coat over my nightgown. Liljan stirs but doesn't say anything when I slip out the door with a bundle beneath my arm.

I slink down the stairways and through the maze of the main house. It is the witching hour between days; the house is still and dark. There's a wafting scent of orchids, the distant chime of a grandfather clock. I tap out five low knocks on Eve's door and wait for a long moment. I no longer care about getting caught. There isn't much left of me to lose.

I just care that she opens the door.

My heart quickens with nerves the longer I wait, lacing my fingers together. Would she answer the door if she knew how much was at stake? That I teeter ever closer to the fragile line between being alive and whatever comes next?

Maybe she didn't hear me, I try to tell myself.

But she always hears me.

Realization darkens within me. I run my fingers over the veins in one of my wrists. The skin is thin enough for me to feel the hardened lines beneath it.

I turn away at the exact moment the door cracks open.

She rubs her eyes and peers out, and despite everything else, my heart feels like the first hint of sunrise.

I step inside her room.

"What are you doing here, Marit?" She looks up at the ceiling, down at the pink shells of her fingernails. Anywhere but at me.

"I miss you, Eve," I say simply. I shrug and swallow down the lump in my throat. "I wanted to say thank you for what you did today. And to tell you that I'm sorry."

"You know, Marit," she whispers. She fiddles absently with

her headscarf. "The thing that hurts worst is that the whole time, I thought you came here for me."

I still. "What do you mean?"

"You have some other reason for being here, don't you? Something else you've hidden from me. It's not just to work here; it's not to be near me. It's . . ." Her eyes fill with tears. "What were you doing in Philip's room today?"

My chest feels tight. "I was trying to make sure he didn't have a reason to hurt you." She looks shocked, and I hurry on. "I was wrong, though. About so much. I didn't tell you about it because — well, if everything was fine, then you'd never have to know. You could just . . . be happy."

"How could you think that, Marit?" she asks. "Sometimes it feels as though you want me to choose between you and the Vestergaards. How am I ever supposed to do that?" She rolls her eyes, yet at the same time a tear slips down her cheek. "It's so unfair."

"I'm so sorry," I say. "Everything I did was to try not to hurt you, and I roughed it all up anyway. The truth is that I don't know exactly how I fit here, with you, either. I haven't handled it well. And, if I'm being honest . . ." I say, and take a deep breath, "sometimes I might be the smallest bit jealous of Helene."

"Helene?" Eve asks incredulously.

My face burns with the shame of that truth. "For being able to give you something I couldn't, and for swooping in when I'm the one who loved you and looked after you for so many years."

I swallow. "It's not that I don't want a better life for you. I absolutely do. I just wish that . . . I could have been able to give it to you."

She nods at my hands. "What's that?" she asks, almost shyly.

"Oh," I say. "I made it for you. Your costume for the salon." I pull it out. Tighten my lips in a line. "There's something special in it."

I open the folds of the tutu and show her the small stitches. "It's in Morse, but it's memories. Of you. Of us."

She comes closer and I say, "This one is about how when you were eight, you hid your cooked carrots in the cracks of the floorboards because you said they tasted like rotten pumpkin mush, and when Sare told on you, you stuck one up her nose when she was sleeping."

Eve surprises me when she giggles. "I remember that. I remember when you stood guard for the next few nights and let me fall asleep."

I say, "I solemnly promised to make sure Sare didn't stick a retaliatory carrot up your nose."

"You kept a lot of your promises to me, Marit," Eve says softly.

Those were my favorite moments, when she fell asleep before I did. When stillness and peace fell over her as real as a blanket of fresh snow in those magical, vulnerable moments right before sleep.

Her fingers trace over another set of my silver stitches. *When you were nine, I gave up my designated cup of milk for the month of March so the cook would bake you a cake. I wanted it to be so good for you, but it was dry and crumbly, and the icing was like tar when you gave me a bite of it.*

"I'd forgotten this," she says. Her fingers curl. "But now I'll remember it forever."

"You choked down every crumb of that cake," I say. "You said nothing had ever tasted so good."

She giggles. "It really did taste like tar," she says.

She pats the bed and I tuck her in like I used to, sealing her up in the sheets like a letter in an envelope. But there's one more confession I have to make. There will be no more convenient lies of omission. No matter how painful the truth is to tell.

"Eve, you know that thing that can happen when you use too much magic?"

"The Firn?"

I nod. "I'm going to have to leave this job. I can't stay here and be what Helene needs or wants any longer."

She sits up straight. "Are you in danger?" She takes my hand in hers, and I'm careful to keep my wrists pointing down. "Don't lie to me, Marit."

"I'm not in danger as long as I leave," I say. "And never use magic again."

She looks at me for a long time with her wide, brown eyes. "Marit, you hurt me. And sometimes you do things that you think are giving me cake when really I'm choking on crumbs. But," she says, "you are the family I chose all by myself. My sister, not through blood. And it doesn't matter where you go or what you do. I want you to be in my life. I love you."

I close my eyes. All I've ever wanted was for someone to choose me. But what I wanted all this time was something I already had. I take a deep breath of air as though I've been cut free from a corset. It's the first moment I've felt better since Ivy died.

"Now do the face thing," Eve commands. "Maybe I can hire you to just live here and do this every night." She closes her eyes and whispers, "I have the best dreams on the nights you do it. Maybe you have some sort of sleep magic, too."

I brush her eyebrows with my thumbs, then sweep them over her cheekbones.

"There. I've brushed away anything ugly or bad left over from today," I whisper. "Now go to sleep, and we'll both wake up fresh tomorrow."

Her eyelids flutter just a little, as if she's dreaming. I love the way she smells like violets and the charcoal from her toothpaste and faintly of palm oil.

There's a long moment of silence, and I wonder if she's gone to sleep.

"Honch, honch, honch," she whispers, squinting open one eye, and I hug her close and let my muffled laughs work deep through me like peals of light.

CHAPTER TWENTY-NINE

I N THE MORNING THE BALLROOM overflows with the scent of flowers and lemons and soap. It is steadily turning into a verdant, living courtyard, like spring erupting in the frozen heart of winter. Swaths of plush green moss form a carpet around the gilded wooden stage, and my curtains gush in dark streams of velvet on either side.

I have another dress and two uniforms to finish for the salon, but at least I got them halfway done before the Firn. It will be close, but if I work hard, I can complete them by hand. I promised Eve two things before I left: I'd stay through the salon to see her dance for the king — and I wouldn't use another drop of magic. They are promises I fully intend to keep.

With nerves fluttering in my stomach, I climb the stairs to Jakob's attic nook. I find him curled over his desk, poring over historic treatments for diseases such as cowpox and smallpox.

"Do you want to take a look at what I found?" he asks, his voice strong and friendly. He gives me an easy smile, to show that there aren't any hard feelings between us; that even after what happened in the greenhouse, we can still be friends.

I nod and he shows me the blackened ring. Yet my pulse warms and quickens at this nearness to him, confirming to myself that friendship isn't what I want.

"I returned the real ring last night. But this one," he says, holding it up to the light. "This blackened one—it's almost as if it's been burned."

Something jogs in my memory. "When I was stitching Philip's wounds, there were all these scars on his body," I say slowly. "Old ones, new ones. Marks that almost looked like burns."

"Were they from whoever attacked him that day?" Jakob's brow furrows. "Or from something else?"

"The new ones could have been. Maybe. But what of the old ones?"

"From the war?"

I hesitate. Perhaps that's all they are.

"Marit," he says. "Dr. Holm accepted my apprenticeship. I'm leaving my job at the Vestergaards'."

Though I expected this, it still feels like taking a swift, silent blow. I knew Jakob was going to leave. I know that I have to, too. And I realize now, that ever since I was six years old, broken-hearted during those first years at the Mill and not wanting to get close to anyone who could leave me, how fatalistic I've been about my future. Or when I was stuck at Thorsen's, disbelieving there was going to be anything other than a life of caution and loneliness for me. But now that the Firn is actually threatening my future, I want to fight for it more. "When will you leave?" I ask, careful to keep my voice nonchalant.

"Next week. I'll stay through the salon and then go." He looks at me and gently adds, "And it's possible Liljan is coming with me."

I still don't have the answers I want. I am starting to accept that I might never know what my father sought to tell me. Trying to find out almost got *me* killed too. But what a brief, bright moment I have had here—a sweet taste of home that has both strengthened and weakened me. It gave me friendship and love and the Firn, and I'm going to leave here with all those things still in me.

I don't regret it.

"I—" I start to say.

But there's a knock on the half-closed door. "Hello," Brock says, pushing it open. He looks between us. "Marit, can I show you something?"

The words die on my lips. I bite back a sigh. "Yes," I say. Jakob gives us a smile that seems distant, as if he's already not here anymore. He pockets the blackened ring and ducks out the door.

My heart feels as though it's blooming thorns, but I turn my attention to Brock.

"What did you find?"

"I know we don't really believe the stones are glass magic anymore, but I'd already started putting out word to the other servants in the area."

"And?" I ask.

"There's no pattern. The missing are young and old, male and female. They went missing on different days, in different places."

"And their magic?"

"All different kinds. Random, even seemingly useless magic, sometimes—like smoothing wrinkles with a touch, or making snow."

"But they *did* all have magic?" I ask.

He nods. "The police didn't pay much attention over the years when it was just servants going missing, one at a time, and no bodies. But now they can work on volume. Now that they have a body, and Philip's testimony, they might finally start paying attention. Maybe something good will come out of this after all. Maybe we will have stopped someone else from being killed." He meets my eyes. "And then at least Ivy's death won't be for nothing."

"I hope she gets justice too," I say softly. "So Philip *was* telling the truth about the attack."

"Is it wrong to feel a little disappointed? Because there's still something I really don't like about that man," Brock says, and I bite back a dark laugh, because I feel the same way.

My eyes fall on the silver stripe of Jakob's skates, lodged between his heavy books. "Brock—can you do something else for me?"

"Anything," he says.

At the picture in my mind, I bend to touch the winking blades and smile to myself.

⁂

With two days left, the Vestergaards are in considerably good shape to host the salon and welcome the king. I haven't told anyone yet, but after the salon, I'm going to Copenhagen to seek employment, whether it's as a dish maid or laundress. Something without magic. Something that keeps me close enough to see Jakob and Liljan and Eve on occasion.

Maybe to even see her rise through the ranks of the Royal Danish Ballet.

Liljan stays up with me late into the night, helping me sew any inner parts of Eve's salon dinner dress where clumsier, more amateur stitches can be concealed.

"Did you tell Jakob yet?" she asks, pulling the silver thread through the eye of her needle.

"No," I say. I adjust my pincushion cuffs. The Firn hasn't grown or spread since I swore off using magic, and it makes me wonder — if enough time passes — if the Firn could ever fade or dissipate. "But I will tomorrow," I say, as much a promise to myself as to her.

So when I'm sitting in the windowsill of my tiny workroom the next afternoon, and Jakob knocks on the door, my heartbeat starts pattering in my chest like softly falling rain.

I check my reflection in the window glass, smoothing and pinning my wayward hair, and then open the door.

"Hi, Marit," Jakob says. The corners of his mouth twitch slightly when he sees me. "I found something that might be of interest."

In his hands is the thick tome on gemstones he gave me for Christmas.

I move out of the way to let him in. Something like thunder is building low in my abdomen.

He taps his finger on the book. "There is an entry here about a stone that changes color. It happens when it is exposed to light."

"Oh?" I ask. I feel a tug of interest as the pages fall open to a small painting.

"The stone is called proustite. It doesn't seem to have immense value, and as far as I can tell, it isn't attached to any particular myths or legends. But I thought you'd like to see it, just in case."

"Proustite," I say. The image is of a small red stone that looks sort of like my father's. *Sometimes called "ruby silver," proustite is a rare specimen with a vibrant red metallic sheen,* I read. *The stone must be kept hidden away and never displayed, because it darkens a little more with every exposure to light, until eventually, it turns to black.*

A stone that darkens, just like Philip's did.

Jakob's eyes meet mine.

He sets the book gently on the table and turns to leave.

But when his hand is on the doorknob, I say: "Jakob—wait."

He pauses and slowly turns to face me again.

"I think I might be able to help you," I say. I swallow as I fiddle with my wrists, heart hitching. "With your research."

I unbutton the cuffs and tentatively hold out my wrists. And if I ever doubted whether he cared for me, that uncertainty vanishes completely when I see his face. It's raw and painful and devastating, and it tells me more than anything he could ever say.

"Marit," he says, taking a step toward me. His eyes are both dark and bright, and he makes a sound low in his throat. "That makes me—" His hands tighten into fists at his sides. "I promise," he says, through gritted teeth, "I'm not going to stop looking until I've found something that could help you."

Though everything in him is clenched, he comes to take my wrists so gently in his hands and runs the very tips of his fingers along my veins, like mining for ore. The sensation is heady and trills over my skin, lighting every sense of feeling I have.

"I want you to take a sample of it with you," I say quietly. "Before you leave for Dr. Holm's."

Because just like Ivy's death might cause the police to pay more attention to the other missing servants, maybe my misfortune could help someone else too. Misery fights so hard to gain the upper hand, but there's always something left in its gleanings: the seed of something good that ensures despair can never quite win. Sometimes I think about how if I could go back and keep my sister from dying, I would in an instant. And yet, if she hadn't . . . I would never have met Eve, or Liljan, or Jakob, at all.

"I will," Jakob says, and I even manage a slight smile.

"That night when we hid from Nina and you first told me about the mines," I say, remembering us together on the glowing-white ice lake, under a sky lit with glittering stars. "You said you might know someone who can teach me to skate?"

He nods, his fingers leaving my skin.

"How about now?" I ask.

I push away from my workstation. I still have Eve's dress to finish. But this feels like my last chance at something, and I realize how much I want it.

I tilt my head to indicate *follow me* and am careful to keep him an arm's length away as we grab the skates stashed in the attic. The Vestergaard house is thrumming at full tilt with people preparing for the performance tomorrow. Servants below us move in and out of the doors, streaming like ants, carrying furniture and flowers, polishing the front windows.

"Nina's going to kill us if she sees us taking a break," I whisper.

"I'm already leaving," he says. "Nina can't fire me."

Me too, I think. Even if she doesn't know it yet.

Instead of taking Jakob through the kitchen and out to the lake, I lead him to the back door. Toward the greenhouse.

Every nerve in my body is electric, and it's making me lightheaded.

But when we step outside, my worries soften and melt into delight.

Brock's done what I asked him to—everything, and more. Pure white wisteria falls in layers as light as a whisper. The strands dangle like delicate curtains of icicles and lace to shut out the rest of the world.

"Here," I say. I part the wisteria and step into the corridor.

Inside is cool and dim, dizzy and lush with the scent of jasmine. Soft bursts of lavender wisteria drape down to where I can reach up and graze them with my fingers.

"What is this?" Jakob asks. He takes a step forward and slides.

The path in front of us is a smooth, translucent sheen. Brock helped me pour a thin layer of water, which crystallized into ice. Rae will melt it when we're done, and Liljan is doing her best to keep Nina distracted. The lush wisteria tickles my arm. I set down my skates.

"Jakob," I say hesitantly. I take a deep breath. I've been very careful not to let him touch my clothes. Not until I was ready.

I take a gliding step toward him and catch his wrist in my hand. I feel the pulse there quicken, just like it did on Christmas Eve. But this time, I pull his hand toward me and place it lightly on my waist. I feel his whole body tense at the exact moment he reads what I've written.

I'm sorry.

I think about you all the time.

I've sewn the secrets into my petticoats.

Where only he could find them.

I'm scared.

I might be in love with you?

"Marit?" he says hoarsely, and warmth stirs in my body, and

something seeps into my chest and through my arms and legs that feels like pure gold.

I bring my face to meet his and feel the heat of his mouth and the softness of it. The way he smells and tastes, his breath catching, his heart beating hard through his shirt. His spectacles slightly knock against my cheek, and I pull him against me and kiss him deeper, my feet slipping on the ice underneath us. The taste of his breath is cool, like snow and mint. I shiver with that pleasure, the tingle and chill that climbs all the way up my spine to the roots of my hair, that yearning of wanting more. And it feels better than I ever imagined. Even if it's only for this moment, I feel that transcendent crackle I thought I'd never get to feel again.

Magic.

From the corner of my eye there are flowers blooming around us, curling tendrils of lavender and iris and Gallica roses, and I know Brock is somewhere nearby—that this is his way of saying thank you for saving him that day in Philip's room. I smile against Jakob's mouth and he takes my face in his hands. I've never seen him look at anyone the way he's looking at me right now, and I think I'll be able to revisit this moment for the rest of my life. Every time I catch the hint of new flowers blooming their short-lived sweetness into the world. Jakob runs his fingertips over the skin just behind my ears. His touch leaves the most delightful shiver, and my whole body—my breath, and the air just between us—heats to a degree that his spectacles half fog over.

Liljan clears her throat, then parts the curtain and takes a step inside. "You two," she says deviously. "Finally."

"Where in prune's name are you, Marit Olsen?" Nina hollers from inside the house. "Why isn't Eve's dress done yet? Mrs. Vestergaard is going to have my hide, and I'm going to have yours!"

Liljan shrugs apologetically at me. "I bought you as much time as I could."

I pull away from Jakob, not used to feeling his warm body this close to mine.

"Are you sure you have to go?" he says.

"Are you sure *you* do?" I ask.

"Yes. Because I'm going to find you a cure if it's the last thing I do," he whispers into my ear. He straightens the collar of his shirt where I pulled it askew. Then he plucks one of the wisteria bursts and hands it to me.

I'm practically floating when I turn and follow Liljan. I twirl the wisteria stem between my fingers and wonder at what powerful magic humans have—perhaps the most powerful kind of all. That we can set other hearts to bloom and burst the way Brock does to the flowers.

CHAPTER THIRTY

THE NEXT DAY FEELS BITTERSWEET. It means an ending for me and hopefully a beginning for Eve.

I peek through the open ballroom doors so I can see what the space will look like for the king.

Five crystal chandeliers hang in a crisp row from the vaulted ceiling. The wooden floors gleam like a lake of honey, and the walls are gilded with golden vines that intricately intertwine with green living ones. I can hear the running of a fountain some-where, beyond the cushion of lush moss that surrounds the carved wooden stage. Fragrant oranges drip off white-blossomed trees like heavy raindrops. Brock brings in still more greenery, his hands dark with dirt, his arms bursting with frilled scarlet poppies that open to look like the Danish flag. What would take months, perhaps years, to transform has been done in a matter of weeks due to magic.

Eve dances in the midst of it, already in her costume. We fashioned glittering glass pieces that look like gemstones to wrap around her calves on satin laces and catch the light when she moves.

At the far wall, almost out of sight, Peder paces in front of a rich mahogany table. When he moves, I glimpse what he's guarding—a map of Denmark, its land and sea and smattering of islands made entirely from multicolored jewels. Philip, dressed in elegant finery, stoops to inspect the map. The red ring on his finger is gone now.

This time, the stone there is a deep emerald green.

When he catches me looking at him, he stops talking and holds my gaze for a beat too long.

It sends a dank shiver down my spine and I turn away.

To my right, Declan leans toward the massive glass windows, looking up at the clouds. "Snow's coming," he mutters under his breath.

The king is set to arrive at four, and the performance will begin at half past. High-ranking miners will be in the audience to assist with Philip's ceremonial presentation of gifts, and then they will all retire for dinner together. I've made the servants new uniforms just for this occasion. The ones who will be visible and serving, such as Jakob, Nina, Liljan, and Brock, will wear the highest quality black fabric that sheens when it catches the light.

I make the rounds, delivering the uniforms to their rooms.

"Nervous?" Liljan asks, taking her livery and pulling it over her head.

I nod. "You?"

She shakes her head, reaching to fasten the little pearled buttons at her neck.

"I know it's just a uniform, but it is gorgeous," I say.

"I don't look like a penguin?"

"No!" I snort, helping her with an intricate braid. "What's a stunningly beautiful bird?"

In the mirror's reflection, with her straw-blond hair, she looks a lot like Ingrid.

"A flamingo," she says.

"I say phoenix."

"I'll try not to burst into flame."

"Or drop a mess on anyone."

"If I do, I'll aim for Nina."

I giggle.

"Good luck," she says, and gives me a kiss on the cheek.

I weave down the stairs, carrying the final uniform to Malthe's room. I raise my hand to knock, but there are lowered voices coming from within the bedroom. I hesitate. And then I hear a voice I recognize.

"I don't have to tell you how big tonight is," Philip says quietly. "This has to go off without a hitch."

I hold my breath and lean closer.

"Are you going to tell her tonight?" Malthe asks. "All of it?"

There's a pause, long enough for me to wonder if they have stopped talking.

Tell her *tonight,* I think. There are only two *her*s they could be referring to.

My stomach knots. Helene?

Or do they mean Eve?

"I don't know what is going to happen this evening," Philip finally murmurs. "Are you ready for anything?"

I carefully press my ear flat up to the door. And then there is a sound.

It might easily be nothing more than a trunk lock clicking shut.

Or it could be the cock of a pistol.

I freeze.

Surely Philip wouldn't try anything dangerous tonight, not with the king of Denmark coming. Not with his heavily armed royal guards crawling through every room in the house.

Still, I feel a wave of nausea. Unease.

I hang the uniform on the doorknob and step backwards, as quietly as I can. My foot causes the stair to creak. I'm not sure exactly what I overheard. Perhaps I should go and find Helene. But what would I say? I don't want to falsely alarm her—or worse, do anything to upset Eve right before she performs the biggest dance of her life. I hurry to my room, looking for Liljan, but she isn't there. I find Jakob's attic still and empty. On his desk are four glass vials, meant for samples of my blood.

It was probably nothing, what I overheard. Just my imagination leaping to conclusions and being overly suspicious, especially where Philip is concerned.

I return to my workroom and pick up the last gown I'll probably ever make for Eve. I have only the final touches left, maybe a quarter of an hour's worth of work—enough time to finish for the dinner tonight. But my foot is tapping, and I feel tighter and jumpier than usual. That conversation has unnerved me.

We all just have to get through tonight, I tell myself—and then I accidentally stick my finger with the needle.

A small droplet of blood beads, and I watch in slow motion as it falls onto Eve's dress.

Blood.

There is blood on Eve's lace.

I swear and quickly dab at the spot, but I manage only to make it worse. I take a breath. Liljan can fix this. I just have to find Liljan, and she'll make it look as if this never happened. But then I am hit with a strange thought. An advanced case of Firn that exists in a living body has to be fairly rare. It's possible that my blood is actually more valuable than the dress it fell on. I promised Jakob he could study the Firn in this state, to help him find a cure. I bite my lip. If I really did overhear something important between Philip and Malthe—if there's a chance that anything will go terribly wrong tonight—I might actually use my magic. If I am brave enough, if it means protecting Eve. But then I'd fill my blood with Firn and lose this opportunity.

I stand.

Maybe, just to be safe, Jakob should take my blood now.

I find him in Brock's room, wearing the suit I made and measured to fit him like a glove. The cut is perfect, and he's devastating in it. His lip curls into a suggestive smile when he sees me, and for a moment, my stomach dips. I gesture for him to follow me.

"What are we doing up here?" he asks, grinning when I lead him to the attic.

I close the door behind us. "Actually," I tell him, "I want you to take that blood sample now."

His smile fades as I unbutton my cuffs. "Are you sure?" he asks.

"I have a strange feeling about tonight," I say. I have that same twinge of anticipation I had at the Mill the day Eve was adopted. That foreboding sense that something is going to happen. "You should do it now. Just . . . in case."

"All right," he says cautiously. He takes one of my wrists in his hand. Finds a fleam with a sharp-looking blade, then swoops to brush his lips over my skin. My heartbeat spikes, and there is a trilling feeling left by his fingertips. "I'm going to breathe the vein. This will hurt a little," he says apologetically. I blink and look away, forcing my eyes to the tome on gemstones. I hid it here last night to keep it safe from Nina's prying, and now I look again at the image of the small reddish stone Jakob thought resembled Philip's.

Proustite.

The caption says: *The unique design that gives proustite its unusual color and value is the very same thing that leads to its destruction.*

That's funny, I think as Jakob finishes. Proustite sounds so much like magic. The thing that makes it valuable is the very same thing that destroys it.

Jakob puts gentle pressure on my arm and then bandages it,

and his eyebrows quirk with such adorably intense concentration as he fastens the pin that I pull him to me and kiss him, and he makes a pleasant sound of surprise. Behind us, the door opens and I hear an exaggerated throat clearing. "Is this going to happen *every* time I find you?" Liljan asks, rolling her eyes. "Mrs. Vestergaard is looking for you," she says to Jakob. "And—" She pauses. "Did you know Dr. Holm was planning to come today?"

Jakob peers out the portal window. "No. What is he doing here?"

Outside, people are starting to arrive. Their carriages stream down the drive, through the falling snow.

"Marit, here. Eat this," Jakob says, digging out a biscuit from a stash within a wicker basket. "Do you feel all right? I can get you some water."

"No, you go ahead," I say.

He pauses to give me a sweet smile at the door.

"Jakob?" I ask. "Just be careful tonight."

"You too," he says. And then he's gone.

I finish carefully rolling my sleeve down my arm. There's a thought brushing up against the back of my mind. I look again at the book in front of me. Hesitate, and shut it.

I pick up a glass vial of my blood—my blood that is valuable, because of the Firn in it.

As the blood swirls and settles, the light catches it. Out of the corner of my eye, the vial almost seems to shimmer.

Those miners were murdered.

To cover something up.

I stop short. I've watched the way Eve's crystal grows in its glass jar, binding itself together. That crystal has built up steadily over time. Like love and hate do. Like the jewels in the mines do.

Like the Firn has inside of me.

The mines are costing Danish lives, my father wrote. He desperately wanted the king to see the mines with his own eyes, he said, or more people would die.

Hanne's voice echoes in my head. *Other servants and workmen, just like Ivy, have gone missing.*

They were all servants.

Servants with magic.

Realization is opening inside me like a hundred flowers in the night.

With trembling hands, I open the vial and drip a few droplets of blood onto a piece of glass, like I've seen Jakob do before. It takes much longer than it should, because my fingers are clumsy.

Perhaps I was closer than I realized when I guessed there was a massive web of deception around the Vestergaard mines.

But perhaps the truth is actually even more horrible than I dared imagine.

I push the sample under the microscope, and when the image sharpens, I gasp.

My blood flows crimson around tiny splinters of crystal, as if someone took a sledgehammer to my father's stone and shattered it into a million glittering little pieces.

The revelation hits me like a fist coming through a glass window.

Hell's bells.

The answer to my father's riddle was right in front of me.

No—it was *inside* me, all along.

Every jewel that built the Vestergaards' massive fortune—every one that glitters from the heads and necks of Danish royals across Europe, that Philip wears in his rings—was made with magic.

Or rather . . . made *of* magic.

The jewels aren't glass, like I feared.

They are Firn.

CHAPTER THIRTY-ONE

Philip
The Day of the Salon: January 30, 1867
Vestergaard Manor

THE SNOW IS BEGINNING TO FALL hard and fast as the chimes ring through the house.

I straighten my cuff links, each one set with a gemstone, and answer the door.

Dr. Holm is standing outside, the snow collecting around his boots.

"Philip," he says. "You're looking much better."

I smile. My oldest friend. From that first night in the morgue, to how far we've come tonight.

"Welcome back, Tønnes," I say, and step aside to let him in.

CHAPTER THIRTY-TWO

Marit
The Day of the Salon: January 30, 1867
Vestergaard Manor

FOR A LONG MOMENT I close my eyes and let the realization crash over me. The horror of what this means is like a growing dark wave, and I take a few deep breaths so I won't faint. The snow falling outside has kicked up and is blowing sideways with a shrill wind. I fumble to cap the vial again and quickly snake down the stairs, through the corridors.

The house swirls with servants, frenetic as the snow falling outside.

"Has it turned to a blizzard?" Dorit asks, looking out the window in disbelief. The kitchen around her is set with glistening pastries and golden brown birds, steaming copper pots and explosions of flour.

The king is coming.

The miners are coming.

The chimes ring out from the front door, and the clock strikes half past three.

No, I realize.

The miners are already *here*.

"Move," Nina tells me briskly. She, too, glances at the flurrying snow. "Lara, bring out every candle you can find and make sure there are stacked cords of firewood near every fireplace."

Out of habit, I reach for my father's stone in my pocket and then flinch back when I realize what I've been touching all along.

"Where's Jakob?" I ask. When no one answers, I turn and run through the underground corridor.

I silently open the door to the upstairs.

The plush rug sinks beneath my feet like crimson-colored moss.

Beyond the enormous ballroom windows, the world is swirling with white. A fire burns bright and hot in the marble fireplace, and there are flickering flames lit in the sconces and the candelabra set on the table. Inside the ballroom, it is a warm oasis, a Garden of Eden blooming right in the middle of a blizzard.

I wait in the shadows. Across the room, Liljan is fussing over Eve's costume, fixing a blossom to the fluttering edges of her skirt and dyeing it to match the glacial blue. The miners mill around in the space between us, dressed in brimmed silk hats and the finest doeskin pantaloons. The room buzzes with a nervous energy.

They all keep stealing glances at the empty chair.

The one left for our king.

"Snow is coming down thick out there," one of the miners says. Gemstones flash on his timepiece, and when he sheds his coat, a peek inside reveals several more jewels, glinting in a rainbow of colors. The sight of them makes my stomach turn to lead. "Can't see a meter in front of you," he says, smiling as he hands his coat to Signe.

When he turns, I glimpse the scarred skin on his cheek. It is in the shape of a fishhook.

My heart squeezes like a fist.

I crouch and pretend to examine a curtain hem, then tuck myself into a hidden space among the fern fronds. Jakob is here, standing next to Dr. Holm.

What are we going to do? I think. If we try to flee, the only place we can go is out into the snow. We can't all fit into the carriages, and if there's any chance of this secret getting out, the miners will kill us on the spot. I picture Ivy lying dead in the snow.

Ivy, and all those other magical servants who went missing over the years. A chill snakes down my spine. We're worth much more dead to these miners than we are alive.

Philip tightens his tie and clears his throat. "Helene?" he says. He's dressed in a fitted dark tailcoat and white cravat, his hair oiled and slicked back. At his call, Helene turns around slowly. "I'd like a private word before the king gets here," Philip says.

Jakob shakes hands with Dr. Holm and excuses himself. I whisper his name when he passes, but he doesn't hear. I press myself farther into the shadows. I'm not leaving Eve alone with all of them. Even from across the room, I hear her nerves in her anxious giggle. She sways a little, as if she's lightheaded.

"Are you all right?" Liljan asks her, reaching an arm out to steady her.

"Eve," Helene says. "If you wish to change your mind, it's all right. You don't have to do this."

"I'm fine," Eve says, brushing away their concern. "I think I'd like some water."

Liljan says, "I'll take her, ma'am."

Helene hesitates. "Go on," she says. "Have her eat a handful of nuts and dates to settle her nerves."

In that moment, I want nothing more than to make a run for it. To grab Eve and plunge out into the blizzard—perhaps even confront the king on the road as he rides in. The realization dawns on me that his guards probably wouldn't let me within five meters of his carriage. Would they even listen?

I stay put, my unease mounting.

"Helene, perhaps your guard would like to give us a moment to discuss sensitive business?" Philip asks.

Peder looks to Helene questioningly.

She looks back at him, thinking for a long moment.

"No," she says steadily. "I'd prefer he stay."

"Very well."

Philip strides past me to close the doors to the ballroom. He makes sure the latch holds tight. I shrink back as far as I possibly can. If he catches me, after what happened in his bedroom . . . I shudder.

Now I am trapped here. And for the first time, I realize how many of the miners appear to be armed.

One by one, they rise and place blue velvet cases on the table in front of Philip. He walks along, his shoes clicking on the wooden floor, and snaps up the lids for inspection. The first holds hollowed-out pinks with glittering edges as sharp as knives. Gold-tinted teals. Apricot crystals that look as though they're caramelizing. I fight off a wave of nausea at the sight. Perhaps each magic makes its own beautiful color. Perhaps that's how you know what sort of power is waiting inside it.

"Helene, I think tonight's events will warm the king's view toward Eve's performance considerably," Philip says. He gestures to the table. "Tonight we will present the royals with this tiara for Princess Alexandra. A necklace for Queen Louise. A timepiece for Crown Prince Frederick. A scepter for the king, and a ring for George, in Greece, with coronets and badges to come for the young Princess Thyra and Prince Valdemar."

"I didn't realize we were bribing the royal family into forcing the ballet's hand," Helene says. Her voice is like a tightly coiled wire. "I don't think that will make things especially easier for Eve."

"Oh, of course it won't be anything as explicit as that," Philip assures her. "But I think they'll be willing to exert their influence wherever they can on our behalf, after tonight. Because we're about to increase the impact of that influence considerably."

"I'm afraid I don't know what you mean, Philip," Helene says. She stands, the train of her violet skirt rustling. She seems as poised as ever, but I see the way her fingers are tightening on the chair.

"I don't want to catch you off-guard tonight and have your surprise on full display to the king. But . . ." Philip says. He extends a brooch to her like a peace offering. It's a dark blood red, with a pin that's as silver-sharp as my needles. "You should know that these are not just any jewels."

Helene hesitates. She takes the brooch from him. Examines it between her long, delicate fingers.

My heart flutters like a torn kite caught between sky and branches.

She really doesn't know.

"These jewels are quite like ballet, actually," Philip says. "Both are things of beauty that hide an incredible strength. Please," he urges. "Put it on." She carefully pierces the pin through the satin of her dress, not taking her eyes from him the entire time.

Philip smiles at her. He gestures to the largest piece on the table: the map made out of jewels showing Denmark.

"This performance tonight is about much more than the future of ballet, of course. It's about the very future of Denmark. It's about magic," he says. "At our fingertips."

He snaps his fingers.

Instantly, a flame appears between them.

Helene gasps and takes an instinctive step forward.

He rubs the flame out.

"Think of this, Helene," he says, watching her reaction. "Queen Louise is playing a strategy game with the marriages of her children, placing them across the nations to help Denmark." He trails a hand across the map made of gemstones. "Denmark is not a Great Power, but we are in bed, quite literally, with all the other Great Powers. And now—with these jewels—we will no longer be a weak, symbolic spouse, bankrupt and frail."

Helene is still looking at the place where the flame appeared between Philip's fingers. "Are you saying that there is magic in those jewels?" she whispers.

Philip nods, a smile cracking across his face. "What we have is not the ugly, brute strength wielded on the battlefield, but a beautiful, quiet strength to be wielded behind the closed doors of those gilded rooms. Sometimes a small show of power displayed at just the right time—a little magic, to enhance either a favor or a threat—can swing a negotiation in the direction we want." I think of the way I poured magic into Eve's tutu that day at Thorsen's, using every little advantage that might sway the decision in her favor. I close my eyes.

Philip continues. "Perhaps even the whispers of the magic that the Danes now seem to possess will be enough to deter larger aggressors. Or perhaps we will someday harvest enough magic like this that our soldiers and armies will be invincible. But for now, we will arm our royals with jewels in their strategic places, and a quiet strength at that level might do more than heavy guns or machinery or boots on the battlefield. It could be that small difference or advantage that changes the future of entire countries—that can spare or wipe out generations."

"Why didn't you ever tell me about this?" Helene says in a low voice. "Why now?"

"There was some uncertainty as to how you'd react," Philip admits. "Now seemed like a good time to ensure that your reaction would be contained. You have a lot to gain this evening. I've done all the work, giving the king jewels to secure access and trust. Tonight he'll find out how much they are actually worth. You can understand why this all must remain highly secret."

She stays silent.

"Denmark has been humiliated step by step over the past fifty years. Our land has been chipped away from us, bit by bit. Think of what influence this could have, Helene. This royal family is a tree with branches spreading strategically into a dynasty across Europe and Russia, with magic wielded around their necks as glittering gems. Suddenly, Denmark is not a weak, dying nation. It instantly becomes one of the most powerful nations in the world."

I hold my breath.

Helene is thinking, the pulse jetting beneath her ear. Her voice is quiet and betrays the slightest tremor. "Philip, where did these jewels come from?"

"From the mines, Helene," he says easily. "Some stones come into existence with magic inside them. The same way it is with people. Where else could they come from?"

She studies him and doesn't answer, surrounded in a room of all men, who are covered head to toe with jewels.

I think of Helene pouring the sugar into the glass jar, showing Eve how to form a complex structure from the tiniest seed.

"Is this going to be a problem, Helene?" Philip asks. The miners all stare her down. "You employ servants utilizing magic around you every day. It would seem you are already at peace with the use of magic for your own personal benefit."

"You'll forgive me if I need a moment to consider what all of this means," Helene says, her poise returning. She still looks suspicious, as if she's trying to figure out something that she's missing. "I'm just not certain why Aleks never told me about this before."

As the clock strikes four, the six miners and Dr. Holm look to Philip for direction. Half are reaching into their pockets for some sort of magic to hold in their hands. Only this time, I don't see dazzling beauty or riches when I look at their jewels. I see danger and power, threats and blood.

The king is due to appear at any moment.

Helene has to know the entire truth before that happens. I am just a servant. No one is going to listen to me. But they might listen to *her,* if she can be reached. If she chooses to do the right thing.

Courage, I think, steeling myself. Courage like Ingrid had, to stand up to these men.

Her name is in my heart as I step from the shadows, the light cutting my face like a piece of glass.

"Helene," I say, relishing the startled gasps I cause when I step out from the ferns. I hold my vial of blood aloft to catch the light —a fire of my own, sparking between my fingers.

"Everyone here is lying."

CHAPTER THIRTY-THREE

Philip

THAT SEAMSTRESS GIRL. The one who stitched me back together, and then I caught her snooping in my room. She's going to ruin everything.

"What is she talking about, Philip?" Helene asks.

"Those jewels aren't from the mines," the seamstress continues steadily. She takes another step forward and holds out a glass vial of blood as though it's a torch. Her eyes blaze. "They've killed people and mined their blood for Firn. Those stones are magic because they came from *people* with magic."

Helene's eyes are growing wide with disbelief as she turns to face me.

"Philip," she says, and swallows. "Tell me that isn't true."

It takes me back to that night in the morgue, with my handkerchief pressed to my nose.

"Tønnes . . . is it wrong?" I'd asked. My eyes flick to him now, then to the door.

This can still be salvaged. If I can get Helene to see reason.

Magic.

We all use magic in one way or another.

Everyone is complicit. Some of us just bear a little more guilt than others.

"Listen to me, Helene," I say calmly, as if I'm speaking to a frightened animal. "This discovery we made saved the mines. They weren't going to last much longer with just limestone—and no one would have wanted those jewels if they knew where they really came from. We only took Firn from people who were already long dead."

At the beginning, anyway.

Everything started off so small, so simply.

It was the perfect storm when Tønnes brought me to the morgue that night. He often apprenticed there after hours, to learn anatomy and help him study to be a doctor—a secret arrangement not strictly legal. But that night, a tree fell onto a man with Firn in his veins. Firn advanced enough to have crystallized. No one knew he had magic, or else the man would have gone straight to the cremator instead. What remained, when Tønnes washed the blood away, were tiny crystals. Magic —crystallized magic—glittering like the shrapnel of gemstones.

And Tønnes came to me, his old friend. Because what better way to hide the discovery of magic crystallized into gemstones than in a mine?

I had hesitated, with that handkerchief in front of my nose. The same way she's hesitating now.

"It's their own Firn that kills them," I continue. "It's no good to them once they're dead. But *we* are alive. And this plan of ours could help keep many other people alive. Many others," I say, my confidence growing. "Perhaps we could also study the Firn in the meantime. Perhaps we could even find a way to help them."

That's what Tønnes said to me, that night at the morgue. It was enough to convince me then. Of course, that's not how things turned out.

My eyes twitch nervously toward the clock.

I need to get this under control, and now.

"He's still lying!" the seamstress cries. "Dr. Holm published false research that said the Firn was ice. He didn't want to help us. He wanted to make sure we never found out the truth."

Damn, I think, tightening my fist. I exchange a meaningful look with the miner closest to the seamstress. He takes a step toward her.

"*Think,* Helene," the seamstress pleads. "Think when you came across Philip and Ivy. You never saw another attacker because there never was one. Philip killed her for her magic and she fought back."

"Did Aleks know about this?" Helene's voice shakes. She looks me straight in the eyes. "Tell me that he didn't know this."

He didn't. But I think he must have suspected something wasn't right.

That's why he left the mines solely to her.

I can see it in her eyes, that she is coming to the same conclusion.

"He asked me not to sell his shares to you," she says slowly. "Ever."

I hid it all from Aleks. The war hero. He would never have approved. And he was too distracted with Helene to notice.

Because Tønnes kept bringing the bodies to the mines, even after he wasn't working at the morgue anymore. Somewhere along the way his reasoning went from "They were already dead" to "They were almost dead" to "They were probably going to die anyway."

And for a while, that was enough.

I swallow.

By the time I realized that he was actually *killing* them for their Firn—seeking them out to harvest their Firn into jewels —I was in too deep. And so were the mines.

Helene is stalling for time now, but she's afraid. She's outnumbered, even with that seamstress and guard here. I see her shaking under her careful poise, see it in the quivering ends of her hair. I remember watching her on the stage, with Aleks next to me. She defeated him.

She will not defeat me.

Snow is falling heavily outside. I glance at the clock. A quarter of an hour past when the king was due to arrive. Where is he?

"Every single jewel we've sold has blood on it," Helene says, gasping. "Does each one represent a life? There are thousands of sales in the Vestergaard records." She chokes on her own voice. "Hundreds of lives in this room alone." The jewels in the map glitter ominously. Helene's eyes and voice harden as she makes her choice. "I will not be part of it."

"This is for Denmark," I hiss. "People give up their lives for the good of the country all the time. That's what war is; that's what a draft is. My father was willing to do it, and Aleks, and I was too. Magical people are a resource this country—this *house* —runs on. You cannot pretend you are not doing the same thing. You use them for the power they bring you, even if it kills them. Magic is the very future of Denmark."

Helene tenses at the booming crack of a knock on the front door.

The time for reasoning and negotiation is up. "I have guards too, Helene," I say urgently under my breath. "Hidden within the king's own regiment. If you choose to breathe a word of this, I'll kill Eve in front of all of you tonight and make it look like an accident. I swear it to you on Aleks's grave."

Her eyes are lit with fire. "He's rolling over in it in disgrace," she spits.

"Your integrity, or Eve's life. You decide which is worth more to you," I say, and at my nod, the miners reach for the stones that hold the sort of magic that can cause harm. All it will take is for us to hold the light of a flame in front of the jewels for just a moment, long enough for them to warm. It wasn't such a stretch to compare the Firn to ice, after all. The heat seems to melt the magic, making it flow right into the body. *Sometimes,* I think, remembering the scars on my body, *they have to get hot enough to burn.*

I whirl to face Peder and say: "You're outnumbered. Don't

be a fool. Keep the seamstress contained, or I'll kill Helene and then you."

I accompany Helene to answer the knock, and we stand together, my arm firmly on her elbow.

The front door swings open.

"Hello?" she says, fixing a smile on her face.

There's a single courier standing outside. Behind him, the drive is blinding white, with snowdrifts already settling halfway up the carriage wheels.

"His Majesty King Christian IX sends his regrets," the courier says. "The weather is too ominous for the journey and he wishes to postpone."

"Does he?" I ask. A bruise is starting to bloom on Helene's arm beneath my grip. "Good. We want him safely at Amalienborg and out of harm's way."

"Please—" Helene says, but I jerk her arm and firmly shut the door in the messenger's face. Snow and chunks of ice have tumbled into the foyer and are melting at our feet.

She stares at me, her face so close to mine. The crystals in the chandeliers sway gently above our heads. The scent of orchids spills over the foyer vase.

"Madam?" Nina says. She stands at the entrance to the servants' corridor, her voice tentative with concern.

"Go back to the kitchen, Nina," Helene says calmly. "I need you to look after Eve. Don't let her out of your sight."

"Helene," I say. "We thought there was a chance things might go this way."

Tønnes steps forward from the shadows.

Beyond him, my mining men—the ones who have been by my side for the past ten years, helping to weave this web—all stand.

I dead-bolt the front door behind me.

CHAPTER THIRTY-FOUR

Marit

HELENE AND I ARE TRAPPED.

She moves quickly toward the servants' corridor, but Dr. Holm blocks her. I look around wildly, frantic. The miners' faces swim in front of me, carrying the shades of every possible reaction. Guilt, shame, anger, arrogance, murderous rage.

Fear.

All I can think is that I have to reach Eve before they do.

They each take a step toward me, their rings glittering with magic, forcing me into the foyer, so that they can form a perimeter around Helene and me. They tighten like a drawstring around us, blocking the exits.

"Philip," Helene says. She shakes with quiet rage. "Tell me. Did you kill Aleks over this?"

"No," Philip says, and he actually looks taken aback. "I loved my brother. I would never have hurt him."

But there is something that I catch out of the corner of my eye. A look, like a glint of sunlight on a wave, there and then gone. The smallest smile on Dr. Tønnes Holm's face.

Philip sees it too.

"You expect me to believe that you were hiding all this and you let him live?" Helene's laugh is bitter as she turns to Dr. Holm. "You said the autopsy revealed a problem with his heart. I *trusted* you."

"Tønnes didn't hurt him either," Philip says. "Aleks's death was natural." But for the first time, I see a crack in his composure. Of doubt.

Next to me, I can feel Helene's guard slowly reaching for his pistol in infinitesimal movements. *Please let this be over soon,* I pray. I'm careful to avert my eyes, not wanting to give him away. With the armed guard on our side, we have the slimmest chance of escaping. Of surviving long enough to get help.

But Dr. Holm suddenly turns on his heel.

"Wrong choice, Peder," he says, and, as easily as gliding through churned butter, runs him through with his sword.

Helene gasps.

I sputter, "Run."

Dr. Holm caught Peder off-guard, but he startled the other miners, too.

It gives us just the distraction we need.

I grab the massive vase in the foyer and hurl it at their feet. It shatters into a hundred jagged pieces of glass and orchid petals, buying us precious seconds as the miners jump out of the way.

I dart toward the servants' corridor, pulling Helene with me.

We throw open the door and stumble into Nina and Brock.

They were hovering inside, listening, and Brock wields a fire poker over his shoulder. I slam the door closed behind us and Helene grabs the fire poker from Brock and wedges it through the latch just in time.

There are angry footsteps right beyond the door. "I knew something was wrong," Nina says, trembling. Someone jangles the handle, then bangs on the door.

"There's still time to prevent anyone else in this house from dying," Philip calls through the wood in a calm voice. "We can come to an agreement that will prevent any more carnage today."

It is then that I notice Peder's blood is spattered on the collar of my uniform.

"I'm not sure how long this will hold them," Helene says, backing away.

We turn and sprint through the corridor.

When we erupt into the kitchen, everyone turns to look at us. Their jovial, expectant faces turn to shock as they take in Helene's disheveled hair, the panic in our eyes, the blood on our clothes. The clattering of preparations comes to an abrupt stop.

"Bar the doors and windows," Helene orders. "Now."

"What's happened?" Dorit splutters. Brock springs past her and dead-bolts the ironclad delivery door.

"The men in this house are here to hurt us. There is no way out, and there is no one coming to help," Helene says. She strips off her satin gloves. "We have to hide and defend ourselves until the snow slows enough for us to get out or send for help."

"What?" There is a collective note of disbelief as the mood abruptly shifts from joyful anticipation to dread.

"Where is my daughter?" Helene demands.

"Here," Eve says. She steps forward, the glass embellishments glittering on her legs. Her cheeks are flushed.

Brock is screwing the windowpanes shut, and Rae and Declan grab wet logs from beside the stove to barricade the glass.

"We need weapons to protect ourselves, if it comes to that," Helene announces. "And a place where Eve will be safe."

Eve says, "No. I want to help." She looks so earnest in her delicate costume, but there is steel just behind her expression. A knife wrapped in lace. "Where's the guard?"

Helene grimaces and shrugs tellingly toward the blood on my clothes. Rae gasps, and the room takes on a new level of seriousness, darkening like the sun behind a cloud.

"What do they want with us?" Lara whispers. She tugs at the ends of her hair.

"Magic," Helene says. "It's where the jewels come from. They've been harvesting magic to use for themselves." She strips the brooch from her chest. Throws it onto the table, as though the touch of it has burned her. We stare at the stone in horror.

"We have to move quickly now," she continues. "They'll hunt you for your magic, and Eve and me because we know too much. Prepare to hide, defend, and protect until the blizzard passes. We're like fish in a barrel in here, and if we go out in this storm, we will die."

We hurry to pull the heavy kitchen table and the linen

trunks in front of the back door to the greenhouse, stacking on chairs and my sewing machine and the heaviest items we can find. Once we've secured the entrances, Jakob says: "Now, weapons."

We scatter through the servants' quarters, grabbing kitchen knives, emptying the cupboards of crystal and china. Nina unlocks the silver cabinet and throws heavy candlesticks onto the pile. We break the china into long shards that can be used as daggers. Brock brandishes his gardening shears, and I send my sewing scissors across the counter with a clatter. Jakob packs as many medical supplies as he can manage in a bag. "Just in case," he says grimly.

"This is not a death sentence," Helene says as we survey our collection of makeshift weapons. "They came to this house expecting a performance with the king, not a fight. And we know this house better than they do." At Helene's nod, Liljan sets a simple rendering of the house plan flooding across a tablecloth. Jakob uses it to quickly point out the back stairways and secret nooks that are unknown to anyone but us.

He says: "We also know our own magic better than they know theirs. Theirs is foreign—but with all those stones, they probably have magic we aren't even aware of. We will have the best chance of surviving tonight if we can take them by surprise."

"How many of them are there?" Lara asks.

"I counted six miners in the ballroom," I say. "Then Philip, Dr. Holm, and Malthe. Our goal is to all survive until we can safely send for help."

Rae bites her thumb nervously. "And what are they doing right now?" she asks.

We stop moving to listen.

All I hear is dead silence.

It is too quiet.

"They know we're in here," Brock says. "We have to hold the kitchen as long as we can and then keep them guessing after that. We can disappear inside the main house, try to draw them apart, and form a counterattack if necessary, or we aren't going to make it through the night."

We split into groups and designate a rendezvous point. Helene, Brock, Dorit, Rae, Signe, Oliver, and Nina will stay back and take the west side of the house. Declan, Lara, Jakob, Liljan, Eve, and I will take the east wing. My body may be useless when it comes to using magic—*but,* I think grimly, *at the very least, it can still act as a shield.*

We freeze at the sudden sound of scraping along the gutter.

"What was that?" Rae whispers.

"They are coming," Helene says with forced calm. "Hide, subdue, knock them out, kill them if you have to. Strip them of their weapons and jewels by whatever means necessary. Do not hesitate. They will kill you if they get the chance."

They are bigger than almost all of us. We have no traditional weapons to go against their pistols, swords, and revolvers. The Firn in their stones gives them magic, while our magic gives us Firn. Our cost is their gain. And then my nose pricks with the acrid smell of smoke.

Someone has climbed up to the roof and covered the kitchen chimney.

"Douse the fire," Nina hisses.

There's a bang on the delivery door. They are surrounding us, stationed at every exit. While we were forming a plan, they were too. We are trapped.

Lara screams as the galley windows shatter. We fall to the floor. Someone must have harvested magic like Ivy's to make the windows explode like that. The force sends the stack of logs tumbling. They splinter against the stove and land among the fresh shards of glass.

We crouch, trembling, as a shrill wind comes gusting through.

Rae crawls to the stove and places a palm on the copper pot, instantly setting the water inside to boiling. She waits for a miner's hand to reach through the blown-out panes. Half a moment later, jewel-covered fingers fumble with the window's iron latch. The miners are going to unlock it from the inside and then climb in.

Rae heaves the pot instead. The boiling water makes a sizzling sound when it hits the man's fingers.

He lets out a horrifying scream and staggers backwards.

"They've surrounded every exit," Brock confirms.

But that means that for the moment, they're divided. Which means this is our best chance to infiltrate back into the main house and stall for time by making them hunt for us.

"At least if one of us survives, there's a chance the truth gets out," Jakob says.

"We'll cover you here and provide a distraction," Helene says.

"Then we'll do the same for you," Jakob says.

"Get Eve to the rendezvous point safely," Helene says to me.

"I will," I promise.

"This is *my* home," Helene reminds us with fierce determination. She looks around at our grim faces. "No," she corrects herself softly. "This is *our* home."

She pulls out a serrated knife from Dorit's collection. Rips through the satin layers of her skirts to free her long, strong legs. "And we are going to defend it."

Jakob hands me a candlestick that's as heavy as lead, and Brock says:

"Run."

⌘

At the end of the underground servants' corridor, there are men waiting for us.

We can hear two of them talking on the other side of the door.

Declan places his finger on a knot in the wood, creating a tiny peephole around the level of our knees. He kneels to look through it, giving him an unnoticed view into the main house.

We collectively jump at the sound of a small explosion coming from the kitchen behind us. Eve tenses, drawing close to me. I pull her tight and give her a squeeze, feeling the rapid-fire beat of her heart. Declan peers through the peephole.

And then he quickly backs away when we hear a sudden dripping sound.

The door handle is starting to melt with some sort of magic. The dribbling metal conducts like lightning to the fire poker we've used to block the door, and the poker starts to drip, drip, like liquid mercury.

I look meaningfully at Liljan. She is careful to avoid the drops of metal that sizzle at her feet and crouches near the bottom of the door. Beneath it, she sends red color slipping back across the floor like blood. The miner on the other side seems to pause when he notices. "What is that?" he whispers.

Declan looks through the peephole and counts silently to us with his fingers.

On three, we jointly burst through the door.

The force of it hits the first man square in the jaw. Malthe is standing behind him. He fumbles to draw his pistol, but he's outnumbered. He gets off a wild shot before Jakob hits him over the head with a candlestick.

Liljan rips off the ties from our aprons and I quickly bind the men's hands and feet with the strongest knots I can make. Then Jakob douses the rest of the aprons in laudanum and puts the stunned men face-down in it. We strip them of weapons and all their jewels and leave them bound, drugged halfway to Sunday, in the servants' corridor.

But when we reach the foyer, we freeze.

The miners have been busy planning, just as we were.

Because it is snowing inside the house.

The foyer appears empty. The doors are all closed, the windows still fully intact. But they've set snow to fall inside by magic, with drifts gathering into an inch of powder on the rugs, sliding halfway up the base of the grandfather clock, settling like silt on the table, and still falling soft and white and steadily from the ceiling. The house is so silent I can hear the gentle ticking of the minute hand.

It's too quiet.

My foot slides on the soft powder.

Now they will be able to track our footsteps through the entire house.

The snow will act like a map, leading them straight to us.

"Step in each other's footprints," Jakob whispers. "So at least they won't be able to tell how many of us there are." I nod and swallow, but the snowfall makes it hard to move quickly. Icicles dangle from the chandeliers above our heads, sharp and piercing. The snow is soft and cold against my neck, settling thick as a palm's width over the foyer table and the shattered vase. Peder's body has been left where he fell but it almost looks as though he's merely asleep and dusted with snow.

Slowly, painstakingly, we make our way across the foyer. Creep past the ballroom. Its doors are closed. There is dead silence behind them.

The grand staircase is blocked. Thorny brown vines are threaded through the banisters, crisscrossing and spiked like barbed wire to make the steps impassable. The men have done their best to limit our exits and trap us on the main floor.

I swallow hard at their use of magic. Tonight will be a battle of power and wits.

Whoever makes the most clever use of theirs wins.

I take Eve's hand. Her skin feels warm and soft, and snow-flakes catch in her dark lashes. The house is starting to dim, with shadows painting the walls around us. It gives me an idea.

"Psst," I whisper to Liljan. "Can you fake the walls?"

We know this house like the back of our hands; we know where the doors and rooms should be. The others have to rely solely on what their eyes tell them. She smiles wickedly. She'll make the house change and shift around them — make them doubt everything they are seeing.

"Stiff stuff, Marit," she whispers.

It's only fitting. To last in this house, you have to earn your place.

Liljan waits until we are all inside the hidden servant stair-case, then runs her hand along the wall to mask the door. She adds several fake doors where the wall is nothing but brick.

When she joins us, securing the lock with a click behind her, we are plunged into complete darkness.

The staircase creaks shrilly under our weight.

I grimace with each upward step, hoping the sounds are masked by the howl of snow and wind outside. My heart feels like a panicked bird, trying to get out.

"Wait here," I whisper to Eve when we reach the landing at the second floor. I squeeze her wrist. "Let us make sure it's safe first. Liljan will stay with you."

Eve wrinkles her nose at me but nods.

I push open the door. Immediately I hear the low hum of a man's voice.

And then it stops.

The hallway is dim as we edge toward the room we've picked as our first hiding point: the large guest room in the corner. It's a good lookout, with windows that face in several directions, a single entry point to secure, and eaves to which we can escape if Philip and his men set the house on fire.

Except that the room is already occupied.

I hold up a finger to quiet the others and scan the hallway. There are no drifts of snow to track our movements here. I take a few hesitant, silent steps. The candlestick I'm holding feels slick in my hand.

A single man is kneeling at the hearth. His back is to me, but I can glimpse that one of his hands is wrapped with a fresh bandage—he must be the miner Rae scalded. In the other hand, he holds out a jewel to the flames, as if to warm it. *Is that how they get the magic out?* I wonder. His hair is so light blond it's almost silver.

My foot makes a loud crunching sound underneath my weight, and suddenly he turns.

I look down in horror. I've stepped into a patch of shattered glass, dyed the same color as the floor. I didn't see it until it was too late.

The silver-blond man springs up from the fire, drawing his weapon. He lunges toward me, and I manage to duck out of his way just in time. He grabs Lara instead, his meaty arms wrapping around her frame. She cries out and stops struggling when she feels the cold metal of a dagger pointing at her side.

"Get on the floor and drop your weapons."

I've put us in danger. If only I'd been more careful.

A second man appears behind us from the shadows, short and built solid as a wall. He was patiently watching for us to appear and now moves forward to trap me, Jakob, and Declan. I don't dare move with that knife hovering between Lara's ribs. The second miner walks slowly, deliberately, to the door of the hidden stairway.

My stomach drops.

He turns the knob and peers into the darkness.

Please stay hidden, I pray. Beads of sweat form on my forehead.

The miner holding Lara at knifepoint barks: "Did you find another one?"

"No," the miner says with a strange grimace, squinting further into the darkness. The metal of his sword scrapes shrilly as he draws it out. "I found two of them."

CHAPTER THIRTY-FIVE

Philip

I T'S COLD AS KNIVES when we finally breach the kitchen. The loud explosion cracks through the night. When the sound echoes around the surrounding forest, I have the same thought I did all those years ago when those miners died below the earth.

I underestimated the extent of what human greed can do.

I rip through hanging strands of white flowers and shove in through the blasted back door.

"Helene?" I bellow.

I'm the first one in, with Tønnes, Steen, and Casper close behind me. We push over a barricade and find the kitchen half-destroyed and abandoned. The wind howls through the shattered window shells. Broken glass gathers in piles, like sand, on the floor. I've known Steen for fifteen years and seen what he can do with his massive size. He and Casper climb the stairs, their weight creaking as they methodically break down the doors of every room above our heads.

"It's clear," Steen calls.

The servants must have fled through the corridor to the main house. They must have already come upon Hugo and Malthe waiting at the other end. The rest of us will now follow from behind and trap them.

It's as if the past is circling back to happen all over again.

I didn't kill those men in the mines all those years ago.

But I didn't stop it from happening, either.

I prepare my weapons—a pistol, knife, revolver, and eight types of glittering Firn—and steel myself.

I do not think of what Aleks would do, to see me hunting his wife in his own house.

"Tønnes, is it wrong?" I asked all those years ago.

We are long past those questions now.

"To the house," I say, and point my knife to the servants' corridor.

We fall in line—Steen first, then Tønnes. Then me. We leave Casper behind and start down the underground hallway.

What would have happened if that miner hadn't snooped through the secret corridors of the mines and stumbled across those skeletons ten years ago? Where would all of us be, if not here, plunging through this house in a blizzard?

Claus Olsen was the one who started it all. He was one of the higher-ups in command. He had never been a problem before.

But suspicion had been simmering for a while. The miners didn't really believe that jewels could grow in the mines. Olsen's mistake was to believe that his fellow men would want to shine light on the truth, as he did.

He misjudged the power of greed too.

"What's this?" Steen says ahead of me. He stumbles over something in the hallway. He kicks at it. Swears.

"Are these our men?" he asks.

The leather in Tønnes's boots creaks as he bends to examine the bodies.

"Out cold," Tønnes confirms. "And stripped of weapons."

There's a crash from somewhere above our heads.

"They're trapped," I say, wiping my brow. I brush away the slightest tick of concern. "We still overpower them in size, weapons, and magic."

And now we have a sense of where they are.

I strip down to my vest, securing the gemstones I plucked from the map of Denmark and stashed into every pocket I could find. We creep forward. Snow falls gently in the foyer, silent and eerie. The windows look like sheets of ice. The doors to the ballroom are closed. There are two sets of footprints that spread out in front of us. The first leads to a dead end—a solid wall—and then vanish like a ghost's.

The second set leads to the ballroom.

I move silently, feeling the snow fall like feathers onto my face. I put my finger to my lips. Then to the cold steel of my pistol.

Aleks's portrait watches me from behind his gilded frame.

He never knew that half my miners were planning to turn

me in. They wanted to tell King Frederick where those jewels were really coming from. But the other half wanted in on the scheme.

They set an explosion that killed their own friends. Sealed the truth in before it could get out.

Then there was truly no turning back for me.

I pull at my tie now to loosen it. It feels as though it's strangling me.

My brother wept the day those miners died. I fed him a lie — that it was an unpreventable accident. I told him what would make him breathe easier. Just like I will do with the royal family when this is over — what I tried to do even for Helene. I spare others the weight of the truth and carry the load of it myself while they reap all the benefits. They get to sleep with a clean conscience. It is just like the way that soldiers go to war and come back with the burden of what they saw, what they did, for the greater good of the country. Is there not something selfless, something even admirable, in that?

I pause outside the ballroom and listen.

From inside, there is the faint sound of chiseling.

We have a cache of stored magic — so much more magic than they have — and the flames to release it. *But a cornered animal is always the most dangerous animal of all,* I remind myself. I raise my gun and fire straight through the ballroom doors.

Someone cries out.

In the next moment, we burst inside.

At first all I can see is green, a verdant patch set among the snow both inside and out. The scent of greenery is overwhelming. The ballroom is flooded with blossoms. It's sickeningly sweet, like swimming through perfume. The room is so still it seems abandoned.

But they are hiding here, somewhere.

I snap to light a flame between my fingers and warm the ring on my left hand. I feel the magic stir inside the stone. Feel when the magic then enters my skin and runs through me.

Steen starts stalking around the perimeter of the room, shooting into the greenery. Outside, the snow is thick and blinding white, swirling, like dancers turning. The sun set hours ago, and now the snow reflects the moon, brightening the world outside to an eerie dusk.

"You're going to run out of bullets," Tønnes says, as if he's bored. "Be patient. Save them for when you have a clear target."

We move through the orange trees, our backs to one another for cover, until we reach the center of the ballroom. My eyes fall on what caused the sound of the first crash and then the chiseling. *Ah.* They were trying to destroy the jewels we left in the Denmark map. We took as many as we could carry, determining by color the ones that could be used as weapons. The servants tried to hammer the others, to shatter them to dust.

It's that moment when I realize, vaguely, that something is swinging above my head.

I look up just as the chandelier begins to fall.

I shove Tønnes and dive out of the way.

One.

The chandelier shatters where I was standing half a breath ago. It explodes, like a grenade of crystal.

Two.

The second one follows.

I struggle to my feet again and leap from the path of the third.

My hands are empty when I hit the floor. In my haste and surprise, I dropped my pistol.

It's buried now, somewhere beneath the mounds of glass.

The third chandelier ricochets so hard off the floor that it sends crystal shrapnel flying into a window. The glass shatters but stays locked in place. It looks like a glittering spider web.

These servants are putting up more of a fight than I expected.

Just like Ivy did.

I touch my mouth. My lip is bleeding. My side aches from the injury that little servant gave me when she sliced into me that winter morning.

I didn't know she had any glass on her when I approached. I didn't expect her to morph it into a blade.

I guess that's two things I should never underestimate, I think grimly.

Human greed and servant magic.

Helene suddenly bursts from behind a fern and darts up on top of the display table. She's almost quicker than my eye can follow, graceful and intense with power. Before I can move, she is behind me. She puts a knife to my throat.

I can feel the serrated edges against my skin when I swallow.

Steen groans. He's bleeding, holding his ribs, but he's staggering up to his feet. He barely makes it to standing before he's confronted by two women. They are older than Helene and don't appear to be using magic to fight. One of them merely screams, then hits Steen square in the face with a cooking pot.

He crumples to the floor like a sack of flour.

We all turn at the distinctive sound of a pistol cocking. I can swivel my head just enough to see Tønnes, standing rigid. His jaw is set. He is pointing a gun in my direction. It's trained on Helene.

"Let him go, Helene," he says.

I did not set off the explosion in the mines that day.

It was not my idea, nor my intention, to kill people for their magic.

At first, all I wanted to do was help the mines.

Then all I wanted to do was help Denmark.

And here we are.

"No," Helene says defiantly. Her knife grazes my throat, like a violin bow sheering along a taut string.

Very calmly, I tell Tønnes: "Shoot her."

And then the walls around me begin to shift, coming alive like snakes.

CHAPTER THIRTY-SIX

Marit

"GET DOWN AND DROP YOUR WEAPONS," the miner who is holding Lara demands again. *"Now!"*

I lower my hands and gently release my candlestick. It's wet with sweat and drops onto the floor with a dull thud. I focus on breathing and try not to faint.

Beside me, Declan and Jakob slowly kneel, arms raised.

" 'Ey, what do we have here? Is that the Vestergaard daughter?"

The miner pulls Eve out of the darkness. She lets out a small shriek and then tightens her lips. She doesn't make another sound, even when he throws her roughly to the floor.

Could I actually kill someone?

I don't know.

My fingers curl into fists.

For Eve, I think so.

Jakob releases his weapon so gently it doesn't make a sound. Out of the corner of my eye, I see Declan carefully put his hands, palms down, against the wooden beams of the floor.

"Keep the Vestergaard girl for negotiations," says the miner holding Lara. "Dispatch the other one so she doesn't get in the way."

Lara lets out a small whimper.

Declan sends me and Jakob one furtive glance of warning. We barely have time to flinch before his hands flex and a deep tremor shoots through the wood.

It's a shocking pulse that I feel reverberate through each of my bones. It rattles all the way up to my teeth and knocks everyone who is standing off balance.

The miner holding Lara tumbles backwards, and Lara falls with him. Her head makes a sick thump when it catches the edge of a marble side table.

"Jakob!" Liljan cries, and emerges from the stairwell.

The miner closest to Eve scrambles to his feet. His fingers glitter with jewels when he instinctively raises his sword and slashes toward Liljan. Eve lunges toward him and kicks her powerful foot squarely at his knee. Her kick connects, diverting him just enough to save Liljan's throat. The sword catches her cheek instead and Liljan cries out as a slice of bright red appears down her face.

The miner stumbles backwards, slashing out one more time.

Straight along Eve's right arm.

She gasps and draws it tight to her body.

Declan sends one final tremor through the wood and then jumps to his feet. He wrenches a board clean from the floor and wields it nails-out, advancing toward the miner who held Lara.

Jakob and I scramble for our weapons.

I lob my heavy candlestick through the air to Liljan.

She lets go of her face long enough to catch the weapon and hurls it at the miner who slashed her, striking a blow to his cheekbone to return the favor.

When he crumples, Liljan kicks him hard in the ribs, and he gasps for breath and then loses consciousness. I sprint to Eve and sink to her side. The blossom Liljan pinned to her costume is withered and bruised. She's breathing quickly and lightly, as if she's in shock.

"Jakob," I say. Blood pours out of Eve's arm. The cut is deep.

But the miner with the silver-blond hair is going head-to-head with Declan, and Jakob moves to help. Neither Jakob nor Declan is trained for fighting, and even between the two of them, they can barely hold the man off.

Jakob scoops up a fireplace poker from the bedroom and advances on the miner, the pointed end outstretched.

"How do you get the magic from those stones?" he demands.

He jabs the silver-blond miner in the arm and makes him drop his sword. It clatters at their feet, and Jakob continues to advance, jamming the poker near the base of the miner's throat. "Tell us and I'll hit you where it will simply knock you unconscious rather than through your carotid artery."

The miner swallows, then furtively looks around. His colleague is down, and he's cornered. He slowly raises his hands to his chest.

I watch warily as I wrap a tourniquet made from curtain ties around Eve's arm.

"I'm not going to be able to dance anymore," she says. "If I can't raise my arms."

"Shh," I say, stroking her hand. "Don't think of that now." Liljan presses the ends of her dress to her face to staunch her own bleeding and helps me tighten the tourniquet.

The miner makes a sudden move and Jakob jolts him in the throat.

He passes out.

"Jakob," I gasp, and in an instant, he is here.

"You'll be better at closing this," I say, showing him the gash on Eve's arm. "Unless . . ." I hesitate. "I use my magic."

"Don't you dare, Marit," Eve snaps.

Jakob gingerly picks her up and carries her in his arms.

"You're going to be all right, Eve," he says gently. He looks at Liljan and says, "How are you, Lil?"

She shows him her cheek and he winces. "I like grotesque trivia," she grumbles, "but I never wanted to be *in* it."

"Help me with Eve and Lara, and then I can stitch you up, too," Jakob says, bringing them to the guest room. Declan and I drag the two miners into one of the small side closets, their unconscious bodies heavy as lead. We lock them inside and examine our newly acquired weapons. Each man had a sword, dagger, and pistol, plus fifteen-odd different jewels containing indiscernible magic. I pick up the stone that the silver-blond man held in front of the fire. The jewel is starting to darken.

"We've subdued four of them," I say to Jakob. I finger the darkening stone. "And I think I know how they get the magic out," I say slowly. "When they heat the stones, the magic seems to enter their bodies."

I pour out a dose of laudanum for Eve. Just enough to take the edge off her pain but allow her to keep her wits about her in case she needs to run and hide herself.

"Can we destroy the stones, then?" Jakob asks. "Lil, burn them in the fire so the magic is spent and the miners can't use it against us." She nods and begins to toss the jewels one by one into the flames. They heat like glittering coals and then steadily blacken, and I wonder if pure magic is seeping out of them, pouring into the air like a scent or wisping smoke. What sort of beautiful power did each jewel hold? And now we burn it away and turn the stone to a mere shell, and I can't help but think of it as a life that was utterly wasted.

"That blackened stone we took from Philip's room," I say. "It must have been old magic. Once they're spent, they're ugly as lumps of coal. Just useless, dead Firn."

"Wait a minute," Jakob says, as if an idea has struck him like a match being lit. Eve winces as he starts sewing the wound in her arm. "Say that again?"

But the sudden sound of a crash below makes us jump.

Followed shortly by another massive crash.

It sounds like a lot of glass, shattering.

"Marit," Eve says desperately, turning to me. "Helene. She might need help."

I'm about to say no, that I want to stay with her and make sure she's all right, but the utter despair on her face stops me.

"Yes," I hear myself say. "I'll go."

"I'm coming with you," Declan says, grabbing a pistol for each hand. He offers one to me. I shake my head.

"I don't know how to use that, and I don't want to learn." He digs through the pilfered weapons, sifting them like pieces of gold.

"I'll come back," I promise Eve before she can say anything else. I squeeze her hand. "Be brave, dear one."

I exchange the briefest look with Jakob. His suit is torn and there's blood on it. His glasses are perched on his nose. He looks so grimly handsome, as if he is searching for just the right thing to say.

Just like at the Mill, I hurry to stand, putting off goodbye. If I don't say it to anyone in this room, the small handful of people I care for most in the world, then don't I have to survive?

I have to.

Declan hands me a knife. And we run.

❧

The magic the miners set must have run out, because it has finally stopped snowing in the foyer.

The footsteps we left before are mostly covered over again. We step into the new drifts, and the snow enters my boots like a cold gasp.

The ballroom doors are ajar.

With each step forward, my fear grows.

There's still time to turn back, I think as Declan and I crouch. I could take Eve and we could run far away from here, from the Vestergaards and their horrible mines. We could save ourselves. Tell someone the truth. Seize the future I have always wanted.

I don't want to fight anymore. I want to run from here. I want to forget magic ever existed. I want to be away from the Vestergaards and their endless misery of hurting the people I love.

But then there's another crash inside the ballroom.

"Come on," Declan whispers.

I hesitate for a half second and an old, wretched thought slithers through me. Who would Eve want to survive more — Helene or me?

I shake off the thought as if it is something I can squash beneath my boot. Then I follow Declan through the ballroom doors.

We step from the winter of snowbanks into the heady spring of an orange blossom grove. I peek through the flowering branches, softly moving beneath the cover of greenery. Declan and I crouch under the shielding corner of a marble table. Helene is a mere three meters away from us.

She has Philip at knifepoint.

Dr. Holm steps out from the shadows. I don't think he knows we are here. He raises his gun in Helene's direction and cocks it. "Let him go, Helene," he says.

"No," Helene says.

I squeeze Declan's arm, and Philip swallows.

"Shoot her," he says calmly.

Declan tenses beside me and my mouth instantly goes dry. There is no way we can save her from this distance.

And then I feel something shift along the wall behind me. I bite back a shriek of surprise. The walls around us are moving. Shifting, like green waves or emerald snakes.

The vines — it's as if they've come alive.

I search the room.

Brock is here somewhere.

A strong gust of wind suddenly whips through the house, blowing out the shattered glass that hung like a delicate spider web in one of the windowpanes. The flurry sends a spray of debris into the ballroom, tinkling as the glass falls, and Helene jumps. The blade in her hand takes a small bite into Philip's skin.

A single shard remains in the bottom windowpane. The glass slants up like a shining, jagged iceberg.

Helene shifts her grip on the knife and her voice is like steel: "Did you kill my husband?" she asks.

But instead of Philip, Dr. Holm is the one to answer.

"I wouldn't have," he says. "If I had known he'd leave the mines to you." He sniffs, still pointing the pistol. "Or that you'd be so stubborn not to sell them off."

Philip's face looks so pale and aghast that I almost feel sorry for him.

But then my eyes fall to the floor.

One of the vines is no longer clinging to the gilded walls.

It has pulled away to slither across the honeyed floorboards. At first I think it's just a trick of the wind. But then the vine begins to climb along Dr. Holm's shoe, to coil and wrap itself around his right leg. For a split second he looks down, blinking as if he can't believe his eyes. He lowers the gun from its aim on Helene. Points the barrel down and tries to shoot the vine on the floor.

The sound ricochets and I jump. But the vine keeps coming, tightening around his leg. Advancing with purpose up his torso.

"It was *you*," Brock says from the shadows. A second vine is climbing now, creeping up Dr. Holm's trunk, reaching for his neck. Brock steps forward as Dr. Holm drops the gun and tries to grasp at the vine with his bare hands. "You were the one who attacked Ivy," Brock says, seething at Philip. I think back to him at the glass shop that day in Copenhagen. Perhaps he was already scouting her then, making his plans. Perhaps he even wanted her to recognize him. So that when he met her alone that day on the road, she would make the fatal mistake of stopping long enough to greet him.

One of the miners now enters the ballroom with a yell and runs toward Dr. Holm, trying to slash at the tightening vines with his knives. It hits me with a pang that he looks about the age my father would have been, if he had lived.

Brock's face tightens with fury as he turns toward Dr. Holm. "And you were in on it. You used them. You *killed* her." Dorit, Rae, and Nina step forward to form a barrier around Brock as he grimaces in concentration, and with one look at his face I know exactly what he is feeling. Firn is sharpening like glass knives in his veins. He's reaching down into all the magic he has. Just like I did for him. Just like Ingrid did for me.

With a single snap, the vine around Dr. Holm suddenly jerks. It's enough force to yank him backwards. It pulls him toward the blown-out frame of the window. Toward the last jagged piece of glass that slices up, its edge glinting in the moonlight.

He drops onto the glass with a sickening sound of something being punctured. Then his body falls soundlessly from the window, into the snow-covered night.

Philip goes pale.

It's as though time in the room stops at that moment.

Brock's chest is heaving. The room goes completely still, and Brock closes his eyes, spent.

I always pictured the color of vengeance to be deep crimson red. The color of anger and blood, of proustite, and sometimes of magic.

But today, vengeance is Brock's.

And its color is ivy.

✿

Everything is so eerily quiet around me, even as there is blood and fighting and fear and weariness.

Declan bursts from our hiding place to help Dorit and Nina and Rae.

There are only three adversaries left—Philip and two miners.

For the first time, the battle is shifting in our favor.

We could outlast them and the storm. We could make it out of here.

The two miners are fighting hand to hand with Brock, Dorit, Nina, and Rae.

Declan doesn't reach them in time before Rae's blood goes spattering across the floor.

She falls, forever.

Helene still has her knife to Philip's throat. The weapon trembles. "You've done all this for nothing," she says in a low voice. I creep a meter closer to them, keeping to the shadows. "The king is going to want to know where the magic comes from." Her delicate throat swallows, and I realize: she's stalling.

She doesn't really want to kill him.

"No, he won't," Philip says simply. "Because do you think he cares where his sugar comes from, Helene?" he asks. "Do any of us? Every day, it makes our Danish tea and cakes sweet. Yes, I know that emancipation was signed decades ago. Yet how many people still probably died for the sugar in your own kitchen? For your cacao, your coffee. The cotton and silk in *your* dresses, Helene. The king will not question where the jewels came from or what they really cost. The more people want something, the less willing they are to find out the truth. They simply choose not to look."

Yet my father did, at least when it came to magic. He looked at the truth square in the face and he did not turn away. He risked and lost everything for it. Perhaps simply because he was a good man. Perhaps because the daughters he loved had magic pulsing through their veins, and he knew that someday the victims could easily be us. My eyes well up with a fierce swell of pride. I know the truth now. The choices my father made turned me into an orphan. But they made him a hero.

In that moment, Philip manages to escape Helene's knife hold.

He turns on her.

It has been clear, from the beginning, that she is no match for him physically.

And still. I wait in the shadows. Dorit is holding up Nina, who is limping and looks deathly pale. Everywhere, shattered glass is crunching beneath the scuffles. Declan and Brock are still fighting, but Declan is bleeding from his side and Brock seems exhausted. I can see the Firn inching and curling beneath his skin.

I look from my hiding place to the door. To the promise of safety and escape. To Eve.

Philip knocks the knife out of Helene's hand and sends it clattering across the floor. Furious snow is coming in through the shattered windows, and I think of that night at the ballet, with the royals and Hans Christian Andersen. When Eve and Helene and I all dreamed about the future.

Philip has managed to restrain Helene, and now he pushes her toward the broken window so he can finish the job.

She doesn't even know that I'm here.

Maybe she never has to. Another ounce of magic will kill me. I could hide in the shadows and wait.

But that is a decision too.

Helene is fighting her best as the snow swirls in to bury the parquet floor around her. She is starting to falter, her energy failing. Philip jolts her wrists in front of her. Begins to methodically tie her up.

I look at my own wrists, at the mark of the Firn, as he binds hers.

Eve's mother.

Don't use magic, my father always told me. *Be a Gerda,* he wrote.

Which do I choose?

I know what choice these miners made. They took and spent the lives of others to get magic for themselves. But I have the chance to do the opposite. Sacrifice my own magic for the life of someone else.

All this time, I've been clutching so tightly to a selfish love for Eve, to a future together.

And now, as simply as letting out a breath, I let it go.

Eve can't go back to being an orphan again.

I've worried all along that if she had to make the choice, she would choose Helene over me. But now she won't have to.

I step out from the shadows and reach down for the full force of my magic.

I know what a true older sister would do.

Because my older sister did it for me.

It's as if a space has opened up in my lungs from the last time. As if the magic is quicker to go down to that deep level. Magic is singing through my veins in pleasure and excruciating pain as I untie Helene's binds from across the room. Loosen them enough for her to slip out of them, all without ever touching her.

"Marit," Helene chokes out when she sees me. Philip turns to look at me, surprised. I've caught him off-guard. Bought just enough time for Helene to escape her binds. He whirls around to face me, the knife appearing in his hand.

"Magic *is* the future of Denmark, Philip," Helene says from behind him. "It has saved Denmark from you." She grabs a shard of glass and thrusts it deep into his side.

I stop holding on. To my magic. To the future. In a mirror of each other, Philip and I both sink to the floor. I can feel the Firn race through me, and I wonder what mine would look like as a jewel. What color it would take.

For the first time in my life, I am not afraid of it.

Perhaps because I willingly chose it — and because choosing it meant someone else is going to live — for the first time, maybe I could actually even find the Firn beautiful.

☙

Eve curls up beside me. I feel the familiar weight of her, just like all those nights at the Mill, as she lies down next to me here one last time.

"You're going to be all right, Eve," I whisper. "With Helene."

"Marit, *you're* going to be all right," she says fiercely.

But I'm not, and I think she knows that too, because she leans to cover me with her body, shaking, and I smell her familiar smell, the one that reminds me of rest and happiness, of a thousand nights falling asleep at the Mill. I touch her hand as she runs it, so tenderly, over my cheeks, and I remember what she looked like in all those moments our lives overlapped. Holding Wubbins up to me uncertainly, leaving traces of biscuit crumbs in my sheets, pushing Sare over, scheming about Ness, defending me from Brock. That look of wonder on her face that first night at the theater. Dancing in the light from the street lamp at the Mill when she thought she was alone. Those quiet, vulnerable moments when she was falling asleep next to me and already half dreaming. If all our memories are a duet, now she will be the only one singing. And the song that was mine to sing, the memories of her as a little girl, of Ingrid, of my father, will die now, with me.

Eve traces so gently along my eyebrows.

"There," she says. "I've brushed away anything ugly or bad left over from today. Now go to sleep." She wipes away one of her own tears that falls on my face, and her voice breaks when she lies: "And we'll both wake up fresh tomorrow."

I close my eyes, and suddenly I'm on the staircase and I'm five years old. My sister is humming and making a flower crown. My arms are twining around the banister at my home; the edge of the wood is leaving a mark on my cheek. "For you?" Ingrid says, handing me the crown, her laugh like wind chimes. My father is at the stove, and I can smell the warm milk, the orange zest of Mother's old whipped custard cream.

"I love you, Marit," Eve whispers in my ear.

I feel warmth flooding through me. Because all my life, I was afraid of the future. Afraid that when the end came, I would be alone.

"Eve," I breathe. What more could I ask for than this? The most precious gift.

To spend the last moments of my life with the one who, for me, made it all worth living.

CHAPTER THIRTY-SEVEN

Philip

I WAS LISTENING ON THE DAY the miners found out the whole truth.

The day that sealed everything, that meant there was no more turning back for me.

Half the miners wanted to tell someone the truth — the police, the king. Half wanted to continue the secret and get in on the action.

Their voices rose and echoed off the limestone.

"No one leaves here without agreeing," Steen declared.

I listened to all of it. What happened next. All I did that day was listen.

Sometimes the biggest decisions you make come by doing absolutely nothing.

The miners split.

And half of them killed the other half.

And made it look like an accident.

There was so much blood on all their hands.

There is so much blood on all our hands.

There is blood on me.

My blood.

Helene is looking at me in judgment, watching me from steps away, in her deep purple silk, as I bleed. While she lives in this house built because of the things I did, wearing clothes paid for by the choices I made. Eating food that was made by other people's sacrifice. She asks servants for that in her own house, by using their magic. Trading their lives for her comfort. How is what I've done that different, when it comes down to it?

I'm just willing to look at my hands and see how truly dirty they are. She gets to pretend hers are clean because she doesn't watch it happen right in front of her.

Don't act like you are better than me, Helene, I think but am too weak to say. *Or that what you do is any different.*

At least I have integrity about it.

At least I'm being honest with myself.

Two of my men are lying motionless on shattered glass. One of the male servants is dead beside them.

"We have to help her." Eve is sobbing over that dying seamstress as though the child has lost her own mother.

I miss my mother.

"Eve," that servant Jakob says, cracking open a case filled with medical supplies. "Do you remember what I taught you about variolation in our lessons? About the woman who used old small-pox scabs on her son?" He looks around frantically. "We need weakened Firn."

I'm in so much pain. There's blood coming out of my side

that I try to hold with my hand, but there's a lot of it. It feels like another lifetime that I was a young boy, holding my arm behind my back, with my mother's blood on my sleeve. Just wanting not to feel so afraid. Just wanting my mother to stop crying.

"She always carries that red stone from her father," says Jakob's sister, Liljan. She ransacks the seamstress's pockets, but they are empty. Everything around us is shattered glass, stilled bodies, mangled vines, wreckage.

"It must be in her room," Jakob says urgently. "We don't have time." He falls down beside the seamstress's limp body and plunges a syringe into her. Draining out the Firn, just like Tønnes and I used to do.

Liljan is doing the same to that male servant who killed Tønnes with the vines. My eyes blur. Tiny shards of Firn glitter in the light, like fool's gold in a bloody stream.

"I think I know," Eve suddenly breathes, crawling over the seamstress, "where she might keep it."

Eve turns over the hem of the seamstress's dress. Finds a small secret pocket.

I blink and she pulls out a scarlet stone tucked inside.

"Yes, Eve!" Jakob says. He finishes extracting Firn-filled blood from the seamstress's arm, and then begins to transfuse her with his own blood. "Now we need it weakened—"

"I know," Eve says, and holds the stone over a candle flame, grimacing only slightly when the jewel blackens and the heat burns her fingers. *What is she doing*—releasing all the precious

magic into the air, making the stone as useless as a lump of coal?
I always buried my spent Firn deep within the mines.

Except Eve starts to scratch the girl's arms with the stone.
Scrapes off pieces of it and nicks her skin.

"Don't go, Marit," Eve murmurs gently. "Stay and we'll fight
for each other, like we always do."

Jakob leans down and kisses the servant's eyebrows and the
tips of her eyelashes. Liljan wipes tears away into her sleeve.

That seamstress ruined everything.

I was so close. To what I'd worked so hard for. Spent all those
lives for.

I would have made it worth it.

Will I see my mother again? Surely, if there is someone or
something out there waiting on the other side, they can find it in
them to understand why I did what I did?

I remember being on the battlefield.

I remember watching the little boy with magic.

Aleks watching the ballet.

My mother, with jewels in her hair.

I've lost so much blood. It's making me unsteady.

But I think the last thing I see, before it all goes dark—

That seamstress.

How could one person, one single girl, destroy everything I
tried to do?

I might have imagined it. It's hard to tell anymore.

But the last thing I think I see is that seamstress gasp and
open her eyes.

CHAPTER THIRTY-EIGHT

Marit
June 29, 1867
Copenhagen, Denmark

THE BOOKSTORE SMELLS LIKE LAVENDER, fresh paper, and old leather, and a small brass bell tinkles over our heads when we walk through the door. It's dim and cool, a reprieve from the sticky summer air outside, and the bookstore owner grunts at us from the counter. Jakob walks to the oak panel holding the new arrivals. His fingertips dance along the shelves, and he gets a shy smile when he touches a certain crisp green spine. "This one," he says. His eyes crinkle with pleasure behind his spectacles and he pulls the book from the shelf. "You're going to love this one," he whispers, and asks the owner to ring it up. "It has everything you like."

I tuck the book under my arm, feeling the same way Ivy's orbs must feel when the sun floods through the glass and turns them to pure gold. We make our way across the street to the tiny, unassuming brick office on the corner.

The office sits at the outskirts of northern Copenhagen. It is set in a small, shadowed nook next to a bakery, so it always smells like rising bread and flaky cinnamon pastries. The sign on the front of the office has no words. There is just a symbol: a rope that curves like a lemniscate, the sign of infinity. If you look closely enough, you can see that the rope is actually a vine, sprouting with tiny ivy leaves.

When we step over the threshold and close the door, we both hesitate. Then Jakob gives me a lingering smile and crosses to his side of the office, where he is surrounded by a hundred tumbling books, his cabinets of glass test tubes and cannulas, and various microscopes. I have to force myself toward my own desk to abide by our rule.

No kissing allowed during work hours.

I trace my fingertips over the gold words stamped into the cover of my new book and have just sat down to open it when a small shadow pauses in front of the window. I can see the outline of her through the diamonds of colored glass. She hesitates, and then with the lightest knock, the door creaks open.

It's a young girl, around nine years old. Her dark hair is slightly matted. Her clothes are brown and threadbare.

She takes a tentative step inside. "I heard . . ." she says nervously. "I heard you can help me." She turns in the scuffed toes of her boots and extends a coin with the ivy symbol etched onto it. The coin is our secret signal that she's been sent by someone in the magical community who knows about us. Knows what we can do.

She looks so young.

"May I see?" I ask gently. She nods and pulls up her sleeve.

Blue is edging in a pattern of crystallized frost under the skin on her wrists.

"What's your name?" I ask her.

"Elise," she whispers.

I don't even need Jakob's microscope to see that she's ready. I give him a single nod from across the room.

"Come with me, Elise," I say, offering her my hand. When I send her to change into a plain cotton gown in our washroom, I run my fingers over her clothes. By the time she emerges, the fabric has knit itself back together, stronger.

"It . . . won't hurt, will it?" she asks me tentatively, climbing onto the table in the examining room.

Her hair sticks up in tufts at her temple. It reminds me of when Eve was a little girl.

"Yes," I say gently. "Yes, sweetheart, this will hurt. But it's going to save your life, and the Firn you give today will save someone else, someday. Just like the cure you're getting now came from the generosity of someone who was here before you."

She scrunches her eyes shut and doesn't make a sound as I press the large needle into her skin. "You're doing so well, Elise," I say as I drain as much of the Firn blood out of her veins as I can without killing her. We'll boil the shards of Firn down to form one larger glittering stone, just like Philip and Dr. Holm once did—but we're taking what they meant for death and turning it toward life. We catalog and store the stones, keeping cabinets filled with all different kinds of crystallized magic to sell within the magical community. Their sales pay enough to keep our clinic running, and our customers sign a contract to return the deadened Firn once it's spent. Because that dead Firn is perhaps the most valuable thing of all, in the end—it holds our cure.

When I finish draining two vials of blood from Elise, I unlock the cabinet and select an inoculation from our stock. The injection allows us to introduce the Firn's danger in a much weakened state. Our bodies learn how to form their own resistance, just like a vaccine. And now when the Firn tries to take hold in us, it is attacked and dismantled, instead of being left to build up and steadily crystallize in our veins.

For so long, we had to choose: our magic or our future. Doing the things that made us *us*—that made us feel alive, but at the cost of life itself. Now, every time we take someone's Firn, it's like adding a new knot to a rope that keeps growing; each person who comes in for a cure also gives us a lifeline to throw on to the next person. It's the key that unlocks endless magic.

And it's about as close to sewing up the rips in people as I can get.

"Thank you," Elise says simply when I am finished. She tucks her bandaged arm into her mended cloak, staring at it in disbelief for a moment. "Thank you," she says again, and then she ducks out into the bright sunlight.

I catalog her visit and tally the books to show Helene. Our clinic, and the work we do here, is underwritten by Helene Vestergaard. She is selling off the limestone mines —getting out from under the weight of them, and setting aside money to fund our work for years to come. Our clinic can't give anyone back the past that was stolen. But it can help to make sure that people with magic have a future now.

I run my fingertips down the page and smile a little at the filling columns. Helene wanted to come clean and tell the public the truth about the mines. But it risked putting magical people in more danger than ever before. The confession would place a deadly target on our backs, forcing us to hide our magic or live in fear that someone might try to harm us for Firn. So we convinced her that the best choice was to keep quiet. Now no one will ever know the truth about the Danish jewels that glitter around the royals' necks.

Not even the king himself.

"We better go," Jakob says to me, locking away Elise's newly collected Firn and reaching for his hat. "We're going to be late."

He turns the sign in our window to CLOSED. "Are work hours over now?" he asks coyly, and pulls me in close. My breath catches a little. I've waited all day, anticipating this. I gently touch his collar and then his lips, happiness flooding through me as he leans in. My stomach flips when he grazes a finger just behind my earlobe, and I tighten my grip around his waist. His kiss deepens in a way that makes me understand how many times he's pictured this very moment all day too. "Come on," I eventually whisper into the corner of his mouth, and when he gives a little groan of protest, I laugh. "We can't miss it."

The mountains are flowering with marguerite daisies, and the Vestergaard home rises up behind a lake that glints like a slab of polished azurite. The house has been restored from the massive damage it sustained during the battle with Philip and his men. The windows are new and sparkling in the sunshine. White camellias spill out over their ledges.

There is nothing on the façade that hints at what happened that night. The evidence disappeared as completely as the blizzard melting away. Jakob was the one who ventured out into the early morning snow, once Philip was dead and the rest of the miners subdued. Jakob spread urgent word through Brock's network of servants until we found a connection to a well-placed policeman. A senior officer—a man with a young son who can turn milk to butter without the use of a churn. He arrived at the Vestergaards' with a small but heavily armed group to collect the surviving miners and Malthe only a few hours later.

I'm not sure what happened to them, but the officer assured us that the secret will be safe.

The official word is that the others died in the blizzard.

Now we join several ink-black carriages to park in a line in front of the Vestergaard home. Brock stands at the door to escort guests inside, his hair slicked back with oil. He's dressed in tails. He pulls us aside and knits a fragrant string of white gardenias around my wrist and then stuffs a matching boutonniere into Jakob's pocket. He smirks at us. "If you're late," he says, pushing us inside, "Nina will turn you into hats."

Jakob and I part to change, and I hurry up the stairs to the room I still share with Liljan. Any of us could leave the Vestergaards for other employment now, and yet none of us have. I've found the family I always yearned for and I'm not going to give that up just yet. But the scars left from that terrible night are harder to hide on the inside of the house. A walk through the back gardens shows stone markers carved for Declan, Rae, and Ivy. Nina limps and uses a cane. Eve's arm has a long, thick pink scar that sometimes she bears proudly and sometimes she asks Liljan to hide. Lara's head injury healed, but she often searches for her words. Some days I catch Helene staring off into space, standing alone in front of the portrait of her late husband.

I pause at the mirror now, fastening my gown. On the days when I come downstairs and find Dorit crying as she makes oatmeal—or when I wake and realize that it's getting harder to remember what my father and Ingrid looked like—I can feel the sweet temptation rising, to let hatred and bitterness settle within me just a little bit. Every day, in big ways and small ones, the people in this house get up and make the choice to forgive all over again.

And I will too. I wear a small piece of my own Firn on a chain. It reminds me that magic and love are things I used to fear —things that build up little by little over time, creating something beautiful in the deepest parts of me. But the wrong things can build up too, if I let them.

The Firn on my chain is a lovely glittering violet, always

asking with a quiet insistence: *What will I look like on the inside at the end of my life?*

&

I rush through the house before the performance starts. The kitchen is alive with warm smells of fresh pastry, of simmering braises and honey and cakes and platters of flowers and berries from Brock's garden. It is a magic house even more than before, unlocked from the threat of the Firn.

I join the rest of the guests in the ballroom just in time. Jakob looks jaw-dropping in his black tuxedo, and when he sees me, he swallows hard and fidgets tellingly with his cuff links. For the first time, I made a new dress for me with magic and without any fear. It fits every curve, as though bright blue satin is being poured around me from a pitcher.

Flustered, I take my place in the front row next to Liljan. She squeezes my hand between the seats. Her scar is a silver thread across her face.

Beside me, with his curly hair and shadowed cheeks and a top hat resting in his long fingers, is Hans Christian Andersen. I startle at the sight of him, so close to me in the flesh, and manage to stutter out a greeting. An amused smile quirks his lips. Maybe someday, I'll have the courage to tell him how definitively his stories have woven into my own.

A hush falls over the small, intimate crowd when the violinist begins to play.

Eve is finally getting to perform.

Because Helene isn't interested in getting Eve into the Royal Danish Ballet anymore. Helene is starting her own ballet school and planning a series of special shows, with tickets you can't buy. The performances are by invitation only, where there are whispers of magic and wonder. A new wave overtaking ballet. This is the first show—a preview, to get influential people talking. Next, Helene and Eve will travel throughout Europe and Russia and the West Indies, studying ballet, holding auditions. Learning more about where they came from, and—I heard Helene say in a lowered voice to Dorit—perhaps even where the sugar is coming from. "Philip was wrong about almost everything," she said quietly, and I leaned into the shadows to listen closer. "But people can get almost everything wrong and still get one or two things right." So she and Eve are picking out the little glints of what might be truth. Sifting through the rest of it and starting somewhere.

When they return, we'll morph the east wing of the house into a dormitory and ballet school for Helene to run. Any orphans who show promise as dancers are being given first preference.

We will offer them a place to live, here with us.

And though we aren't certain how much magic exists outside Denmark, the salons have one final purpose. The whispers of magic should act like a beacon of light, drawing out those people with hidden magic themselves. All it takes is one person in each city to begin spreading word of a cure through their own underground networks. And if there is need for a cure in other countries, we will be ready with it.

The curtain rises in front of us. Eve is center stage, standing in the shadows of an arching tree bough. At the moment the song begins, leaves and blossoms fall from the branches and twirl around her still, poised figure.

Eve lifts to her toes beneath the tree, and the green leaves turn russet and orange and are flaked with gold as they swirl to the stage. The violin music is so deep and rich it could be poured into cups like coffee.

Mr. Andersen leans slightly forward.

Eve is a lightning rod, drawing every eye in the room to herself. She dances as though she is lit with fire on the inside, and seeing her also causes something to light within me. There are gasps when the snow begins to fall from the rafters and the audience realizes that the snowflakes aren't made of paper but are cold and soft. The room suddenly fills with the scent of fir trees, as though we have wandered into a deep forest, and a line of luminaries springs to light at the very moment Eve piqué turns past them.

Eve doesn't look like the dancers I saw months ago on the royal stage. She is drawing into something deeper, more desperate, surging with its power behind her jetés. There are flowers blooming and vines curling around her, fireflies rising in sparks above her head — so much beauty, without a single jewel in sight. As the music builds to a climax, she begins spinning like a top set off by a child's fingers — an impossible number of turns, a tangle of arms and legs and a skirt flecked with bright glass, refracting a thousand points of light.

And then when she leaps into the air, I think of all the hours of pain and frustration and sacrifice that only she knows, the cost in her life that went into making this fleeting moment of beauty for the rest of us.

It might not be as dramatic as what Ingrid did for me. But what is love if not life, siphoned out and given away and spent freely for others each day?

Eve lands the leap, the one I saw her miss and hit the floor of the greenhouse in her rehearsals for the king. But this time, she doesn't waver. She nails the jump cleanly. She raises her head, her chest heaving, and she searches the crowd for me. When our eyes meet, my pride for her does the same thing that my hurt for her does: slices through me to a different place, magnified on her behalf.

I feel the goose bumps rise on my skin, the pleasurable shiver.

She did it. That glorious zing.

Magic.

Hans Christian Andersen leans forward even more next to me, his eyes lit. "Life," he whispers. "Life itself is the most wonderful fairy tale."

I know that after tonight, Eve will go on from here. She will leave Denmark to travel with Helene, maybe for months at a time. She will continue to change, and improve, and, soon enough, grow up. But she will always come back.

And I will be here, waiting. Listening for the front door to finally open—for the voice I love most to call out, "Marit! Marit, I'm home!"

She is.

More than anyone else, she is.

With a plum in my hands, I will run to her.

THE END

ACKNOWLEDGMENTS

To Greg, James, and Cecilia: This book was born from that special year we spent in California. I'll always cherish that time with you, roaming the San Francisco Botanical Garden, marveling at the wonders of the Academy of Sciences, and watching *The Nutcracker* at the SF Ballet. Oh, how I love you.

To my parents, Kevin and Sarah Bain: There will never be enough words to say thank you, or how much of a blessing you are. Thank you to Hannah Bain, Andrew and Angie Bain, Donald and Jean Korb, Ralph and Doris Bain, and the Bain, Goldman, and Shane families.

Thank you to Mark and Barbara Murphy and Janlyn Murphy. Your support and love continue to mean the absolute world to me.

To Peter Knapp: Thank you for believing in me, for cupcakes and pep talks and crisp fall days, and for helping make my dreams come true.

To Nicole Sclama: Thank you for your enthusiasm and for bringing this book to life. I am forever grateful to work with you and the entire hardworking team at HMH Books for Young Readers: Celeste Knudsen, Shannon Luders-Manuel, Michelle Triant, Sammy Brown, Taylor McBroom, Mary Magrisso, Susan Buckheit, and Anna Dobbin.

To Sarah Odedina, Helen Crawford-White, and everyone at Pushkin Press: You are an absolute dream to work with, and I'm so grateful and blessed that I've gotten to do it twice.

Thank you to the many people who made California feel like home: Melissa Freeman, the Balsitis family, Carolyne Conner and the Tonella family, Lianne Achilles, Yomei Kajita, Alisa Hosaka, James Minahan, Katie Allen Nelson, Stephanie Garber, Misa Sugiura, Tara Goedjen, Andrew Shvarts, Lucy Keating, and all the other friends, authors, readers, bloggers, booksellers, and amazing people that make up the book community in California.

Thank you to my author friends for your encouragement, invaluable insight, and friendship on this journey: Kayla Olson, Anna Priemaza, Bree Barton, Gita Trelease, Corrie Wang, Lindsay Cummings, Nadine Brandes, and countless others from my debut group.

Thank you to Beth Nelson, Anne McKim, Addie Peyronnin, Jennifer Carter, Chris Iafolla, Anna Tuttle Delia, Sarah Hoover, Sarah Dill, Christie Pickrell, Kristen Daniels Wade, Susi Thannhuber, April Welch, Alexandra Nesbeda, Caitlin Dalton, Wendy Huang, Emily Hall, my incredible Missouri neighborhood crew, the entire Hess CG, and the Amundson family. To all my friends near and far, who have shared your lives with me in Connecticut, Massachusetts, San Francisco, Evansville, Tokyo,

Hong Kong, Indianapolis, and now Missouri, please know that I am thinking of you as I write this. I thank you for your support and your enthusiasm over *The Disappearances*—for showing up at events and sending messages and for the way you make my life so incredibly full.

Thank you to the readers, bloggers, booksellers, librarians, and Bookstagrammers who have championed my books. You have deeply touched my heart.

And thank you to the true older brother, who gave His life so I could find home in Him. You are abundance, forgiveness, and hope. Romans 5:3–4. Your beauty speaks to me everywhere.

More from Emily Bain Murphy